An American Duchess

BOOKS BY CAROLINE FYFFE

Colorado Hearts Novels

Heart of Eden
True Heart's Desire
Heart of Mine

Prairie Hearts Novels

Where the Wind Blows
Before the Larkspur Blooms
West Winds of Wyoming
Under a Falling Star
Whispers on the Wind
Where Wind Meets Wave

The McCutcheon Family Novels

Montana Dawn
Texas Twilight
Mail-Order Brides of the West: Evie
Mail-Order Brides of the West: Heather
Moon Over Montana
Mail-Order Brides of the West: Kathryn
Montana Snowfall
Texas Lonesome
Montana Courage
Montana Promise

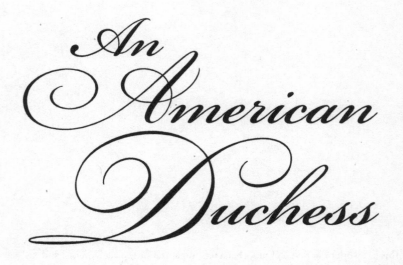

Caroline
Fyffe

Montlake
Romance

Published by Montlake Romance, Seattle

www.apub.com

Amazon, the Amazon logo, and Montlake Romance are trademarks of Amazon.com, Inc., or its affiliates.

ISBN-13: 9781542091671
ISBN-10: 1542091675

Cover design by Shasti O'Leary Soudant

Printed in the United States of America

For my beautiful nieces,
Emily Spillmann and Sophie Meyer,
with love.
You're both royalty in my eyes!

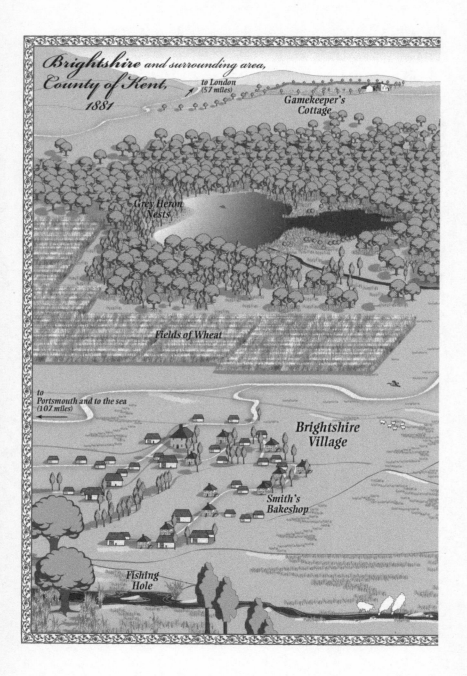

PROLOGUE

The eyes of green and blue come back,
To haunt, to laugh, to flaunt your fame,
But underneath what years have grown,
Remains the stain of utter shame.

Oh, man boy, raised in shadows was,
Returns now from across the sea,
Thinks all is good, but does not know,
Recompense is owed to me.

A pretty bride you bring with you,
What better way to crush your heart?
With emerald eyes and locks of golden hue,
She will regret your days apart.

So now good fortune comes to me,
At long last, victory snatched from defeat,
Beranger, your pain I'll see,
And my revenge will be complete . . .

CHAPTER ONE

September 13, 1881
Brightshire, Kent, England

*T*hey dance just for me, Charlotte Aldridge thought, looking out across the ocean of swaying stalks of wheat.

A light breeze cooled her skin and lifted her mood as she walked beside her pony cart filled with loaves of bread. The spring yield, planted last January, reached greedily toward the warming sun. This crop would not bear as much as the winter harvest but would surely keep the small market town of Brightshire, as well as the countryfolk of Goldenbrook, fed through the winter months. The inhabitants of the nearby hamlet depended on each morsel the reaping machine left behind.

The cart bumped easily along the pitted dirt road, the pony's lead line tossed across the animal's back. A rare Adonis butterfly, known in Kent for its shimmery blue shade, flitted across the path and landed on a stalk of wheat. Slowly, its large wings opened and closed. Charlotte stopped to watch, wondering how a silk dress in that exact hue would feel upon her skin. Feminine, for one. Impossible, for another. She wrapped her arms around her middle, imagining, longing. Then, without so much as a by-your-leave for her breathless admiration, the lovely creature took to the sky and was gone.

She heaved a sigh and ran to catch her cart. Ahead, a stone bridge arched over a narrow brook. From there, the road leading to Ashbury Castle disappeared into forestland. It wasn't visible now, but what she knew from living in Brightshire her whole life was that the road through the forest would emerge into a great open expanse and the five-hundred-year-old castle of the Duke of Brightshire. The tall, square tower and checkerboard-patterned battlements were partly visible over the treetops. Two flags fluttered in the breeze—one bearing the duke's coat of arms and the other Queen Victoria's.

Charlotte sighed again. The scent of wildflowers reached her nose, reminding her of costly perfume noblewomen took for granted as much as the air they breathed. Did they know how lucky they were? Charlotte would be happy with a single dress that hadn't been handed down through the village but was new, hers alone.

She gazed at the tower. There was something magical about Ashbury. But since the death of William Northcott, Duke of Brightshire, and then his son and heir, who had worn the title for less than a year, a cloud had hung over the town. The Northcotts were the most important family in the area and employed many of the villagers. The lucky ones, with jobs inside the castle, relayed the goings-on and tensions from Ashbury on a daily basis. Charlotte's cousin Amelia worked as a scullery maid, and her monthly visit home was anticipated with excitement. During the time the young duke had reigned, Amelia had brought rumors of parties and gambling, as well as tension between the duke and his mother, the dowager duchess. Then the young duke had died in a hunting accident and his body hadn't been recovered for two whole days. The affair had been ghastly.

His death and the fact that a new duke or duchess had not been announced had been the subject of speculation for nine long months.

And now rumors abounded that the knife wound that had killed him might not have been an accident at all—but murder.

The rumors made Charlotte fear for her brother. Thomas was twenty, older by a year, and seemed to be hiding something important about that day. She dared not pry for fear of learning something she would not like to know. She'd heard from Amelia that the young duke often went into the woods with his gun, sometimes just to shoot, and other times to hunt small game. That day the word was he'd gone out alone. That same day Charlotte had gone into Ashbury's woods, basket over her arm, in search of the wild mushrooms that grew around the lake to use in the meat pies they sold at her family's bakeshop. She'd seen movement across a large meadow and up the rise: two men, their backs to her. One was clearly the duke, for his bright red cloak was like no other. He was tall and his wide shoulders distinctive. The other man wore a long duster, much like the one Thomas owned. He'd been partly hidden by trees, making his identity uncertain. Thomas delivered the bread to Ashbury every Tuesday and ran into the young duke now and then; he'd spoken often of the duke's conceit and condescending words. There was no love lost between them.

Soon the men moved out of sight, and Charlotte went about her chore. An hour later, and on her way home, she spotted Mr. Henderley, the gamekeeper, striding through the forest, wearing a long coat, a noticeable limp to his gait. Slipping behind a bush, she waited for him to pass. The gamekeeper's job was to watch for poachers, and she didn't want to get into trouble, even for poaching mushrooms.

Before long, Thomas—now she was sure it was him—jogged out of the tree line. He was too far away to call without alerting the gamekeeper. He looked distressed, and once or twice he glanced over his shoulder. She knew him well enough to believe he'd found some sort of trouble.

It wasn't until she'd heard of the duke's passing that she'd remembered she'd yet to ask Thomas why he'd been on the duke's land. He hadn't had a gun, so he wasn't poaching. But when she inquired, he claimed to have been fishing on the other side of Brightshire. Why had he lied?

In the days that followed, the constable questioned the men of Brightshire and Goldenbrook, hoping to find a witness to what had transpired. A duke's death was serious, and facts needed to be known. The lawman hadn't doubted Thomas's account, but she had. Even before the duke's death, she'd noticed Thomas had begun to behave differently, and his frequent absences from the bakeshop created tension between him and their aunt. He seemed to avoid Charlotte's glance, and sometimes her altogether. Recently, she'd misplaced a hair ribbon and later found the decorative length in the pocket of his coat, of all places, when she was tidying up. Questioning him turned his cheeks ruddy, and he'd shrugged.

She'd told herself that she needed to remember Thomas wasn't a boy any longer, that he had grown up and must have some secrets. With that thought, she'd been able to lay her worries aside—until yesterday. Two women had come into the bakeshop whispering about the duke. They'd heard rumors there might have been a fight of some kind and he'd been killed. One woman had whispered that Thomas, the baker's nephew, had been questioned by the constable. Charlotte's back had gone stiff at that—as if the constable's questioning made him guilty. All the men had been questioned! All of them. It had taken every ounce of restraint for her to simply smile and help the women with their purchases.

Charlotte glanced longingly at the clouds, wishing she had the ability to fly away from her problems like a sparrow. She reached out and stroked Sherry's neck under her flaxen mane, taking note the small beast was hot and would soon need to rest. Only twelve hands tall, the old Welsh/Hackney cross had a cottonlike forelock and more than a few gray hairs around her muzzle and eyes. The scabby, fly-bitten area under her belly never seemed to heal no matter how much lard Charlotte slathered on.

A plume of dust appeared on the road ahead.

Someone is coming from the castle!

Charlotte had traveled from Brightshire to Goldenbrook many times before, but today she'd turned off her usual route and was now headed toward the dense forested woodlands that led to Ashbury. A whisper of uncertainty filled her chest. She thought of the dead duke, the gamekeeper, and her brother. Had something more than an accident transpired that day? Was the responsible person still lurking in the woods?

Not someone, but a group!

Taking Sherry's lead, Charlotte guided the pony off the side of the road, making room as she waited for the procession to reach her. The gleaming black coach trimmed in gold was escorted by two riders and followed by the same. Were the duchess and Lady Audrey inside? Her heart thrummed against her ribs.

"Easy, little mum," Charlotte mumbled, more to calm herself than the already drowsy pony. "We'll be on our way soon enough."

As the coach passed, Charlotte curtsied, keeping her gaze respectfully anchored to the ground even though she hungered for a glimpse of the women's gowns. A quick insubordinate blink earned her a flash of bright scarlet and of cobalt trimmed in gold.

Such beauty! Oh, to see the dresses in full!

And then they were gone.

Charlotte waited until they were down the road before she nudged Sherry awake. "Walk on, little mum," she whispered. "Fairy tales are not for girls like us." The ache inside was real. Insistent. She pushed it away. "We have work to do and need not while the day away with silly daydreams. We certainly don't need to anger Aunt Ethel."

After crossing the arched cobblestone bridge, they entered the dark, forested lands that lay before the castle. Still early in the day, there would be plenty of light filtering in and around the densely knit trees.

"Watch your step," Charlotte whispered as they approached a deep rut. She didn't like this stretch of road. The mile-long tunnel of living green was spooky. Though the temperature was sunny and warm outside the forest, within the darkness a puff of cold air chilled her shoulders. Unnerved, she glanced behind at the disappearing daylight and then placed her hand on Sherry's warm withers as they walked along.

The hamlet children spoke of witches and gnomes and fairies in the forest. Every now and again, the tale of the Lost Baby resurfaced—how the weeping could be heard on foggy nights, as the child cried for her mama. Aunt Ethel had scoffed at the myth, saying the account was nonsense. But why, then, did folks still come scurrying into Brightshire from time to time, saying they'd heard *something*—like a child whimpering in the trees?

The branches overhead swished, and the leaves of a holly plant tinkled. A mixture of alder, ash, and aspen filled the forest, as well as elderberry and buckthorn. She particularly liked the white bark of the silver birch and the delicate flowers of the burnet rose plants scattered over the mossy ground. The forest smelled musty and old.

Suddenly, a dog streaked out from under the brush and rushed her wagon.

Sherry reared and turned a half circle, ready to bolt for home. Charlotte jumped forward and grabbed the trailing lead line to keep her from running off. Loaves of bread flew to the ground, rolling here and there.

"Stop that!" Charlotte yelled at the gangly golden retriever barking playfully at Sherry's legs. "Get back before I take my boot to you!" Although loud and obnoxious, the animal didn't appear dangerous. She needed to see if any of the toppled loaves could be salvaged.

"Bagley," a voice thundered. "Heel!" The command was followed by a tall stranger, who appeared out of the foliage.

The interloper barked again and grasped one of the loaves on the ground as Charlotte herself took hold. A tussle ensued. She lost her balance on the uneven path and fell onto her hands and knees. The dog, his prize clenched between his jaws, bounded off into the bushes.

Embarrassed, she climbed to her feet and brushed dirt from her palms. She felt a warm trickle of blood before the pinch of pain.

The man started in her direction. "You're hurt, miss."

She snatched her injured hand behind her back as she fished in her pocket for her kerchief with the other. "I'm fine, it's just a scratch, but your dog has stolen my bread!" Humiliated by his fretful gaze, and how she must have looked playing tug-of-war with his unmannered beast, she made a show of picking up the other loaves. "*And* your dog scared my pony. Where are his manners, sir?" With nothing left to do, she turned to face him.

He was tall and held a rifle in one hand, and his booted feet were spread wide. Fear streaked through her. Was he a road robber, here to steal the rest of her bread and anything else she had? He made no move toward her.

"I'm sorry." He dipped his chin. "About your baked goods and the scrape on your palm. Bagley's still a pup, more or less."

Robbers didn't go around with unruly upstarts, did they? When he did step closer, she realized he was younger than she'd originally thought, maybe five years older than she. His clothes were clean and free of patches and visible mending. He wasn't a farmworker or peasant. A long coat, one much too warm if he were to venture out of the shade of the woods, fell all the way to his tall, black boots. A thick belt around his middle held a small leather bag, a sheathed knife, and what looked to be a coiled leash for his rascally scamp.

Not quite ready to forgive and forget, she said, "The missing loaf will cost you threepence, sir. I'll not charge you for the fare that landed on the road unless the castle turns it away."

"I have no money on me. I'll have to pay you later. Just tell me where."

The deep timbre of his voice pricked her senses. "Smith's Bakeshop in Brightshire."

"I've not seen you before," he said. "Who should I ask for?"

Who was he and why was he trespassing on the duke's land? "Miss Aldridge. My brother usually delivers the bread to Ashbury. He's sick today, and so his job fell to me." Sick? Ha! Early this morning, after Aunt Ethel was too busy in the bakeshop to notice, Thomas had climbed out his bedroom window and shinned down the wall with the dexterity of a mountain goat. At sundown, he'd no doubt appear with six or seven large golden trout.

Giving so much information, she felt she'd earned the right to ask who he was. "And you are?"

"Tristen Llewellyn, from Wales. Mr. Henderley, the gamekeeper, is my uncle."

Mr. Henderley's nephew? "Have you taken his job, then?" She remembered the older man's limping gait the day of the duke's death.

"No, just helping out until he's back on his feet."

Bagley was back, wagging his tail as if he hadn't just found trouble. He trotted around his master several times and then sat by Mr. Llewellyn's side, as docile as a little lamb.

Now that she knew who he was, she allowed herself to relax. "Do you always let your dog go around frightening people?"

Tristen shrugged as amusement filled his eyes. "He's in training. We've just lost the scent of a trail we're following." He gazed down at the dog. "He'll get better with time."

"A trail?"

Mr. Llewellyn nodded. "Aye, a poacher, but I'm not sure. My uncle believes that during his convalescence, men have become bold. I've yet to encounter any in person but have found the signs. Footprints. Bloodstains. Pheasant feathers. Things like that. You should keep an eye out when you travel."

She turned the pony and cart back in the direction toward Ashbury, not liking that news at all. She thought of Thomas and wondered how he filled his days. Not only with fish, she suspected. "Pheasants?" she murmured.

A frown tilted Mr. Llewellyn's brows. "That's right. This *is* bird season—pheasant, grouse, partridge. But I'm sure that's of no interest to you."

"Oh, and why not? We bake the finest meat pies in all of Brightshire, Goldenbrook, and beyond. If we don't know what type of birds to expect from our hunters, how can we gather the most pleasing herbs and produce to complement the taste? I'll be expecting some nice woodcock—*after* October first, that is."

A smile played around his lips, and he gave a slight bow. "I withdraw my narrow-minded judgment of you, Miss Aldridge, and beg your pardon. I'll bid you good day. But please, stay on the road. There's been more than enough evidence of poachers."

"I'll do that, Mr. Llewellyn, but I'm from the village. The poachers are probably my neighbors and friends." *And brother.* "I have nothing to fear if all they are after is game." When his brow lowered she gave a conciliatory smile. He was only trying to be helpful. "But there have been robbers, so yes, I will be careful. And thank you. Good day."

Hours later, and finished with the daily deliveries, Charlotte swished the currycomb over Sherry's coat as the mare stood quietly in her stall, munching hay. After that, she cleaned the chicken coop and collected the morning eggs, which remained untouched in their nesting boxes. She was responsible for the chickens, but since she'd been sent to do Thomas's job, hers had remained undone. Taking the back door steps quickly, she stopped in the open threshold of the bakeshop, encountering a blast of oven heat.

"There you be!" an angry voice snapped.

From the square worktable inside the kitchen, Aunt Ethel, her hands deep in a large bowl of bread dough, glared at her. Her short jacket, with elbow-length sleeves, was covered by a full white apron. A blue-checkered scarf circled her neck and tucked into her bodice. The white cap atop her graying brown hair looked like a toadstool. After rising, the dough she worked now would be baked into loaves overnight.

"Did ya deliver ta Goldenbrook too? I know how that enchantress that lives there scares ya."

"She's a midwife, Aunt, not an enchantress. I'm not frightened of her." *Or you.*

Speaking back on any account was always a risk. Aunt Ethel loved to paint her in the worst possible light. Frightened, lazy, brazen. Aunt Ethel and her sister, Ruby, the woman who'd raised Charlotte for the first three years of her life, had inherited the bakeshop from their parents. When Ruby passed away from a gangrenous arm nicked by the hatchet that was used for butchering, responsibility for her children, Thomas and Charlotte, fell to Aunt Ethel. While Ethel put up with Thomas because he was Ruby's true son, Charlotte didn't fare as well. Ethel never let Charlotte forget that she was a foundling, not blood.

"Ain't you the sassy one? If I wasn't up to my elbows in bread dough, I'd teach ya a little respect."

"I'm not being disrespectful, Aunt." They locked gazes. "Give me one minute to change my clothes and refresh myself, then I'll spell Verity out front. I'm sure she'd like a cup of tea since you were short-handed today."

Aunt Ethel's eyes narrowed.

Charlotte made room for the basket of thirty-five eggs between the tall stack of mixing bowls and spices and extracts. Upstairs in the room she shared with her cousin Verity (and Amelia when she was home), Charlotte stripped off her soiled clothes and put on fresh.

Out front, Verity was waiting on a customer, so Charlotte took a damp cloth and began to wipe the empty bread shelves that had been full this morning.

"You're back," Verity said, giving her older cousin a smile once the woman walked out the door. "I'm glad. You'll never guess who came in."

Charlotte tipped her head, waiting. Verity liked to drag out the telling.

"Well, don't you want to know?"

"Yes, please tell. If not one of our usual customers, I'm stumped."

"That handsome gentleman. You know the one. With a mess of brown hair and eyes that speak of romance. I almost fainted when he came through the door."

Charlotte stopped wiping. "The duke's cousin?"

"Yes." Verity's chestnut curls bounced under her kerchief as she nodded. At seventeen, she was one year younger than Amelia and three years younger than Thomas. "I almost lost my voice when I asked him what he wanted. Oh, Charlotte, he's so attractive. Have you ever seen the like?"

"What did he buy?" Charlotte couldn't resist teasing her.

"Two raspberry tarts, just like before. What do you think that means? Some kind of message?"

Oh, Verity, you have the heart of a romantic. What will we do with you? "Two raspberry tarts? That he has an appetite, and raspberry is his filling of choice."

Verity waved her off. "You're no fun, Charlotte. I like to pretend he comes in to see me. Is that so wrong?"

Charlotte walked over and draped a loving arm across Verity's shoulder. "Of course that's not wrong. And who knows. Maybe you're right."

It could be true, she told herself as Verity melted into a pool of delight. Hope kept one's spirit alive. Gave something to dream about other than the hardships and unhappiness of each passing day. She'd not steal that from her cousin.

"Charlotte!" Aunt Ethel shouted. "Get out there and get us a cockerel for supper. Wring its neck and pluck it clean. I'll do the rest when I'm finished here."

If only there were a way to tell her aunt that Thomas would most likely show up with a string of fresh trout, and save the cockerel to live another day.

"Go on," Aunt Ethel continued. "It's the second Tuesday of the month. Amelia comes home from Ashbury to spend the night. I've made a currant cake with sour milk frosting and cinnamon biscuits. Light a fire under your feet, you indolent girl. One night a month ain't near enough time to spend with my darling daughter." There was some muttering Charlotte couldn't make out. "Amelia's made something good of herself. Just think, working at the castle."

Verity shrugged despondently at Charlotte, knowing she fell short in her mother's eyes as well.

"Charlotte, you hear me?"

"Yes, Aunt Ethel. Going right now."

Charlotte passed through the kitchen and was about to leave out the back door when the town crier, an orphan boy of ten, bounded past her into the kitchen waving a small piece of paper over his head.

Aunt Ethel gasped in surprise.

At the sound of the commotion, Verity poked her head in from the front.

"What's the news?" Charlotte asked. *What else can go wrong today?*

"The Duke of Brightshire has been found—in America, no less! Ship docked late last night in Portsmouth. Tomorrow he'll be on his way to Brightshire! And bringing an American duchess with him from a place called Coloradee."

CHAPTER TWO

Emma Brinkman Northcott gazed out the opulent train car window as a tangled mass of feelings churned inside. In Portsmouth, after they'd disembarked the ship, she'd been told that the next morning a train would transport them to Cranbrook, where she and Beranger would have a suite at a local hotel so they could eat and rest and prepare for the last leg of their journey. From there, a coach sent from Ashbury Castle would carry them the rest of the way to Brightshire.

To her disappointment, Emma hadn't been able to see much of Portsmouth in the darkness, but this morning, boarding the train, the sun had peeked over the horizon in splendid pinks and reds, and she'd been treated to a storybook land of quaint cottages with thatched roofs, tiny cultivated rose gardens, and tidy barns. Her spirits leaped to life— here before her was her future. The train chugged through golden grain fields of ripe wheat, oats, and other crops. There were black-and-white dairy cows, picturesque villages dotted with stone buildings, colorful doors, flower boxes, and women dressed in neckerchiefs, bloomers, and darling little hats.

Everything from the villagers to the buildings and farms looked as if they belonged in a fairy tale. Things here were so different from her home in Colorado! Long, rambling ranch houses were replaced by stone cottages. Dirt roads were now cobblestone streets. Stock horses, so useful for gathering cattle, were now draft horse giants pulling heavy-looking wagons. And the overall feel was old, *very old*, ancient. Had her American roots begun somewhere here?

She sat back and closed her eyes. The last few months had been an incredible dream come true. When she'd met Beranger North on a business trip to Santa Fe, she'd had no idea that the handsome mining expert with the slight accent and two different-colored eyes was really Beranger Northcott and destined to inherit a dukedom. Beranger hadn't known himself until his uncle, Lord Harry Northcott, arrived to take him back to England to claim his title as Duke of Brightshire. He and Emma had wed that same night, transforming her instantly into the Duchess of Brightshire. That had barely been a month ago. The thought was still so unbelievable.

For a moment, she felt a pang of longing for the four sisters she'd left behind. She imagined them being here with her. Lavinia would be cooing over the women's charming hats, Katie venturing off the road at each stop to inspect the types of trees that grew in England—because of the type of lumber they would produce—Mavis would chronicle every aspect of the voyage in her journal, and Belle would be alive with excitement over the different breeds of horses that filled the pastures and streets.

"Your Grace?"

The moniker almost felt like a joke. Emma didn't fit the role of Your Grace, Duchess, or anything else. But she was determined to try. Coming to England and accepting the roles wouldn't be fair if she and Beranger wanted to change everything. That wasn't the point. They both intended to adhere to customs as well as they could.

And yet there were so many customs to remember, so many proto-cols to follow. Curtsy, bow, incline a head? Look here, don't look there. How she wished for just one of her sisters to help soften her arrival.

Alone in her and Beranger's luxury sitting car, Emma watched Gertrude Bucket, the woman Lord Harry had hired in Boston to make the voyage to England with them and tutor Emma on English propriety, make her way down the rocking passageway, being careful to keep her balance. The slight, middle-aged woman was the embodiment of decorum. She followed Emma around like a lonely puppy dog, whispering dos and don'ts in her ear often enough to make Emma want to scream. Gertrude made Emma feel like a country bumpkin, which wasn't the case at all. Emma and her sisters had been raised in Philadelphia, first by their mother until her death, then by guardians; they'd all graduated school and had socialized to some extent in genteel society. Then, last year, they'd inherited one of the largest, most successful cattle ranches in Colorado when their father passed away. The Five Sisters Ranch.

"Miss Bucket, you found me," she joked, hoping for a smile.

The woman just stared, a bemused expression on her face. "I most certainly did. As I specifically mentioned before, you should not be anywhere on this train alone. It's unseemly." An upward motion of her hand was the signal Emma should sit straighter and lift her chin.

Begrudgingly, Emma complied. "But I'm in our private car. I'm safe."

"I'm always available to accompany you." Gertrude gave her a stern glance as if she thought Emma a child. "You told me you were going to lie down, and I just came from checking your sleep car. When you weren't there, you gave me a start. Please be more considerate in the future."

"Emma, my love, there you are."

As usual, Beranger's appearance chased away her misgivings. Never once when she was in his arms or by his side did she have any uncertainties over leaving her family. Only when they were parted, and she was left alone with her thoughts, or alone with this woman who whittled down the remains of her confidence, did she wonder if she'd made a mistake thinking she could live up to the expectations of a duchess.

"Please excuse us, Miss Bucket. Emma and I would like some time alone."

Gertrude didn't look pleased she'd been supplanted. A watch appeared in her hand like magic, and she clicked open the lid.

"Teatime has arrived, Your Grace," she said, emphasizing the title. Gertrude didn't like Beranger being so informal with his bride, and had told him so—but only once. "The duchess has yet to grasp the significance of the ritual. This is our last teatime before we arrive. Would you not like her to practice yet again? You'd not want her to flaunt her ignorance to proper society."

Emma saw Beranger tense.

"We appreciate your dedication, Miss Bucket. You can take tea with Lord Harry. He's in his suite reading and will enjoy having someone to converse with."

Her eyes lit up.

"Please turn the latch as you go."

She gave a slight bow and hurried away, locking the door behind her.

"You're incorrigible," Emma whispered for his ears alone. "Lord Harry will kill you if he finds out you sicced Gertrude on him."

Beranger lifted a shoulder, and the lopsided smile, the one that made her fall in love with him, appeared.

"But he won't find out unless you tell him." His eyes, one blue and one green, sparkled with mischief. He lowered his face to hers.

With a hand to his chest, she pushed him back. "Don't."

His brows shot up.

"Not after last night on the ship. How can you even think of kissing me? I've never been so sick in all my life."

"Oh, I can think of that, and a lot more, my darling wife. Is this not our honeymoon? And since last night was spent on violent seas, preventing any honeymooning from going on, and since now we are safe in this train car, and the door is locked, I thought I might entice you."

He brushed his lips along her shoulder and then up to her ear.

She sighed and leaned into his body, feeling the luscious pool of heat warming inside. "But what will Lord Harry think?" She was barely able to get the words past her lips.

"That we're honeymooning," he whispered.

"In that case . . ."

Emma tried to relax, but troubling thoughts kept popping into her head. What would England be like? Would the people there approve of her? If she didn't learn fast enough, would she hinder her husband? Be an embarrassment to him, as Gertrude implied?

Beranger lifted his head from her neck. "What's wrong?"

"Nothing. I'm enjoying myself."

He straightened and studied her long enough for heat to spring to her face.

"I'm frightened," she finally admitted, sorry to have ruined the mood.

"Frightened? Of what? We'll be in Brightshire tonight. Nothing to be worried over."

"What if I'm a terrible duchess? What if I let you down?"

"You could never let me down, Emma. Be an American. That's who I fell in love with. Be yourself and you'll win everyone's hearts, not just mine."

His searching gaze eased away her fears.

"If you say so, *Your Grace*," she whispered teasingly. She ran her hand over his broad chest, all the while pressing closer. Taking the initiative, she brushed her lips across his and then softly kissed each corner of his mouth. "Your every wish is my command."

The light was back in his eyes, and more, something much deeper and indescribable. Soon they were swept away on a wave of desire.

Later that day, as Emma slumbered beside him in the rocking coach they'd boarded in Cranbrook, Lord Harry and a sleeping Gertrude Bucket on the seat opposite, Beranger turned in wonder to gaze at his wife. All his years in America, he'd never imagined he might have what he'd found with her. The thunder of true passion. The melding of two hearts to such heights that after each time, he was left in wonder and thanksgiving. He could hardly believe such happiness was real. Before her, he'd never known what true love was.

Strawberry locks framed the face of an angel, and long lashes rested against her creamy, soft cheeks. If they were alone, he'd be tempted to take her back into his arms. Instead, Beranger glanced out the window to watercolor splashes of orange and red tingeing the horizon. The familiar sights of England, of his homeland, couldn't dispel the unease he carried inside him.

After his mother died when he was just an infant, Beranger had been taken in by his father, William Northcott, Duke of Brightshire, who'd been willing to acknowledge the illegitimate boy as his own. The decision had infuriated his wife, Radella, the duchess, and her fury had soured the very air Beranger breathed for the first thirteen years of his life. The woman had seemed formidable to a small boy, but she had also been frightened of him, convinced, because of the different color of his eyes, that he'd brought a curse with him, one that was preventing her from conceiving another child after her firstborn, Gavin. She'd used every trick to drive Beranger away, and his father seemed to turn a blind eye to her measures. Then, at thirteen, Beranger overheard the duke finally capitulating to his wife's requests to send Beranger to Italy. That night, Beranger stole a horse from the duke's stable and, with only a knapsack and handful of money, rode to the harbor and sold his freedom away for four years as a deckhand aboard the *Destiny*. At seventeen, he arrived in America a free man and proceeded to make his own fortune in the gold and silver mines.

In Emma, though, he'd found something more precious than all the treasures in the world. When Lord Harry arrived with the news that Beranger's father had died, as well as his older brother, Gavin, their world had been turned upside down. Even more unbelievable was the revelation that Beranger wasn't illegitimate after all; his father had loved his commoner mother so much that he'd secretly married her before he'd married the duchess. That meant Beranger was the true heir of Brightshire and Gavin the illegitimate brother.

After Beranger ran away, the duchess had gone on to have a daughter, Lady Audrey, and both women no doubt mourned Gavin's death. Despite that, Beranger held no fear of the upcoming reception with his stepmother, the woman who'd ruined his childhood. He was a grown man; she had no power over him now. But when he glanced at Emma, still blissfully asleep, worry tilted his brows. They'd met and married so quickly. What if she hated Brightshire? The weather was drastically different from Eden, Colorado. The people and customs as well. In Eden, she had a shop and the family's ranch to tend to; here she might be bored to tears. She and her sisters had been so close; Emma had never been away from them for more than a day. She'd never displayed an ounce of regret at accompanying him, and yet a part of her surely wished she were back home. He'd seen the way her gaze continually strayed back the way they'd traveled—toward America, and the West—when they walked the ship's deck.

He sighed and looked out at the passing landscape.

"Beranger?" Lord Harry said quietly, so as not to wake the others. "I wonder at your soulful expression."

His uncle seemed to have a nose for trouble. Had been that way ever since Beranger was a boy.

"Just enjoying the sunset."

Harry smiled. "I'd say more is on your mind than that. I think you're worrying over your future. And dwelling on your past." Harry reached out and clapped a hand on Beranger's knee. "I could always read you like a book, my boy." He let his hand fall away. "You don't have to pretend with me."

Beranger turned again to gaze out the window. The sun had set, and all the previous color in the sky had turned into wispy white clouds. He checked to see that both women were still sound asleep. "Emma's on my mind. When the five sisters were called back to Colorado last year to inherit their father's cattle ranch, they learned that John Brinkman had written each of them a personal letter to be given to them on their birthday."

Harry's face lit up. "Why, we celebrated Emma's birthday on the train east to Boston. That was a jolly good time."

"Exactly. She was under instructions not to read the missive until her birthday, yet it remains unopened to this day, tucked away in one of her trunks."

Harry grasped his chin, thinking. "I see. Have you asked her why?"

"I don't have to. It's evident she's homesick."

"Perhaps. Or maybe the rough seas made her forget."

Beranger shook his head. "As much as she denies the fact, she's melancholy. Her eyes betray her. That letter from her father is her last connection to home, and she's savoring the occasion the reading will bring for as long as she can. I don't blame her in the least, but I'm . . ."

"Frightened? Saying so is not a sin."

Beranger nodded, unable to meet his uncle's eyes. "I don't want to make her unhappy. She's made to smile, to laugh. The joy she's brought to my soul is immeasurable."

"Beranger, you of all people should know what it's like to adjust to a new country. Have faith in her. Love shines from her eyes each time she looks at you, dear boy. Don't rush her. Stay steadfast in your love for her, and all will be well."

"And if you're wrong?"

"Then we'll cross that bridge when we arrive to it—and not before."

Beranger felt as if he were eight years old again and in the boxing ring with Gavin. Unschooled, he had experienced some fear until Uncle Harry had given him a few invaluable suggestions on how to gain the upper hand. The man had never married, and Beranger sometimes wondered why, but perhaps his advice was worth taking. Deciding to try it, a semblance of peace drifted down upon him, one he hadn't felt since Emma's birthday. He'd buck up and see where that got him.

Beranger smiled. "I can't wait to see my stepmother's face when I walk through that door."

Harry raised a brow in censure. "Don't look for trouble. That will find you on its own. I sent a cable to alert your stepmother and sister, as well as the staff, so they'll be well prepared. Everyone will be excited to greet the Duke of Brightshire and his beautiful duchess."

"I hardly think that will be the case—them excited to see me. My sister alone will be disappointed not to inherit the title." For a duchess to inherit was almost unheard of, yet exactly such an intent had been written into the letters patent first granting the title Duke of Brightshire to one of their ancestors. Surely, Lady Audrey would be resentful that Beranger's return prevented her the honor.

Harry nodded. "I'm sure. But she'll get over that as soon as she meets you and Emma. She has other issues to fill her time, like finishing her schooling so she's able to make a good match and get married. Since she turned fourteen, there have been plenty of gentry visiting Ashbury with their eligible sons."

"She has a good dowry, then?"

"Oh, yes. Your father made sure of that. One that will attract every young buck in the land when the time is right. Lady Audrey wanted to come out next year at sixteen, but your stepmother is insistent she wait until seventeen so she'll be able to run a proper household of candor and grace, speak fluent French, Italian, and German, sing like a bird, *and* play the piano." An amused tilt wrinkled his brow. "I'm glad I wasn't born female, I can tell you that. At any rate, Lady Audrey may even be relieved to be rid of the duty that comes with the title. She seems to enjoy flitting about like a butterfly."

In an instant, Beranger was transported back to his boyhood and days spent running free in the forestlands with peasant boys whose families worked in or lived near the castle. There'd been a girl too, the closest thing to a sister he'd had at the time. Phoebe Parker. She was the only female he knew who liked catching frogs, swimming in the river on a hot day, or climbing the craggy cliffs on Ashbury's moors. He wondered if she were still in Brightshire.

Beranger leaned into the velvet seat of the coach, listening to the clopping of the horses behind the carriage, two of which they'd brought on the ship from America and were being led by riders on their own mounts. He wasn't thirteen any longer, so he'd better decide how he was going to navigate his new life.

CHAPTER THREE

Beranger tried to keep his anxiety at bay as the coach raced along the roadway, the evening light dancing across the many landmarks he remembered from his boyhood. Their arrival at Ashbury was imminent.

"I can't imagine what I'll do all day," Emma said, donned in the fanciest dress she'd brought from Eden. "After having my own shop . . ." She lifted a shoulder.

Beranger glanced at her and smiled. "I'm sure we'll be bombarded with social invitations as soon as the word gets around that the Duke and Duchess of Brightshire have returned to Ashbury Castle." At least, for her sake, he hoped so. In reality, he had no bloody idea how the *ton* would react to his reappearance to claim the title. No idea at all.

Lord Harry, now freshly shaven and changed, but still looking somewhat worse for wear after the long day of travel, yawned. He rolled his shoulders and said, "As a duchess, you're free to do anything you'd like. You needn't worry. Give yourself time to settle in. Enjoy the scenery. You may find England much to your liking. Most everyone in your country, except the American Indians, has come from somewhere in Europe. Perhaps researching your lineage and where your people hailed from might be entertaining."

"I can do that? I'd find my father's and mother's ancestry fascinating to know."

Beranger rubbed her hand. "Of course, my love. Nobody is going to force you to be anything you aren't. And I wouldn't want that. We both have to work to keep our ideals and not let anyone"—he let his gaze stray lazily to Gertrude, who was now staring out her window at the slight rebuke—"browbeat us into submission."

"Thank goodness," she said on a breath. "I cannot imagine myself sitting around day after day, doing nothing but strolling a beautiful garden followed by several hours of needlework and tea drinking."

Lord Harry looked perplexed.

"Please don't get me wrong, Lord Harry," she said. "I don't mean to sound ungrateful. You know how I love to dress for an occasion. In fact, I feel extremely underdressed tonight."

His face lit up, losing all its worry lines. "You'll have plenty of opportunities to do that."

"And I'll work on my posture and manners until nobody will be able to tell I wasn't born right here in jolly ol' England. I'll remember that the first floor of the castle is called the ground floor here, and the second floor is called the first." She took a deep breath and slowly released it. "I want to make you all proud. As well as the people of Brightshire and beyond. And of course, Americans."

Lord Harry beamed. "In my cable, I instructed Pencely to send for the dowager's dressmaker. I'm sure she'll be waiting with her entourage and bolts of expensive fabric."

Emma tapped her lip. "Mr. Pencely is the butler, but there are also footmen, valets, housemaids, and a personal lady's maid. Housekeeper, cook, several helpers in the kitchen . . ."

Beranger chuckled. "You've got a good start on it, sweetheart. Better than I do. When I was living at Ashbury, I was kept well out of the way. I have just as much learning to do as you." He lifted her hand and kissed it.

"Look!" Emma pointed through the dim light outside toward an old woman watching their approach from the roadside. Her scraggly brown robe hung on her thin frame as she leaned on a tall staff. She carried a straw basket on her back. "Stop the coach! She looks about to drop. Maybe she hasn't eaten for days."

Miss Bucket, donned in her own best dress, gasped. "You can't stop for every peasant, ma'am! There are thousands of them. You'll ruin your reputation before you even arrive."

"Emma's right," Beranger said, ignoring Uncle Harry's look of distress. His life had expanded—he was responsible for so many others now. What good was he as a duke if he didn't help the people around him? He pounded the ceiling of the coach, and the driver brought the horses down to a walk and then stopped. "We will give her our hamper of food."

A footman opened the door, and Beranger lifted the straw hamper and descended. To his surprise, Emma followed.

The woman straightened when she realized they meant to speak to her. Her wrinkled, elongated face ended in a pointed chin, from which several wiry hairs protruded. Eyes glittering with intelligence took in their approach, not in the least bit intimidated.

"Ma'am, you look hungry," Emma said. "We'd like to offer you this basket of food. Or, if you're in need, a ride to your destination."

All right, they could do that, he supposed. If the woman was on foot, she couldn't be going far—darkness had already fallen—although he didn't like the way she was looking at him: as if somehow, somewhere, they'd known each other.

"I live in Goldenbrook," she said.

The road to Ashbury turned off before arriving in Goldenbrook, but the hamlet wasn't much out of their way. Surely this woman knew whom the coat of arms on the door belonged to and where they were going.

"Can we take her there?" Emma asked before Beranger had a chance to respond.

He nodded.

The woman's black eyebrows arched, and she smiled at Emma. "Such a kind heart has this one. I will accept, and be in your debt. I'd not want to lose the contents of this fine basket to an outlaw."

She was not speaking of the elongated basket on her back but the one she stared at in Beranger's hands.

As they settled back in the coach, Gertrude slipped onto the back bench next to Emma, and the woman took the seat next to Lord Harry. Beranger instructed the riders at the rear to guide their American horses on to the stable at Ashbury and the driver to take the short detour to Goldenbrook.

"You spoke of outlaws?" Beranger inquired. "I've been away sixteen years, but back then there wasn't much crime around Brightshire. Decent people didn't have to worry over their goods."

"Or their lives?" the old woman questioned.

"No, not that either. Is that what times have come to now?" he asked, glancing at Lord Harry. His uncle had hinted at changes, but had not been specific. Perhaps he'd thought Beranger wouldn't have wanted to return if he'd known each and every detail. Lord Harry's lips were pressed in a thin line.

She cackled softly and sang, "Brightshire forest, thick and dank with leaves, sounds are silenced in your green-thatched eaves . . ." Then she smiled. "But perhaps not so much danger for someone like me." Her widened eyes landed on Emma. "But a pretty miss surely should not be out when the sun disappears and the shadows take wing." She pointed a crooked finger in their direction. "Be warned so as not to be sorry."

Emma inched closer to Beranger.

He didn't appreciate the crone's humor in trying to frighten Emma. He knew her kind. Old ways and superstitions were more prevalent here than in America. Storybook rhymes were full of wicked witches less daunting than this old woman—and as a boy, he'd heard every single one. He hoped Emma didn't take her seriously. She'd show up in a day or two at Ashbury and offer, for a few coins, to read Emma her fortune.

The woman studied his eyes now in the illumination of the lanterns the footman had lighted when they'd gotten out to speak with her. A knowing smile curled her lips, making the hair on the back of his neck prickle. "So—you have returned."

Did she mean something different than him coming back to claim the title? He thought she did. "I have. Along with my wife. This is Lord Harry Northcott of Newchurch and Miss Gertrude Bucket of Boston."

Gertrude squirmed uncomfortably under her gaze.

"And you are Master Beranger," the old woman said, bringing her attention back to him. "I recognize your eyes. I remember you running through the woods like a wild elk."

Recognition stirred in the back of his mind.

The crone turned to Emma, who gripped his hand more tightly. "And who are you?"

"She is my wife, the Duchess of Brightshire. Seems I've come up in the world." They had entered the hamlet of Goldenbrook. "Where shall we stop?"

"Here, Your Grace," the old woman said. "Your coach can't manage the woodlands where I live."

Beranger followed her gaze to the few dwellings. Grimy windows flickered with candlelight. In the deepening twilight and low mist that had begun to creep along the cooling earth and moss, the community appeared unnerving—deserted, even, although that was plainly not the case. He thumped the ceiling, and the coach halted.

The door opened, and she was helped to the ground by the footman.

Beranger passed out the heavy basket of food.

"Wait," Emma said softly, stopping the woman as she backed away, her arms full. "You never said who you are. What is your name?"

Beranger cut his gaze up to the darkened sky. He'd have to speak with Emma, make her understand she was not in Colorado any longer. He hoped he could help her comprehend the difference without making Brightshire, and now Goldenbrook, sound unappealing. Things here were different. Older. Strange things occurred.

"My name? No one of consequence has ever asked my name before. They'd rather me get out of their sight. But since you've asked, Miss Emma, I'm Mathilda Tugwer, duchess of the swamp." She tittered like a young girl at her joke.

Gertrude bristled at the disrespect shown by the old woman's intimate form of address.

"But most folks around here know me as the midwife. If you ask for that, I can be found." She turned a sly eye his way. "You may be in need of my services someday soon, Your Grace."

"We'll be on our way," Beranger stated, ignoring her outlandish statement, his patience all but gone. But as the coach turned around, headed on toward Ashbury, he wondered how the old woman had known Emma's name.

Fear streaked through Emma. "So many servants!" she breathed when she saw the domestics lined up to receive their coach. Their black-and-white uniforms stood out in the light of the gas lamps. She swallowed hard. The riders who'd gone ahead with the horses while they'd taken Mathilda Tugwer to Goldenbrook must have alerted the house to their pending arrival.

Emerging from the forestlands a moment ago, Emma had been robbed of breath when the silhouette of Ashbury Castle had come into view. Golden light gleamed from windows, making the place look magical. But it was not at all how she'd imagined. She'd seen pictures of castles with moats filled with water and a massive gate to span the channel. This was more like a huge, elegant house.

Excitement twirled inside as the coach rolled to a stop in front of the five-story building. Several squared-off pillars reached for the sky, and two flags gently waved a welcome, as if to say: *The duke is home!* The footman opened the door to a rush of fresh air. Beranger descended first and offered Emma his hand. Thankful for the feel of his warmth in this moment of uncertainty, she looked up into his eyes.

"Here we are."

"Yes, here we are," she replied, pushing down her wobbly stomach. As she stepped out of the coach, she caught sight of the moon as it peered from behind a silvery-white cloud, casting their shadows before them. *How many years of nobility have done as I am doing right now? How many marriages have been made? How many soldiers sent into battle? And now, I, Emma Fortitude Brinkman Northcott, am doing the same. The thought is unnerving.*

Servants bowed and curtsied as they walked the gravel path to the front door, older ones smiling affectionately at Beranger, and the younger ones less at ease, not knowing what to expect of their new duke.

Beranger stopped before a tall, stately man. "Mr. Pencely," he said warmly.

"Your Grace," the butler said, his arms straight at his sides. "We were delighted to learn Lord Harry's search for you in America was fruitful. My heart is full at this reunion. Too many years have passed since you left us."

He turned his attention to her. "Your Grace," he said with all the respect in the world. "Welcome to Ashbury."

Emma gripped Beranger's hand as they passed through a foyer guarded by several suits of armor, a plethora of swords crossed on the wall, and an impressive coat of arms tapestry. They were barely inside the grand house, and already she'd never experienced such opulence.

An impressive staircase of dark walnut filled one side of the entry-way, large portraits of a regal-looking lord and lady the other. The room glimmered thanks to crystal gas chandeliers. The ceiling was so tall she couldn't guess the height. Pencely led them to a set of tall double doors where another suit of armor stood at attention.

A feeling of wonder chased away Emma's trepidation about meeting the dowager duchess and was replaced by exhilaration and anticipation. *This is my wonderful new life. With my magnificent husband, whom I love with all my heart.*

They entered the room.

Standing near the center, the dowager duchess and Lady Audrey were, in a word, stunning. The older woman wore a vivid blue velvet gown accented with creamy white lace at her collar and wrists. The close-fitting bodice showed a fine figure. Her chestnut hair was styled with tight curls on her head and around her oval face.

Lady Audrey reminded Emma of a mixture between Mavis and Lavinia. She had her older sister's wide blue eyes and Lavinia's glossy brown hair and heart-shaped face. Her narrow-sleeved, low-cut emerald gown displayed just a small swell of her breasts and was adorned with flouncing, a multitude of bows, and thick ribbon. On anyone else the embellished garment might have looked silly, but Lady Audrey shone, beautiful like a star in the heavens.

Emma allowed Beranger to guide her forward. He halted before his stepmother and half sister, the women's expressions unreadable.

"Duke," the dowager duchess said, putting out her hand to Beranger. "Welcome home."

Beranger took her hand in his. What would he say? Emma wondered. Or call her? Gertrude had rehearsed with her what she'd thought the reception would be like, what to expect, but nobody had really known. Emma sensed Lord Harry behind her and knew her tutor would be there as well, judging her performance.

"Dowager Duchess," Beranger said. "My happiness at being back at Ashbury is immeasurable. You look well. I'm pleased."

Watching Beranger's genuine smile and the heartfelt expression in his eyes, Emma recalled all the ways this woman had schemed time and time again against her husband when he was only a boy. Yet in an instant, he'd signaled that bygones were bygones. Her esteem of him grew even more.

"I'd like you to meet my wife, Her Grace, the Duchess of Brightshire, formerly Emma Brinkman of Colorado."

The dowager duchess turned to Emma. "Duchess," she replied, smiling so sweetly Emma felt like she was truly glad to meet her.

"My stepmother," Beranger said to Emma. "Her Grace, the Dowager Duchess of Brightshire."

They didn't waste words here in England. Beranger's stepmother, still smiling, took Emma's outstretched hand and patted it.

"Ma'am," Emma replied with a slight nod.

"And you must be Lady Audrey, my sister," Beranger said, a certain pride ringing in his tone. "I'm delighted to meet you. I didn't know you existed until a month ago. The fact that I have a sister is a great surprise to me, although it shouldn't be." They did the dignified hand holding, but then Beranger pulled her into a hug.

Flustered, Lady Audrey stepped back, toward a distinguished-looking young gentleman who'd been standing behind her. She performed a slight curtsy, murmuring in a silky, practiced voice, "Yes, Duke. And I you. I've heard a lot about my half brother, Beranger, and his different-colored eyes."

Direct and to the point. Beranger introduced them, and Emma tried to get a feel for if they'd be friends, but the introductions had moved on to the fellow instead.

"Brig! Welcome home," he chortled. "What a great surprise for all of us. Too bad Gavin's not here as well. We lived through many adventures—some good, some not so good, and I believe even though you were younger than your brother, you were the ringleader."

Emma hoped she didn't look hopelessly lost already. At least Beranger had explained that the nickname Brig, shortened from Brightshire, would be used by friends and family, and that his father had gone by Brig for most of his life. That she could call him Brig, Brightshire, Beranger, or *my love*. He'd let her know with kisses that he preferred the latter.

The man speaking to him so warmly turned out to be the Honorable Justin Winters, a distant cousin. Emma had been frantically thinking through Gertrude's lessons when Beranger had whispered that she need only address him by his name and that others would call him "Mr." and not the cumbersome title "honorable."

"Ringleader, yes. Truer words were never spoken," the dowager duchess agreed, smiling prettily.

Justin ignored the dowager's comment. He wore dark brown trousers of fine fabric. His slim-fitted jacket was open to a high-buttoning waistcoat, stiff collar, and a knotted necktie.

"You're a sight for sore eyes, Brig! I was only eleven when you ran off, you heartless fellow. We were all worried." His gaze cut to the dowager and then jumped to Emma. "I hope he didn't tell you he wasn't loved, because he was. At least by me. I practically worshipped the ground he walked on. Playing with him was always much more exciting than with Gavin. The late duke had a tendency to stay around the manor, while your husband enjoyed riding into the unknown hills, cave crawling, and exploring lake bottoms. Never a dull moment with this Northcott."

Emma glanced at the dowager, who never seemed to let an expression cross her face that wasn't expertly controlled. She was a master at hiding her thoughts. On the ship, Lord Harry had shared that when she found out Gavin was the illegitimate son—the sin she'd unmercifully wielded over Beranger's head—she went into seclusion for months.

After she emerged, the topic never once crossed her lips. Now here she stood proudly, as if the balance of power between her and her stepson had not shifted an inch in the sixteen years Beranger had been away.

Beranger held up a hand to stop the singing of his praises. "Justin is two years younger than myself, Emma, and being he was only a boy, he does not remember things as clearly as he should. I assure you—our childhood was not nearly as exciting as he claims."

Justin smiled at Emma. "I can't wait to hear about your adventures abroad. I want to know all about America and you and your sisters—American heiresses and owners of most of a Colorado town called Eden, am I correct?" He gave another bright smile, but she didn't miss the way his eyes flickered toward the dowager and back. "We're all family now. And as family, I'll be the first to enlighten you of the peril threatening Ashbury. I'm not sure even Lord Harry knows," he said, glancing at the older man, "because much of it has befallen us while he has been away."

Beranger's smile disappeared as Lord Harry stepped forward to join him. "Oh?"

"Gavin liked to gamble more than was prudent. Much of the fortune is gone. A large section of farmland has just been sold to keep this place running. I believe, Brig, you will have your hands full keeping things afloat."

CHAPTER FOUR

Tonight is special. The duke has returned. But what a time to be thrown into the scullery without a whit of knowledge as to what was expected. Charlotte scoured a black spot on the bottom of a large copper kettle, scrubbing diligently—washing dishes she knew, but interacting with castle folks, even servants, was foreign to her. She'd spent most of her years in the back of her aunt's bakeshop with a head filled with dreams.

Charlotte had been taking three cakes out of the wall oven the morning after Amelia's return home when Aunt Ethel came storming into the kitchen, her nightcap askew, her wild gaze flying about.

"Amelia is burning up," she'd said. "Get me some wet rags and some ice."

Ice? Here in the bakeshop? There was no such thing. Charlotte had offered to go for the doctor, but her aunt informed her that she'd already woken Thomas up to dress. Charlotte had been ordered to wash and dress and take Amelia's place at Ashbury.

"If she doesn't show up this morning," Aunt Ethel said, "she'll be fired. You know how mean that duchess can be."

Charlotte complied, lucky to catch a ride with the milkman, but she'd had no news concerning her cousin's condition since she'd left. Thomas was supposed to bring word, but he'd not come.

Straining now, she lifted the heavy copper pot and dipped it into the rinse water, whose surface had collected a shiny film. *That* would need changing soon too. She set the pot upside down on the drainboard with the pile of other pots and pans she'd scrubbed, then paused to stretch her back in several directions. The ache of this work nearly made her long to be back in her aunt's kitchen.

How in Saint Gabriel's name did the cook and her underlings go through so many pots and pans? She dared not slow her pace. Soon one of the kitchen maids would arrive with another armload to be washed.

Toweling off the damp dishes and kitchenware, she put them away, trying to stay out from under the footmen and maids. The pots and pans to the kitchen. The china and crystal to a long cupboard in the hallway between the two rooms, which was locked with a key each and every time it was opened and closed. The key, attached to a long burgundy strap, was draped around her neck. If anything went missing during the time she had the key, she'd be responsible.

A kitchen maid sailed into the scullery. "Amelia! Where's the large saucepan? The one that's dented on the rim." She frantically glanced around. "Have you hidden it to cause trouble?"

Hidden it? How outrageous. "I'd never do such a thing," Charlotte stated as she turned from the sink, feeling defeated and tired.

The maid tipped her head. "I keep forgetting you're Amelia's cousin." She drew her lip between her not-so-straight teeth. "Do you have any idea? It's Cook's favorite." She rummaged wildly through the items Charlotte had just finished washing, knocking a pan to the stone floor. "Not here anywhere." Her gaze narrowed. "Where'd ya hide the bloomin' thing? I know your type. Anything to get attention. Don't care how or why."

Servants brought Charlotte caked-on, greased-up, and burned things all day long. How was she expected to remember where everything went? "I *do* remember the bent saucepan—but an hour or two ago. You're sure it's not already being used somewhere in the kitchen?"

The girl's lip curled.

These people are not your family. You're not in the bakeshop any longer . . . "Have you checked the lower kitchen shelf next to the medium-size cupboard where the dishes go?"

"Ain't there. Besides, that's just fer fry pans."

How in the world do they expect me to remember one pan among so many?

The maid planted her hands on her waist. "I've searched everywhere. Come on, you're gonna help." She grasped Charlotte's arm and tugged her into the other room. "Otherwise, we'll both be plucking feathers for a month . . ."

Ah, a job I'm good at.

The kitchen was hopping like a hutch full of hares on hot coals. Servants were jumping this way and that, preparing the evening meal for *the lost duke*, as they called him, who'd returned after sixteen years away.

Charlotte pushed her hair from her eyes with the back of her hand and quickly searched the places she'd been, retraced her steps, and finally found the pot buried beneath several others in a large, heavy drawer.

"Be more careful where you put things!" the cook admonished after the emergency had been averted. The woman had been kind on their first meeting, but now that dinner was being served, her eyes looked cold and hard. She was only as good as her help.

Feeling chastised, Charlotte went back to the scullery, wondering again about Amelia's condition.

"You're new here," the footman said, following her into the scullery.

"I'm only filling in for my cousin." She dropped her gaze to the two sinks of water, which still needed draining. "As soon as she's well, she'll be back."

"I see." He was tall with a nice smile and dark hair. Amelia had said footmen were hired for their good looks and stature. To say he was handsome was an understatement.

"Jos!" the cook hollered. "These beef cakes need to go up."

"Are you Jos?" she whispered, alarm spiking up her neck.

He nodded. "Jos Sleshinger."

"You better get to work." *Before you get me in trouble.*

He turned on his polished heel and was gone.

Relieved to once again be alone, she tested the water on the stove by dipping in her baby finger.

The same kitchen maid, who was Amelia's roommate in the servants' quarters on the top floor, clattered back into the scullery carrying an armload of china. "Be sure you empty your water and clean the sink before you start on the dinnerware."

"I'm doing that now," Charlotte responded, reaching into the cold, slimy rinse water to pull the drain. "But thank you for the tip. I appreciate you pointing things out."

"I was the scullery maid before your cousin, and I'll make sure you don't get unmindful of your duties. If you do, I'll get scolded."

Charlotte tried a timid smile. Later tonight she'd be alone in a room with this girl. She wished they could become friends. "I'm sorry, but in everything I've learned today, I've forgotten your name."

"I'll bet a shilling you ain't forgot Jos's." She raised a censuring eyebrow before marching away.

Charlotte glanced down at her grease- and grime-stained apron and began to laugh. Before she knew it, she was bent over the sink as she dried her eyes with her apron strings. What she'd thought was funny had turned into despair. She was exhausted and desperately needed a cup of tea.

"Is there something funny in that sink?"

The keys! She'd mistaken the jingle of keys for silverware being taken from the drawer in the next room. She whirled around. Mrs. Darling, the housekeeper and head over all the women downstairs, stood before her. If the missing pan hadn't lost Amelia her job, Charlotte's warped sense of humor might. What should she say? Beg for forgiveness?

"I, ma'am, er, no . . ."

"I distinctly heard you laughing, Miss Aldridge. I'd like to know why."

She knows me.

"I guess I'm a little tired. And, well . . ."

Mrs. Darling's eyes softened. "You've been flung into a difficult situation." She came into the room and looked around. The large ring of keys she was known for was fastened to a leather belt she wore around her middle. As stern as she looked, Charlotte sensed she was fair.

"I'm changing the wash and rinse water now, to begin on those," Charlotte said, looking at the china. "But first, I need to rid the sink of grease." She glanced at the clock. It was almost nine, an hour before the staff took their own meals in the servants' hall. But not the kitchen staff. All the rules had been spelled out to her more clearly than her actual duties.

Mrs. Darling lifted a brow. "Tonight will end soon enough. And then you'll rest. Tomorrow will be easier."

With that, the housekeeper was gone. Charlotte took heart. *This too shall pass. And who knows, once I'm back in the bakeshop, I might even miss all the activity. Things have a way of becoming something different once they're over.*

Taking the large bar of soap, she lathered her rag and cleaned the sink. Going to the stove, and being careful not to burn herself, she wrapped the thick towel around the handle of the pot and, with both hands, carefully carried it to the sink, poured a portion of water in to rinse the sink, sloshed it around, and repeated the process. Her arms shook with fatigue. Once the sink was clean and she'd plugged the drain, she dumped in the rest of the water with great relief.

The strong feeling of being watched made her turn. She wished the scullery had a door, so she'd not be so visible to anyone passing. She expected her grumpy roommate or the housekeeper again. Maybe even the bold footman.

She almost dropped the empty pot on her feet.

"Excuse me." The young man Verity had mentioned visiting the bakeshop—the Honorable so-and-so—stood there. He pointed to a bright scarlet stain on the front of his white shirt.

"W-wine?" she asked, struggling to speak through her suddenly dry throat.

He shook his head, his charming smile making her light-headed. "Something better. Raspberry currant sauce. Would you know where I might find some hot milk, pretty miss? I hate to ruin a perfectly good shirt."

CHAPTER FIVE

I n the wee morning hours, Beranger, who'd been unable to find sleep, pulled Emma closer to his side and drew the heavy counterpane over her shoulders. Since the fire had dwindled to coals, the bedchamber had cooled considerably.

He lay in the huge bed, one arm resting behind his head, the other holding Emma, her head resting on his chest. Darkness still hovered outside the windows. Intent on seeing the sunrise, she had requested they leave the drapes open. He'd complied, eager to do her bidding and ensure her happiness. She was everything to him. He'd not let her be hurt or regret their decision to wed. As if reading his thoughts, she sighed in her warm cocoon and snuggled closer, running her palm over his naked chest.

Justin's news last night had come as an unwelcome surprise. *Damned Gavin! Never knew when to quit and walk away.* Now his ineptness was threatening what had been in the family for centuries. For a moment he'd considered that perhaps things were not as bad as Justin made them sound. He'd always liked to be the purveyor of drama and misfortune when they were children.

Beranger had stayed beside the dowager as the others ambled off in conversation.

"You're a man now," she'd said. He'd watched her lift her chin in a fashion Beranger remembered all too well as her gaze tracked between his green eye and the vivid blue one that was the signature color all the male Northcott heirs had inherited. She'd been formulating what to say, how to put him down, where to land her spear of words to effect the severest injury. She'd done it since he was a child.

"Don't stare at me so with those queer eyes," she'd hissed at him when she'd come into the stable unannounced.

Only nine years old, Beranger had stepped out of the stall, a pitchfork in hand, sweaty from mucking the stalls. Her sudden appearance, and the sight of her hatred, had made him stumble, and he'd had to catch himself on the stable door to keep from falling.

"You unnerve me to my soul. I can't imagine what you're thinking when you look at me that way. Why can't your father see you clearly, as I do? Now go away, go hide until I'm gone. I don't like to be in the same room when it's just the two of us."

"So tall. Handsome," the dowager duchess said now, her voice smooth. "I had not thought I'd ever see you again. I have suffered many years of guilt over your disappearance. I'll admit, at first your absence was a relief, but as the years passed, I came to realize my part in your disappearance. I hope your years in America have served you well."

He hadn't expected her soul baring, and yet, he should keep in mind she *was* a master of deception. Had she really suffered from guilt? He hardly thought so. Could they begin anew? Be the family they never were before? She most likely would be repulsed at the idea. But a festering grudge only hurt the grudge holder. He had Emma and wanted a good life, not one where he'd have to be wondering about his stepmother's intentions all the time. He refused to be that person. "They have," he said. "In fact, I owe you a debt. If I hadn't gone away, I'd not have met Emma. For that, I'm extremely grateful. I can't imagine my life without her."

Her gaze slid to Emma, who was conversing with Lady Audrey. He was relieved that the two seemed to have taken a liking to each other. Once all the newness of England wore off, Emma would miss her four sisters more than she knew. Perhaps Lady Audrey could help fill the void.

The dowager continued. "From what I learned from Lord Harry's cable, you knew her only a short time before wedding her. She isn't much more than what the Americans call a mail-order bride, is she not? She hardly knows you or the place she will now call home. I hope she will be happy here."

Her self-satisfied smile caused his stomach to clench. She believed her words would anger him, hurt him. Hadn't the embarrassing predicament she found herself in, her bigamous marriage and the illegitimacy of her son, softened her in the least? Perhaps she was just making a statement and hadn't meant it as a slight to Emma. "Hardly that. And she's resilient. I'm sure she'll adjust quite well."

"As much as you may try, you can't understand these types of challenges for a woman. But I'll keep an eye on her and help whenever possible."

If only that were true. He'd made a pact with himself aboard ship he'd not let his boyhood insecurities concerning his stepmother affect him—but he did not desire harmony so much that he'd let Emma be chewed up by unkind comments meant to slice her heart in two.

He leaned close and lowered his voice so the footman standing at the door wouldn't hear. "Let me make myself perfectly clear. There will be no shenanigans where Emma is concerned. Not like when I was a boy. I had to put up with your torments back then, but she does not have to now. Are we understood on that subject?"

Her eyes snapped with anger, but still she smiled. "Duke, I'm surprised you'd think so little of me."

"Emma was not, or is not, a mail-order bride. That comment was to hurt me on my homecoming to Ashbury. Do you agree?"

"I misspoke, never intending for you to take my statement in that light. I'm sorry."

Well, good. We both know where we stand. Maybe she means her words. I've never heard her apologize to anyone before.

He'd changed the uncomfortable subject then, expressing his condolences on the deaths of his father and half brother.

At the mention of Gavin's name, she'd glanced at the darkened window across the room for several long moments.

"There is one thing I've yet to come to terms with," she'd said.

"What is that?" He had the power to put her out if he wished. He'd never do that, despite what she'd tried to do to him throughout the years.

"When Gavin took the title," she began, "since he had yet to marry, he allowed me to remain in the wing I'd shared with my husband for all the years we were married. The rooms hold so many memories. My marriage, the birth of my children . . ."

Realization dawned. "You don't desire to move to Lily House?" Located on the other side of the garden, the dwelling was where the dowager resided once a new duchess arrived. Lily House was a smaller version of Ashbury and just as beautifully decorated.

How would Emma react to the dowager remaining not only in Ashbury but in the bedchambers reserved for the duke and duchess? The dowager's feelings were understandable, he supposed. She'd lost so much, her husband and her son, in a short amount of time. If he kept a close eye on her, perhaps there were things Emma could learn from her. Would his wife prefer to have the dowager duchess close to answer questions and give advice? He couldn't *always* be here. There would be times he would be away. He'd make this concession for Emma, even though the dowager's moving out wouldn't bother him in the least. "If you'd like to remain in that wing for the time being, that's fine. I have no pressing urge to take the second floor. Emma and I will be well content on the third floor, where we are now."

"Your generosity is exemplary. Thank you."

And they would be content. So much had happened in the last two months. Not only had he found his soul mate and married, something he'd thought would never happen, but he'd learned his father had actually married his mother—a commoner. How that had transpired was still a mystery, but the ceremony had been kept secret, even after Beranger's birth.

My father was weak. Allowed my grandfather to rule his every move, dictate who he was supposed to marry.

Disdain welled up within. How hypocritical was the aristocracy? If Brightshire expected an aristocratic English duke upon his return, they'd be sorely disappointed. He was more American in thought and deed than English.

"You're awake?" Emma murmured into the darkness.

"I am. How did you sleep, my love? Are you rested?"

She made a catlike sound deep in her throat and stretched against him. "Very well, thank you. This bed is heavenly compared to the one on the ship. I'm thankful to finally be in Brightshire—on solid ground. Oh, Beranger, Ashbury Castle is astounding. More than I ever dreamed. You should have warned me."

"If I had, you may have refused to come."

"Never." She sat up, and the counterpane fell away to expose her silky chemise. "Wherever you go, I'll go as well."

Seeing her like this, only the filmy garment between them, was tempting. But she was worn out from the trip and last night's lengthy meal. They'd let the servants do their unpacking at their arrival, but before bed, instead of calling the maid, Beranger had insisted on helping Emma undress.

"Emma, have you read the letter from your father?"

He felt her still.

"Not yet, but soon. I want to be settled first."

"Settled? Aren't you curious as to what it says? If I was in your shoes, I don't think I could wait."

She didn't respond.

"When you do, you'll tell me?"

"Of course. Now, happy anniversary, my love," she said, finding his lips.

Was she trying to distract him? He pushed away his doubt and made sure she knew how much he liked her attentions. "Our anniversary was yesterday."

"I'm just early for next month."

He chuckled.

The morning was still dark and, unable to see anything of the horizon, Emma burrowed back under the covers.

"It's like a dream come true," she whispered against his neck. "Who would have thought something as fantastic as becoming a duchess was my destiny." She drew a short distance away. "Beranger, I don't *feel* any different. I'm the third daughter of a cattle rancher, a sister, a wife. That's all. All these lords and ladies are going to know I'm a fraud."

"You're *not* a fraud. And everything that you are is more than enough," he growled, rolling her onto her back and finding her lips.

A short knock sounded. A moment later, the door opened to the glowing light of the gas lamps in the hall. A maid came partway into the room holding a tray.

"It's still dark," Beranger bit out, angry at the interruption. He didn't bother to pull the counterpane over his shoulder.

"I'm sorry, Your Grace," the girl replied in a quaking voice.

She looked terrified, holding a tray of white porcelain dishes, cups and saucers, and crystal water glasses. Breakfast fit for a king and queen. Things he'd experienced after making his millions in America, but not here at Ashbury. His room as a boy had been at the end of the servants' quarters, a whole two floors away from Gavin. And he rarely ate in the dining room with the family because his eyes were too spooky for the duchess. They made her lose her appetite. That had been fine with him, after the rejection had faded. He'd liked the servants better anyway . . .

The chambermaid grimaced. The tray was heavy.

"The dowager duchess thought you and the duchess would like some tea and scones with clotted cream and orange marmalade," she said softly. "But I can come back later, if you'd prefer."

Is my stepmother already interfering in my life by having breakfast sent up hours early—or is she really trying to be nice?

Beside him, Emma sat up, clutching the counterpane to her throat, her strawberry hair tousled. "That's not necessary, miss," she said, looking around for the robe draped on the end of the massive bed. She jumped up and slipped it on. "Please come in. Those scones do sound delicious."

Beranger sighed and burrowed deeper under the counterpane, refusing to get out of bed. The chambermaid—Hyacinth Green, which Emma learned by asking her name, age, and how long the girl had been at Ashbury—was all smiles in less than a minute. The tray was deposited on the side table.

Beranger levered himself up on his elbow. "Would there happen to be any coffee in the kitchen?"

"Coffee, Your Grace?" the servant repeated.

Emma's eyes brightened. "Yes! Coffee! I remember my first cup brewed over campfire flames and under the stars. We were out riding the ranch, exploring the far reaches of the acreage." She sighed, and her eyes went dreamy. "All to the chorus of the coyotes and an owl. I've never had a better cup since."

Hyacinth looked doubtful. "I'm not sure, Your Grace. I'll have to check. I've not seen any in the kitchen."

"I've had enough tea to last a lifetime," Beranger said gruffly. "I need coffee—strong and plentiful. The duchess does as well."

Emma put out a placating hand. "Could you ask for us, Hyacinth? Watching the sunrise with a cup of coffee will remind me of Colorado."

She looked through the covered dishes on the tray like a child inspecting the presents under the Christmas tree.

"Yes, Your Grace. Straightaway." The pretty sixteen-year-old twirled easily now, free of the tray, and made to leave.

Emma hurried ahead and opened the door for her.

Beranger stifled a laugh. It was touching the way she tried to make the chambermaid feel comfortable. She didn't yet understand the way of service like the English did. Emma would learn the staff didn't want to have their jobs done for them, because if that occurred they would have no way to support themselves. They'd discuss the subject later, over coffee—if the kitchen had any—and see if he might be able to make her understand.

If he didn't, there was no doubt his stepmother would. And that conversation would not be pretty. He wondered if he'd made a mistake allowing her to remain in the wing that should rightfully be theirs. He needed to talk to Emma about it. Would she understand why he'd decided to allow it? How could she, if he hardly did himself?

CHAPTER SIX

C harlotte zipped around the scullery, preparing for another day. She barely noticed her aching muscles and strained back as she polished the stove and brought in more firewood. She swept the whole room and polished the window that looked out on the service door. Today felt like her birthday, Christmas, and New Year's all wrapped up in one. All because of the Honorable Justin Winters. Memories of last night had her stepping high. With persistence, and scalded milk, she'd been able to remove most of the berry stain from his shirt, but not completely. She'd been astounded by his patience as she worked on the crimson blot. He'd casually talked of this and that and even mentioned that he'd noticed her in the bakeshop a time or two in Brightshire and was surprised to see her arrive at the castle yesterday. He'd even called her pretty.

Verity would have swooned with envy.

Was the stain on his shirt on purpose? She couldn't help but think that was possible. *So he could come down to the kitchen to see me?*

"Why're you standing there wasting time?" Margaret Malone— Charlotte had made a point of remembering her name this time— appeared in the doorway, holding a tray of pots and pans. The kitchen's daily routine was already underway.

Margaret's tone, as sharp as any darning needle, went straight through Charlotte. She'd tried to befriend the kitchen maid last night before bed. And again this morning. But Margaret didn't seem to want to be friends. Thankfully, this morning Thomas had left a note on the scullery sideboard for Charlotte to say that Amelia's fever had broken and the doctor expected her to make a full recovery within the week. Charlotte would soon be back at the bakeshop, making bread, cakes, and meat pies like normal.

"I'm heating the hot water, what else?"

"Should'a put that on *before* ya blackened the stove and swept the floor. Now you'll be waiting for the water to boil and be backed up for most the mornin'." Margaret shook her head in dismay, but the gleeful look in her eyes gave her away. "Mrs. Darling *won't* be pleased. You best be prepared to be scolded."

"Tomorrow I'll put the water on first thing. Nobody mentioned that to me."

"I shouldn't need to mention something so basic. Anyone would know what to do."

Actually, Margaret was right. If she hadn't been mooning over Mr. Winters since before she'd opened her eyes, she would have thought of the simple step. "You're right, Margaret. Thank you for pointing out my error."

Having finished unloading the dirty saucepots, crusted cake tins, and blackened frying pans, the maid hurried away. Within a moment, she was back.

Annoyed, because Margaret had indeed caught her waiting pointlessly for the water to warm, as she'd predicted, Charlotte straightened. "Yes? Did you want to say something else?" *Go on and castigate me again for being stupid. I can take it. I'm used to Aunt Ethel . . .*

"Mrs. Darling wants to see us in her office."

Charlotte blinked. "Us?"

Margaret nodded.

Charlotte followed her out the door, past the servants' hall, to the end of the corridor, where a brass plate hung on the door. It read: "Mrs. Darling, Housekeeper."

They looked at each other, and Charlotte knocked.

"Come in."

The room was cozy. Mrs. Darling sat behind a writing desk, glasses Charlotte hadn't seen before perched on her nose. As well as other writing implements, a feather pen sat in a cradle, its soft white plumes disturbed by their entrance. A side glance at Margaret revealed the stark whiteness of her face. She was frightened to death. Charlotte had the bakeshop, and in a sense, so did Amelia. But what of Margaret? Did she even have a home to return to if she was fired?

"Ma'am," Charlotte began, feeling responsible for some reason for the grumpy maid. "You wanted to see us?"

Mrs. Darling nodded. "I know you're both busy at the start of the day, so I'll not keep you long. I've been informed that you, Miss Aldridge, show talent as a baker at your family's shop in Brightshire. From this time until Amelia returns, you, Miss Malone, will return to the scullery, and you, Miss Aldridge, will assist in the kitchen—as Margaret does, but I'd like you to work alongside the pastry cook as well. Now that the duke and duchess have arrived, some new fare in the kitchen will be nice."

A knife sliced through Charlotte's heart. *Poor Margaret!* She would not take this well. The demotion was a huge step back, and all of them, including Mrs. Darling, knew that fact clearly. The scullery was the bottom of the ladder.

"B-but, ma'am . . . ," Margaret began.

"It's only for a time, Margaret. Charlotte is needed in the kitchen, where her talents will shine." She smiled and stood, signaling the discussion was over. "Effective immediately."

Charlotte chanced a quick glance at Margaret as they left. The girl's face appeared chiseled from stone. Charlotte felt compelled to say something, a few words to soften the blow. A sentence or two, to let Margaret know she hadn't gone looking for her job. That as soon as Amelia returned all would go back to normal. *It would, wouldn't it?*

Margaret beat her to the punch. Halfway to the scullery, she grabbed Charlotte's arm and pulled her to a stop. "I didn't have an easy life like you, working for your family. I come from the workhouse, and before that, a cottage home since I was one year old. With no ma or pa, work's all I've ever known. At twelve, I got my first job in Throwly, working seventeen-hour days for a gentleman and lady with three young'uns. They made sure to get their money's worth out of lazy ol' Margaret. That job lasted two years, then I got taken on here, in the scullery, being a helper to the scullery maid. When she took to her grave, I showed Mrs. Darling I could do the job myself. Took me three years to advance, and your cousin took over." Tears welled in her eyes. "I made something of myself. I'm a kitchen maid at Ashbury Castle."

"You *have* made something of yourself, Margaret! And you should be proud."

"I'm not pretty. Some might say I hurt the eyes. That's why I have to work harder than anyone else, because of my looks. Chambermaids are pretty—in case the gentry sees 'em. Footmen too." That was all she could get out before one large tear rolled down her cheek.

"Please don't cry, Margaret. I had no intention for this to transpire. I didn't request to work in the kitchen. I'm just filling in so Amelia won't lose her job. I'm sure as soon as she returns, you'll be back in the kitchen, just that fast."

Margaret wiped her tears using the backs of her shaky fingers, then her eyes narrowed. Her grief hadn't taken long to turn into anger, and perhaps hatred. "You won't get away with this, Miss Nicey-nice. You'll be sorry you stole my job."

Margaret continued toward the scullery. And Charlotte just stood there feeling miserable.

I wonder how Mrs. Darling found out I do most of the fancy baking?

Her conversation last night with Mr. Winters came back to her. Had he spoken of her with the housekeeper?

A thrill of impressive proportions skittered up and down Charlotte's back.

CHAPTER SEVEN

From across the table in the breakfast room, which was completely different from the grand dining hall they'd eaten in last night, Emma watched Beranger in a deep discussion with Lord Harry. She'd never seen him so intense. Between her bites of egg, some sort of beans, and a crumpet she'd taken from the tray of sugary delights resting on the sideboard, she caught words such as *poker*, *debt*, and *Gavin*.

"And what is this?" she whispered to the footman who was filling her cup from a fine silver pot. The English even brewed their coffee differently; Emma would be able to stand a spoon in the dark sludge if she so desired. She poked at the curious-looking item using her fork.

The footman pulled back and raised one brow. "That's black pudding, Your Grace."

She noted the firm texture. "It doesn't look like pudding. It looks like sausage, but the color is strange." She took a tiny bite, chewed, and then swallowed. "It's tasty," she said, as if conversing with the footman was a natural thing to do.

"That's because it *is* sausage, Your Grace."

A bubble of irritation surfaced inside. She was learning quickly that English reticence sometimes made simple things difficult. "Then why call sausage pudding? Clearly, it's not. And I've never seen black sausage before. What makes it so?" She cut off another portion and considered the odd flavor. *Not pudding indeed.*

Across the table Beranger and Lord Harry had stopped speaking and were watching her with amused smiles.

Annoyed, she swallowed and glanced back at the footman, who seemed to be growing more uncomfortable by the second. "Can you explain?"

"Pig's blood turns black with air. At least that's what I've been told. I've not watched the process myself. The blood is gathered when the hog is slaughtered, so—"

Emma gagged and reached for her water.

Beranger and Lord Harry roared with laughter.

The poor footman hurried away.

After rinsing out her mouth, she took several gulps of her heavily sweetened and creamed coffee and then glared across the table at Beranger. "You're supposed to warn me, Beranger! Not let me make mistakes."

"When is eating a delicacy a mistake, my love?" He smiled innocently as he gestured to his plate. Tiny bits of leftover black pudding were evident. "And is this any different from eating mountain oysters, as I heard the ranch hands refer to on the Five Sisters?"

"I don't eat bull's testicles, and I don't eat pig's blood either." She shivered. "Not willingly, anyway."

She looked away before she said something she'd regret and wondered where everybody else was. Last night she'd learned that Beranger's cousin had been staying at the castle for quite some time. Possibly even since Gavin's death. The fact that these grown men and women didn't have any sort of job at all was puzzling. They spent their days talking and eating. What kind of a life was that?

As if her thoughts had conjured them, the dowager duchess, Lady Audrey, and Justin came into the room.

"Shall you let us in on your joke, Duke?" the dowager asked, looking between the men. "We heard you two all the way down the hall."

They availed themselves of the buffet table and sat, Beranger's cousin taking the empty setting next to Emma.

"Lord Harry was just telling me about an incident that happened in a bar in Santa Fe. That's an American town I'm well acquainted with, having lived and worked there for over a year. It's nothing you'd find amusing, I'm sure."

He lifted his coffee cup and locked eyes with Emma over the rim. His gaze said he was sorry and that they were on the same side.

"As a matter of fact," he went on, since he still held everyone's attention, "Santa Fe is where Emma and I met. In a women's apparel shop."

Please stop. Don't say that I was taking you to task for flirting with the sales clerk.

"Emma was the most beautiful woman I'd ever seen. She stole my breath, and my heart. Isn't that right, my love?"

Heat scorched her cheeks. All eyes turned her way. Even the footmen's, if the burning sensation on the back of her neck meant anything. She'd scold Beranger later. She didn't like being the center of attention, especially around his stepmother.

"What can I say?" she said with a good-natured smile. "I fear my husband needs glasses. He's in fine form this morning. You all should be on your guard."

Lord Harry coughed playfully into his hand and mumbled, "And why not? These few days are his honeymoon, you know . . ."

"Leave the poor girl alone!" Justin chortled. "You're both incorrigible. Give her some time to settle in, then, I'm sure, her being an American, she'll take you down a peg or two, no doubt."

"No doubt," Beranger echoed. "I've seen her do it to a man who wronged one of her sisters."

"*Really*, Justin," the dowager duchess admonished, stirring some lemon into her tea. "You're beginning to sound like an American yourself." She took a sip and then dabbed her lips with her napkin.

The dowager's posture was impeccable, as was Lady Audrey's. Emma straightened even more and lifted her chin the tiniest bit. "I'm curious about life in the castle. What do you like to do for fun, Lady Audrey?" Emma asked.

Lady Audrey looked surprised. "For fun?"

"Well, yes. I love to read and ride my horse." She realized how silly that sounded after the words were already out of her mouth. "My sister Belle took up shooting when we moved to Colorado and is a sharpshooter." She was rambling. But like a toboggan on ice, she had no way of stopping the momentum until she reached the bottom of the slope. "Mavis likes numbers, puzzles, and civics. Lavinia, hats, anything and everything hats—although in the last year she's taken up the painstakingly slow and patient art of rock sculptures. And Katie—" *My gosh, what does Katie like? I can't think of a thing.* "Well, Katie likes just about everything. She's a successful businesswoman. She runs a lumber mill." She sounded like a fool. Why had she gone down this road in the first place? Worse: she felt a wave of homesickness.

Even when Lady Audrey lifted a stiff shoulder, her posture never suffered. "I sing and play the piano. I do stitching and enjoy writing verse. And paint. I so enjoy my watercolors." Her brow lifted. "*And* I socialize."

"We've had more visitors than ever at Ashbury of late," the dowager added smugly. "Lords who have known your father, and his before that," she went on, directing her gaze at Beranger. "Along with their eligible sons. She will have her pick when she decides to marry."

Beranger lowered his coffee cup into the saucer. "That's good news indeed."

"And *I*," Justin blurted good-heartedly, "like to do whatever my benefactor or benefactress is doing at the moment. I'm a jack-of-all-trades, except perhaps building, like your youngest sister, Duchess." He winked at her. "Someday, perhaps, you can show me how to brand a calf, since we don't do that in England. We don't have the wide-open plains like Americans. Our lands are marked and fenced."

Emma found herself relaxing and liking Beranger's cousin.

"I hope we can see some of your paintings, Lady Audrey," Beranger tried again, bringing the conversation back to her. "Do you do landscapes?"

His half sister dropped her gaze to her plate. "Yes. But nothing worth seeing yet."

Disappointment crossed Beranger's face. "Well, soon, I hope. Now"—he placed his napkin beside his plate and stood—"Lord Harry and I have work to do. Accounting ledgers to look at and a trip to London later today, for a vote in tomorrow's House of Lords. There's a bill I'd like to vote on concerning voting rights for more classes of Englishmen."

The dowager's smile was cool, but she said nothing.

Emma frowned and stared at Beranger. When had he made the decision to go away? And without saying a single word to her. Of course, he'd take her too, wouldn't he?

He caught her gaze. "Until a proper lady's maid is hired for you, Emma, Hyacinth Green will fill in. She can pack the things you'll need. Two nights won't require much."

Thank God! Relief flowed from her head to her feet.

"The duchess can't possibly go." The dowager's voice was pleasant but firm. "She's just arrived. Important people want to be introduced. And we have much to go over. The Dowager Countess of Sarre is coming for tea tomorrow, as is Lady Coldred. You remember the local baroness, don't you?"

"Those visits can wait."

Beranger didn't sound as firm as the dowager. Emma looked between the two.

Sadness sagged the dowager's features. "Perhaps you don't remember Harriet Ninham, Dowager Countess of Sarre. She's ninety-five with a delicate heart. She might not make next week. As a boy, you experienced the concept of duty from afar, but never had to conform, to graciously forfeit of yourself. Our main duty is hospitality and graciousness. Now that you're duke, you may not realize the enormous importance of your station, and that of your new wife." She turned her gaze on Emma.

"I'll be happy to stay behind," Emma said, fuming. How dare the dowager paint Beranger in such an ignorant light? If she expected Emma to fall to pieces over a simple social event, she was wrong. Emma would show her she could handle herself in any situation.

"You're sure?" Beranger asked.

Had a look of relief just crossed his eyes? "Absolutely."

"We'll cut our stay to one night. That'll be sufficient time for us to visit our solicitor and make an appearance at the House of Lords."

He came around and helped her from her chair.

"Don't rush back on my account," she responded, gazing into his eyes. "I have your stepmother and sister to count on. If you need more time to finish your business, take the opportunity while you're in London." Her heart squeezed painfully at the thought of sleeping even one night without him, but she kept her tone light. "What on earth could go on here beside chitchat and drinking tea? Besides, I do want to get to know the place."

He pulled her into his arms for a quick embrace and whispered against her ear, "Are you sure? I'd like you to come along. See London."

Wanting to show him she could take care of herself, and that he need not worry, she nodded. "I'm sure. You'll be better able to concentrate on business if I stay here." She was well aware of the others watching. "Go and have a good time, and don't worry. We ladies will have our own fun while you're away."

CHAPTER EIGHT

Deep in thought, Tristen Llewellyn crossed the open lawn and approached the castle greenhouse, intent on delivering a message from his uncle the gamekeeper to the gardener, telling him their evening game of chess would have to be postponed, for he wasn't feeling up to the task. The building, on the south end of the garden, was not far from the servants' door that led to the kitchen. From the other direction, Tristen saw a flash of sapphire along the line of trees and knew it to be Lady Audrey's walking cape. She usually went out this time of day for air, and to enjoy the fall colors.

A burst of heat hit Tristen as he entered the greenhouse. Stuffy air filled his lungs. Striding down the aisle, he passed rows of planters with new sprigs of green he couldn't identify. Others were tall and mature. He recognized the wide leaf of green tobacco not yet ready to be harvested, but that was about all. Aunt Rose would be able to name every plant. She and Uncle Arson were good to have taken him in. Life back in Wales felt like a distant dream. At one time, he'd thought he'd study to become a master mason, like the grandfather who had raised him. Hard substances in his hands roughened his skin, grounded him, and made him know that only small changes were needed for a true conversion. Carefully chipping away at an inlay was like watching a beautiful flower bloom. The hours he'd assisted his grandfather—or even just watched—were some of the best of his life.

Then suddenly his world had changed overnight.

For a moment, he gazed at his hands in the bright enclosure. *Not soft, but nothing like before.*

"Hello?" Tristen called and turned a complete circle. "Anyone here?" The place was small, but visibility was hampered by plants and boxes. The gardener could easily be missed if he were squatting down. The message from his uncle wasn't urgent, but Tristen had obliged because Uncle Arson had a difficult time now even getting out of a chair. If unsuccessful here, he'd check the expansive garden next, and if that didn't pan out, he'd be on his way.

Yesterday, he'd come upon more tracks in the forest, most certainly made by poachers. Empathy for the poor made him sigh. The penalty for poaching had been steeply increased by the last duke. Three months behind bars and worse for a repeat offense. They needed the game to feed their families, but he had a duty to his employer. The risks of closing his eyes to the illegal practices were countless. For Lady Audrey, or any other innocent person walking in the woods, stumbling upon the crime could be extremely unsafe. Desperate men were dangerous.

Unsuccessful in his endeavors inside the greenhouse, Tristen opened the door to leave and practically ran into someone with a wicker basket draped over their arm. "Miss Aldridge!" he said, recognizing the young woman he'd encountered on the road only two days ago. Hadn't she said she worked at the bakeshop in Brightshire? A small world indeed.

Amusement sparkled in her eyes. "Mr. Llewellyn, what a surprise."

"What are you doing here? I thought you worked in Brightshire?" He glanced at her hand, remembering her hurt palm.

"My cousin is the scullery maid in Ashbury's kitchen, and she's taken ill. I'm filling in until she can return so she won't lose her job. But right this moment, I've come to gather a few fresh herbs for the rosemary-walnut bread I'm baking."

Her pleased expression made him smile. "How is your palm? May I see?"

Her eyes widened.

"It was only a tiny scratch, Mr. Llewellyn, and is now healed. There was never a need to worry."

Without asking, he gently took her hand. What she'd said was true. Only a tiny scrape remained on her palm, but the rest of her hands appeared red. Scullery work was not easy. And now she was baking too?

He let go and leaned back, feeling the edge of the building with his shoulder. A bit of sunshine had appeared from beneath the clouds, and he told himself that was the warmth he felt on his face. It had nothing to do with the touch of the hand he'd just been holding. "How does the scullery maid bake bread? I'm confused."

"Actually, I've been promoted to assistant baker, and the poor girl who used to be in the scullery is back there until my cousin returns. I feel horrible about it. Margaret Malone is none too happy about her demotion either."

Margaret? The girl had taken a shine to Tristen the day he'd arrived. He did his best to be her friend without encouraging any infatuation. He, an ex-convict who would himself be out of a job once his uncle's strength returned, had nothing to offer any woman. Not a scullery maid like Margaret—and *certainly* not beautiful Charlotte Aldridge.

At his silence her smile faded. "I wasn't looking to take Margaret's place—it just happened. I never said anything to Mrs. Darling about my baking, but I think Mr. Winters—"

"Mr. Winters?" Tristen tamped back his irritation. He'd seen him hanging around the kitchen before. That man never missed a pretty face. "Oh?"

Charlotte shook her head dismissively. "I'm sure it's nothing. He came to the kitchen with a berry stain on his shirt, and we spoke for a bit. He'd have no reason to mention me to Mrs. Darling, I'm sure."

Tristen wasn't sure about anything at all, now that the warmth he'd been feeling had been dispersed by a gust of icy annoyance. Miss Aldridge was none of his business. Whom she spoke with didn't concern him in the least. "I best be back to work," he said, ready to resume looking for the gardener. "Good luck to you in the kitchen."

An hour later, morning preparations had come and gone, and Cook was working ahead on the noon meal.

Charlotte, in deep contemplation, whipped the spicy scented batter of her family's one-hundred-year-old gingerbread recipe. If she'd made this recipe one time, she'd done so a thousand and needed no words on paper to remember the ingredients and proportions.

She'd told Alcott Brown, the pastry cook, a man in his thirties with shy eyes, a pleasant smile, and a prematurely receding hairline, that she couldn't give the castle her family's secret recipes. However, she could bake as many of their specialties as needed, for as long as she stayed. Aunt Ethel had been emphatic that she do *anything necessary* to keep Amelia's job safe. Making a few gingerbreads couldn't hurt. And, she thought, feeling a smile, perhaps if the duke and duchess liked her delicacies, they'd put in a weekly order from Smith's Bakeshop, in addition to the weekly bread they had delivered each Tuesday. Aunt Ethel would be pleased.

Pouring the batter into her already greased pan, Charlotte used her spatula on the sides of the large bowl. Her thoughts drifted again to Mr. Winters and their encounter the night before. The instant he'd asked for milk, she'd scampered away and gotten some from the cook— for nobility, she'd told her. Why had he seemed so interested? She a maid. He a member of the aristocracy. When the milk had been scalding, he'd stripped out of the blemished garment to a thin linen shirt underneath that indecently showed his muscles, but he didn't even seem to care.

After she'd done all that she could, he'd taken the garment from her, brushing his arm against hers.

A flurry of excitement by the stairs interrupted her daydream. People had descended into the kitchen.

Charlotte glanced at her apron, thankful she'd been careful and had also secured her hair using twice as many pins. No stray locks would escape her cap today.

"Our new duchess," Alcott whispered in Charlotte's ear. "As well as the dowager duchess and Lady Audrey."

The young woman had strawberry-blond hair and a beautiful smile.

Mr. Pencely, the butler, followed behind.

Mrs. Darling's heels clicked hurriedly down the corridor from the opposite direction as she rushed to receive them. Greeting the new duchess, she explained that Cook had asked for her to show them around and introduce them to the staff.

"Much younger than the last," Alcott said, nodding toward the strawberry blonde. "I wasn't here when His Grace was a boy, but many knew him well. The older servants speak highly of him." He shook his head. "But who knows how a man has changed in sixteen years?"

The small group came farther into the kitchen, and the new duchess glanced around with interest, nodding at the things Mrs. Darling pointed out. The new stove alongside the old, the gas lamps that had been added a handful of years back. The water closet down the hall. The icebox.

The duchess seemed enthralled. She actually smiled at a footman and then at a maid.

Mr. Winters came down the stairs and joined the group. His gaze traveled around the room until he saw Charlotte. He inclined his head, his lips curling just the slightest bit.

She dropped her gaze, and heat scalded her face. Had Alcott seen? Had anyone? Looking up through her lashes, Charlotte noticed Margaret's glare from the scullery door, her mouth pulled in a frown.

"Dinner last night was delicious," the duchess said to the cook. "The duke and I enjoyed ourselves immensely."

Charlotte thought she saw the dowager smile snidely and look away.

Cook inclined her head. "My pleasure, Your Grace. If there's anything you or the duke want special, let Mr. Pencely know and he'll tell me. Nothing's too grand or rare. Just ask."

"That's kind of you," the duchess replied. "I'll let my husband know."

"Her name is Emma," Alcott whispered at Charlotte's side, then turned to take a sheet of Chelsea bun cake out of the oven. A light, sugary scent of cinnamon and lemon filled the room.

The group peeked into the scullery, and the new duchess said something to Margaret, as Charlotte stayed all too aware of Mr. Winters's whereabouts. Feeling like she might faint, she forced herself to watch Alcott run a knife around the edges of the pan.

As if he'd read her thoughts, Alcott smiled woefully and said, "Our two classes are worlds apart, Charlotte. No servant ever crosses the line without getting burned. Be sent away without a referral? That's the end of their life in service. Most end up back at the workhouse—or worse."

Mrs. Darling led the group in their direction. Charlotte didn't have time to even straighten her cap before the new duchess and the old, along with Lady Audrey, stood before them. Mr. Winters stood at the back of the group, smiling—and making her hands shake.

"And this is our pastry cook, Mr. Alcott Brown, and his assistant, Miss Charlotte Aldridge. He's been at the castle for five years and Miss Aldridge only two days."

"I'm pleased to make your acquaintance, Mr. Brown," the duchess said. "And you as well, Miss Aldridge. Charlotte's such a beautiful name. A beautiful name to match a beautiful face."

Heat scalded Charlotte's cheeks again. She made a deep curtsy, not knowing exactly how she should respond. "Thank you, Your Grace," she finally said. The duchess's outstretched hand meant she intended to take hers. Charlotte slowly reached forward.

"I feel a bond, Miss Aldridge. We arrived at Ashbury Castle on the same day and are learning the ropes together, so to speak. That must mean something, yes? And you strongly resemble my younger sister Katie, who I left behind in Colorado and miss terribly."

The deep affection in her voice froze Charlotte's tongue. She imagined she saw the duchess's eyes mist up.

"I feel we may be friends," the duchess went on, smiling into her face.

A look of displeasure pulled the dowager's mouth. "It's time to rest before our outing later, then the dressmaker will have you for several hours before the evening meal." She started for the stairs. Lady Audrey and Mr. Winters followed.

"Thank you, Your Grace," Charlotte mumbled, keenly aware of everyone's gaze on her. Alcott and Mr. Winters looked surprised, as did Mrs. Darling and the cook. But Margaret Malone, her eyes narrowed to slits, turned back to the scullery and stomped away.

CHAPTER NINE

"You're awfully quiet, my boy," Lord Harry said, climbing out of the coach. "What's bothering you?"

The coach clattered away, and they began their walk toward the office of the solicitor Beranger's father had used for years. A filmy mist hung over the ground, making the air chilly even for September. Tall buildings blocked the sun. Back in Colorado the sun would be shining, the air warm and clear.

"I don't like leaving so soon. Not with Emma staying behind."

But deep down, I wanted her to stay, his mind argued. *Until I'm sure of my reception in London, sure I'll be accepted as Duke of Brightshire, in the courts and especially in the House of Lords. If I'm going to be shamed, I don't want her to witness it. Only time will tell if others still think of me as illegitimate.*

"That couldn't be helped. Gavin left Ashbury in dire straits. I hadn't realized the coffers were near empty. And there may be more debt than we know of. Such was the case of the land we lost several months ago. He'd told nobody he'd gambled the acres away until the new owners showed up on the doorstep. The news hit everyone hard. Your family and the tenants alike. They fear for their positions. Each time you have to sell land, the new landlord may throw them out. They've lived on those lands for generations."

Beranger nodded. The estate had been successfully passed down through his lineage since the fifteenth century. Ashbury would not be ripped from the Northcotts on his watch.

Lord Harry gave a low grunt. "Ours is not the only grand estate in jeopardy, Beranger. Many lords have done just as your brother did, and your father, for that matter. Paid little attention to detail, believing the resources would always be there as their luxurious lifestyle bled bank accounts dry. Then the cheap imported American grain has all but put most tenant farmers under, making payment to their lords nearly impossible, and the same thing is happening with other crops too. Something must be done. I'm thankful you're home to tackle the problem." He clapped Beranger on the shoulder. "Not only that, but more than a handful of lords have gone looking to America to solve their problems. Marrying an heiress to bankroll their lifestyle and save their reputations is an easy fix. Such arrangements happened all the time, and still do, I'm sure."

Beranger scowled. "Americans *want* the titles."

"And the English *need* the cash to save their tattered reputations."

Surely no one thought that of him and Emma, did they? He hadn't even known he was a duke until his uncle had turned up in Eden. By then, Emma had already captured his heart. If she'd refused to come to England with him, he might not have ever returned.

"Turn here, the way is faster," Lord Harry said, striding down a small side street. The narrow road, deserted except for shadows, was almost an alley. Brick walls lined the way, interrupted by a door or dark window every so often. Behind them, the sounds of the city faded, making the click of their heels on the cobblestones more noticeable. About a half a block in front of them, moving in the same direction, appeared a solitary man.

Then, out of a doorway ahead, three rough-looking scoundrels emerged and pushed the man to the ground. Several punches were exchanged. Beranger saw the glimmer of a knife blade.

"Hell!" Beranger pushed the leather satchel holding Ashbury's account books to Lord Harry and ran forward. Grasping one assailant by the back of his shirt, Beranger threw him headfirst into the wall. The man slumped to the ground. His fellow attackers hadn't noticed Beranger's arrival. One pressed the knife blade to the victim's throat and demanded money. The other watched, his fists clenched at his sides.

"I have something for you," Beranger growled, spinning the second ruffian around. He landed a powerful blow under his jaw that actually lifted the man into the air. When the fellow landed, he stumbled back, catching one foot, and fell to the cobblestones. Staggering to his feet, he took a quick look at Beranger and Lord Harry and ran off in the opposite direction.

The one holding the knife jumped to his feet and vaulted forward to meet Beranger. A snarl twisted the ugly scar that ran down the side of his face. Crouching, the two circled each other. Evil gleamed in the man's eyes.

"May as well stick *you*," he panted. "Hand over your money if you want to walk away alive. Him too!"

For one instant, Beranger's mind flashed back to his first month on board the *Destiny*, when he was only thirteen. The sailors had gone ashore. The midshipman, although twenty-one years old, was small and reedy, and the men often teased him that Beranger was larger. Somehow, the shy midshipman found himself beset upon by three drunken sailors from another ship. They pushed him from one fellow to the next while they laughed and sneered. When the first punch was thrown, Beranger jumped in the fray and held off the beating until the *Destiny*'s burly cook and purser arrived, both shouting and itching for a fight. Beranger had been celebrated as a hero that night and carried on the men's shoulders into the pub, where they proceeded to get him drunk.

The victim on the ground stirred. For one instant, the attacker glanced his way. That was the moment Beranger needed. He kicked out. The knife sailed into the air. He lunged forward, taking the man down to the hard stones, and the two rolled several feet. The brute was stronger than he appeared and was able to land a punch to Beranger's jaw. Furious, Beranger flipped the man to his stomach, pinned his hands behind his back, and forcefully drove his face onto the stone street.

The man howled in pain and stopped struggling.

Sitting atop the criminal, Beranger wiped away a trickle of blood at the corner of his mouth.

The victim had recovered and staggered to his feet. Seeing his assailant on the ground, he stripped off his braces and handed the lengths to Beranger, who secured the brute's hands and feet. Glancing to the wall, he saw that the first attacker had awakened at some point and sneaked off as well.

The victim, though bruised and dirty, smiled and put out his hand. "I owe you my thanks, and perhaps my life."

They shook vigorously.

"Stanton Wellborn the third," the man said. "And whom shall I give the great credit of saving me?"

"Beranger Northcott," Beranger responded, not at ease using the title he'd recently acquired.

Lord Harry shifted his weight. "His Grace, the Duke of Brightshire, sir."

"The Duke of Brightshire!" Wellborn clearly looked taken aback. "But I heard you had died in a hunting accident quite some time back. Was that rumor?"

"Not rumor. That was my older brother."

Wellborn's brow furrowed. He looked to be in his early thirties and was nicely dressed despite his disheveled hair and the long tear that had opened his shirt beneath his gentleman's jacket. Once more tucked under his arm was a leather briefcase, much like the one Beranger had thrust into Lord Harry's arms before the fight. "Then you are the only other son of William Northcott?" He didn't wait for an answer. "The one who has two different-colored eyes? It's too shadowy here to see, but am I correct?" he asked.

"You are."

He nodded, and a grin appeared. "I've heard of you! Actually, I was up in Scotland, and the subject came up there as well. You're famous, I'd say. The eyes, their ability to curse. I don't believe in curses, but some do."

Uncomfortable, and aching at several points in his body, Beranger shifted his weight. "No curse, just a stepmother who spread the superstition far and wide." He glanced at Lord Harry, who stood quiet. "But I had Lord Harry, my good uncle here, to help offset her malice."

Wellborn clapped Beranger on the shoulder. "I'd tell anyone the Duke of Brightshire was my lucky charm today. By the gallantry you have shown, I have no doubt that is true for others as well."

Now even more uncomfortable with the man singing his praises, Beranger said, "I suggest we move on before someone else tries to finish off what those three started. We can alert a constable to this fellow's whereabouts."

Lord Harry and Wellborn nodded. In three short minutes, they were back on the busy main road.

"So much for your shortcut, Lord Harry," Beranger said. "Next time, we shall stick to the more well-traveled streets." He looked at Wellborn and chuckled. "I'm sure you will as well. You're feeling fine then to make the walk home, or wherever you were going?"

"I am. But I must thank you again for your bravery. Not many would jump into a fray when outnumbered."

Beranger shrugged. On board the *Destiny*, he'd learned early on that to be a man was to step up when the time arose, if you ever wanted someone at your back in a time of need. "Ideally no man would stand by when another is outnumbered. What I did is nothing to be singled out for."

Once Wellborn had taken his leave, Harry handed Beranger his handkerchief without a word. Beranger dabbed at the crusted blood at the corner of his mouth. He hadn't taken a blow since a bar fight in Eden when Emma had marched inside in support of her sister Katie, disregarding the room full of drunken men. A swirling goodness warmed his gut. After the fight, Emma had tended to his cuts and bruises. Then and there, he'd promised himself he'd win her heart, no matter how jaded she was about love. The doing hadn't been easy, but oh, the chase had been worth every bit of grief she'd given him.

"How's the jaw feel?" Harry asked, stopping in front of a tall brick building. A list of names on a brass placard was anchored beside the door.

"I'll live." Beranger glanced up. This was only the second time he'd been to London in his life. The first time he'd accompanied his father's groom when his father had gone to see this very same solicitor. Beranger had only been about five at the time, and compared to Brightshire, everything had seemed so large, so busy.

"Stay with the coach and mind the driver, Beranger. Do not run off. This is not Brightshire. London is large and fast-paced. People don't tell the truth. Everyone here will want something from you. Be good. Do as I say."

Beranger remembered the deep longing he'd felt during that brief, rare moment when the duke had squatted before him and tousled his hair. The duke never touched Beranger like he did Gavin, never offered his younger son words of encouragement or wisdom. The only time he'd seen pride in his father's eyes was when the duke was addressing Gavin. And if his stepmother, the duchess, was present, the duke barely spoke to him at all. Lord Harry had explained many times that Gavin was older. As the heir, he was the child they doted on. But Beranger had felt there was more. Because he was illegitimate, his father was loath to touch him.

"When I get home tonight, I'll look in on you. If you were good, I'll bring you something."

But his father hadn't looked in on him that night and had barely said a word on the trip home. Once they'd returned to the castle, Beranger had watched from the hallway as the duke lavished gifts on Gavin, his heir.

"Your silence is worrying me," Uncle Harry said. "You must have some good feelings now that you're home in England. Please tell me that."

"I'm just recalling my first visit to London. I'd been surprised Father asked me to come along, but I later learned the duchess had a special gathering planned for Gavin and didn't want me around. She said she could feel my gaze even when I wasn't in the room. The duke hadn't wanted my company—just the opposite," Beranger said gruffly, palming the doorknob.

Lord Harry grasped his arm. "Not a good memory."

Beranger shook his head. "They rarely are, concerning my family."

"That's the past. Let that go, or resentment will eat you alive. Bitterness and hatred rarely care who they destroy. You've married a delightful girl, you've been named Duke of Brightshire, and the world has essentially been placed at your feet. Soon you'll be a father, I'm sure. Don't waste everything you've gained by staying stuck in the past with a father who was weak and a brother who didn't deserve you. The people in Brightshire are delighted you're home. Prove to them their memories of the resilient, clever, and courageous thirteen-year-old boy are correct. Show them you have come back a man, and you have all those qualities and more."

Moved by his uncle's words, Beranger reached out and placed a hand on the older man's shoulder. "Thank you, Uncle. If only you'd been my father, my life would have been vastly different."

"Our life circumstances make us who we are. I wouldn't want you any different."

They pushed open the door and stepped inside, then set about the business of saving Ashbury Castle from ruin.

CHAPTER TEN

A lone in the kitchen that night, Charlotte finished up the Blackwell tarts and two Eccles cakes for tomorrow's tea. Cook had asked for several delicacies, and Charlotte had offered to make them, giving Alcott a rare night off since he'd never before had such an accomplished assistant.

Flattered at his compliment, Charlotte had taken a short nap after her nightly shift, then risen at midnight and made her way to the kitchen through the silent castle. She'd found the journey alone down four stories a bit unnerving and wondered if Amelia had ever done so herself.

The clock chimed two o'clock. As soon as she cleaned up her dirty mixing bowls, baking pans, utensils, and her cup of tea, she'd head to bed so she'd be able to rise on time at five thirty.

She liked the kitchen best like this. The quiet and calm were more like the bakeshop and not the raucous castle kitchen, where something was happening all the time. This tranquility fed her frame of mind, and soon she was imagining the things she'd never actually have: pretty dresses, fine surroundings, dancing in the arms of a handsome man.

She stretched and glanced around, satisfied with her night's work. No one to shout orders, no icy stares from Margaret or suggestive expressions from the footman. No Aunt Ethel to criticize her every move. This was the longest she'd ever been away from Brightshire and the bakeshop. She hoped sales were good and that Thomas was staying out of trouble.

A sudden cool breeze skittered up her neck. Feeling like she was being watched, she turned.

Mr. Winters stood on the last step of the stairs. Surprise, then pleasure, flitted across his face. "Good evening, Miss Aldridge," he said, coming closer. "I hope I didn't startle you. I expected to find the kitchen empty. A late-night snack is not all that uncommon for me."

"You didn't startle me, sir," she said smoothly, hoping God would forgive her for a small white lie. In truth, his sudden appearance had her breathless. Still, she didn't want to appear an ignorant peasant in the presence of gentry. The difference in their education alone was daunting. She could hardly believe he took the time to speak to her at all. Last night had been a shock, and now . . . ? She didn't understand.

"Does my cousin work you all night, Charlotte?"

She blushed. He must have heard her tell the duchess her name. Was it improper for him to use it now? "No, sir. Alcott usually does the baking, but, well . . ."

"You're helping him? How nice." He came closer and looked at her pastries.

"I'm finishing up a few special requests from the cook for tomorrow's tea. Where the new duchess will meet some—" She snapped her mouth closed. He knew well what tomorrow was. Much better than she did, she was sure.

Mr. Winters watched as she nervously gathered up the dirty utensils and bowls. He wore a fine waist-length jacket over what looked to be a nightshirt. Thank goodness he'd donned his slacks and hadn't come down in just a nightshirt, expecting to be alone.

"As you were saying, the tea tomorrow is growing exponentially," he said, tipping his head. His gaze roamed the room.

He can't be nervous, can he? She'd not heard the word *exponentially* before, but she guessed more cakes and biscuits would be needed for tomorrow than had been expected. Good thing she'd prepared a few extra.

"It seems you've already heard that the dowager duchess received a cable tonight," he went on. "Lord Charles Northcott of Sevenoaks, the duke's oldest uncle, may arrive, his entourage in tow. The castle is filling up." He gave a broad smile, exposing his straight white teeth, something that was rare among the countryfolk. "Just like old times. Dinner parties, hunting excursions, cigars and whiskey, pretty ladies everywhere you turn. It's been some time since Ashbury has seen those days. Almost everyone is relieved the duke has been found."

Does that mean someone isn't *happy His Grace has taken his proper place?* The story about him not being illegitimate—and being the true heir—was quite astounding. *I wonder who would be unhappy at his return. Perhaps that was just a slip of the tongue.*

"Is there something I can get for you, sir?" she asked, coming to her senses. She should have asked him straightaway, before he'd launched into conversation. The housekeeper and butler slept only down the hall. Not upstairs with the other servants. What would happen if they heard the conversation and came out to investigate? Her insides squeezed at the unsuitable situation. "If you'd like, these cakes and biscuits are still warm." She waved her arm across the counter of sweet treats, hoping he didn't say yes. "Or are you hungry for something else? Bread and cheese, perhaps? Or some leftover lamb?"

Would she get in trouble for rummaging around the leftovers for Mr. Winters? She had no idea. Back home at the bakeshop, Aunt Ethel kept all leftovers under lock and key. Food was difficult to come by, and not to be wasted or taken for granted. Practically nothing went into the slop jar. "Perhaps I can find you a stray chicken leg. Or some beef?"

Boldly, he came forward and picked up her hand. "It's true, I did come in search of food, pretty Charlotte, but now I've lost my appetite. You look so charming in this apron. Do you mind me telling you that?"

My word! What is he doing?

She stood there like a deer facing down a lion, too frightened to move. Surely he didn't expect an answer to his question? Was she reading something into his words, letting her imagination run wild? Maybe he was just a very nice, very friendly man. A spicy aroma wafted past her nose, and she realized he must have applied some sort of perfume. Did *men* wear perfume? Not in her world.

His eyes grew wide, and he gently let her hand fall as he stepped back, giving her room to breathe. "I've frightened you. I'm sorry. I'd never want to do that."

Nervous under his observation, Charlotte reached for the empty butter dish and gingerbread-covered spatula, appalled at her shaky hands, and placed both into a used mixing bowl.

"I'd best get on with my work," she said, piling on several more dishes and hurrying toward the scullery. She set the dishes next to the sink and ran her hands over her apron to settle her runaway nerves. The kitchen was silent behind her. What was Mr. Winters doing? Just standing there and waiting for her return? She couldn't bring herself to turn from the sink and look.

In the next room over, where fresh game was hung until it was butchered, she thought she heard the door clatter open. *Now what?* Alcott hadn't mentioned she'd have all kinds of visitors passing in and out through the night. If she'd known, she wouldn't have offered to stay here alone. Gathering her courage, she slipped quietly into the adjoining room and found the door ajar and a tall, wide-shouldered silhouette looming.

Tristen Llewellyn.

"Hello?" she said cautiously, but at the same time relieved. "Mr. Llewellyn, is that you?"

He came forward a few tentative steps in the darkness. "Miss Aldridge? I had no idea you'd be working this late."

"I'm preparing for a tea tomorrow—baking, that is."

"Just give me a moment to hang these jumpin' hares and I'll be gone." He cradled his shotgun in one arm and in the other gripped three large rabbits by their hind legs, their long, wobbly bodies stretching toward the hard stone floor. "They're gutted and cleaned. Cook'll want 'em as soon as she rises."

Charlotte made a pleased sound in her throat. "Wouldn't we love those at the bakeshop? Nothing better than fresh rabbit pie, chock-full of carrots and potatoes."

Mr. Llewellyn was quite attractive with his height and wide shoulders. She couldn't see the color of his eyes now, backlit as he was by the moonlight outside the door, but she remembered from earlier today in the sunshine by the greenhouse they'd been sky blue and sharp—

A sound in the scullery made Tristen snap toward the doorway. Too late Charlotte felt more than heard Mr. Winters's presence.

Mr. Llewellyn frowned.

Did he think he'd stumbled onto a tryst? A woman's reputation was a fragile strand of webbing, easily plucked away and unrepairable. In the blink of an eye, her character, the only real thing she possessed, could be destroyed.

Without a word, Mr. Llewellyn set his kill on the wooden counter along the wall, as well as his long gun. He rearranged a brace of grouse to make room for the jumping hares and then hung them. Finished, he strode past her and Mr. Winters in silence through the scullery, and stopped in the kitchen, his gaze finally alighting on her baked goods.

"As I explained, I'm preparing for tomorrow," she said rather defensively as she hurried to his side.

A head taller than Mr. Winters, Mr. Llewellyn's jaw was covered by dark stubble, and his hair was windblown. Tonight, his long coat would help against the brisk weather outside. He shifted his weight.

"Mr. Winters came looking for a midnight snack," she hurried on. "Imagine that. I was just trying to think of what I could offer—" She snapped her mouth closed, embarrassed.

"At two o'clock in the morning?" he asked in a tone that could chip marble.

Mr. Winters stepped forward. "My intentions are decent, Mr. Llewellyn."

Before he could respond, Mrs. Darling, wearing her housecoat, slippers, white cap, and an extremely annoyed expression, appeared at the end of the corridor. She looked between them. "*What* is going on?"

"I'm baking, ma'am," Charlotte answered quickly. "As I was requested." If Mrs. Darling got the wrong impression and sent her packing, Aunt Ethel would be furious. She needed to be careful.

Mrs. Darling's gaze took in Mr. Winters and then went to the gamekeeper. "Mr. Llewellyn, you're here late—or should I say early?"

"Yes, ma'am," Mr. Llewellyn said. "Couldn't sleep, so I went out for a walk. I brought in three large hares."

"A walk with your rifle?" Mr. Winters asked skeptically.

Charlotte thought she saw some resistance in the gamekeeper's expression when he bobbed his head in respect.

"Why not, sir? Rabbits are out at night."

"I just hope you know what you're shooting at in the darkness. Take my poor cousin, His Grace, the departed Gavin Northcott. Hunting accidents do occur."

Was that a threat implied—or an accusation? Now in the full light of the kitchen, Charlotte saw Mr. Llewellyn's nostrils flare.

"I arrived at Ashbury long after that, Mr. Winters."

"The hour is late, Mr. Llewellyn," Mrs. Darling said.

He respectfully inclined his head. "Yes, ma'am. I'll be on my way. Good evening."

Mrs. Darling anchored her censuring gaze on Charlotte. Did the housekeeper believe she was up to no good as well? And so soon after her elevation from the scullery. Her cheeks warmed under the unfair scrutiny. *I was just doing my work!*

"I'll be turning in as well," Mr. Winters had the good sense to say. The housekeeper wouldn't dare blame one of the family for any transgression. The fault would be placed at the *loose* kitchen maid's feet.

Mrs. Darling waited until the men had gone and then went to the stove and shook the teakettle. Charlotte had forgotten she'd put on water to heat before Mr. Winters had arrived.

The older woman turned. "Would you like a cup?"

"Y-yes," Charlotte sputtered. She'd been expecting a scolding. Who knew, maybe one was still on the way. "That sounds nice. Thank you."

They brewed two cups, and Mrs. Darling actually carried both into the servants' hall, where Charlotte, being kitchen help, didn't usually sit. She switched on the gas lamps. "We'll sit here for now, since everyone else is asleep," the housekeeper said. "No one will mind." She set the cups opposite and motioned for Charlotte to take a seat.

Charlotte settled herself, relieved to get off her feet, and took a sip of the soothing liquid.

"How do you like working at Ashbury, Charlotte? Are you settling in?"

Charlotte glanced up from her cup. "Yes, ma'am. I like it here. I hope I'm settling in quite nicely. There's so much going on."

"That there is," Mrs. Darling responded, a small smile appearing. "And probably more than you know. Your baked goods look delicious. I think the duchess will be pleased. I wouldn't be surprised if she asks you to stay on. Would you be inclined to say yes, if she does?"

Charlotte tipped her head in disbelief. "I have the bakeshop, ma'am. I'm needed there." *Although here is ever so much more fun.* "And you mean in addition to my cousin, correct? I'd not like to take Amelia's place permanently. She counts on her service here."

"And we on her. No, not one or the other, but both. The day before you came to Ashbury, the dowager duchess fired a kitchen maid for, shall we say, an insignificant infraction." Her mouth flattened into an angry line. "I'd like to keep you, Miss Aldridge, if that's possible."

What will Aunt Ethel think? Do? Charlotte's excitement pushed away her fear. "I'd like that very much."

"I thought as much. But I must warn you, young women in service are a tempting target for unscrupulous men of both classes. You must guard your honor. When a young woman chooses to go into service, she is expected to give up what she may have had in another kind of life, if you understand my meaning. Service becomes your family. Any undesirable involvement will get you dismissed without a letter of recommendation. Period. Do I make myself clear?"

Charlotte nodded, then sipped her drink. The faces of both men flashed in her mind. Mr. Winters had seemed to imply something untoward about the duke's hunting accident. She'd been worried over Thomas, and his possible involvement, but she'd seen Mr. Henderley too in the vicinity that day. If she lived here, closer to the people— Mr. Llewellyn—perhaps there'd be a way to find out what the game-keeper was like, and what he'd been doing limping through the forest.

Then again, she thought, maybe some secrets were never meant to see the light of day.

CHAPTER ELEVEN

The evening hours had flown by in the blink of an eye. Before Emma realized the time, Hyacinth was helping her undress and prepare for bed. The young chambermaid unfastened the many tiny buttons that ran down the back of her deep scarlet gown. Finished, she clumsily lifted the fabric over Emma's head, completely destroying the coiffure that had taken a full hour for the dowager's lady's maid to create. Emma didn't care. The night was over and she was going to bed, but Hyacinth had been simply frantic, moaning and primping and trying to repin her locks.

Alone now, the quiet bedchamber surrounded her. She snuggled deep into her covers, the heavy counterpane bolstering her ragged nerves. *Oh, Beranger, I miss you. I should have heeded your words and gone along. I'm not ready to handle this new life without you by my side.*

The day had progressed well, with a visit from the dressmaker and a handful of seamstresses who'd measured her to their hearts' content, showed her page after page of dresses, gowns, and riding outfits. Styles for teas, social events, walks in the garden, and grand balls. She would need a whole chamber alone to house the clothing, but, by the way they'd spoken, that's exactly what she'd have. They'd measured her feet as well, and her head for hats. Her sister Lavinia would be so envious of the bonnets, sunhats, headbands, and elegant evening headdresses they'd described in detail.

Then this evening, there'd been another long seven-course dinner in the grand dining room for only the four of them. Everything was ornate, down to the sparkling white tablecloth trimmed in gold thread. The dowager and Lady Audrey had seemed totally unimpressed.

Emma had been thankful for the lively dialogue and funny stories of Beranger's distant cousin Justin. He'd kept the conversation moving nicely and drew her out by asking more than a few questions about Colorado. Wanted a detailed description of her sisters and what they did, their businesses, and how they spent their time. The English were fascinated with the American West and thought cowboys, outlaws, and gunslingers were one and the same. They had no concept of the vastness of the land and how large the states and territories were.

Emma scrunched her pillow and rolled over, trying to get comfortable. *I wonder what my love is doing right now?* She huffed and felt her eyes sting. *He's sleeping, of course, like I should be. He'll be home soon enough tomorrow, and all will be well.*

The bed felt massive. She thought of their previous night together and blushed in the darkness. Marriage was wonderful. The hidden secrets had been well kept, and although she'd had some ideas, they paled in comparison to reality. She'd been a fool. Especially after she'd put up such a fuss to her sister Belle about never wanting to fall in love.

Unable to get comfortable, Emma turned to her other side and tucked her folded hands beneath her cheek, staring at the candle. The tiny yellow flame flickered in the darkness. The bedchamber was chilly, as she'd found most of the castle to be, even though it boasted fifteen fireplaces that burned all day long. Keeping a grand place like Ashbury running smoothly took a vast amount of work.

A sound outside her window stopped her thoughts. Their bedroom was located on the fourth floor—*No, third,* she corrected herself. High enough that nothing could harm her. Still, she felt edgy.

Angry at her wakefulness, Emma climbed from the bed and pad-
ded silently to the carved bureau, where the letter from her father was
propped against an empty vase. She stared at the envelope for several
moments, a deep longing tightening her throat. Why hadn't she opened
it yet? The handwriting appeared shaky, a stray line here and there in
her name where one should not be.

Father had been dying.

She reached for the envelope, but then let her hand fall away. She
wasn't quite ready yet.

Feeling melancholy, Emma returned to the bed. Her door was
locked, as was her window latch. Keyed up, she knew sleep would elude
her for hours.

Fingering the counterpane, she counted sheep for ten minutes.
When that didn't help, she counted the rooms she knew in the castle.
This was not the grandest room by any means. Beranger had told her
that he hoped, at some point, the dowager would want to take Lily
House. He'd been surprised that Gavin hadn't moved her there already,
but perhaps he'd been waiting till he took a wife himself.

Frustrated, she sat up. She'd never fall asleep at this rate. All she
could see was the face of Mathilda Tugwer. The witch from the Brothers
Grimm's "Hansel and Gretel" fairy tale had nothing on her.

*I need to stop! At this rate, I'll never get any rest. Tomorrow, at the tea,
my eyes will be puffy. I'll not be at my best. I must conquer my fears and
take hold of my imagination.*

She glanced at the door. If only she could have a cup of sweet warm
milk. Within a few minutes, she'd become drowsy and fall asleep.

She supposed she could pull the velvet cord, as she'd been instructed,
but then Hyacinth would have to come down to Emma's chamber, see
what she wanted, go to the kitchen, and rouse somebody that could do
Emma's bidding and return again upstairs. A lot of work for a cup of milk.

No, this was Beranger's castle now, and she was Beranger's wife.
She'd go fetch her own milk. How difficult could that be?

She stood, slipped on her robe and a pair of socks. Taking the candle, she silently went to the door and listened. All was quiet.

Summoning her courage, she opened the door and slipped out onto the mezzanine. Darkness bubbled up from below. The stone balustrade was thick and opulent. She turned left, went to the bend, and turned right to find the wide staircase that connected each floor. With a tripping heart, she quickly descended the floors without making a sound.

Gooseflesh rose on her arms and legs from the chilly air. A breeze made the candle's flame dance. *Is a window open somewhere?*

She passed the large tapestry of a field of grazing deer, and then a long row of huge portraits. *It's nice to see you all again,* she thought, making herself smile. When she got to the bottom, she stopped. Which way to the second staircase that led to the kitchen and servants' area? She'd been so busy with the dowager duchess and standing for the dressmakers, she'd been to the kitchen only the one time. And then the group had been talking, and she hadn't paid attention.

A drop of scalding wax fell on her hand.

Shocked more than hurt, she gasped so loudly she actually extinguished the flame. The light that had been guiding her evaporated into the darkness. A creepy feeling slithered down her spine.

"Don't panic," she whispered, hearing only the pounding of her heart. Swallowing down her fear, she waited for her vision to adjust to the darkness and then continued carefully onward.

Her intuition told her left. A moment later she found the green-cloth-covered door that opened to the staircase that led to the basement. Doubtful that anyone was up at this time, she was surprised to see golden light filtering up from below, making her descent much safer. At the bottom, she followed the sound of murmured voices and came upon none other than Mrs. Darling and Miss Aldridge sitting at the large table in the servants' hall. The cups they were drinking from clattered to the tabletop.

CHAPTER TWELVE

C harlotte blinked in astonishment. The Duchess of Brightshire stood before them in her nightclothes, holding an unlit candle. Leaping to her feet, Charlotte almost knocked her chair over as she remembered to curtsy at the same time.

Startled, Mrs. Darling bolted to her feet as well. She rushed forward, sputtering, "Y-Your Grace, is something wrong?" A note of panic marked her voice. She glanced at Charlotte as if a kitchen maid would have the answers to her questions.

The duchess put out her hand, a surprised smile on her lips. "I'm sorry if I frightened you." She glanced at the gas lamps, her smile growing. "My candle went out, and I had to proceed in the dark." She laughed, stepping closer. "I'm thankful I didn't fall and break my neck. And now to find you two is a delightful surprise."

Charlotte glanced at the housekeeper for direction. She didn't quite know what to do, or what was expected of her, but she was moved by compassion. She'd known nothing but kindness from the duchess. Perhaps she was as befuddled as Charlotte at being plunged into this new world. "May I brew Your Grace a cup of tea?" she asked softly. "I can deliver it to your room in less than five minutes, as well as biscuits fresh from the oven."

"Yes, thank you," the duchess replied. "A cup of tea sounds lovely. But only if I may join you here in *this* room. I'm lonely upstairs all by myself. And I like the feel down here much better. I'm so happy to find you both. Would you mind horribly?"

Heat rushed to Charlotte's face. The duchess taking tea in the servants' hall? She hadn't been here but two days, yet she knew that was not commonplace.

Mrs. Darling made a swishing motion, and Charlotte hurried away. Standing next to the warm stove, she listened to their quiet voices while she worked, steeping the tea and arranging a selection of baked goods on a plate. "Here you are, Your Grace. I hope this will settle your nerves."

The duchess smiled her thanks.

Mrs. Darling dipped her head in appreciation of Charlotte's fast thinking.

The duchess sat, but when Charlotte and Mrs. Darling remained on their feet, she patted the tablecloth. "Please, sit," she said with exasperation. "Where I come from, everyone is equal. I'm not used to special treatment and don't know if I'll ever be. I hope my American ways won't be a disgrace to Beranger." The duchess brought her cup to her lips and blew on the hot liquid. "Please, go ahead before your tea gets cold."

Charlotte and Mrs. Darling sat and sipped from their cups. She wondered what she could say to entertain the duchess, but Her Grace beat her to it.

"What I really came all this way for—and the way *is* long," the duchess said, then laughed, "is my crutch. Would you believe at my age I sometimes need a cup of warm milk to fall asleep? I've been lying in bed for hours. I miss the duke, and thought, *Why not?*"

Their gazes touched, and Charlotte felt herself relax. The American's simple charm was appealing, and nothing like what she'd heard of the lofty Lady Audrey or her mother. Alcott had said the dowager duchess never interacted with the staff and only spoke to them when absolutely necessary—or when she was firing someone. And it was mostly the same with Lady Audrey.

"I'll warm some milk before you leave," Charlotte said. "So you can take a cup to your room."

"Thank you. And you must show me how, so in the future I won't have to bother anyone. I can't imagine this will be the only time I'll need it since I'm—well . . ." The duchess sucked in a deep draft of air and quickly looked away to hide her face.

Shocked, Charlotte glanced at Mrs. Darling and then extended her hand and gently patted the duchess's arm. "There, there. Everything will be all right." *It would, wouldn't it?* "Please have some tea before it cools. You'll feel better."

The duchess dabbed at the corners of her eyes with her napkin. "Please forgive me. It's just that I miss my sisters. We've never been apart." Unshed tears glittered in her eyes.

"That's quite all right, Your Grace," Mrs. Darling said, seeming to have gotten over her shock. "I can understand how different living in a castle must be for you. How strange and uninviting, surrounded by servants. Is there any way I can help?" She glanced at Charlotte. "How *we* can help, I should say."

"I just want a friend." Her gaze tracked between them. "I want to get to know you both. Is that all right or against the rules as well? The dowager duchess was quite explicit on the subject of friends, and who they could and could not be."

What should she say? Surely what she was suggesting was not all right at all, at least with the dowager duchess. Not from the stand-point of things Charlotte had heard from Amelia and even in the last two days from Margaret. She glanced at Mrs. Darling to see how she would respond. Surely, being the housekeeper in Ashbury for many years, the woman would have an answer to this question. One accept-able to everyone.

"Of course we're your friends, Your Grace. But you have other friends as well. The duke's family. The dowager duchess and Lady Audrey. And what of the woman who arrived in your group?"

"Gertrude Bucket." She lifted her cup and took a sip. "I suppose you're right. Gertrude is my friend, but she took to her room claiming a headache and hasn't left since. I've tried to visit her a few times, but she always turns me away, claiming she doesn't feel well enough to talk. The voyage to England was arduous. Choppy seas and winds kept us in our cabins for days."

Mrs. Darling smiled. "Maybe sharing about your sisters will make you feel better."

The duchess's lips wobbled upward. "Yes, that's a good idea. Well, let's see. Two of my sisters, Belle and Lavinia, are happily married and settled. Katie, the youngest, the one who resembles Charlotte, has recently had her heart broken. She'd anticipated a proposal, but he turned out to be a handsome rake. A woman from his past came to Eden. And that was that."

Charlotte bit her lip. How sad. Two men's faces popped into her mind, and she firmly dismissed them both. She'd not let either break her heart.

"And then there's my oldest sister, Mavis," the duchess went on. "She's a widow. The man she's fallen for, our sheriff, is a handsome devil in his own right. His eyes light up like the sun whenever Mavis steps into his office, but he's dragging his feet for no apparent reason. Watching is difficult. I can see how much she loves him, but she holds her feelings inside because she doesn't want to worry her sisters."

Charlotte and Mrs. Darling exchanged another glance.

Mrs. Darling gently patted the table between them, as if she wanted to comfort the duchess with a soothing touch but didn't dare. "Don't worry overmuch, Your Grace. Things'll work out for the best. Sometimes a woman wades through several common brown frogs before she finds her prince."

The duchess nodded thoughtfully, as if weighing Mrs. Darling's words. "Thank you. I'm feeling much better. Thank you for caring. Sometimes all a troubled heart needs is someone to listen. You're both very good listeners, indeed." Her smile grew stronger and warmer, and she drank the last of her tea. She pushed the plate of biscuits forward. "Neither of you has eaten any of these delicious cookies," she said, and then realized her mistake. "Biscuits. So many details to remember—you'd think I'd get this small one correct. Please have some."

Charlotte and Mrs. Darling indulged. The duchess seemed calmer with food in her stomach and a few minutes of conversation. She quickly pried out Mrs. Darling's first name and learned that Charlotte was a baker in Brightshire filling in for her sick cousin. With the new duchess's friendly interest, Charlotte's brief life story tumbled out—that she had an older brother named Thomas who delivered the bread to Ashbury every Tuesday, Charlotte's quick-tempered aunt, even how she imagined herself wearing a beautiful blue dress.

After they'd all relaxed for a while, the duchess grew serious.

"The tea tomorrow has me anxious. Would you, my new friends, be so kind as to offer me a few suggestions to calm my nerves?"

CHAPTER THIRTEEN

For Beranger, the miles between him and Emma seemed far too many. Each bump of the carriage plucked away at his already thin agitation. The important vote in Parliament had been postponed for reasons he didn't know. What he did know was that Gavin had left the coffers of Ashbury all but empty. Drastic measures would have to be taken, or else they'd have to sell more land to pay taxes.

Lord Harry shifted in his seat. "Stop brooding, my boy. We'll take one day at a time, that's all. The one bright spot is that your step-mother was spending Ashbury money fixing up and renovating the old place almost faster than Gavin could lose the funds at the gambling table. We may be broke, but almost everything that needed fixing has been repaired, replaced, or updated. The castle looks better than I ever remember."

Beranger stared as the coach bounced along. "True enough. And you trust this solicitor, Alfred Batkins?"

"He's served the dukes of Brightshire for as long as I can remember, even before your father, when I was just a boy."

"That wasn't my question." Fatigued, Beranger rubbed a hand over his face. He'd gotten little more than two hours of fitful sleep last night worrying over Emma. "Batkins is as old as sand. Perhaps he's missed something important. Or perhaps he's the problem itself. I don't trust anyone until they prove to me they've earned my trust. And I don't know him from Adam."

"Yes, I remember that about you. You're always watching and waiting. Seeing what presented itself. I think your scrutiny has served you well. But about Batkins, I don't know what to say. He's partner at one of the most respected firms in London. To question him may prove counterproductive. I'd suggest you go about business, for now, as if he's part of your trusted inner circle."

The coach slowed while passing through Brightshire. When they made the last turn that led to Ashbury, Beranger's dark mood began to lighten. He'd have Emma in his arms soon. And if he could manage some privacy, perhaps they could spend the remainder of the afternoon alone, in their chamber. That shouldn't be too much to ask of anyone, should it? As the horses' hooves clattered over the bridge and headed for the woodlands that had been his refuge as a boy, a rush of warm sentiments gripped him. They entered the forest, the interior of the coach plunging from brightness into darkness.

"I'm sure the Dowager Countess of Sarre as well as Lady Coldred have enjoyed spending time with Emma," Lord Harry said, a happy chirp to his tone. "Perhaps there are some cakes and biscuits left. I've a gnawing ache inside my belly."

"Hell!"

"You've forgotten the tea?" Lord Harry let out a chortle of laughter. "I've been wondering why you've been so quiet. You've been thinking of Emma and returning home. Well, that's understandable for a newly married chap." His smile widened. "She'll be busy for the next two hours, at least. Just because teatime is coming to an end doesn't mean the lady guests will be on their way. They'll still need to take in the gardens, make a full day of it."

Beranger growled. He'd wanted to depart London directly after breakfast but had been detained by several lords who wished to discuss yesterday's votes and get to know him—and they had not shown any hint of the rejection he'd feared. There were important issues that needed to be addressed. Those decisions would affect the people who lived in Brightshire and the surrounding areas. Regular folk, who relied on their lords to make the choices that would protect and preserve them as they did their best to live well and prosper. He'd never expected to be a duke, but since he was, he wanted to do right by the people. But how did a person even begin to do that? Especially if he had no idea what those regular people expected of him?

The coach rolled by a young man crouched at the side of the road holding a rifle. By golly, Beranger wanted to get home, but he also wanted to know the happenings around Ashbury. Here was a way to begin gathering that knowledge by seeing what, on the castle lands, had caught the fellow's attention. He reached up and pounded the ceiling.

The coach rolled to a stop. Without waiting, Beranger opened the door and bounded out. "What's this, my lad? Is there a problem?"

The fellow stood. He must have realized he was face-to-face with the new duke by the way he looked at Beranger's eyes.

"Your Grace."

Beranger pushed away his impatience to be home. Each person he met deserved his full, undivided attention. He only had one chance to make a first impression. He wanted that to be good. For the people to trust him. He wasn't his father or his brother. Beranger would do things his way. "Is there a problem here?"

"Possibly, Your Grace. Early this morning, I'd spotted some tracks. As I went deeper into the surrounding woods, I spotted the blood. Now I end up here." He pointed to the ground, where drops of blood tinged the leaves. "Either someone was hurt, or they've been poaching and this is animal's blood. I'm not sure."

As if on cue, an adolescent-size golden retriever crashed through the underbrush to skid to a halt by the fellow's side. A bright red tongue rolled out the side of his mouth, and his sides heaved from running. He couldn't have looked happier.

Beranger straightened. "And you are?"

"Tristen Llewellyn."

"Ah, you're Henderley's nephew, then, from Wales. Helping him gamekeep."

"I've been helping for two months now."

From habit, Beranger stuck out his hand, and they shook. The youth's eyes went wide. Beranger turned to Lord Harry, who had come to his side. "An hour or two, you say?"

"I'd guess that, yes," Lord Harry replied. "You may as well find something else to bide your time, because you're not going to get within twenty feet of the duchess until then. Did you want to visit good ol' Arson?"

Beranger looked Tristen in the eyes; the young man was as tall as he was. "I do. If I hadn't had to make this fast trip to London, I would have already looked in on him and Rose." He put out his hand toward the coach in invitation. "Come along. You'll ride with us."

"I couldn't. I'll meet you there," Tristen responded. "I have Bagley."

"The dog's welcome." Beranger stopped by the driver. "To Henderley's."

Inside the coach, the three large men got comfortable. Bagley leaned on Tristen's legs.

"Your aunt and uncle were always good to me."

Tristen smiled, his hand resting on his dog's head. "They're good to me as well, Your Grace."

"Does Rose still work in the kitchen?"

"Aye, she does. But she always finds time in her day for Uncle and me. We're the luckiest of men."

"Yes, that's just the way I remember her. Always taking fine care of me and any other urchin she could corral. Tell me, did they ever have any children of their own? I know they wanted a family."

He shook his head.

The coach came out of the forest, passed by the castle, and continued on around back, down a winding road for a quarter mile. The home, larger than a cottage, sat back in the trees and held a magical kind of charm—like wood elves or gnomes resided there. The small garden, still well kept, looked to be producing quite nicely. Hanging from the tall sycamore beside the front porch was the wide-seated rope swing. He'd spent many an hour here contemplating his place in the family that seemed to wish him gone. Back then, the front door had been painted red, but it was now a shiny blue. Window boxes at the upper bedroom windows brimmed with color. Along with everything else, Rose's talent with plants was even more impressive than the gardener's at Ashbury. Emma would fall in love the moment he brought her here, where, he realized, he felt most at home. The Henderley household had provided much of the familial love Ashbury didn't.

He eagerly drank in the sight as the coach rolled to a halt, deeply wishing he'd thought to bring out some sort of gift. A thank-you for all the love and memories he'd held close to his heart on the open sea and for his time in America. He could hardly wait to get inside.

"Beranger!" Arson Henderley belted when the group came through the front door. "You're a sight, my boy. When I heard the news of your return, I could hardly believe my ears. Come over here so I can greet you properly. You too, Lord Harry. Good to see you, man."

Arson Henderley sat in a chair by the window, a lightweight blanket resting over his legs. His face was thin, and he'd lost at least fifty pounds, if Beranger's assessment was correct. But his smile, his eyes, were all the same, just older and rather tired. Beranger rushed forward, engulfing his old friend in his arms.

"What's wrong, Arson?" he asked after he stepped away. "Why can't you greet me on your own two feet? Your nephew didn't say."

"Doctors don't know. My legs are gradually losing their strength. I used to be able to get around slowly inside, but whatever is wrong with me keeps advancing. There'll come a time when I won't be able to get out of bed."

Beranger just gazed at him, trying to determine the seriousness of his condition. It sounded grave, but perhaps in London—or in America—the doctors knew more about this sort of affliction. Later, Rose would give him the full truth. Just like old times, Arson was not a man to talk about himself or his troubles.

Arson reached out an arm to Tristen, beckoning him closer. "But I have this fella—and thank God for him. He's doing a good job with your woodlands. Keeps track of the game that's taken out and is swifter on his feet when after poachers. The accounting book never looked better. His arithmetic is near to perfect. You couldn't have a better man looking out for you, Your Grace."

"Beranger," he corrected. "I'm not Your Grace to you. I owe you my sanity, my life."

"Poppycock." Arson laughed. "You're the duke, and we will address you accordingly. Did Tristen tell you he's from Wales? Only son of my dear sister, God rest her soul. He's a better shot than I am, I can brag on that." Arson's smile was filled with pride. Here was the son he'd never had.

"I'm happy to have him aboard." He needed to say more, put Arson at ease. "This house will always belong to you and Rose, Arson. Even when—"

"I can't get out of bed?"

"That's right."

For the first time in Beranger's life, a look of disquiet crossed his old friend's face.

"We don't take charity, *Your Grace*. We're keeping up due to Tristen. We won't fall short."

Beranger hadn't meant to sting Arson's pride, but it appeared he had. Later, in private, they'd revisit the conversation, and Beranger would remind him of all he and Rose had done for him. Meanwhile, he wanted to discuss all this talk of poaching. He remembered the local boys and servants' children he'd run with as a youth. Their families had been poor. Even one deer from Ashbury lands would feed many mouths. During hard times, the risk of being caught poaching was worth it.

But why should it be that way? As steward of these lands, the Duke of Brightshire owed to them a decent standard of living. Maybe the previous dukes hadn't felt that way, but Beranger did.

Ashbury was about to change the way business was carried out—he'd see to that, even if the other lords around the countryside didn't approve.

CHAPTER FOURTEEN

E mma sat straight as an arrow, trying to remember every instruction Mrs. Darling had given her last night concerning today's tea with the local dignitaries. She should have paid more attention to Gertrude Bucket's instructions, she admitted, but somehow the urgency of preparing for today had finally made the lessons sink in.

It was a good thing too that Emma had Mrs. Darling to rely upon. Gertrude's illness—combined, Emma suspected, with a bit of a miffed feeling that Emma had turned elsewhere for direction—had prompted the woman to announce that she missed Boston and would be returning as soon as possible.

Hyacinth had helped Emma dress for today's gathering in a blushing-pink gown made of fine, delicate linen, delivered by the dowager's dressmakers only this morning. She adored the gorgeous garment. The narrow skirt had just the barest of back padding and hugged her waist like a glove. The feminine capuchin collar made her neck look like a swan's. She'd never felt more beautiful. The rest of her trousseau, so to speak, would be finished by the end of the week.

She smiled at the ladies in the group: the dowager duchess; Lady Audrey; Harriet Ninham, the ninety-five-year-old Dowager Countess of Sarre; and Lady Eugenia Coldred.

Lady Sarre, who was almost completely deaf, gazed at the small, untouched slice of cake on her plate. The group had already consumed the savory items and scones and were on the desserts. "This looks delicious, Duchess."

She'd said the exact phrase at least thirty times since Emma had poured the tea. Her thick black wig of curls, adorned with a small tiara, looked rather strange in contrast to her naked eyelids. As eccentric as she appeared, she was a lamb, and kind to a fault.

Seventy-five-year-old Lady Eugenia Coldred, a local baroness with bluish-gray hair and a shrill voice that could wake the dead, nodded emphatically. Both women had been exceptionally kind, and Emma found no fault with either. Through the last two hours, three cups of tea, and two sweets, they'd explained in detail their titles, who was related to whom, which title came from where, and their families' connections to the dukedom, if they existed.

Most of the connections went over Emma's head like a kite in the wind. Thankfully, Beranger's uncle Charles and his family had sent a cable this morning explaining they'd been delayed. As uncharitable as it sounded, Emma hoped they'd stall their arrival for a year. She already had enough on her plate contending with more highbrow relations. But it did make her wonder about his absence. Lord Charles was next in line for the dukedom after Lady Audrey—for as long as she didn't have any children. Did he resent Beranger's good fortune?

Keeping her posture painfully erect, Emma—in complete opposition to what Miss Bucket had advised about raising her cup and saucer chest high while extending her baby finger (such a position, declared Mrs. Darling, was rude and implied elitism)—delicately gripped the top of the handle with thumb and index fingers and brought the teacup to her lips. Tipping the china toward her, she took the tiniest of sips, thereby executing the movement perfectly. She looked at the liquid, for to do otherwise was also rude. She caught Lady Coldred's smile of approval.

"Duchess," Lady Coldred said wistfully, "you move and speak as if you were born and raised here in our good country. Such beauty and poise. Lady Sarre and I are delighted to be counted among your first guests." She clinked her cup back into its saucer.

Truly touched, Emma felt warmth rise to her cheeks. The endearment wrapped around her heart after the hollow flattery from Beranger's stepmother.

"Thank you so much, Lady Coldred. I find your country so charming. I'm doing my best not to humiliate my good husband, the duke. Alas, each day is a school day, as my eldest sister, Mavis, is fond of saying. I find that so true here."

Emma didn't miss the dowager's sour nod of agreement—because she'd been the recipient of the like all afternoon. The woman could barely stand being in the same company as a backward hick from America. The ice queen rarely said a word, and instead tried to undermine Emma's confidence with glacially cold, hawklike stares with her lips curled just the tiniest bit at their edges.

If the dowager thought Emma would crumple in fright from her asinine tactics, she was wrong. She wouldn't flee back to Colorado at the first hint of discomfort to lick her wounds and cry on her sisters' shoulders. The highbrow, too-good-for-anyone-else dowager duchess would soon learn just how tough she could be.

And at this point, Lady Audrey was no better. She was a replica of her mother, only younger. Every once in a while she'd mumble a word or two through her sugar-sweet smile but avoided any topic of interest or intellectual exchange. She never voiced her opinion on anything. Beranger's sister appeared friendly to her whenever Beranger was near, but that evaporated the minute they were alone, or around her mother. Surely, she was nursing her anger over being bumped out of inheriting the title. Emma had come to England intending to win over both stepmother and half sister for Beranger's sake. So they could all be friends, because now they were family. But the more time they spent together, the more apparent it became that the dowager duchess and Lady Audrey didn't want to be friends, let alone family.

"Yes, yes." Lady Sarre nodded as if she had actually heard the compliment her friend had just voiced to Emma. "Fairly and always. Whenever and now." She glanced at her teacup and then around the room, confusion clouding her eyes. "This looks delicious, Duchess."

Moved by compassion, Emma reached out and placed her palm over the old countess's unsteady hand. The loving gesture seemed to startle everyone in the room. Not caring what the others thought, Emma let her hand linger. "Thank you, my dear lady," she said.

Lady Sarre's bare eyelids fluttered, and then a smile crept across her face.

"Oh, *the duke*," Lady Coldred said on a breath. "He was such a handsome child. I daresay, I look forward to his return so I can see what kind of a man he's grown into. He had the most peculiar eyes."

Emma cut her gaze to the dowager duchess and lifted a brow. "Yes, quite beautiful. I've heard some small-minded people believe they're bad luck—maybe even hold a curse—but he's brought me nothing but love and happiness. I think such superstition laughable. I didn't know such silly delusions even existed."

The dowager lifted her fork to her lips but held Emma's gaze, her eyes cold and hard.

Was the woman capable of bodily harm? At that moment, Emma would have had to say yes.

"Bah, you're right," Lady Sarre agreed, oblivious to the dowager's fury. "Only peasants believe in curses. One blue, one green. His gaze drew everyone's attention, and I've never seen the like since. But what a fine, *fine*-looking boy. Of course, because of the conditions of his birth, none of us ever dreamed he'd someday be the duke." Using the edge of her trembling fork, she carefully cut her cake and put the small

103

bite into her mouth. The skin of her neck rippled as she chewed. After swallowing, she dabbed her lips using the corner of her napkin. "I still don't quite understand those circumstances. They've changed, haven't they? What was it I was told?" Her gaze touched each face. "How could His Grace William first be married to His Grace Beranger's moth—"

Thankfully, before the woman could say any more, voices sounded from somewhere in the castle. The deep laugh could belong to none other than her husband. Emma's heart took wing. All she'd endured until his return melted away. She looked to the doorway, praying he'd come looking. Oh, how she wanted to fly into his arms! But as much as she loved this gorgeous dress, she wasn't even sure she could trust herself to walk fast in all her finery. She had yet to master such tiny shoes.

"I believe Beranger has returned," she said, making her first slip of the day by calling her husband by his Christian name at a formal function. But she hardly cared.

And then, there he stood in the doorway, looking impossibly handsome. Their gazes locked. He strode into the room, and all the women's faces—excluding his stepmother and sister's—shined like the sun.

Looking rakish and windblown, he held out a palm. "Dowager Countess and Lady Coldred, so good to see you. You're both more beautiful today than sixteen years ago." He glanced at the dowager duchess and his sister and nodded politely. "I found my stepmother the same. There must be something magic in the springs that feed Brightshire."

Emma didn't know how he could treat his stepmother so kindly, but it impressed her every time.

He graciously took the hand of each guest and kissed their fingers. "Thank you for welcoming my wife so warmly into the fold. Because of your tutelage she can do nothing less than shine."

Both elderly ladies appeared spellbound.

"Oh, yes, Duke," Lady Coldred cooed. "Anything we can do, we are happy to. Just ask."

Not caring what was proper, Emma stood and went to his side, and he took her hand in his own. *Oh, how I love him.*

"Ladies, I'm stealing the duchess for only a moment. I promise to bring her right back."

The guests nodded, affection brimming their gazes.

His stepmother gave her famous blank face.

Lady Audrey appeared indifferent.

Excitement burned as Beranger led her down the hall into the library. Inside the room, which was blessedly empty, he wrapped her in his arms as he used his boot to close the door. His head lowered to hers. The kiss was deep and needy, and she thought she'd die from the pleasure. She'd walk a hundred miles barefoot for one minute in his arms. Pulling back, he scorched a trail of voracious kisses down her neck and across the tops of her breasts, revealed by the capuchin collar. The sweetness of his love almost brought her to tears.

"I missed you so much," she breathed, barely getting the words out.

"And I you, my love," he responded, his lips still branding her skin. "And I you. More than you could ever know. I should have taken you with me. My mistake was not insisting you come along. The moment we set away, I felt hollow without you by my side."

Breathing rapidly, she whispered, "So your trip was good, meaningful?"

He took a healthy draft of air as if he'd just sprinted a steep hill and pulled far enough away that he could see into her eyes. "In a manner of speaking, yes. Although I don't like what I found out. It's true what Justin has alluded. My foolish brother has all but ruined the manor. There are barely funds to pay wages—let alone taxes. Something must be done quickly to turn the estate around. And I'm not even sure, at this point, that feat can be accomplished."

"Beranger, I'm so sorry! I had hoped you'd have good news to report. That you'd discovered some secret account Gavin hadn't known about."

"No such luck. I'll have to pay the taxes and operational costs myself this year. And possibly next year too. Ashbury has been the Duke of Brightshire's responsibility for centuries, and I won't be the duke to let the manor see ruin and the property split up until nothing is left. From what I was told, a number of the larger estates are going that way without enough cash to help."

"I have money, Beranger."

"Never. That won't happen. Besides, my money invested in America is more than enough. I'll liquidate a few things quite easily," he said. "I'll not lose Ashbury under my watch."

Emma stroked his cheek, bringing his attention back to her. His expression was almost painful.

"And because I went to America and made my own fortune," he went on, "I'm now in a position to save our holdings—not just some, but all." He searched her face. "Do you mind?"

"Mind? Of course not. I think it noble that you're willing to invest. Who knows, perhaps the false narrative that sent you to America was predestined by God to save all this." She waved her arm to indicate the gorgeous room where they stood. "Few could do the same."

A smile grew across his face, and his eyes softened. "Thank you for always believing the best of me. I'm determined to turn the operation around. The estate *will* pay for itself, but the question is when."

She placed her hand against his warm cheek, loving him all the more for his concern. "Don't look so cast down, my love. Surely we'll think of something. I'm an American, and by a lot of accounts, so are you. We're resourceful. We've only just begun."

He placed another quick kiss upon her lips. "That we are, and have! Now, tell me how you fared in that enormous bed all alone. Were you frightened? I hardly slept a wink for thoughts of you."

"I did fine," she said, deciding to keep her two o'clock visit to the kitchen to herself so he'd not think her silly. She stepped away and put out her arms so he could see her gown. She did a slow turn. "My new gown, my duke husband."

Admiration shone in his eyes. "Beautiful, but not as beautiful as what's inside."

He took her in his arms again, but she frowned and stared at his folded silk necktie, not wanting to look into his face while she voiced her concerns. She drew in a breath. "Beranger, if something evil came to pass, Lady Audrey would become duchess, correct?"

She dared a quick glance at his face. A crooked smile pulled his lips, but that couldn't dispel the feeling she'd developed when she'd challenged the dowager a few minutes ago. Was the woman capable of doing something awful?

"Why would you have such a silly question?"

"Because. When your brother passed and you couldn't be found, Lady Audrey prepared to take the title and everything with it. She, and her mother, can't be happy now that you've returned and spoiled those plans. I just don't want to see anything happen to you."

"Anything like what?" He playfully touched the end of her nose. "I'll get a bunch of cats to test my food?"

"Don't be flippant. I feel useless to help. Who would I even turn to if I suspected some sort of foul play?"

"Emma, you're being silly. You need to get back to your tea before your old guests fall asleep." He kissed her again. "If you did have a worry, and either I or Lord Harry weren't around, you could go to the gamekeeper and his wife, Arson and Rose Henderley. They practically raised me. You can trust them. I do. Rose is a kitchen maid."

"Oh, I met her yesterday when you were gone. A very nice woman. All the staff are. As a matter of fact, I like them more than I do your family."

He rubbed his hands up and down her arms. "I can't argue with you there. Put your fears aside. Nothing will happen, except you might be sought after if you don't return to the sitting room."

He kissed the top of her head. "Go back to your duty, and tomorrow we'll go riding. I'll show you Brightshire and Goldenbrook. I'll introduce you to some of my oldest friends. Would you like that?"

Nodding, she made herself smile for him. He hadn't been in that room when Lady Coldred brought up Beranger's stepmother and the secret marriage that had transpired before her own. The look the dowager duchess had sent said everything. She'd not forgotten. And she'd not forgiven.

The deck was stacked against Beranger, Emma was convinced. If he didn't want to acknowledge that, she'd have to be all the more watchful for them both.

CHAPTER FIFTEEN

O n Saturday morning, Tristen strode toward the castle kitchen,
three pheasants slung over his shoulder, tied with twine about
their feet. Yesterday, Cook had sent a note to the cottage requesting
fresh pheasant for tonight's dinner. In addition to catching poachers,
Tristen's job entailed raising game birds on the duke's lands, managing
their habitats, and controlling the predators such as weasels and other
critters that got at the eggs or took the young. When the duke and his
guests were in want of leisure activity, he released game birds for them
to hunt.

Bagley romped by his side, distracted by every bush and tree he
passed. Tristen was beginning to have his doubts concerning the young
dog. A great hunter needed to pay attention more and play less.

Emerging from the forest on the road that led from his uncle's cottage, Tristen slowed his footsteps. The duke and duchess were crossing
the meadow from the stable, riding side by side on very different horses.
The duke's mount was huge, black, and went with a prancing gait,
whereas the duchess's mount was small and nondescript and ambled
along with his head low and relaxed. An odd pair for sure. Both mounts
were undoubtedly different from the leggy thoroughbreds and feisty
Welsh cobs that were often seen in these areas, or even from the giant

workhorses. Before his troubles in Wales had started, he'd considered himself a horseman to a certain mark, but now that life was gone.

The duke, some two hundred yards away, saw Tristen and put up a hand.

Tristen waved back, amazed the duke had taken notice. But would he feel differently knowing that his game was entrusted to a former convict? For now, his history was safe with his uncle and aunt, but if the truth ever came out, surely he'd be sent away. Then what would he do? How would he make a living? Not many were willing to take a chance on an ex-jailbird.

He approached the meat room's door with the intention of slipping in and out, but when he opened the door, Bagley darted inside. "Bagley," Tristen called, not too loudly, hoping the scamp would mind.

A shout of surprise went up in the kitchen.

There was no option but to follow into the large, open workspace.

The room was crowded. The servants stood around laughing as his dog wolfed down something he shouldn't.

Mrs. Darling scowled.

Mr. Pencely, the butler, who was the man his uncle reported to, frowned even harder. Pencely knew Tristen's past—but in deference to Uncle Arson, who'd been at Ashbury all his life, he'd allowed the young man to stay. Now Bagley's mischievous nature was risking all that goodwill.

"Bagley, heel!"

Everyone turned.

Aunt Rose came his way, eyes twinkling, though she kept a serious expression on her face. "I tried to stop him, Tristen, but I wasn't fast enough. That rascal needs to stay outside." Her gaze slid to the butler, who was shaking his head ruefully. Tristen grabbed Bagley's collar and dragged him toward the door.

"After you tie him up, come back in for some cake," Mr. Pencely called. "We have a celebration going on."

Embarrassed—what sort of gamekeeper would he make if he couldn't even train his dog?—he took Bagley around to the garden and secured him in some shade. Returning, he deposited the pheasants in the meat room, then joined everyone in the kitchen. He noted with relief that the celebratory cake looked unmolested. Miss Aldridge was there, watching with amusement. She knew the truth about his dog.

"We're celebrating Amelia's return," Aunt Rose said, slicing the cake. "Though Charlotte has been a good replacement while Amelia was sick, and we'll miss her, we're glad to have Amelia back. And any excuse to have cake is welcome."

He *had* worked up an appetite this morning tromping through the grasslands on the hunt, the only place he felt free of the bars that had held him for years. He liked pheasants better than chickens because at least the former lived free, rather than in coops. He knew the feeling of impotence of being caged and respected the wild animals on the estate, letting them live their lives in freedom until they were needed.

Alcott, his apron covered in pastry flour, grinned. "We're thankful she's come back to us shining with health."

Basking in attention, Amelia laughed. Charlotte stood at her side.

"Yes, we're so pleased," Mrs. Darling added. "We couldn't be more delighted."

Tristen nodded politely at Amelia, a girl he'd met several times, whenever he had a kitchen delivery. She was pretty, with a coquettish smile and a scattering of freckles across her nose, making him think she liked to get outside when she could. Did her return mean Miss Aldridge would be leaving?

As Charlotte and Amelia began handing out the sliced cake, Mr. Winters passed through the servants' hall in sight of the celebration. Tristen frowned. He was taking liberties by entering the servants' space as often as he did. It wasn't difficult to imagine what he'd come in for. But was Charlotte aware? Would Winters turn her head with silken words and then leave her in a family way after he'd had his fill? Tristen hoped she was smarter than that.

Margaret sent him an adoring smile. With cake in hand, she came his way.

"How you be, Mr. Llewellyn?" she asked, her white apron already spotted with grease.

"Good, thank you. I guess now that Miss Smith is back, you'll be returning to the kitchen," he replied.

She nodded and swallowed a bite of cake. "Mrs. Darling will be giving me word later today, I'd think. I won't miss the scullery." She held up one reddened hand. "And what of you? I see Bagley hasn't learned many manners yet. Is he coming along at all?"

Bagley had a reputation. And not a good one.

"Picking up more all the time—it's just his doggy brain keeps forgetting what he's learned."

Charlotte came his way, then hesitated when she saw him speaking with Margaret. She looked around and tried to find someone else who needed cake, but he was the only one left.

He hadn't encountered her since that night in the kitchen when Winters was there. Had Tristen made her uncomfortable? He hoped that would never be the case. But perhaps it was that she welcomed Winters's attention and felt his censure without him even voicing his concerns.

She held out the offering, and their gazes briefly touched. Beside him, Margaret straightened as if ready to go into battle.

"Are you packed and ready to go home?" Margaret asked. "I saw your travel case out this morning. I thought you'd be gone by now."

Margaret Malone, the bane of my life!

When rising in the wee hours each morning, Charlotte attempted to be as quiet as possible, but Margaret wasn't as considerate. She stomped around like an elephant, making as much noise as she could. She never refilled the water jar when she used the last or allowed Charlotte to open the window to let in the cool night breeze. The worst was her silent treatment. She was surprised Margaret had spoken to her now.

Charlotte smiled, first at Margaret and then Mr. Llewellyn, offering him the plate of cake. Their fingers briefly touched, sending a spark of awareness up her arm. "I am, later today."

"Thought as much," Margaret replied. The cake on her plate was already gone, but a small crumb had fallen onto her chin and jiggled when she spoke.

Charlotte briefly brushed her own chin, widening her eyes slightly as a subtle sign.

Margaret didn't take the hint.

Mr. Llewellyn did. He reached forward and gingerly removed the morsel, then held the crumb out so she'd know what he'd done. Margaret's face flushed a bright red, and she turned calf eyes up at the handsome gamekeeper.

"But, actually," Charlotte began—not wanting to be cruel, but Margaret had a way of driving her to distraction—"Mrs. Darling has asked me to stay on. I'll be going home for a few days to find out if that's possible. I'm not sure I'll be back, but I hope so."

Margaret's mouth gaped. "Stay on?" she spat, then her eyes narrowed. "Because of Mr. Winters? I saw him down here laughing with you this morning. Your face turned pink at everything he said. He's way above you, Charlotte. Most likely, he put in a request so he can get to know you."

"Margaret!" Charlotte gasped. Yes, Mr. Winters had been quite solicitous toward her, but she wasn't willing to let it go further than that—at least not until she'd sorted through her feelings. The last thing she needed was Margaret spreading rumors. "Please, think before you speak! Each time he came into the kitchen, he was looking for something, that's all." She didn't dare look at Mr. Llewellyn. Did he share the same low opinion of her?

From the corner of her eye, Charlotte noticed Rose coming their way. "I couldn't help overhearing you might be returning," Rose said, her eyes bright. "That's wonderful." She looked at her nephew and then back at Charlotte. "What time do you plan to depart? I'd feel better if Tristen escorted you through the woods. They never used to be so unsafe, but of late . . ."

Alarm streaked through Charlotte. "I'm fine walking alone," she replied quickly. "Mr. Llewellyn has work to do. I don't need his help."

Mr. Llewellyn straightened sharply, as if he too found the idea off-putting. "I am busy, Aunt Rose, I don't—"

Rose waved away his excuse as if it were mist in a breeze. "I insist. Tristen said just last night he'd discovered more tracks around the woods that shouldn't be there. Not when the pheasants are nesting. There may be poachers about, or outlaws." She laid her hand on Tristen's arm, but his expression didn't change. Charlotte could see he was none too happy regarding this turn of events. "I'd feel better knowing you're with him and will accomplish the walk unmolested. It won't take that long."

Tristen's gaze seemed to reach out and touch Charlotte.

Margaret's audible squeak of distress was almost funny after what she'd done, besmirching Charlotte's name in front of Tristen. Charlotte didn't feel one speck of guilt.

"But, but, she can ride back to Brightshire with the coal man," Margaret blurted. "He's arriving any time and always has room on his front seat for whomever." She glanced around in alarm. "Myself, Amelia, and even Cook have traveled with him from time to time. More too. He's a nice man and won't mind at all."

Rose tipped her head in thought. "That's a possibility. What time did you plan to leave, Charlotte?"

"I promised to bake a few more items for Mr. Brown before departing. I won't be ready until about three, so . . ."

Rose nodded firmly, as though that decided it. "The coal man never stays past one. Tristen will be by at three to collect you. Does that give you enough time to do what you must?"

Charlotte squirmed. She didn't want to make the walk under his disapproving gaze, especially after what Margaret had insinuated. "Please, that won't—"

"My aunt is right," Tristen finally said, although his tone was none too happy. "I make a point of being out there at differing times of the day and have yet to walk those acres. It's no inconvenience at all, Miss Aldridge. The forests are my responsibility. Leaving you to make that walk alone would be taking a risk. But bear in mind to bring your raincoat. The clouds have been gathering all morning."

What was the use in arguing? "Very well. I'll be ready at three and meet you outside by the entrance to the forest."

He nodded, then forked a large bite of cake into his mouth and seemed determined to be polite even if he did disapprove of her. "Did you make this, Miss Aldridge?" he said after swallowing. "It's awfully good."

Just what I need. More reasons for Margaret to hate me. "Yes, I did indeed."

CHAPTER SIXTEEN

Beranger, this is beautiful! What a wonderful way to spend a Saturday afternoon," Emma said, her voice ringing with deep emotion. She gazed at the land lying between the manor and Brightshire, having taken the long way around to see a river and the many meadows. They visited the small lake and marshlands, and a mountain peak where you could see far into the distance. "Each place we visit I like better than the last. I understand now why your memories are so vivid. Your homeland is beautiful. The air is so crisp, clean—and brisk." She hugged her arms around herself. "I'm glad we came."

He turned in the saddle. They'd stopped a few minutes back, and she'd given Dusty, her trusty gelding from Colorado, rein enough to reach down and grab a mouthful of grass. Early this morning Beranger had let everyone know he'd be occupied until the following day. He refused to be called away for problems that would still be there for him to consider tomorrow, next week, and most likely next year. He and Emma hadn't had a proper honeymoon aboard ship, and he intended to remedy that now.

"That makes me happy. I'd like to take you on an extended visit to London. To see the symphony, Big Ben, and Westminster Abbey."

She looked utterly charming in the riding habit the dressmakers had delivered—almost a native Englishwoman, except that no amount of talking could convince her to try an English saddle over her western. He'd told her to wear her riding britches from home, if she preferred, but she'd declined. She was an American, and he didn't want one hair on her head to change.

"And Buckingham Palace, Beranger? I definitely want to see that, but not the queen. I don't think I'll ever be ready for that."

His loud bark of laughter spooked Charger. The horse jerked to the side, his large, intelligent eyes wide. Easily keeping his seat, Beranger reached down to calm the gelding with a pat on his neck. "No, my love, we won't be meeting the queen anytime soon. As a matter of fact, I believe my father only met her once in all the years he was duke. I wouldn't be ready for a visitation like that myself. Although I'm sure she'd be interested in meeting a beautiful American like yourself. I'll have to keep that in mind."

They started off again, her riding close enough to reach out and playfully slap his thigh. "Don't you dare tease me, not today. This is the first we've been alone since the ship, practically. There're so many servants in the castle I never know who is walking by my bedchamber door. It's disconcerting."

He cocked his head. "You had help on the ranch, didn't you?"

She arched a brow in mock surprise. "Help? Yes. A cook and a housekeeper. Nothing more. That can't compare to the multitude of servants here. The dowager duchess is in the process of hiring a proper lady's maid for me, though I'm not sure I like a stranger helping me in and out of my clothes several times a day."

"I happen to remember a bunkhouse full of young men just waiting to do your bidding—take Trevor Hill, KT, Moses Poor, and others. Did I dream those ranch hands, Mrs. Northcott?" He teased her with the American address. "They were there to help."

"They were there to ranch, not assist me in and out of my clothes."

He conceded with a nod and a chuckle. "You have me there."

Emma laughed. He'd never seen her so free and relaxed. They topped a rise and had a nice view of Goldenbrook, the hamlet where they'd dropped the midwife, Mathilda Tugwer, the evening of their arrival. Had that only been four days ago?

Using her saddle horn for leverage, Emma pushed taller in the saddle to get a better look at the hamlet below.

In the general view, a dozen cottages sat scattered on one side of a common area, across from more on the other. Some were clean and neat, others run-down and shabby. Two women stood outside doing their laundry. A baby sat at their feet in the grass. A group of children dashed in and out of a nearby shed, perhaps playing a game of tag. Several benches were haphazardly dispersed about, and a swing hung from the sturdy branch of a tall elm. From here he could see patches of kitchen gardens, flush with emerald-green lettuce leaves, strings of climbing beans, and lime-colored plants laden with red tomatoes. The Gilded Goose, a small country tavern at the end of the commons, was a place Beranger remembered well. The menfolk went there every afternoon to sate their thirst after long days in the fields.

Unaware they were being watched, one woman fished a bedsheet out of a bucket of water and handed one end to her companion. The two twisted the material until most of the moisture had been extracted. With wooden pins, the wet linen was fastened to the short line between their homes.

"Is that Brightshire?" Emma asked. "I've only been through at nightfall on the day of our arrival. I was so nervous that day I don't remember a thing. It seems so small. And where are the people?"

"Not Brightshire, but Goldenbrook."

"The hamlet? Where are the shops and businesses? How do they live? Just houses set out in a field, not much more. I'm surprised."

"Most of the inhabitants have found work in Brightshire, which is only three miles away. Or they've moved to London to find employment in the many factories springing up like garden weeds. They used to work the fields for landowners around these parts, but all that has changed with modern machinery. Fewer men are needed to put in crops and keep the fields."

"But three miles is a long way in a storm, or if you have a sick child. I would think some sort of doctor here would be nice." Her intent contemplation formed a *V* between her brows. "Is there a school?"

"A small one."

"It feels so isolated. This is also where Mathilda Tugwer lives, yes?"

"You remember her name? She can do you no harm, Emma. You have nothing to fear from her. Still, I would caution you about . . ." He paused and searched for the words to help his wife understand. "Becoming too friendly. She's not really a gypsy, since she's lived in these parts for years, but I'm sure she'd not be averse to making a few coins by telling your fortune, or mixing a tincture to chase away blues or help you sleep." He reached over to smooth back some strands of her hair caught by the wind. "I'm not saying she doesn't have healing abilities, I just don't want to see you be hurt in any way. You're trusting to a fault sometimes. Be kind, but be cautious." He couldn't tell what she was thinking.

"You want me to stay away from her?"

"Not really that. Just don't let her pull you into anything that makes you uncomfortable. There is a difference." He pointed at movement below in Goldenbrook. "Would you like to see the hamlet closer?"

"Would you?" she asked.

"I would. For old times' sake. Actually, more than that. Each day I'm back, more of the hurt of my childhood falls away. I'm happier than I believed I could be. And, if I'm truthful, I'd like to show you off. I may be the new duke, but I still sometimes feel like the illegitimate son who lurked in the shadows. I want everyone to meet my beautiful wife."

Squeezing Charger with his calves, Beranger led the way down the trail.

The women working between the cottages stopped what they were doing and took notice. The children came to a screeching halt in a billow of dust. The baby was the only one who seemed unaffected by their arrival.

Beranger and Emma halted some ten feet away. "Good day," Beranger greeted.

Their eyes were large. By now they'd caught sight of the duke's coat of arms on Beranger's saddle pad. They curtsied, and the children ran off behind the shed.

"Can you tell me if Rodrick Simmons is still the proprietor of the Gilded Goose?" During his early teens before he left to sea, Beranger used to stop in from time to time and have himself a half-pint of warm ale, even as a boy. He could taste the bitter bite now from memory.

"Oh, yes, Your Grace," the older woman said.

Beranger recognized her as Mrs. Parker, the mother of a girl named Phoebe who used to run with the boys whenever she could sneak away from her chores. He wondered what had become of her.

"Old man Simmons still pours the ale, if 'e's sober. If not, 'is son will do the job if 'e's around." She looked over to the quiet pub. "Mr. Simmons is gettin' on since you was here last. His 'ealth ain't what it used ta be. 'E'll be mighty happy ta see you 'gain. As am I, Your Grace. I used to love your pretty eyes. You go on an' say 'ello." She smiled at Emma and gave a small nod. Both curtsied again.

A warm feeling of goodness flowed through Beranger. During his years in America, it was the bad memories that had mostly stuck with him, the reasons he'd left this land. But being back was helping him to remember good memories too. He hadn't thought much about all the people who would be affected by his return, and if they would or would not remember who he was. His findings were proving more moving than he'd ever expected.

"Tell me, Mrs. Parker, what's become of your daughter, Phoebe? She used to play in the woods with the lads all those years ago. She could keep up with us, no trouble at all." He looked around, thinking the place almost looked deserted. "I've thought of her over the years, I'll admit."

The woman's face brightened with pride. "Why, she's made a good marriage, Your Grace. Yes, a good marriage indeed. Wed the blacksmith."

Leo Lewis. Bully. Five years older and uncaring who he picks on.

"You remember Leo? His pa died, leavin' 'im the forge and livery. Most these wee ones ya see scattered are theirs. I keep 'em most days—seven, to be exact." She glanced around, her wide smile revealing several missing teeth. "Keeps me young, running after 'em. You might see 'er if you're 'eaded ta Brightshire. Just think, the duke asking after my daughter."

"We are," he replied. "I'll be sure to look her up. Good day." Turning Charger, he preceded Emma over to the Gilded Goose and dismounted.

Going from the overcast sky outside into the utter darkness of the Gilded Goose rendered Emma almost blind. There was a crackling fire in a huge stone hearth, astounding because of the small size of the pub. Two fellows sat on rickety stools in front of an uncommonly low bar top, bent over their drinks. They didn't even look around at the sound of their entrance.

"We'll only stay long enough to say hello," Beranger whispered as he drew her along by the hand. "Rodrick Simmons was kind to me back then."

"I don't mind, Beranger. Remember, I've been inside Eden's saloon."

Beranger chuckled, low and deep. "And I went a round of boxing with those drunken fellows because of it. Yes, I remember. That's exactly why I don't want to stay."

Emma pretended to pout, letting the wicked gleam in her eye tell him she was teasing. "But I'd like to taste the ale."

"Come on up ta the bar, young fella," a familiar voice called. "Bring your lady. We won't bite."

The speaker was an old man with hands deep in a bucket of water as he washed glasses on the low bar.

"Mr. Simmons, remember me?"

The man quickly looked up.

"Beranger Northcott, back from America."

The two men at the bar clambered off their stools in astonishment and stood with their mouths agape.

"Is it really you, Beranger?" Mr. Simmons mumbled, squinting. He reached for a towel and quickly dried his hands. "You were but a lad the last time I served ya a half-pint. Look at ya now." He chuckled. "Even then you could hold your beer. Now you're tall and strong—the picture of health. By God, you standing before me does this old man good. The day you ran off was a sad day. Took the heart right out of the shire, ya did."

The old fellow tottered out and wrapped his thin arms around Beranger, hugging him fiercely.

A burly man, who must have been listening from the back room, came through the door behind the bar and glared. "I heard the news yesterday, Pa. True, it's him all right. And 'e's the Duke of Brightshire, now that Gavin's dead in his grave."

Mr. Simmons swung around to his son. "What's this you say? Duke of Brightshire? Shame on you for not saying something sooner! I'd have been ready for Beranger's visit. He'd never forget a friend."

"Aye. I remember you, *Your Grace*," the younger version of Rodrick said with a sneer in his voice. "The sneak has returned to claim the title after Gavin is cold in his final resting place. What is the shire coming to?"

The two standing men listened with interest. "Murdered with his own knife," one of them mumbled. "Foul play that's never been established."

Frightened, Emma gripped Beranger's hand. Only yesterday she'd had the conversation with Beranger about him being careful. And now this? They'd been told, and believed, Gavin's death had been an accident. Her worst nightmare was coming true right before her eyes.

"Why do you say that?" Beranger demanded. "Do you know something, or is the beer talking? Speak up!"

Mr. Simmons's son stuck out his chest. "That brother of yours used to gamble with us, not that these men have much to lose, but that didn't stop *the duke*. He'd clean us out on a regular basis and smile as he went out the door. Even with the financial struggles at *your* castle, we had less to lose than him. Braggart and a cheat. I say he got what he had coming!"

CHAPTER SEVENTEEN

"I s this everything?" Tristen asked, glancing at the small carpetbag Charlotte had just set at her feet.

A few minutes before three, she'd reached the specified meeting place at the edge of the forest to find Tristen waiting. She shouldn't feel so nervous, she told herself. If only she had her pony and the cart to focus her attention on, give her something to talk about. She glanced at her belongings and then up into the gamekeeper's stonelike expression. "Yes, this is all."

A breeze had come up in the last few minutes she'd been waiting. Tristen retrieved her bag and took a step away.

"Please, I can get that. The carpetbag's not heavy, and I'm used to fetching and carrying things for myself."

With his rifle cradled in one arm and the handle of her bag gripped in his other, he gave an affirmative nod. "I'll carry your bag, Miss Aldridge. As I mentioned before, the clouds have been gathering and are heavy with rain. I doubt we'll get all the way to Brightshire without getting drenched. We best hurry. I'm surprised you didn't bring an umbrella."

"I don't have an umbrella, sir."

"No need to call me sir. Tristen is fine with me."

He didn't look at her as they stepped out of the cloudy sunlight into the overgrown tunnel of forest to begin the journey. The path instantly darkened, and she was suddenly more than grateful for Mr. Llewellyn's presence, even if he did look a little put out with the chore.

"All right then, Tristen, I will. And you must call me Charlotte in return." She glanced around and then up at him. "And where is Bagley? Did he find trouble and have to stay home?"

From the corner of her eye, she saw him sigh. "He did—again. His endless barking startled a nesting pheasant off her eggs. He needs to learn what he's to chase and what he's not to disturb. Since he can't seem to remember the difference yet, he's home in the shed."

She chanced another look at him. "The shed?" she said, unable to mask her distress.

His frown softened. "More a small barn with other animals. It's plenty large, with food and water. He's not being punished. I just don't want him dashing around causing mischief."

A gust of wind sent the treetops dancing above their heads, the great canopy of green and yellow swishing loudly. The briskness of the dropping temperature produced goose bumps on the backs of Charlotte's arms. An eerie feeling skittered up her back. Thank heavens the bread delivery was Thomas's job and not hers. Her vivid imagination would have made the trip unbearable on a day like today. Every twig that snapped or leaf that rattled made her peer over her shoulder.

"Have you met my brother, Thomas?" she asked, trying to banish her nervous thoughts. "He's the one who usually delivers the bread to Ashbury and comes through once a week."

"Thomas Aldridge? No, I haven't. The woods around the castle are quite extensive, though, so I never know where I'll be. I can't cover every mile every day."

"No, I wouldn't think so."

A distant keening, the sound resembling the cry of an infant, whispered faintly by on the wind. Charlotte shivered and stopped in her tracks. She'd heard the superstition enough times. "Did you hear that?" she asked. "The lost baby." She wrapped her arms tightly around herself and looked up at the trees. The forest had darkened even further. "The poor thing sounds so sad."

Tristen stopped and looked back at her—being his stride was so much longer than hers, he'd already gotten quite a few paces away. A curious tilt brought his brows together. "That's the wind in the trees. There's no lost child here or anywhere else. Just because others believe such silliness, you shouldn't."

"So you've heard the myth, then? This is the first time I've heard the sound for myself."

"Aye. And that's all it is, a superstition." He gave her a critical look. "I didn't take you for the gullible sort, Charlotte."

I really can't blame him. Until I heard the eerie wail today, that's exactly what I thought of others who came into the bakeshop with stories of ghosts and apparitions. But the cry does sound just like a baby, heartbreaking and sad. What am I to think?

"No, I'm not superstitious—but I do have an active imagination. I always have, and sometimes it leads me into trouble."

"Like imagining a member of the peerage and a country girl could fall in love?"

She jerked to a halt, not believing what she'd just heard. What should she say? She'd never be able to change his preconceived notions about her—especially after what Margaret had shared.

"No. But that's my business and not yours."

A self-satisfied expression appeared on his profile.

She'd like to tell him to just turn around and go back the way they'd come, but the forestlands had grown even darker. Rose's warning of poachers and outlaws echoed in her head.

"I don't want to see you get hurt, Charlotte," he said. "I'm looking out for your best interest."

"No need," she said coolly, lifting her chin. "I can take care of myself."

The baby's cry sounded again, and she regretted her words. It wouldn't do to alienate him just now.

"Maybe—maybe that wasn't the lost baby," she said, her pace slowing again. "But just a woman somewhere nearby with a cranky child in tow. Sound does carry on the wind, you know. It has to be real."

"It's the wind," he insisted. "The sound never happens on a calm day."

They'd come to the bend in the road where the track made a sharp turn. She wondered why the road had been cut that way and not straight through. The next section of road, which would lead to Brightshire, was much longer than the one they'd just traveled. A soft pitter-patter of rain sounded on the leaves above. Tristen had been right. She wouldn't arrive home without getting wet.

"Where do you think the sound comes from, then?" she asked, with nothing left to debate and fearful he'd pick up again with her private affairs.

He slowed to walk next to her, his expression growing animated. "When he wanted to search out the sound's origin himself, my uncle found a fissure in the craggy granite outcrop to the northeast."

"Have you been there?"

"Not yet."

"Then why hasn't he spread the word and put a stop to the fears? That would be the kind thing to do. Many folks believe in ghosts, and the crying baby doesn't help."

"The fissure doesn't help."

"Yes, that's what I meant."

Tristen smiled, surprising her. He was stingy with his smiles, and they seemed to wield a great power. Even the mysteries of the forest took on new appeal.

"Because the legend of a baby's ghost in the duke's forests keeps many of the poachers at bay. Uncle Arson says without the tale, poaching would be worse." He gave her a long look. "I can't say that I blame him. All he wants is to avoid confrontation where men might get hurt. Besides, he didn't start the rumor, just didn't lay it to rest."

His uncle? Avoid confrontation? Feeling brave, she asked, "Does your uncle have a temper? Or get into fights?"

"What? Of course not! That's an odd thing to ask."

She lifted one shoulder innocently, as if she hadn't had an ulterior motive in mind. "Just wondered. By the way it sounded, I thought perhaps he went around looking for trouble."

"He's the most even-tempered man I know."

She was mulling over his response when a sight up ahead made her feet slow and then finally stop. The discussion of ghosts and apparitions had her edgy, even if Tristen had given her reason to believe the superstition was just a myth. A shiver ran up and down her spine.

A good quarter mile away was a shape in the middle of the road. Not tall like a man, or large as a horse, but not small enough to be a boulder or a parcel fallen from a wagon. Then suddenly, the silhouette moved, its dark surface writhing and flapping.

Frightened, she grasped Tristen's arm and pulled him to a stop. "What's that? I can't tell from here." Her whispered plea came out a garbled mouthful. Her fear mounted when he didn't respond directly.

"Don't be frightened," he said, low. "Could be a beggar. Bent over or sitting in the road."

"In the center of the road? How strange."

"Not much traffic. Plenty of time to move if a carriage or cart comes along. Come on, or we'll never get you home before the rain starts in earnest."

She could tell by the way he never took his eyes from the thing in the road that he was more concerned than he let on. She was glad he had his gun. Was this some sort of trap set by outlaws?

Her mouth felt filled with sand. Every rumor she'd ever heard whispered in her village went through her mind. Tristen marched on, seemingly unaffected by the fact she still clung to his arm. But she couldn't bring herself to let go for fear he might dart off the road, leaving her alone with whoever or whatever that was. Slowly, needing more contact, she let her hand slip down his forearm to his hand, where he, without question or missing a beat, enfolded hers within his own.

As they neared, whatever, or whoever, moved again.

The baby sounded once more, soft and lilting on the wind.

Charlotte thought she might melt into a ball of fright. Tristen glanced at her and shook his head, not even having to hear her words to know what she was thinking.

The object grew in height and turned around.

Charlotte let out a sigh of relief and let her hand fall away, suddenly regretting the loss of the warmth from Tristen's palm. "It's only Mathilda Tugwer. I know her. She lives in the hamlet and visits our shop every few months. Although she looks frightful, she seems harmless enough. She's a midwife and has always been kind to me. I wonder what she's doing on the road to Ashbury. Do you know her?"

"I don't. But I've seen evidence of her in the woods. A small track here or there. Plants that have been broken at the stem as if someone had been gathering. My uncle told me of her."

They were within speaking distance, so Charlotte called her name.

"Ahh, the baker girl," the old woman replied in her creaky voice, a smile pulling her thin lips upward. "How is my Charlotte these days?"

"Fine. But you gave me quite the scare. I didn't recognize you from farther away." The lovely scent of wet earth wrapped around them, and raindrops dotted the road. "If the rain is coming through the canopy, it must be pouring out there."

Mathilda tilted her head and laughed at the exact moment a crack of thunder boomed overhead. The sound appeared to come from her. Tristen stepped closer to Charlotte—as though, perhaps, it was he who was now a little frightened.

For several long, uncomfortable moments, the midwife's gaze roamed Tristen's face. Charlotte edged forward slightly.

"This is Tristen Llewellyn. The gamekeeper's nephew. He's working at Ashbury until Mr. Henderley is back on his feet."

The woman's eyes narrowed with interest. Charlotte was used to Mathilda's hooded gray cape, stringy black hair, and haunting silver eyes. She had a sweet tooth for plum tarts and apple strudel and could be seen passing through Brightshire just past sundown one to two times a week. Charlotte was not frightened of her, maybe because the woman had been around for as long as she could remember and had assisted the birth of many a country wife—or even an unmarried wench. One night, after Charlotte had sneaked her a glass of plum wine from the bottle Aunt Ethel kept hidden behind her cooking oils, Mathilda had whispered that she'd known a woman once who'd greatly resembled Charlotte. She'd given an account of her pretty face, blue eyes, silky dark blond hair. And how her voice sounded like bells on the wind. When Charlotte had asked if that woman had been her real mother, Mathilda had shushed her questions, but the light in the woman's eyes spoke volumes. Later, Aunt Ethel had cursed Mathilda as a fool and liar and told Charlotte never to bring the subject up again.

"Tristen Llewellyn," Mathilda repeated.

Tristen gave a nod but remained silent.

"Did you hear anything a moment ago, Mathilda?" Charlotte asked, wondering what she'd say regarding the superstition.

"You mean the lost baby?"

Charlotte bobbed her head. "Yes, exactly that."

"I hear her all the time, at least whenever I'm in the woods."

"Would that be often, madam?" Tristen asked. "I walk the woods every day, and I've yet to see you."

"But I've seen you. And no, not often, but when I feel the urge, or need willow bark or wild herbs."

She held out what looked like a list of words, perhaps of the plants she was hunting for. Charlotte was surprised that the woman could write at all. She hoped Tristen wouldn't bring up the fact that she was trespassing on the duke's land. Mathilda had so little.

Charlotte looked between them. "Is the lost baby a ghost? The story has been around for so long, she must be."

"Nobody knows, not even me." A sly-looking smile spread across her face. Was she trying to frighten Tristen?

Mathilda stepped closer and touched Charlotte's hair.

Charlotte steeled herself not to cringe back.

"How old are you now, my little baker?" the old woman asked. "The years go by so quickly, I sometimes forget."

Forget? Had the woman known her longer than she'd thought?

"Nineteen." The woman's eyes glowed, and uncertainty swirled inside Charlotte.

"Yes, that's right. You best be on your way. Darkness is falling more quickly with the storm." She looked at Tristen. "You will see her safely all the way into Brightshire? To her home?"

"I will."

"Good. Then you won't mind if I take this trail out to the bog where the large willows grow, now will you? I must replenish my stock."

"I won't." He looked down into Charlotte's face. "We'll be off."

They took a few steps and Charlotte turned to say goodbye, but Mathilda had already vanished into the forest.

The rain above intensified from the soft pitter-patter to a deafening drumming on the forest canopy above. Thunder sounded again. The sky had looked dark, but she hadn't expected such a storm. "May I have my carpetbag to retrieve my shawl?"

Tristen watched her dig for her garment and then wrap it around her head and shoulders.

Now that the rain had begun in earnest, he was striding quickly, and she had to run to keep up. She glanced at her bag, rocking with

Tristen's stride. She'd have to set it by the kitchen fire to dry once they reached the bakeshop.

Tristen switched the carpetbag to the hand that held his rifle and took her hand in his own, causing a flutter of butterflies once again when his rough, warm palm came in contact with hers. "Think you can run? Temperature's falling, and we lost time speaking with that woman. I'd feel better to have you home. The darkness can cover a multitude of scoundrels. There've been rumors the duke's death wasn't all that accidental, and no one has been detained for the crime, if there was one."

With her hand wrapped in his, she nodded. *But the culprit you're worried about might be your uncle.* Because he loved his uncle, Tristen would welcome that information as much as she welcomed the thought that the culprit might be Thomas.

CHAPTER EIGHTEEN

The wind began to howl, and dark, foreboding clouds swirled above, preparing to unleash a torrent of rain. Beranger glanced over to see Emma shiver and cursed himself for letting her go out today without proper rain clothing. They'd both be soaked before they arrived back at Ashbury. And he hadn't liked the worry in her eyes when they'd left the pub. Hearing that Gavin may have been murdered had disturbed them both.

"Let's canter," he said, the wind whipping Charger's mane. "Do you feel comfortable doing so? I'd like to try to reach Brightshire before the clouds let loose. It'll be closer to head there than return to the castle."

"Yes, as long as you lead. Dusty's better following."

A bolt of lightning cut across the sky as they cantered through sheep pastures and entered Brightshire from the side. Large drops of rain pelted the dry earth, shops, and anyone foolish enough to be out on such a day. "Here, this way," Beranger shouted through the wind.

Trotting though the empty streets, Beranger cut toward the livery, with two reasons on his mind. One, they'd leave the horses there until the rain let up, and two, he'd like to see his old friend Phoebe Parker, now Phoebe Lewis. He gave a mental shake of his head. It was difficult to believe she'd married Leo.

On both sides of the road, shops and buildings were stalwart, some with brightly painted doors or window casings, looking attractive even in the rain. A thick green moss covered the north sides of the steeply pitched roofs, while the other sides were clean shingles. Lamplight brightened windows, and he wondered if any of the places had had gas lamps installed, as the castle had. He'd missed this town, he realized with a surge of affection.

The bulky, crisscrossed timbers above the double-door entry of the livery appeared a thousand years old. The large, sturdy building, the walls proudly straight, seemed exactly as Beranger remembered from his youth.

They clattered inside the open doors and pulled up. Darkness enveloped them amid the scent of hay, horse manure, and wet wood. When Beranger's eyes adjusted to the gloom, he noted three or four burning lanterns. He remembered the two rows of stalls.

He dismounted and tied Charger's reins to an iron ring.

"Hello?" a deep voice called.

"Hello, Leo," Beranger called back as he helped Emma down. They tied Dusty beside Charger and waited.

Leo Lewis's tall silhouette appeared in the threshold of one door. The cloth he'd been wiping with fell to the ground.

"Beranger Northcott," a woman's voice called out from the second set of doors, which were now open. "The prodigal son returns."

At first, Beranger didn't recognize the woman standing in the doorway. She'd grown taller, almost as tall as him. Her hair, still dark, was pulled back, almost scraped against her scalp. He recognized Phoebe's voice more than he did her face. There wasn't a trace of her usual friendly smile, or the laughter that had always been in her eyes, but there was something in her stance that rocked him back into memory. Happiness pushed him forward. "Phoebe. Your mother told me I'd find you here."

Her chin edged up, and he noted some darkness around one eye.

"So that's how you recognized me. You wouldn't have if you hadn't had help. I've changed, but you haven't, much."

Leo stepped forward, a frown on his sweaty face. Where at eighteen he'd cut a fine figure of a man, it now appeared he'd put on many pounds around his middle and lost a good amount of his formerly thick, black hair. He'd been quite vain about that hair, boasting no woman alive could resist it.

Emma edged closer to Beranger.

After introductions, a child began to cry from somewhere in the back room. Phoebe nudged her husband. "I told ya Beranger had come home, Leo, so stop scowling at me. You need to unclog your ears and listen. News hit the village a few days ago."

Feeling the tension between the two, Beranger reached for Emma's hand. This reunion wasn't quite what he'd expected; perhaps leaving quickly was best. "I'd like to leave the horses until the rain stops."

"Sorry, we're all filled up," Leo replied.

Not everyone is glad to see me home.

"Fine," Beranger replied, although he knew it to be a lie. "We'll be on our way, then."

He gathered the reins and turned to the door. Lifting his arm over Emma's head in a useless attempt to shield her from the rain, they ran out into the storm. He understood Leo—the man had never been friendly—but he didn't understand Phoebe's reaction. He'd thought she'd be just as happy to see him as he'd been to see her, but the tension in the room could have been cut with a knife. Was Leo so jealous she was unable to show any type of affection? Or maybe Phoebe was tired. With seven children, her life couldn't be easy.

He ducked under the eave of a dry-goods shop, pulling Emma under with him. "Are you hungry?" he asked, looking around in the dusky light as the street filled with puddles. "I think we should find somewhere to wait out the storm, since the livery didn't pan out."

"Is there a restaurant or pub in Brightshire? Surely people have to eat."

"A few, but probably not the kind you're used to."

She smiled up at him as her wet hair began to sag around her face. "Anywhere dry is what I'm used to. As long as it's warm and they have coffee."

"I can't promise coffee."

"Well, tea, then. And something hearty. I've worked up an appetite. Stew or soup sounds good."

"Then follow me. I know the perfect spot."

Tristen rushed through the bakeshop door behind Charlotte, drenched to the bone. The two had run most of the way to Brightshire, her hand in his, only stopping to catch their breath when needed. Although four o'clock had yet to fall, darkness prevailed. The September storm had grown into a tempest. He wasn't looking forward to the trip home.

As the door banged closed behind them, an older woman, who must be Charlotte's aunt, nearly dropped what she was holding. Angrily, she took a step away from the long glass display case that ran the length of the room. Golden-brown loaves of bread, as well as other baked goods, sat on a large rectangular tray on a nearby table. "My word!" she screeched.

Charlotte turned to Tristen, a wide smile on her lips. "Never in my life did I expect a thunderstorm like that, Mr. Llewellyn!" she said through a round of laughter. "I'm soaked through. Look at me." She put out her arms and turned a full circle, still breathing hard from their run.

Mrs. Smith's screech sounded again. "Charlotte, look at you! A drowned rat is prettier. You're a disgrace, girl."

Charlotte ignored the insult as if she were used to hearing much of the same. She pulled off her sodden shawl and brushed wet strands of hair from her face, all the while holding his gaze. Merriment danced in her eyes. He tried to ignore how pretty she looked.

And how jealous he was that Mr. Winters had her attention.

The angry woman turned from Charlotte and her dripping clothes to him. Her eyes narrowed. "And who might you be?"

Tristen felt wet and conspicuous. Water cascaded down his coat and trousers, pooling at his feet. The puddle around them grew. "Mrs. Smith, I apologize for drenching your bakeshop floor. Now that you're home safe and sound, Miss Aldridge, I'll be on my way." He inclined his head and started for the door.

"Please, wait." Charlotte put out two supplicating hands. One to the woman and one to him, stopping his departure. "Mr. Llewellyn is the assistant gamekeeper at Ashbury, Aunt Ethel. Amelia knows him from his visits to the kitchen. He was good enough to see me safely home through this storm."

Ethel Smith's appearance softened so quickly the transformation was almost funny.

"A pleasure to meet you, ma'am," he said, feeling uncomfortable and more than antsy to get back out into the storm. Something inside him said out there was safer than in here with Aunt Ethel. "I'll be going now . . ."

"Oh, no, Mr. Llewellyn," Aunt Ethel said. "Please stay and warm up. If you're friendly with my sweet Amelia, you're welcome to stay—as a matter of fact, I insist. Come warm yourself by our fire. Dry off and rest. Verity, my younger daughter, will serve you something to eat as well. The walk back will go better with a full belly." Her eyes brightened. "We have some ale too I can offer. Wait until the foul weather eases up."

Charlotte smiled, seeming unaffected by her aunt's clear affection for her daughters and the way she practically ignored Charlotte. Tristen wasn't sure why he cared, but something about her aunt's dismissiveness irked him.

"I was just about to suggest that," Charlotte said. "It's the least I can do to show my thanks." She looked at her aunt. "Is there a meat pie I can heat for this fine gentleman who was so good to see me home?"

"There is," her aunt stated. "Jumping hare and potato. And it's still warm from the oven. Amelia makes a splendid version of it when she's home. No one's can hold a candle to hers, not even Charlotte's."

The aunt's grin revealed a missing tooth on the left side. Her back was slightly bowed, a posture developed from years of kneading, he presumed. A white apron covered most of her clothes, and a puffy white cap over graying brown hair topped off her look. She didn't resemble Charlotte in any way, shape, or form.

"Didn't you come in here a day or two ago?" Ethel asked. "To pay for some bread you said you spilled from our cart."

"I did, Mrs. Smith, yes."

"Honesty in a man is a quality that's becoming harder and harder to find."

Another young woman appeared through a door at the back of the shop. A young man stood back, watching.

Charlotte crossed the room and took the girl's arm. "This is my cousin Verity Smith and my brother, Thomas." She smiled up into her brother's face, a look of pride crossing her eyes.

Thomas would stand eye to eye with Tristen if he came closer. He had his cousin's shade of hair, darker than his sister's. In fact, Tristen realized, Charlotte resembled none of her relatives at all. The way Charlotte accepted her aunt's scornful treatment brought a surge of admiration. He doubted he could be so charitable living under these circumstances.

Tristen nodded back politely, feeling at a disadvantage in his dripping clothes.

Ethel, eyeing the growing puddle at his feet, said, "I insist you accept our hospitality, Mr. Llewellyn. Verity, take him to the kitchen while Charlotte helps me stock this display case." She glanced at the bread and sweets on the tray. "My niece hasn't done a lick of work for days. Go on with ya, before you create a lake in here. The fire's warm. We'll join you soon. Thomas, pour him a mug of ale."

Verity led the way through the narrow door into a much larger kitchen. There was an oven on the far wall, and a fireplace in the middle of the side wall. A large work area took up the middle of the room, with a pot rack hanging above. A table was crowded into one corner, and two rocking chairs in front of the fireplace had kitchen towels draped across the back, drying. The establishment was neat and clean and filled with a variety of wonderful smells that made his mouth water.

"Here, sir," Verity said, her brown eyes lowering shyly as she led him to the fireplace and turned one of the rocking chairs so he could face the hearth and warming flames.

Thomas went to get the jug of ale from a shelf.

"Have him remove his boots," Aunt Ethel called from the front room, "so his socks can dry out. I'm sure they're wet through, by the amount of water they brought in, and—"

The bells above the door jangled loudly, drowning out whatever more the aunt had said. Someone else had come into the shop. There was a flurry of voices and what sounded to be a cry of happiness from Charlotte.

Verity rushed to the door between the rooms, and Thomas followed. Tristen thought he might as well see what was happening out there as well. As good as the warmth from the fire felt, his curiosity was more of a motivator. Had a suitor just arrived, one Charlotte was fond of? Could it be Mr. Winters? Even though he had no claim on the girl, he was powerless to stop his stockinged feet from crossing the short distance to find out.

CHAPTER NINETEEN

When the bells above the door sang out, Charlotte turned from the display case to greet whoever dared venture out in such a storm. Astonishment hit her like a streak of lightning. The duchess! Here in the bakeshop. She looked much the same as she and Tristen had only moments before—soaking wet and happy. The next moment the duke himself stepped in behind her, laughing and shaking water from his tall frame. The duchess's riding habit, which must have been lovely at some point, was saturated all the way through. The hem was almost black with mud, and the once-crisp bows drooped like a sad dog's ears.

The duchess's blue lips trembled, but her eyes lit with excitement, not seeming to feel the discomfort from the cold. The strawberry hair Charlotte remembered, which had looked so soft at their after-midnight meeting, drooped over her forehead in sopping-wet hanks.

"Your Graces!" she blurted, curtsying and looking from one to the other.

Soon Verity and Thomas joined the group, as did Tristen. The tiny shop front shrank with the new arrivals.

Charlotte cut a quick glance to her aunt, whose eyes were as large as saucers. Her mouth resembled an open barn door. Being upstaged by anyone always soured her mood, and especially her niece. But some-thing had to be said and done, and doing so was up to her.

"Welcome to Smith's Bakeshop," Charlotte said to the tall duke. This was the first time she'd seen him up close. "We're honored by your presence." She felt the others hovering in the doorway behind her. "Please come in and make yourself comfortable."

"Charlotte!" the duchess gasped. "I'm so happy to see you. I didn't realize this was your bakeshop, but I should have known from all the stories you shared with me and Mrs. Darling in the kitchen that night. Why, you're drenched to the bone, just like us."

Unbidden, Charlotte's gaze slipped to the side, where Tristen was watching the interaction.

Aunt Ethel and the others looked confused, glancing about with tipped heads and puckered brows. Charlotte hadn't told anyone of her tea with the duchess. The memory warmed her through and through.

The duchess grasped the duke by the arm. "Beranger, this is the kitchen maid I told you about, the one who was so kind to me and made me feel at home. Doesn't she look like Katie? She and Mrs. Darling have made me feel very welcome." She rushed forward and enfolded Charlotte in a tight hug, not minding her wet state in the least.

"Thank you for being so caring with my wife," the duke said. "Your kindness will not go unrewarded."

Charlotte blushed. "I don't want anything in return. But please, come into the back kitchen and dry off and have something to eat. Mr. Llewellyn, your gamekeeper, was just about to do the same after walking me here and getting drenched for his reward. We have more than enough and insist you be our guests."

She'd seen the duke's gaze find Tristen, and he'd given him a nod of greeting.

"Oh, and you must be Mrs. Smith," the duchess said. "And Thomas, and Verity," she added, bestowing gracious smiles on them all.

"Why, I, well . . . ," Aunt Ethel sputtered, her hands flapping around and eyes blinking in surprise. Verity too appeared stunned speechless by their prominent guests, while Thomas, his eyes guarded, hung back, which wasn't his usual way with strangers.

"We would love to join you if we wouldn't be taking too much advantage," the duchess said. "When we went out for our ride, the skies were overcast, but we never expected such a downpour." The sound of the rain on the bakeshop roof made hearing difficult.

Thomas stepped forward and glanced out the window. "Would you like me to bring your horses in out of the weather, Your Grace? We have a small barn around back."

"Thank you, I would," the duke responded.

Aunt Ethel gazed unbelieving at the duke with a funny expression on her face. "I remember you. The boy with the strange eyes."

A smile grew across the duke's face. "It's nice to see you again, Mrs. Smith. I was in your shop many times as a youth—especially summertime. The memory of your strawberry tarts makes my mouth water."

"Please, this way," Charlotte said, noticing again the duchess's blue lips. She needed the warmth of the fire.

Everyone made room for the duchess around the fire, and she insisted that Charlotte join her. Charlotte caught Aunt Ethel's scowl at that. She'd prefer the honor be bestowed upon one of her own daughters. Then the idea of dry clothes was tossed out by the duke, who seemed concerned over his bride's health. Within fifteen minutes, the duchess was outfitted in some of Charlotte's garments—none too fancy, but better than her damp riding habit. Charlotte changed as well, gathering apparel from Verity and some from Amelia to make do.

Back downstairs, the men, drier but still damp, were at the table feasting heartily on meat pie and ale. The bakeshop kitchen had never felt so cozy. The duke placed several gold coins on the table, much more than the meal and the use of clothes were worth, but he insisted on paying them for the fine hospitality and clever conversation.

"I'll return to Ashbury and summon a coach for you and the duchess." Tristen, now finished with his meal and looking sated and a bit drier, stood. His gaze found Charlotte's.

She flushed. "It's still raining out there."

"Can't help that. I can take the shortcut through the woods."

"We appreciate that," the duke said. "You can take my wife's horse. Mine is leery of strangers. I wouldn't trust him in a storm like this. Nothing against you, Llewellyn."

"Have you ever ridden a western saddle?" the duchess asked, sipping from her teacup. "Because you're about to."

He shook his head. "I've not, but I'll manage."

Aunt Ethel brought in a plateful of sweets and placed them in the center of the table for dessert. "Please help yourself, Your Graces," she said. "And you as well, Mr. Llewellyn, before you leave. And be sure to check in on Amelia once you're back. Such a sweet, fine girl there never was."

Charlotte ignored the ripple of hurt her aunt's comments created. She was used to them, after all the years of walking in her younger cousin's shadow, but even though Mr. Llewellyn had accompanied her home, had even gotten drenched for her, her aunt never even considered that he might be a potential match for her, rather than one of her own daughters.

Thunder boomed outside, making the women gasp and the men laugh. Who would have thought they'd be entertaining the duke and duchess in Smith's Bakeshop?

The duchess tipped her head to one side and smiled. "And what of you, Charlotte? Why are you here and not at Ashbury?"

Charlotte could feel Tristen's solemn gaze on her face. She didn't know if this was the best time to broach the subject of her returning to the castle for good, but then, when *would* the time be right? "I was only filling in for Amelia until she was better. She resumed her duties today, so now I'm free to come back to the bakeshop. But"—she glanced carefully at Aunt Ethel—"I've been offered a position by Mrs. Darling, if my aunt will let me accept."

She looked around at the kitchen, suddenly wondering if she was ready. This place did feel like home, despite her aunt's unkind treatment. Yes, Aunt Ethel had raised her, but Charlotte had worked every single day to pay off that debt. She shouldered much more of the work than Verity, and while Thomas was expected to do the manly, outside chores, like chop wood and cut hay, he did little overnight baking and pastry making. She'd hate to leave him, but Aunt Ethel had never been quite as harsh with him. He'd find his way.

The duchess put out a hand to Aunt Ethel. "I'm so delighted your daughter Amelia is feeling better. And you must be so proud of Charlotte. She's a marvelously accomplished baker, no doubt thanks to your fine training. I hadn't realized she was only with us temporarily. Mrs. Darling and the cook handle the staffing." Her gaze implored Aunt Ethel and then her husband. "Oh, I do so hope you'll allow her to return to us."

CHAPTER TWENTY

The eyes of green and blue come back,
To haunt, to laugh, to flaunt your fame,
But underneath what years have grown,
Remains the stain of utter shame.

Beranger, your pain I'll see,
And my revenge will be complete . . .

CHAPTER TWENTY-ONE

Two weeks came and went in a blink of an eye. The first of October saw the fields of Brightshire bare of their offerings of wheat, oats, and barley. The harvest had been generous, and Emma had gone with Beranger on several afternoons to watch the activity of the tenant farmers, enthralled at how the people of Goldenbrook joined together to glean the fields of all they had to offer after the horse-drawn mechanical threshing machines went through at a nice clip. Beranger had marveled at the new developments. What used to take fifty to sixty men to accomplish with sickle and reaping hooks was now done by two or three horse-drawn combines and a handful of men. In the beginning of the century, Luddites had shunned technological change as more and more machines took over their jobs—but the machines had won out.

The comments Emma had heard in the Gilded Goose continued to haunt her. Beranger insisted he wasn't in any kind of danger, but she kept a sharper eye out than ever. Was it possible someone had murdered Gavin? And if so, what were the scoundrel's feelings regarding the new duke? The constable had assured them his men had reopened the investigation, now months old, but what could that accomplish?

Dressed in one of her many new gowns, Emma breathed deeply at the library window as she studied the tree line of the woodlands, willing her thoughts away from her troubles. The ever-changing color of the leaves was beautiful. Deep orangey-red on some trees and bright yellow on others, with a rainbow of shades in between. Emma thought she'd never seen anything quite so stunning except the gorgeous view of the San Juan Mountains from Eden's Main Street.

Home?

Although deliriously happy here in Brightshire, she longed to know how her family fared—Mavis and Katie, mostly, for as she'd told Charlotte and Mrs. Darling, they were the sisters whose hearts had been suffering at the time of her departure. She'd written her sisters as soon as she'd arrived in Brightshire, but who knew how long the letter would take to arrive in Colorado, especially with the ocean crossing. She hoped happiness abounded for both—and she longed for the day she'd be able to share with them some happy news of her own.

Although alone, Emma discreetly touched her tummy. She'd discovered the women of England didn't express their feelings with the same exuberance as Americans. She'd observed as much with the serene Lady Audrey and was always aware of the dowager's watchful eye. A boisterous laugh hadn't crossed Emma's lips since she'd arrived without eliciting a disapproving scowl from the woman.

Is a tiny babe nestled in my womb, warm and protected, a combination of Beranger and myself, knit together with love by God? The thought brought an instant swell of affection. They'd been married about a month and a half, and conception was certainly possible. But she didn't feel any different. And she didn't get queasy at certain smells and the thought of food, as she'd heard would happen.

Even in her contentment, Emma felt a need to be doing something useful. Since arriving she'd done little of importance. Lately, she'd been thinking of returning to Goldenbrook. The hamlet had seemed cozy, the residents helpful to each other, their small gardens colorful and charming. Yet, with the colder weather descending, she worried about how they would fare and wondered if there weren't aspects of their lives that could be improved upon, for the children's sakes if nothing else. The tiny houses and lack of shops or any kind of commercial advantages, besides the Gilded Goose, made the place seem as if it was stuck in the Middle Ages.

She'd made the mistake recently of asking the dowager whether there were things she could do to help them. Beranger's stepmother had let her feelings be known quite well on that subject. It wasn't the duchess's place, she'd said, her face filled with revulsion. The poor could take care of their own—and had been doing so for centuries. But Emma didn't care what she thought. She had to follow her heart, as their father had advised in his letter to Katie.

Father.

Their mother, fearful for her children's safety on the remote Colorado ranch, had taken the five sisters Back East to Philadelphia when they were all still young. Yet their father had never stopped loving them, and upon his death, he'd bequeathed them his fortune. Even more meaningful than that were the letters he'd written them on his deathbed, to be given to them on their birthdays. Her sisters would be appalled if they knew she hadn't opened hers yet. She'd promised to write to them and share the contents since they'd shared theirs.

Beranger had become obsessed with her desire to delay reading her father's words, almost insistent that she correct the oversight right away. But once the letter was opened and the contents read, what from home would she have left to look forward to? She didn't have the heart to tell Beranger that was the reason holding her back—that a part of her still longed for Eden, and still thought of it as home. The beauty here in Brightshire moved her, but she didn't have any memories of these hills, these rooms, these faces, to make them special like they did for him. They didn't have the ability to make her heart sing, or laugh, or cry. Memories were the magic that accomplished those deeds.

Yet perhaps reading the letter would resolve some of her homesickness. *Tonight I'll remedy my misguided ways and read Father's letter,* she vowed. *Then I'll sit down and write a long letter home and let everyone know what Father said.*

Turning from the window, she took in the lovely library filled with hundreds of books. Reading them all would take an eternity. But then, they were about England, Wales, and Scotland. Not America, Colorado, and the West.

The door opened, and the dowager duchess sailed in, followed by another woman. She appeared middle-aged, with a kind face.

"There you are, Duchess," the dowager duchess said, her tone a mite dismissive. "Hiding out again? I've looked everywhere, the garden, kitchen, and even the stable." She turned to the woman at her side. "The duchess is from America. They have different ideas of decorum than we do, but you'll get used to her ways."

"Yes, here I am." Emma's tone sounded slightly defeated even to her own ears, but she didn't care. She glanced at the window. "Just taking in the fall colors." She tried not to bristle at the dowager's superior attitude, as if an American were nothing better than a beetle under her boot heel to be mercilessly crushed.

The dowager nodded. "Very good. Meet Carmichael, your new lady's maid. She comes with the highest recommendations from one of the best houses in Wales. And she's available and can start today."

Hyacinth, the chambermaid, had been filling in until a proper lady's maid could be found, but Emma had grown used to the shy girl's ways. She'd known this day would come, and yet she liked Hyacinth and had mixed feelings about giving her up for this stranger. For whatever reason, she wasn't in the mood today to acquiesce to the dowager's wishes. "I'm quite used to Hyacinth, thank you," she said. There was no way around hurting Miss Carmichael's feelings, she supposed. The dowager should have consulted with Emma before bringing the woman in.

"Hyacinth is no longer with us."

Emma gasped. "What?"

"The fact that she had no proper training was evident in your hair and appointments. She's packed and gone. No use trying to run after her."

Emma reached up and touched her softly done hair, having asked Hyacinth to avoid the tight curls the women in England seemed so fond of. She preferred her hair down. "I don't see anything wrong with Hyacinth's ability. You had *no right* to fire her without speaking with me first. I'm duchess now."

A sly smile spread across the dowager's face. "Indeed, you are. You should begin behaving as such."

The witch. "Why would you do such a thing? What reason could you possibly have? She's been at Ashbury for a year without complaint."

"Is that what she told you?"

It had been. In a private conversation while she'd helped prepare Emma for bed. Not in those exact words, but close.

At Emma's silence the dowager's brow rose. "The girl has had plenty of time to excel at her duties, but she has not. I've been watching."

Emma fisted her hands. "No, that's not true. You didn't like that she and I were friends. That's why you fired her. And what of Hyacinth's chambermaid duties? We still need someone for those."

"I will tackle hiring her replacement next."

For whatever reason, the dowager glanced at the toe of Emma's shoe, visible beneath her gown. There must be something improper with her choice. *Rules!* She was becoming sick of them!

To her credit, Miss Carmichael kept her feelings hidden behind a stoic mask, as if she didn't hear a word.

Beranger's stepmother closed the distance between them and lowered her voice. "I didn't mean to vex you *again*, Duchess. I must remember how extremely *sensitive* you are. But you have to realize, there are things a duchess must know and do. If she does not, she will embarrass her husband. The manor will fall into chaos. The respect that the

Northcott family has held for centuries will dissipate, all because of your *American* ways." She lifted her already elevated chin. "Beranger needs you now more than ever. Does he not deserve at least that? With his *past*, he still has many uphill battles to wage to gain respect, without having to explain to the *ton* why his American duchess blunders in her choice of fashion or manners simply because she was not adequately educated. Do you really want to turn this woman away? She's made the long trip at my request, and is ready today to assist you."

It wasn't in Emma to fight so nastily, and she'd not gain anything by continuing to argue in front of Carmichael. A small part of her whispered, *Isn't the dowager duchess the expert? She's right that you don't want to embarrass Beranger.* Best to back off and regroup. But she vowed that she would find out where Hyacinth had gone and try and entice her back. The poor girl must be heartbroken.

Emma allowed her gaze to slide over to Carmichael, who must have been around thirty or thirty-five years old. Her hands were clasped together at her waist as she gazed out the large diamond-paned library window. Her dark brown hair was neatly done, and she wore no cap. Emma didn't notice much about her face or color of eyes, except she had a small freckle, much like a beauty mark, on the tip of her right eyebrow. Her starched navy-blue dress fit her figure, and she was neither thin nor plump. She appeared strong.

Emma dipped her head and said, "Welcome to Ashbury, Carmichael. From this day forward, you'll report to me, *not* the dowager duchess. Is that understood?"

The dowager smiled like a cat who'd just lapped up a bowl of sweet cream.

Carmichael nodded. "It is, Your Grace."

"Wonderful," the dowager duchess said, undaunted by Emma's outburst. "Oh, did I mention the duke is waiting for you in the stables? I suggest you run off and see what he wants."

"Waiting? For how long?" Emma's anger shot up several degrees—his wicked stepmother had purposely delayed her. "Shall I change? Does he intend to ride?"

"I have no idea, my dear. You had best go find out. I'll settle everything with Carmichael and show her to your rooms. I'm sure she'll want to put your wardrobe in order and see what you're lacking."

"I'll handle that."

The dowager put a hand to Emma's arm. "The duke, Your Grace."

Carmichael stood silent.

Emma flushed. Why did the dowager always make her feel like a recalcitrant child?

"Very well," Emma agreed. She was anxious to see Beranger. He'd gone out after breakfast, leaving her and Justin discussing the weather in Colorado. The extremes, the snowfall as well as the droughts. His cousin never seemed to tire of hearing about life in the American West. Perhaps that explained her homesickness today, why she felt so out of sorts.

The dowager waved a hand at her, encouraging her to scoot. "Go find the duke. You know how men can be if left to their own desires. His eye might begin to wander . . ."

The lance sliced deep, even though nothing could be further from the truth with Beranger. Was the evil woman determined not just to tear down Emma but to undermine their marriage? All Emma wanted was to be away from her.

"I'll bid you good day," she said to Carmichael. Walking slowly, she left the room, holding her chin high. Today the dowager duchess had gone too far. She had crossed the line—and Emma would see to it that there would be repercussions.

CHAPTER TWENTY-TWO

F inished with his morning inspection of the forest, Tristen waited for the duke to join him in the stables, at the end of the lengthy wing at the north end of the castle. He strode down the long corridor of stalls, glancing at the fine horseflesh contained within. This was one of his favorite places to pass the time.

Stable hands moved quietly through the area, going about their business, while laborers cleaned the stalls and swept the aisle to a shine.

Along with being an outdoorsman, Tristen was an equestrian through and through. There was little he liked better than to ride, groom, or even just watch a well-put-together animal grazing in a field. Where he'd acquired his love of the animals, he wasn't sure. But the sentiment had sustained him all those years in confinement.

"Llewellyn," the duke's deep voice rang out.

Tristen turned, and they clasped hands. "Your Grace."

"Dammit, I can't get used to being called that day in and day out. And not even being called Brightshire or Brig. Please, call me Northcott, or North, if you will."

Tristen's admiration of the man grew even more. "I couldn't, Your Grace. Doing so wouldn't be right."

The duke's smile was understanding. "All right, but at least when we're alone. Can you do that for me?"

"Aye. I'll try, but it won't be easy. But only if you're sure."

The duke placed a hand on one of the stall doors and looked inside. "I am. Today I feel like changing a rule that's been passed down for thousands of years." He smiled, and they walked on.

"What did you want to talk about? I was surprised to receive your note."

Beranger strode to the next. "I'd like to speak about the health of your uncle. I need to know everything you do so I can help Arson to my best ability. How old is he now? I've lost track."

"I believe he's forty-six. He hasn't been too specific with me about his health. Sometime back, about nine or ten months ago, his legs began to weaken, and the plight seems to be spreading to the rest of his body. The doctors he's seen can't tell him anything. That's all I know."

They arrived at the stall of the large black gelding the duke had brought with him from America. The animal thrust his muzzle forcefully over the half door and pushed Beranger's chest as if demanding his owner take him out for a ride.

"You've had him a long time, then?" Tristen asked. "Where'd he get his scars?"

The duke rubbed the gelding's thick neck. "No, actually, I haven't had him long. He was pulling a Wells Fargo stagecoach I was traveling in."

"Ah, a stagecoach," Tristen said wistfully. "I can't imagine a stagecoach without picturing a swarm of angry Cheyenne warriors, adorned in war paint and eagle feathers, giving chase. Have you seen some Indians, Duke?"

"I have." His smile ebbed away. "But they're not quite the way you envision them anymore. It's a shame the way they've been treated. Lied to. Such a proud people reduced to dependency on small reservations." He shook his head. "Anyway, the Wells Fargo crew ran Charger farther than they should because they didn't like his aggressive temperament.

I overheard their plans to kill him, so I bought him with the intention of setting him free. Problem was, he didn't run off, but rather followed the stage to Eden. I've been working with him, and he's gentled down considerably."

Tristen saw a kindred spirit in this animal. He tried to be worthy, but serving a ten-year sentence in prison had blighted his reputation. Perhaps here, with the duke's trust in him, he might be able to gain a little of his worth back. "I thought he looked clever. The smart ones know how to adapt. He was lucky to find you."

"I'm the lucky one. I met the duchess around the same time—in a ladies' shop, of all places—and—"

"Beranger?" a female voice called out.

They turned to find the duchess hurrying forward.

"I'm so happy to find you," she said. "Your stepmother didn't tell me you were waiting for me until a moment ago." She frowned. "I hope I haven't kept you waiting long." She looked at Tristen and nodded. "Mr. Llewellyn. How are you today?"

She wore a gown made of mint-green fabric. The hue suited her coloring and made the vivid green of her eyes even more pronounced. "Very well, Your Grace," he responded.

"I'm delighted to hear that. You look well and happy. And drier since the last time we met." She glanced at her husband. "I feel so lost without Lord Harry around. I almost went looking for him a little while ago before I remembered he'd gone home to Newchurch. Ashbury feels empty without him."

Beranger lifted his wife's hand and kissed the back. "I agree. But he needed to check on his holdings. We have to remember he's spent months in America searching for me. He deserves time to get his own life back in order." He leaned back, looking mysterious. "Besides that, he's doing some business for me, so I don't have to go away again."

Her eyes lit up. "Business? What about?"

"Our money problems here at Ashbury may be over. I'm planning to announce something tonight at dinner, if all goes well." He exchanged a satisfied look with Tristen. "Now, is there a specific reason you were searching for Lord Harry? Perhaps something your devoted husband can help with?"

"Not really. I just found myself alone in the library when we usually have a nice morning talk. And it's just that the dowager . . ." She glanced away.

Tristen wondered if he should discreetly absent himself to give them a few moments alone. The duchess seemed melancholy. Perhaps she was simply missing home. He remembered how he'd felt his first few weeks in prison, aching for the familiar.

But before the duke could ask her what was wrong, the duchess shook her head and said, "Oh, never mind." She gave them both a wide smile, then glanced around, taking in the high arched ceilings, the brick walls, the gorgeous woodwork. There wasn't a shaving or stalk of straw or hay in the walkway. She moved toward one of the stalls. "My little quarter horse looks like a pony among these thoroughbreds and warmbloods." She laughed when Dusty nibbled at the lace on her sleeve. "What is that I hear?" she asked, tipping her head. "Birds? In the stables? I don't see many in the rafters."

"Pigeons. Come. I'll show you." Tristen started down a narrow cutoff. The duchess followed and then the duke. Turning sharply to the left and into the shadows, Tristen led them up a short stairway and emerged onto a wooden landing. "It's left over from long ago. The birds used to carry messages before the telegraph was invented. Well, I should say, their ancestors did. I don't think much of anything is done with them now."

Emma cut a look at Beranger. "There're so many. Why do they keep them if they're of no use now? Can't you let them go?"

Tristen understood her feelings and had the same himself. "Since they're domesticated, they'd just return and try to get back into their cage. It's all they know. Best to let them be."

"And keep multiplying?"

"It's difficult to tell their sexes."

Her expression became thoughtful. "Beranger, can a pigeon be trained to fly into Brightshire, to Smith's Bakeshop? I'd love to be able to message with Charlotte, since her aunt couldn't bear to let her return. She's my one true friend, and I miss her at Ashbury."

Tristen raised a brow. Charlotte had a way of collecting hearts, it seemed. He had to admit there was something charming about her, even when she was debating superstitions. He couldn't stop a little smile at the memory of her warm hand in his own.

"What do you say, Tristen? Is that possible?" Beranger asked.

"I don't see why not. Pick out two."

"Two?"

"I thought Miss Aldridge could keep one as well, and be able to message you, if you'd like."

There was no doubt how the duchess felt about that. Delight shone in her eyes. "How long will the training take?"

"I don't know. I've never worked with pigeons, but I'm sure my uncle will have a thing or two to suggest. He's a well-learned man. I'll keep you informed."

Birds fluttered here and there in their large cage, excited to see people. Some flew about wildly, while others sat placidly on the perch, watching. They tipped their heads this way and that, their beady eyes curious. The loud cooing was almost annoying.

"And I'll work on finding new homes for all of these beauties," she said. "I don't want to leave them like this. I've always loved birds. I can't wait until at least two of these can fly into the sky. It's a shame for the poor creatures to be penned their entire lives. They need to get out now and then, into the sunlight, spread their wings on the wind." After the birds settled, she pointed to two of the smaller ones, cuddled side by side on the far end of the perch. "How about those two, over there? Do they look too young to be trained?"

"I'm no expert, but I'd think the younger the better for what you have in mind," Tristen replied. He took one of the dusty bird carriers off a shelf behind them and unlatched the gate. "You best step back." He motioned to his already dusty garment. "This will become dirtier when I step inside."

She and the duke backed up to the wall.

Amid a cacophony of noise, Tristen went to work. Several minutes later, he had the two the duchess had pointed out safely in the small cage. Stepping out of the fluttering madhouse, he brushed off the dust and feathers, thinking tonight would be a good night for a bath.

The duchess rushed forward, concern in her eyes. "Thank you, Mr. Llewellyn. They aren't hurt, are they? I didn't realize they'd be so wild. The commotion reminded me of the yearly roundup at the ranch. At branding time, cattle and cowboys are everywhere, whooping and hollering. It's quite a sight."

That's something I'd like to see. Cowboys, the West, America. Tristen lifted the cage so she could more easily see inside. "Don't be afraid to talk to them. They'll learn your voice and recognize your face. As with most birds, they have very good eyesight and sense of hearing. Keeps them alive in the wild."

The duchess beamed with happiness as she gazed at the birds crowded to the back of the cage. "Something all my own. Like Dusty."

The duke cut his gaze to his wife. "Everything here is yours, Emma," he responded sincerely.

Her smile was real as she lifted her head and they locked gazes. "Not really, Beranger. Except for you, my horse, and now these birds. Everything else is yours, and your family's. But I'm not complaining. If given the chance, I'd do everything over exactly as I have. And I'm feeling more and more at home each day. Don't look so sad." She reached up and gently smoothed his brow.

A bit embarrassed by the intimate scene playing out before him, Tristen turned back to the large cage of birds.

"We best be off," the duke said.

Tristen turned back and followed. As they were about to cross the threshold, the duke listed sharply to his right, bumping his shoulder against the jamb. He weaved and almost went down on one knee.

The duchess grasped his arm. "Beranger! What's wrong?"

The duke had both hands out, fingers splayed, as if trying to keep his balance. "Nothing, Emma, I'm all right," he replied with a garbled tone. "The floor tilted sharply, but it's passed."

His pallor had gone white, and when he tried to smile, his lips pulled down in a grimace. The episode hadn't passed, Tristen was sure. The duke was only putting on a brave face for his young wife, so she wouldn't be frightened.

"Most likely the greasy pork I ate this morning or the poached cod in the kedgeree. It did taste a little fishy. Just give me a moment." His stride was unsteady as he approached the stairs they'd have to descend.

"Mr. Llewellyn, please take my husband's arm as he descends. I don't want him to fall."

"Emma, I'm fine."

"You're not, or weren't. I've never seen that happen before. I'm worried."

Before Tristen could get to the duke's side, he took the steps and then, at the bottom, reached up to assist his wife. The next moment they were back in the aisle of the barn, and several horses looked their way.

Tristen hoped nothing was seriously wrong. He liked this duke very much. He didn't want to see him go the way of the other, not now, not for a good sixty years.

CHAPTER TWENTY-THREE

F our hours later, Tristen found himself in front of Smith's Bakeshop, holding a small cage containing one of the duchess's pigeons. He stopped and glanced about before grasping the knob and entering through the door. A small cluster of bells rang out his presence as wonderful yeasty smells enveloped him. The display case was full. A murmur of voices from the kitchen reached his ears. Nervously, he glanced down at his attire. Before making the trip, he'd bathed and shaved, not understanding why he felt the need to look his best.

Footsteps sounded, and Charlotte's cousin Verity hurried into the front. Her eyes widened.

"Mr. Llewellyn," she said, sounding pleased. She glanced back at the door she'd come through. "Is there something I can get for you?"

The pigeon cooed softly, and Verity took a step back, surprised.

Charlotte appeared in the doorway, a streak of flour across her cheek and her forehead moist with perspiration. She smiled broadly, making him feel like the sun had just peeped out from behind clouds. The girl worked hard. He'd never seen her enjoying a moment of pleasure—walking through a field of flowers, soaking her feet in a cool spring, or sitting in a soft chair reading a book. Always working, helping, or doing for others.

Behind her, Mrs. Smith appeared. Even she looked pleased to see him. Mrs. Smith pushed past her niece and came to his side. When she saw the cage, her brow fell.

"What's this?" she asked.

"A gift from the duchess."

One of Mrs. Smith's brows twitched. "Oh?" She looked into the cage. "One pigeon? Won't make but half a pie."

Tristen laughed, undecided if the woman meant to be funny. "Not to eat, ma'am. To train to be a carrier. So the duchess can be in contact with Charlotte." He searched out Charlotte's gaze, relishing the pleasure that crossed her face. "She told me to tell you she misses you at Ashbury and wishes to be in contact. This way she can easily invite you to tea. If that's all right with your aunt, of course," he said, now studying the older woman's expression. She was not a soft woman. Although he guessed she'd have to be strict to be responsible for feeding four mouths besides her own. "If yes, I'm here to build a small coop to keep the bird and begin his training."

"I won't have a flying rat in my shop," Mrs. Smith grumbled, settling her hands on her hips and lifting her chin. "I don't care who's asking. They carry mites. And I don't see why she needs to be messaging Charlotte. She has Amelia in the kitchen, if she wants ta be friendly with someone. The whole affair is strange to me."

Mrs. Smith gave Charlotte a sidelong gaze that spelled trouble. Tristen hoped his arrival wouldn't cause more heartache for her. He'd witnessed her disappointment when her aunt refused to allow her to return to the castle.

Charlotte hurried forward. "We don't have to keep the pigeon in the shop, Aunt Ethel. He's better off in the barn with the other animals. I'm sure the duchess intended that all along. I'll care for him, and you won't even know he's there."

"I'll know when you're out there fussing ta see if ya have a message. I can just imagine it now."

"There's plenty of room in the loft, by the window," Charlotte went on quickly. "I think it's perfect." She looked at Tristen. "It's male, then?"

"That's yet to be determined, but the duchess seems to think so. She's named this white-and-gray one Romeo and the other, which is pure white, Juliet. We'll just have to hope she's right."

Verity clasped her hands in front of her chest, and her face colored a pretty pink. "How romantic," she uttered on a deep breath. She glanced away when she saw him watching her.

Mrs. Smith jabbed a finger at him, her face still etched with annoyance. "That's mighty presuming of the duchess. Must be her American ways. Still, I don't want—"

"And she's sent along five pounds for any inconvenience my being around during training might cause you," he added. Anyone would be crazy to turn down money like that. The duchess was either very shrewd or very generous—*or both*. He dug the money out of his pocket and held out the offering.

The frown fell off the woman's face, and she snatched the money from his palm. "In that case, Mr. Llewellyn, you can go about your business in the barn. That is as close as Romeo is going to get to Smith's Bakeshop, unless he's in a pie. And I make no promises he won't end up there if he becomes a pest. Do I make myself clear?"

Tristen nodded, having won. "Absolutely."

"Or if Charlotte loses too much time out there doting on the thing. It's bad enough she tends so lovingly to that old pony. Whenever I can't find her, I know where to look."

With the decision made, a smile burst onto Charlotte's lips. She hurried forward. "Come with me, Mr. Llewellyn. We'll go out front and circle around so we won't take him through the kitchen." Charlotte passed by him out the front door. "I'll show you where to build the coop. Thank you, Aunt Ethel," she singsonged.

Tristen turned on his heel and followed before anyone else contradicted her idea. This was the closest he'd been to Charlotte in two weeks. He'd been hoping for her return to Ashbury each time he visited the kitchen, but he'd been disappointed each time. He wondered if that pesky Mr. Winters was still sniffing around. Charlotte deserved better than that man. And Tristen would take it upon himself to see her innocence wasn't jeopardized.

She hurried along in front of him as if she feared her aunt might revoke permission at any moment. Across the alley from the back of the bakeshop, she opened the rickety door to the barn. Inside, the aromas of grass hay, grain, and feathers made him sneeze.

"God bless you," Charlotte said, a sweet smile on her lips.

The pony he'd seen pulling the bread cart looked up from her manger with a mouthful of hay. Her flaxen tail swished away several flies. The building, which was more a shed than a barn, also held a good-size rabbit hutch, and he presumed they bred rabbits for the meat pies they sold. On the far side of the dirt floor was a chicken coop, with a portion wired off to keep the poultry in.

He gestured with a nod. "They're fenced in on the outside as well?"

"Oh, yes." She pointed to a hen-size hatch door that was now closed. "That goes to a small yard behind. But they're fenced and protected from foxes and dogs and hungry nomads of all sorts."

He'd never given much thought to a business like this before, but running a bakeshop wouldn't be easy with all the butchering and cleaning one would have to do. He wondered if Charlotte actually did that herself or if the chore fell to her brother. He couldn't imagine the delicate and shy Verity wringing any necks or chopping off bunny heads. Nor could he see Charlotte or Amelia completing the task either. But Aunt Ethel filled the bill perfectly.

Her apologetic smile twisted his stomach.

"I know what you're thinking," she said. "We have to survive somehow, and this bakeshop has belonged in the Smith family for many, many years before me. Still, butchering is difficult to think about. Especially when the new babies come along and, after a while, become so friendly, as if me or my cousins are just another one of them, a bunny or chicken, only larger and strange-looking. They trust us . . ."

She turned away.

Without thinking, he set a comforting hand on her shoulder, and a bolt of awareness whizzed up his arm. Instantly, he drew back. He had a past, one that was not respectable for a woman like Charlotte. An ex-convict had no place feeling anything for a woman like her.

"It's not your fault," he said softly, looking at the rabbit hutch to keep from staring into her eyes. The chopping block he'd missed before came into view. "You give them a good life while they're alive. That's better than some get."

Several bunnies poked their twitching noses through the wire mesh. He'd been behind bars, just like them. Paid the price for his temper. But that hadn't brought back the life he'd so abruptly ended. Though the man's death had been an accident, Tristen had been stewing for a fight. He'd started the argument, and he'd landed the punch that had sent his opponent—someone he didn't even know—into an iron fence. If he hadn't run off, perhaps the judge would have been more sympathetic.

No, he'd gotten a just punishment. Now he had to get on with his life. But watching Charlotte now, he knew it would never be the life he longed for.

CHAPTER TWENTY-FOUR

E mbarrassed, Charlotte took the ladder rungs one hand over the other. The loft wasn't large, but the roof was tall enough to store hay, which meant she could easily stand, but Mr. Llewellyn would need to hunch over, just a little, like Thomas had to do when he came up here. She liked the loft. As a girl, she'd often escaped her aunt's complaints by sneaking away when the work was done and climbing up into the warmth—or cold, depending on the season. The privacy was golden. She loved the sound of the rain on the roof so close to her head. She could imagine a limitless world from up here. And now, she'd have her very own carrier pigeon, to write notes with the American duchess. She blinked away her surprise and delight.

She made her way to the loft door and pushed it open, showcasing the lovely view of Brightshire. Winding Creek was only thirty or so feet away, and the cobbler and dress shop next door were even closer. With her emotions finally corralled, she turned back to face Tristen.

He'd followed, with the pigeon cooing uneasily in its new surroundings.

"I didn't mean to upset you, talking about the animals." He was searching her eyes. "People need to eat, there's no exception to that. And make a living."

"How is the duchess?" she asked, to move away from the hurtful subject. "I haven't seen her or anyone else from Ashbury for two weeks." Her face turned pink. "Well, Mr. Winters did stop by for some tarts. But only for a moment."

"I'm not surprised." With a set mouth, Tristen placed the carrier onto a mound of grass hay and gazed out the window at the scenery.

She flushed. Had she said something to anger him? His manner had gone from friendly to annoyed. "This is where I thought the coop would work, here out of the way." They should hurry or Aunt Ethel would come out.

As she pointed, an Adonis butterfly flittered into the open loft window and landed on the pigeon cage, its large wings beating slowly. She gasped. "Look!"

"That's a male," Tristen said.

"How do you know?"

"Females are chocolate brown. The male uses the vibrant color to attract a mate."

Her cheeks heated. She liked that he knew so much about animals. "I can see how a female would be attracted," she whispered, not wanting to frighten their visitor away. She chanced a quick glance at Tristen, thinking he needed no blue coloring to help him. Not with his expressive eyes, strong jaw, and chiseled lips. "Isn't that the most exquisite color you've ever seen? Every time one of these beauties crosses my path"—she moved a bit closer—"I imagine a gorgeous silk dress covered in glittery stones. Then the music begins and I . . ."

Embarrassed, she snapped her mouth closed. How silly he must think her. A country baker, dreaming of Adonis-blue gowns and dancing in a ballroom. Conscious of his eyes on her, she watched as the butterfly took to the air and glided out the window without so much as a by-your-leave. Thank goodness, she thought. She'd been silly enough since Tristen's arrival. First the talk of butchering and now dancing in a ballroom. She reached for a safe topic he'd know something about.

"And your aunt and uncle, how are they?"

"Well enough. My uncle's been a bit out of sorts with the topic of the young duke's death being resurrected. Seems the new duke has spoken to the constable, for whatever reason, and the constable came out to see if my uncle remembered anything out of the ordinary that day. The duke and the duchess heard disturbing talk in Goldenbrook that the duke's brother may have been murdered. The duke wants the questions investigated and answered."

Charlotte tried to keep her apprehension off her face. "Murdered? Why would they think that?"

Tristen shrugged. "The position of the wound on his neck would be difficult for him to do in a fall."

She thought of that day. Tristen's uncle limping away. Could he have actually killed the duke and been hurt in the process? The thought was too horrible to imagine. And what about Thomas being there as well?

His gaze roamed her face. "Something on your mind, Charlotte? You look alarmed."

She swallowed. She hadn't meant to draw attention to her dark thoughts. "I was just thinking that you and your uncle seem very close. It's nice you were able to join him here in Brightshire in his time of need."

Tristen's face softened. "We are. Very close. It's more he was nice to ask me. I needed a new direction, and he and my aunt supplied that. I admire him greatly. And owe him a lot. I'd do anything he asked of me. I hate to see his body and legs weaken."

Do you know him, really, Tristen? Is he capable of murder? I just don't know. "I see."

Romeo cooed softly, the sound pleasant.

"So will this work?" she asked. "You're not planning to leave him here in that small cage today, are you? He can't even stretch his wings."

Tristen shook his head and then began feeling around the side of the structure next to the loft door. "Not at all. I'll build something right here, not too large, but he'll be able to easily land and then enter his cage. If things go as planned, Juliet and he will be trained to fly back and forth between your bakeshop and the castle. The distance is nothing for them, and they can make it in a matter of minutes. Almost as good as those telephones that are being installed in some of the wealthier places."

"A telephone! Now that would be magic. I've never seen one. I think I'd be frightened to speak into a wire."

He plucked a piece of grass hay from his shoulder and glanced over at her. The light from the window hit his eyes. More beautiful than the Adonis butterfly.

He put his attention back to his work. But why was her heart beating faster than usual?

"I'm to charge the lumber I buy to Ashbury," he said, "but it won't be much. I'll do that as soon as I take a few measurements and then be back sometime tomorrow to begin work. I'll stay out of your aunt's way. I can tell she doesn't like me."

"No, that's not true. She likes you fine, Tristen. She just doesn't like things revolving around me. If the pigeon had been sent here for Amelia, she'd be more than happy, even without the payment. But I don't care." She hadn't meant to complain. But she didn't want him thinking her aunt's behavior had anything to do with him personally.

Something flickered in his eyes. "I best get to it."

"Yes, and I need to go back to the bakeshop too, before she comes out to see what I'm doing. I have several batches of scones to make, as well as some ginger and brandy snaps." She looked down at the cage, and her heart warmed. "But first, I'll fetch a saucer of water for Romeo to hold him until you take him home. We wouldn't want anything to happen to him before he has a chance to fly."

Tristen's words about his uncle echoed through her head, worry underscoring her pleasure. The duke had inquired with the constable about his brother's death—but that didn't mean any new suspicion would fall on Thomas. She was the only one who could put him in the forest that day, and she'd never do that. Taking one day at a time was critical.

She glanced up to find Tristen watching closely. What was he thinking? She had no idea, but his moods seemed to change with the wind. She found herself wanting to do things that would bring those rare smiles to his face. Then something in his eyes transformed once more, sending heat to her toes, and she took that opportunity to hurry down the ladder, the warm goodness making her feet fly.

CHAPTER TWENTY-FIVE

E mma whirled around the bedroom, panic pushing up her throat like sour bile. Since returning from the stable after their talk with Mr. Llewellyn, she and Beranger had been passing a quiet afternoon in the sitting room connected to their suite. After the frightening way he'd lost his balance in the stable, she hadn't had the heart to saddle him with the happenings with the dowager and Hyacinth. Besides, she wanted to handle the matter on her own. She'd told him the minimum, that she had a new lady's maid named Carmichael. But then she went directly to find Mrs. Darling, who had blanched when she'd told her to find Hyacinth at all costs. Emma supposed she was probably the first person ever to stand up to the dowager.

A frightening thought had occurred to her: Had Beranger's step-mother somehow taken her revenge for their earlier conversation? Was his illness some sort of curse?

She was being silly, of course. And Beranger already seemed to be feeling much better. But when she returned to their suite, she discovered—

"Beranger!"

He glanced up from the open ledger in front of him and pushed up from the desk, his mouth pinching into a hard line. Without saying a word, he rose and strode to her side. "What is it, Emma? What's wrong?"

He reached for her trembling shoulders, but she pulled back, barely able to voice the words rolling around in the empty cavern that had been her heart. Hot prickles broke out over her body, and she raced through her mind, trying to put the last twenty-four hours in order.

"My letter from Father! It's gone!" She rushed to the highboy where she'd placed the letter the very first day of their arrival. The private words from the man she'd only known for the first few years of her life were more important to her than anything, including this entire estate. His dying words were more precious than anything she owned, with only Beranger's love taking precedence.

"I saw the letter this morning," he said, almost angrily, as if trying to convince himself she was wrong. That somehow the letter hadn't disappeared. "Right there!" He pointed to the spot, conspicuously empty. "I've been waiting for weeks for you to read it." He ran his hand over the delicately carved wood furniture. Grasping the side of the highboy, he hefted it away from the wall and looked behind. Finding nothing, he settled it back against the wall and opened the top drawer, sifting through the array of monogrammed handkerchiefs and gloves with his large hands, searching, hunting, hoping.

She grasped his arm. "It's not there! It's not anywhere! I searched all the drawers before I called to you. I looked carefully through each, making sure," she said as he closed the top drawer and began to search the second. "And how would it get in a drawer, anyway, if I didn't put it there? I'm not feeble. I would have remembered something that important."

As if not hearing a word she'd said, Beranger dropped to the ground to place his cheek to the cold stone floor to peer underneath. A moment later he reached forward and ran his hand this way and that under the dresser.

"Someone's stolen it! There can be no other explanation," Emma said heatedly, controlling the wobble that was threatening her voice. *And I know who!* "I've searched every corner of this room, keeping my panic at bay, wondering the whole time why anyone would touch a personal letter—let alone move it." She gazed into his worried eyes. "But that's the point. They didn't move it while cleaning. My letter isn't here. Someone has taken it on purpose. But why? There's no value except to me."

Beranger strode to the decorative fabric pull that would sound a bell in the servants' hall and yanked down so forcefully Emma was surprised the thing didn't come out of the ceiling. "We'll get to the bottom of what's happened this instant."

Despair and self-incrimination pushed painfully inside. "Why didn't I read Father's letter when I had the chance?" Emma collapsed on the side of their large bed, burying her face in the pillow. "On my birthday, when I was supposed to. Like Father asked, and all my sisters have done. Those were Father's wishes, and I disobeyed," she whispered against the pillow, struggling to hold her tears at bay.

The bed sagged. Beranger took her shoulders and began to draw her near when there was a swift knock on the door. He stood and Emma followed, wiping her eyes.

Carmichael came through the door and gave a small curtsy. "Your Grace, is there something you need?"

Beranger practically pounced as he strode angrily forward. "Yes, there is," he thundered. "A personal letter is missing. It's been on the dresser for days—since we arrived. What have you done with it?"

Carmichael blinked several times and then gazed at the dresser, doing a good impression of being surprised.

"You're mistaken, Your Grace. I saw the letter," she said, "and it was on the dresser when I left these rooms." Her voice was steady and clear, her chin lifted defensively. "Do you think I'd like to lose this fine job on the very first day? I can assure you, I would not. But if you trust me so little, maybe I should go now."

Emma stepped forward. "You recall seeing the envelope on the dresser when the dowager duchess brought you up to show you around?"

"I do, yes." She walked over to the dresser and glanced around. "And you've searched the drawers and the rest of the room?"

"We have," Beranger said, none too nicely.

Emma followed Carmichael to the dresser side of the room and said, "As you know, I was in the library when I met you and then went out to the stable. If I could narrow down the last time it was here, that might help." The enormity of what had happened filled Emma with such devastation a tear escaped and ran down her cheek. *No one would take that letter except to hurt me. Can the dowager really be that evil? Or*—a small voice asked, though she didn't like to believe it—*had Hyacinth somehow sneaked back into Ashbury and taken it for revenge?*

"I'm sorry I can't help you more, Your Grace. The dowager duchess showed me your wardrobe and accessories. I was intent on remembering as much as possible for dressing you tonight. She and I also looked through your dressing table, and your implements for hair styling, nothing more. I'll confess, I was concentrating on what she was telling me. Let me ask the chambermaid. She was in here today as well, changing your sheets and tidying up. Perhaps she'll have something meaningful to share." Her gaze traveled between Emma and Beranger.

"Very well," Beranger said, his expression sharp enough to cut steel. "Do that right away. I want that letter found. There is no other acceptable solution. It's somewhere, and I want it back unopened! Do I make myself clear?"

"Undoubtedly, Your Grace." Carmichael backed out of the door and quietly pulled it closed.

Her new lady's maid was gone, but the devastation in Emma's heart remained. Her letter had disappeared. There was a very good chance she'd not get it back. Wanting to spare Beranger the misery on her face, she turned to the window and gazed at the beauty of her new land, the familiar cloudy sky, the feeling of so many miles between her and Colorado. A moment later, she felt him at her back.

He placed both hands on her shoulders. "We'll find it, Emma," he said softly. "I promise you that. I won't leave a stone unturned. I know how much that letter means to you. I'll find it if it's the last thing I do."

She didn't want him pledging something he couldn't deliver. She was at fault, not him. The thick anguish in his voice was enough to bring her to her knees. He'd accepted a heavy mantle of responsibility by becoming the duke. She saw that daily in all the many decisions and plans that occupied him. She wanted to be a source of succor to him, not a source of stress.

"The letter's disappearance has nothing to do with you, my love," she said softly and turned in his arms. "I should have read it weeks ago and then tucked it away in a safe spot. You're not to blame."

"I *am* to blame, Emma. This is my house. This never would have happened if I hadn't brought you to Ashbury." With the tip of his finger, he gently lifted her chin and lowered his lips to hers.

The kiss helped. Life would go on. She loved Beranger, and nothing would ever change that. Setting aside her worries to enjoy the moment, she ran her hands up his shirt, feeling his chest muscles bunch with anticipation.

"We'll get through this," she whispered against his lips. "Nothing can change the way I feel when I'm in your arms."

Her statement put a little spark back into his eyes. He opened his mouth to respond, but took a staggering step back, reaching out as he wheeled away and caught the bedpost to keep from falling.

"Beranger!" she screamed, the horror of the sight blinding her. The vertigo he'd experienced earlier that day had worried her, but he'd brushed the occurrence off so successfully she'd believed him. But now . . .

She clutched his arm, as if she'd be able to keep him on his feet if his legs buckled.

"I'm all right," he slurred. "I'm just—"

"You're nothing of the sort! What happened? Are you light-headed again? Or do you have pain somewhere?"

Oh, please, God, please. Don't let him die.

His gaze slid to the bed, and she helped him to its side, holding him with one arm and ripping back the counterpane with the other. With no words between them, he allowed her to assist him slowly onto the mattress, his eyes closed. Once he was sitting, she helped him lie back. Straining, she lifted his legs and tugged at each boot. Once his boots were off, and he was somewhat comfortable, she ran to the cord and rang for help.

Returning to Beranger's side, she kept up the litany in her head: *Please, God, don't take him from me. Please, God, don't let him be in pain. I love him so much, God, please don't take him from me now.*

Only a moment passed before Carmichael returned.

"The duke is ill! Send his valet here at once, but first, tell Pencely to send for Brightshire's doctor." *Brightshire does have a doctor, doesn't it? A capable doctor with modern knowledge?* "Send a basin of cool water and clean towels immediately, and ask the cook for some broth."

The woman stood there staring at the still form of the duke on the bed.

"Go, please! There is no time to lose."

Carmichael nodded and was gone.

Emma glanced back at Beranger. His expression gave little away. His eyes were still closed, but she knew he wasn't asleep. Her throat closed painfully. The vertigo in the stable had been a warning. And now this. She should have paid more attention. Made him come straight back and lie down. Called the doctor then. Maybe all this could have been avoided.

Her heart constricted.

Then again, maybe Beranger's troubles were just beginning.

CHAPTER TWENTY-SIX

Emma twisted her hands together. *If only Lord Harry hadn't picked this moment to go home. I feel so alone.*

The elderly doctor, bowed at the shoulders and practically blind, had just left the gallery, leaving Emma alone outside her bedroom door with few answers—and with even more fear and anger than she'd felt before he'd arrived. Could a person feel both emotions at once?

The doctor, a sharp-faced man with a chiseled nose and pointy chin, as well as a forehead so narrow from brows to hairline that his appearance was of one who didn't have a brain in his head, had been tending the Northcott family for years, and had an ego to prove the fact. Too many years, in her mind. Surely he couldn't keep up with all the new science being discovered daily—he could barely see to read. Dr. Gannon's office back in Eden had been filled with medical journals, dog-eared and rumpled from many perusals. Reading was a doctor's best source of ongoing education. She wouldn't trust a thing Sir Anthony Bellround said, even if she hadn't taken a violent dislike to the man the moment they'd met. She'd had to fight her prejudice through his entire examination of Beranger.

"His Grace seems fine now, if still a little dizzy," Dr. Bellround had said once they were alone in the gallery, a mocking half smile pulling his lips. She'd been thankful he'd held his tongue until Beranger was out of hearing distance. "We'll wait a few days and see what happens. Could be the strain of returning home. He broke his stepmother's heart, you know." His nose wrinkled as if the aroma of spoiled eggs was on the air. "I remember him as an irresponsible boy, and now . . ." The implication that he had grown into an irresponsible man was clear. "The only thing wrong with the duke is that he's not used to the pressure of running a manor like Ashbury. It's not something that can be learned in a month. Mother Nature has a way of compensating, like putting him to bed. Forcing him to stop and take it easy."

"That's the most ridiculous thing I've ever heard!" she'd blurted without thinking, and was rewarded with another look of disdain. Beranger was the most levelheaded and intelligent man she knew. "We've been riding, visiting, and catching up on the books, but—"

He put up a palm, halting her speech, and tipped a bushy gray eyebrow at her. "You best leave the medical matters to me, Duchess, and go about your socializing. Your husband will be fit as a fiddle in time for dinner tonight, I'm certain. I don't see why he isn't up yet."

Her anger spiked. *This man is a fool!*

"Thank you for your advice, *sir*," she'd said curtly, then gestured to the stairway at the end of the gallery as a way of dismissal. She'd not use him again. Beranger was better off in her hands alone.

Before the doctor had arrived, Beranger was able to tell her his chest was fine, and he had no pain. That he was just a bit light-headed now, and feeling better. He'd wanted to get up and sit in a chair, but she'd not allowed it. On and off, he lapsed into restful slumber while she paced the expensive Persian carpet.

She returned to the quiet room.

"Emma . . ."

Beranger's weak summons brought her rushing to his side. She dropped to one knee so she could be close to his face.

"I'm feeling better," Beranger whispered. When he wet his lips with his tongue, she brought him the glass of water from the nightstand and helped him drink, shocked at how weak he appeared. He might feel better, but he looked even worse.

"Not too much, my love," she said, gently taking the glass away. "Not yet. You don't want to upset your stomach any more than it already is."

"It's not my stomach," he said, low. "It's my head. Most of the spinning has stopped. Please don't make such a fuss over me. I don't know what this is about, but it'll pass. I don't get sick."

His gaze roamed the tall ceiling, and she wanted to cry. He was trying to figure this puzzle out as well.

"I'm sure the doctor is correct in his diagnosis. The anxiety of coming home to England has overwhelmed me, as has finding Ashbury in dire straits."

"So you heard?" At least his hearing was still sharp. She was surprised he'd been able to hear them out in the hall.

"Yes."

"Dr. Bellround is a fool with a head filled with cotton. He reminds me of a weasel."

Beranger chuckled. "You like him that much, huh?"

"He'll not be out again. I'd like to see his face when he learns I've hired a physician from New York. I don't believe for a second anxiety of any kind could put you into bed. No, something else is the problem. And I'm not ruling out foul play."

He arched a brow. "Emma, just because there are rumors about my brother—"

"You won't end up like Gavin. But I don't want you to worry about a thing. You're to rest and nothing else. And that's an order."

His eyes opened wide.

"Not used to such language from me?" Emma said.

"No, I'm not. But I like how it sounds."

"Good, because I'm not to be trifled with when your health is at stake. Is that understood?"

He chuckled and then squeezed his eyelids together, contradicting his earlier assertion about feeling better. She was sure he was still spinning just as much as he ever was—and as much as she was with worry over him.

Does this have anything to do with the questions Beranger is asking about his brother's death? Or am I grasping at straws? She gazed anxiously into Beranger's eyes, though he seemed content to just stare back at her.

He reached out a shaky hand and laid it against her cheek. "My love."

Perhaps he'd read her thoughts or seen the despair in her eyes. Whatever the reason behind his caress, she leaned into his warm palm as she silently prayed for strength. And for his quick return to health.

Life could change so fast. She felt tumbled and bruised, as if she'd been seized by a tornado. But she would be strong, vigilant. She wouldn't let anyone hurt Beranger, or worse. She would be ready.

CHAPTER TWENTY-SEVEN

Tristen had to read the words on the note twice. Ashbury's hall boy waited for a reply, his face red from running the distance between the castle and the gamekeeper's cottage.

"What is it?" his uncle asked from his chair by the window.

"The duke has fallen ill, and the duchess requests my presence. She bids me come straightaway."

"But why you?" Arson asked.

"I don't know." He looked at the boy. "Tell her I'll come immediately."

The boy nodded and dashed out the door.

"Does she give any more details? Has Sir Anthony Bellround seen him?"

"There's no more information." He glanced around, wondering if there was anything he should take along. Why would the duchess summon him, of all people? He couldn't imagine. "Will you be all right alone until Aunt Rose returns?"

Uncle Arson stayed alone most every day, but today, when Tristen had returned from Brightshire and the bakeshop, his uncle had seemed more melancholy than usual. Tristen had been keeping him company over a game of chess.

"Of course I'll be all right!" he barked out angrily. "I never *liked* that doctor. I hope the duchess calls in someone from London. Advise her to do that, if she asks."

Tristen pulled on his coat and draped a scarf around his neck. Him, advise the duchess? Surely that was not the reason she sent for him. Should he take his rifle? The atmosphere around the estate felt edgy, and now this. But no, he'd leave his gun here, even though he usually carried the weapon everywhere he went.

"And if you're going to stay over, get word to Rose on how Beranger's faring before she comes home tonight. I don't like the sound of this so soon after his return. Something's not right."

"I don't like it either. Earlier this morning when we were in the livery, he became light-headed and almost fell. The episode shocked us all."

"You better get going. Will you take a horse?"

He shook his head. "I can get there almost as fast on the footpath. I don't want to take the time to tack up and then have to go to the livery." They exchanged a long glance, and then Tristen hurried out the door, trepidation swirling inside.

Arriving at Ashbury, he entered through the servants' door and hurried down the hall past the housekeeper's and butler's private rooms. He wasn't sure what would happen when he asked to be taken upstairs to the duke's quarters. Would he be stopped? He'd never been past the servants' hall and kitchen area. Alcott, the baker, told him where to go.

The green door at the top of the servants' staircase opened in a hallway outside several other large rooms. He heard the duchess's voice ringing loud and clear.

"No, you may *not* see Beranger. I'm restricting all visitors until he's better or until I know what made him sick in the first place. The doctor gave me no reasonable answer, so I must take all precautions."

"But I'm his mother!"

"Stepmother! Who's never cared a whit about him from day one. Don't pretend like you do now."

The dowager!

"I've been duchess of Ashbury for years. You *can't* refuse me!"

The dowager duchess's voice rang with disdain. She'd never spoken to Tristen directly, but he'd heard her voice a time or two. He'd not like to be on the receiving end of her scorn.

"Watch me! I'm finished pretending not to hear the things you say to Beranger. Or ignoring your pointed jabs. Since his return, he's been nothing but kind to you. He's bent over backward to make you feel welcome—in *his* home! He's protected you from slander when the awkward circumstances of *your* marriage, and *your* illegitimate son, became known. Funny how the tables were turned, isn't it? I've never before met a woman as spiteful. And you're a stepmother, someone who is supposed to love a son, even if he's not her own. You should be ashamed of yourself. So, no, you may not see Beranger until I give the okay. If you try to go against my wishes, I'll banish you to Lily House. You'll learn I'm not as forgiving as your stepson. You choose, Dowager Duchess, which it will be?"

Feeling uneasy just being in the castle, let alone lurking outside the door to hear the dowager's dressing-down, Tristen paced the hall. He didn't like eavesdropping, but what was he to do? The duchess had asked him to come straightaway.

"And, before you go, there's also the little matter about a personal letter from my father that's disappeared from my room today. What do you know about that?"

There was a gasp of astonishment from within. "You accuse *me* of stealing from *you*? How dare you!"

"How dare I not! You were in my rooms unaccompanied. What else am I to think?"

"Carmichael was with me the whole time."

Tristen was amazed that the dowager duchess sounded defensive instead of dismissive. The duchess had her by the throat.

"Did you see the letter on my dresser?"

"No, I did not. There was no letter in your room. And I do not appreciate your tone at all."

"Then you're lying. Carmichael said she saw the letter on my dresser when the two of you went into our rooms. She distinctly remembers seeing it propped against a vase."

"She must be mistaken."

Deciding it best to retreat to the servants' hall and send a note with one of the footmen that he'd arrived, Tristen had just turned on his heel when the dowager huffed out of the room. She stopped abruptly when she spotted him only a few feet away. He dipped his chin as her face turned bright red. From all he'd heard from his uncle about her bulldog toughness over the years, he would have thought she would not be predisposed to embarrassment.

The duchess came out as well. When she saw him, her face lit with pleasure. "Mr. Llewellyn! Thank you for coming so quickly. I'd like you to stay in the castle with Beranger and myself until we can figure out what has brought on his vertigo. He had another episode not long ago like the one in the livery. Can you do that, please?"

The dowager duchess glowered. "He's the gamekeeper! He has a house of his own!"

The duchess tipped her head as if just finding that out now. "Of course, I know that, but that has nothing to do with why I asked Mr. Llewellyn here. Thank you, though, for your input. Now, please excuse us, we have things to attend to. I'll speak with you later."

The older woman's face hardened into an expression that was almost frightening. Oh yes, Tristen had heard the stories of her sharp tongue and even quicker temper, how she fired servants at the drop of a hat. But until this moment, that's all they'd been—stories and rumors. If looks could kill, he thought the new duchess might well be in her grave.

When the dowager had finally disappeared down a hall, the duchess rushed forward, her determined expression gone. She grasped his hands in friendship as if he were her port in a storm. "Again, thank you for coming so quickly. I didn't have anyone else to turn to. I pray you don't mind. Beranger is sick, although he won't admit the fact. I'm beside myself. I don't know if his food has been tainted, or if he's come down with something that could kill him." Her voice broke on the last word. "My imagination has taken wing in five different directions. I didn't know who else to trust."

If he were to guess, he'd say he was only a couple of years older than the duchess, and her imploring face before him gave him pause. He, Tristen Llewellyn, was her most trusted confidant in the castle? Only a handful of months ago he'd been released from prison. Surely, Pencely would have something to say about that when he learned about this summons. "I pledge you my trust, Your Grace, with anything you need. Just ask. I'm honored you called for me."

"As I stated to the dowager duchess, I'd like you to stay in a room across the hall from us. When I'm away, I want you to stay *with* him. Make sure no one tries anything."

"What about his valet? He knows the duke better than I."

"Not much better. Besides, I trust *you*. I'm new and have no idea who is friend and who is enemy. Because of the last duke dying in the way he did, I'm frightened. Perhaps some evil person has a vendetta against the Northcotts—all the Northcotts—and is out to kill each and every one. I won't let Beranger be the next target. I just pray we're not too late. His dizziness has me extremely worried. I've known him long enough to realize this is out of the ordinary for him."

"I see."

"So you'll do it?"

"I will."

"You must understand there may be an element of danger for you. But I don't know. Everything is speculation at this point."

He nodded.

"And you'll fall out with the dowager duchess, and most likely Lady Audrey. You may be blackballed forever."

"Yes, I picked up on that. I was never in with them, Your Grace. I'm willing to risk it." It seemed as if a great weight lifted from the duchess's shoulders.

"Thank you. My lady's maid is with him now, but I don't dare leave him alone for long. I'm not sure about her either." She gestured to the staircase. "We must hurry back."

Tristen followed the distressed duchess, ignoring all the strange looks he received from footmen and chambermaids. The walk to the third floor took several minutes. When they entered the room, they found the duke asleep and the duchess's lady's maid reading silently by his side.

She stood when they entered.

"Thank you, Carmichael. Mr. Llewellyn will take over for you now."

"Yes, Your Grace," she responded and headed for the door.

"Were there any visitors while I was gone? Did anyone try to come in?" The woman turned back. "No. Everything was quiet."

"He was sleeping when I left. Did he ever wake up?"

"No, Your Grace."

As soon as she was gone, the duchess rushed to the bedside and felt Beranger's forehead. She let go a sigh.

"He feels the same. Not warm in the least." She turned to Tristen. "I have one other errand to run, but I'll still be in the castle if you need me. Ring that bell at any change, no matter how small. Someone will be up right away. Don't hesitate to use it—over any little thing."

"Not to fear," he responded. "I'll use it first thing. No one will get close to the duke unless it's you."

That brought a smile to her face. "Thank God I have you, Mr. Llewellyn! And I hope to have another trusted ally here if things go my way. I'll return as soon as I can."

With that, Tristen found himself alone in the opulent room with the duke still asleep in his bed. How the tables had turned. He didn't know what he'd done to deserve such trust, but he knew he'd be willing to protect this man and his wife with his life. Not that he thought that would be necessary. Surely the duchess was imagining the conspiracy against Beranger, and he'd just picked up some illness that would pass in a day or two.

He strode across the floor to gaze out the window at the wooded lands beyond the clearing. He was used to being out there and not in here. Now he was the duke's most trusted ally. How would the duchess feel if she knew his past? That he'd killed a man with his own hands.

CHAPTER TWENTY-EIGHT

I know this is a strange request," Emma stated, working to keep her voice calm and void of all jitters as she took in the circle of servants around her. She elevated her chin a tiny bit to evoke respect, but was sure to keep a small smile on her face. She wasn't used to speaking in front of a crowd.

"I need a volunteer who won't mind leaving Ashbury—perhaps for a few days, maybe longer—to work at the Smith Bakeshop in Brightshire. Whoever decides to help will be generously rewarded on top of your regular salary. But I must have a volunteer by the end of this meeting. I can't tell you the work will be easy, but I hope you will consider doing it for your new duke."

The cook and the other kitchen staff stood around her as she offered her proposition. Amelia Smith, in the front of the group, looked clearly confused.

"I'd like Charlotte Aldridge to return for a few days, and I do not wish to leave her aunt Ethel shorthanded." She glanced around the faces, hoping one of the young women would speak up. The obvious choice would be Amelia, of course, but she'd have to wait for the young woman to offer herself freely. Emma didn't want to force someone to do something they didn't want to do. Besides, she hadn't cleared anything yet with Ethel Smith, and that cranky woman, in all honesty, might tell her to go jump in a lake. She most probably would say no anyhow, but Emma had to try. Besides Tristen, she wanted her friend to talk to. She didn't trust anyone else.

The jangle of Mrs. Darling's large ring of keys preceded the housekeeper before she emerged from the hallway that led to her personal living quarters. She halted and looked around, surprise on her face. Before she noticed Emma, she called out sharply, "What's this? Has an extra teatime been added that I don't know about? You best get back to work, people. Hurry on.

"Oh, I'm sorry, Your Grace. I didn't see you standing there. Is there something I can help you with?"

Yes, that was it. She should have gone to the housekeeper first thing. If anyone, Mrs. Darling seemed honest and good. She would know who in the kitchen could be spared, and who would have the right disposition to go into Brightshire. "Yes, I think you can, Mrs. Darling. Thank you." Emma stepped through the staff, hoping this could be resolved right away. "You see, I need Miss Aldridge to help me with a special task, but I need one of the kitchen staff to volunteer to take her place in the bakeshop, so they aren't left shorthanded. Only for a few days until Lord Harry returns. Will that be possible?"

Clearly surprised, Mrs. Darling's gaze flew to the cook's and then to Pencely, who had come down the stairs and looked irritated.

"I know it's an odd request, but I can make it, can't I? I am the duchess . . ."

"*Of course* you can, Your Grace! I didn't mean to question you or imply otherwise." A murmur seeped through the workers gathered in the room. "Let's go to my room and I'll have some tea sent in and we'll dis—"

"I'll volunteer, Your Grace! If you give me the chance, I won't let ya down."

Silence descended over the room.

Emma turned to find a plain-faced young woman pushing through the group. Her white apron was stained burgundy, and a good portion of her hair poked out from under her cap. Emma remembered meeting her the day in the kitchen when she'd met Charlotte but didn't remember her name.

"I'm sure I can do whatever is needed there for however long. I'm up for the challenge, as long as there is indeed a reward for going."

Mrs. Darling snapped straight. "Margaret!"

Emma put out a hand. "No, that's fine, Mrs. Darling. The first rule of a good business transaction is for all parties involved to know everything there is to know." She glanced around and smiled. "Yes, Margaret. Five pounds will be yours if you take up my offer."

Everyone sucked in a breath at the staggering amount the duchess had offered. Cries went out by others who wanted to be chosen instead.

"Thank you all, but I believe the position has been filled. Margaret, I'll let you know about your departure as soon as I hear back from the bakeshop. I've yet to receive permission from Mrs. Smith. Is that acceptable to you, Mrs. Darling? Can we spare Margaret for a few days?"

She blinked several times and then nodded.

Excitement and something else shone from the kitchen maid's eyes. Was that pride? Or camaraderie? Whatever, it had a good effect on Emma. One more small part of her puzzle had fallen into place—providing both Charlotte and her aunt Ethel agreed. For now, she'd stay positive.

Amelia caught Emma's gaze and glanced away, but not before muttering loud enough for Emma to hear, "Mother is going to be furious with Charlotte for this. She's not going to like her being called away."

All Emma's enthusiasm zipped away. Was she creating more trouble for Charlotte by summoning her? At this moment, she had no choice— no choice at all.

CHAPTER TWENTY-NINE

Tristen was never good at waiting. Not when he'd been a boy, not when he'd been in prison, and not now waiting for the duchess to return. As soon as she was back, he'd go down to the kitchen and relay the news about Beranger to Aunt Rose to take home to his uncle. He'd promised to keep Uncle Arson informed, and he felt time slipping away.

A rustling on the bed made him turn from the window. The duke was sitting, arms straight and hands pressed into the mattress as if he couldn't sit up without the support.

Tristen rushed over. "How do you feel?"

"Like I've been stuck on a runaway carousel and I can't get off." He brought his gaze up to Tristen's face. He grimaced and looked away. "And I'm still spinning, but not as bad as before. I never realized vertigo could bring a man to his knees." He took a deep breath and closed his eyes.

Tristen waited.

"What are you doing here?"

"The duchess sent for me. Asked me to stay with you until her return."

"I see. When she returns, I don't want you to let on that I'm still woozy. I need to get out of this bed, dress, and go down to dinner." He turned slowly and looked at the window, his complexion almost green from the motion of moving his head over his shoulder. "What time is it? How long have I been lying here?"

"I've been sitting with you for about an hour and a half. No one's been here but me."

"Why did she send for you?"

"She's frightened. Fears someone has targeted you, and has perhaps fed you some poison, or something like that."

Beranger groaned and lowered his head into his hands, not looking like he felt well at all. "When will she be back?"

"I don't know."

"I've landed her in a mess. I don't know why I'm sick, Tristen. I've never been sick a day in my life that I can remember. That said, I doubt anyone is trying to kill me. And if they were, poisoning would be too obvious. If they wanted me out of the way, a fall from my horse would be much less suspicious. Accidents do happen."

Tristen cocked an eyebrow. "Like your brother, the young duke? He caught his heel while hunting and accidently fell, sticking his neck with his own knife?"

They stared at each other for a long minute. "Fair assessment. I'm surprised it's taken me coming home and starting to ask questions to make others realize that Gavin's death may not have been so accidental at all."

Tristen, once again crossing the room, nodded. "Perhaps the duchess isn't that far off the mark. We should at least keep an open mind."

Beranger grasped the thick bedpost and slowly pulled his bulk to standing. His nostrils flared as he leaned his head against the post. "I've never felt so helpless. And from a little wobbly head. I'm astonished."

Tristen felt a smile growing. "The duchess turned the dowager duchess away from seeing you. She was a tigress, and no one was going to get near her cub. I was very impressed."

Beranger's head jerked up. "Crikey. The girl has spunk. I'm glad she's gotten over her attack of timidity. The dowager duchess has had her spooked for days. Were you there? What did the dowager say?"

"I was waiting in the next room and could hear the words exchanged. The dowager was none too pleased and put up a good fight, but your wife was very clear she didn't care a whit and that no one, under any circumstances, was to bother you in your room today. No one!"

Beranger laughed. "If she can stand up to the dowager, I best get on my own two feet and out of this bed. Next she'll be after me." He took a step forward, then another. On the third, he rocked so violently to one side, Tristen had to jump forward and grab him around the middle.

"You best sit down. You don't want to fall and hit your head."

"You make me sound like an old man. I'm not but a few years older than you."

"I'm not the one suffering from vertigo."

Beranger pulled free and walked to the window. "True. But I'll be up when my wife walks through the door and—"

The bedroom door opened, and the duchess breezed in. Behind her was Charlotte. The duchess hadn't said a thing about fetching her. Tristen blinked, thinking of their talk in the loft only a few hours before. Since then, she'd plagued his thoughts. She was thoughtful, and he was attracted to her—but with his past, she deserved so much better. He wanted to train the pigeons to make her happy. And to show her how clever he was. And perhaps have a way to be in contact with her himself. Perhaps they'd make it a three-way conversation.

"Beranger!" The duchess ran the length of the room to her husband's side and grasped his hands. "Beranger, when did you get up? You still don't look well. Come back to bed immediately."

Tristen could tell Beranger was doing everything in his power not to sway or show any signs of weakness. Should he keep what he knew to himself for the duke's sake, or assist the duchess in getting him back to bed?

"How long have you been up?" she asked her husband again. "How do you feel? Has the dizziness passed?"

"Long enough to know this is some strange fluke, Emma. I'm fine." He glanced at Tristen and then Charlotte, who had remained by the door across the large bedroom. "As I was telling Llewellyn here a few moments ago, I can't ever remember being sick in all my years. I'm as healthy as a horse. Please stop worrying about me." He waved Charlotte in closer. "Now what have you done? Summonsed poor Miss Aldridge too? Please excuse my state of dress, Miss Aldridge. My wife seems to be overly cautious where my health is concerned." He actually laughed. "Thank you for coming at her request."

The duchess looked back and forth between them. "Beranger, I hope you don't mind I invited Charlotte to Ashbury. I needed some people around me that I feel comfortable with, who I can trust and confide in. With Lord Harry away, I feel like I've been marooned on an island. I didn't know what else to do."

"Of course I don't mind, sweetheart. Anything you want is fine with me. Ashbury is plenty large enough for an army, if you'd like. But please know, you can trust everyone here, my love. You're just spooked, and I don't blame you. I guess it feels like a conspiracy to you, being in a new country—and with my stepmother watching your every move." He smiled at her and at the others in the room and then looked at the clock sitting on the fireplace mantel.

The duchess followed his gaze. "Thank you for understanding. But let me see you back to the bed."

"I'm up and staying. And will sit at the dinner table in an hour."

Her brows crinkled, she turned to Charlotte and Tristen.

"Since my husband has given me carte blanche to do as I wish, as any good husband should, let me ring for a maid to show you to your rooms. I'd like both of you to be our guests for dinner tonight—and every other night you're here. You've come at my request, and that is the least we can do. I'll hear no refusals."

Tristen held his breath. The duchess glanced into Beranger's face as if to see if he would refuse her.

"Of course, my darling. I wholly agree."

Charlotte blanched. "I couldn't, Your Grace. That wouldn't be right. I'm a kitchen maid . . . I, well—"

"Nor I," Tristen said. Eating with the family was a frightening thought. His aunt Rose had described the nightly occurrence in detail, how the diners took a whole hour or longer to dress in formal attire, then took hours to eat a seven-course meal, all the while making small conversation and abiding by centuries-old rules of etiquette. That felt as enjoyable as having a tooth pulled or having one's blood let. He wasn't going. "I couldn't think of it. Watching over the duke is one thing, and dining formally with the family quite another."

Charlotte put up a hand. "Perfectly said, Mr. Llewellyn. Besides, I have nothing to wear to such an evening. And the dowager duchess and the rest of your family would . . ."

Tristen nodded. "I would be very uncomfortable."

"The dowager duchess has no say in this. Only a little over three weeks ago, I was just like you. I never dreamed I'd dine in a castle as a duchess. But I did, and it was lovely. Beranger and I will be honored with your presence."

"That's true," Beranger added.

"I have a gown that I've never worn and that will look gorgeous on you, Charlotte." The duchess rang for a maid. "Get settled in your room and I'll have the dress sent over. We're about the same size, and I know you'll look stunning. Carmichael can help you do your hair as well. I'm more than happy to share. And Mr. Llewellyn, we'll find something for you as well. Never fear, tonight will be amazing."

Tristen cut a look at Charlotte. Her eyes had gone dreamy. He remembered how beautiful she'd looked when she'd shared her dream of dancing in an Adonis-blue gown. He'd not spoil her chance to feel like a princess by refusing to go. If he didn't eat at the duke's table, neither would she. This was the least he could do to make her fantasy come true.

A resounding clang that resembled a giant cymbal echoed through the hall and into the room.

The duchess rushed over to Charlotte. "You have an hour to prepare. That's plenty of time, even if you'd like a hot bath. Please say you'll join us. Beranger is feeling better, so we have something special to celebrate."

The duchess's gaze slipped back and forth between him and Charlotte. He needed to act fast.

"We would be honored." Tristen spoke up.

Emma clapped her hands. "Wonderful."

Beranger looked at Charlotte. "And you agree, Miss Aldridge?"

Charlotte nodded, a sentimental smile appearing on her lips.

A soft knock sounded on the door.

"Please come in," the duchess called. A chambermaid stepped inside, looking doubtful. Seemed the word had gotten around about the duchess's stranger behavior of late. And the missing letter. "Please show Mr. Llewellyn and Miss Aldridge to the two suites across the hall, and then send for a bath for Miss Aldridge, and Mr. Llewellyn, if they'd like. When you're finished with that, please let Carmichael know she'll be dressing Miss Aldridge as well as me tonight. So there is no time to lose."

CHAPTER THIRTY

After her bath and donning the gorgeous sapphire dress the duchess had sent over, the lady's maid named Carmichael had swiftly, with years of practice and skill, swept Charlotte's hair up in a soft, understated style that suited her oval face. The woman had been soft-spoken and kind, ignoring the fact that Charlotte was only a country girl from their kitchen, being treated like royalty by the American duchess. That fact must be making some waves in the castle. Charlotte didn't want to cause ill feelings with her friends and associates in the kitchen, and especially not her cousin Amelia. She didn't know why the duchess had taken to her so, except for the fact she resembled her younger sister and had, quite serendipitously, been available to her in her moment of need that late night in the servants' hall.

A knock sounded on Charlotte's door. She took another look at herself in the mirror, not recognizing the woman before her. Her heart skittered up and down her throat. The time had finally arrived.

The knock came again. Charlotte opened the door, feeling more beautiful than she ever had in her entire life.

Tristen stood there, dressed in dark formal attire. His eyes grew large. "Miss Aldridge, you look—"

"Silly? I know. I feel like a fish out of water."

"No. Not silly at all. *Beautiful.* Let me be the first to tell you."

"Thank you, Tristen," she said, warmth kissing her cheeks. The look of appreciation—and something else—in his eyes made her take a sudden deep breath. She wondered if Mr. Winters would be at dinner as well. He'd come into the bakeshop a couple of days before and stayed long enough to draw attention from her aunt. His whispered comments were becoming more daring, she reluctantly admitted to herself. He'd taken her hand and traced a finger across her palm when they'd been alone. Surely he didn't know how he was coming across, him being so far above her. Would she be happy if he was genuinely interested in her? She really didn't know.

Once again, Tristen's gaze traveled to her face and then up to her hair, ending back in her eyes. When they dipped for an instant to her lips, a jolt of surprise made her take a tiny breath. Though startling, his eyes held not a hint of the lusty appraisal she'd seen now and again from a man leaving the Silver Sixpence Pub in Brightshire, when she'd happened to pass by the establishment on an errand.

She brushed at the delicate fabric of her sleeve again, feeling her face heat. "Thank you again." If she wanted to encourage him, she'd tell him how attractive he looked—but she didn't dare. Even though he must have combed his dark locks, they still gave the impression he'd been out in the wind.

He stepped back and held out his arm. "May I? I went down earlier, and the duke asked if I could come fetch you. They're ready to go in." She slipped her hand into the crook of his elbow. "I can't get used to this large place. I'm used to the woodlands, meadows of tall grass, and the chatter of birds, not the echoes and emptiness of a castle. It took me more than ten minutes to find my way to the dining room." He smiled at her. "But have no fear, I know the way now."

After an endless trek on Tristen's arm—and she was thankful for that to steady her runaway nerves—the two found the drawing room, where the others waited to go into the dinner.

Mr. Winters arrived at the exact same time. He also looked quite handsome in his dark formal attire. "Miss Aldridge, you look amazing tonight. I was delighted to learn you'd be joining us." His gaze slid off her face and lingered where it should not.

Tristen hugged her hand next to his side and cleared his throat.

Mr. Winters gave him an amused look, made a small bow toward Charlotte, and hurried into the drawing room.

"May I speak candidly, Miss Aldridge?"

Her face still burned from Mr. Winters's appraisal. "Of course," she replied quietly, not wanting to draw attention. "What is it?"

"Frankly, it's Mr. Winters."

She waited.

"I know he's been showing you attention. Please be careful."

"You mean a man like him couldn't be interested in me?"

"No, on the contrary. I'm sure he's *very* interested. As a matter of fact, I can tell that he is. But that's what I'm fearful of. I just want to say this to you in case no one else has: men of his standing don't marry women of yours."

Women of yours? She knew she should be offended, but the night was so beautiful, and Tristen looked so earnest and handsome, and he was just watching out for her welfare. She took no offense. Hadn't Alcott said the same? And Mrs. Darling too. "Thank you, Tristen. I shall keep that in mind whenever he is around. But I'm sure you have nothing to worry about." She glanced at the doorway. "Shall we go in?"

Charlotte tried to control her amazement at the grand chamber. Three tall windows, reaching all the way to the ceiling, were adorned in a lovely floral fabric with burgundy flowers and tiny yellow blooms on a creamy background. They were a focal point and would have framed the outside view of the castle gardens beautifully if there had been light to see. A large bookcase took up one wall and gorgeous artwork the others. Numerous chairs and sofas were set about, each with its own side table accented with a vase or other decorative object. The lavishness almost stole Charlotte's breath.

The dowager duchess and Lady Audrey stood together in conversation. The dowager wore a soft yellow gown with a sparkling tiara almost hidden in her hair. Lady Audrey dressed in a vibrant pink, which suited her creamy skin tones. The garment had an abundance of drapes made from a gauzy, sheer fabric that made Charlotte's fingers itch to touch. The girl was so slender the crisscrossing of see-through drapes enhanced her shape.

Feeling like an impostor, Charlotte allowed herself one quick glance at the ladies and then steered her attention away. It seemed someone had alerted them that there would be guests for dinner—guests that would usually be serving them in some way—because they showed no surprise when she and Tristen entered. In fact, they showed little emotion at all. Neither disdain nor acceptance. Charlotte wished she could be so controlled, for she feared a look of sheer terror might be etched upon her face.

Mr. Winters smiled from where he stood with the duke and duchess when they entered. His warm attention brought a blush to her face, and she pondered what Tristen had said, what he'd warned.

The duke stood next to the large fireplace, as if he were overseeing a grand undertaking. He exuded an air of confidence she hadn't seen in him before. The duchess, garbed in green velvet, with tiny glittering rhinestones at her collar and cuffs, was gorgeous.

When Emma saw her and Tristen, her eyes lit up like matching emeralds. She excused herself from their conversation and hurried over.

The duchess took Charlotte's hands in her own. "This dress suits you!" She pressed her cheek affectionately to Charlotte's. "You outshine everyone in the room."

After greeting the duchess, Tristen left to go speak with the duke and Mr. Winters.

"I hardly think so, but thank you. And thank you for lending me this dress."

"My pleasure." She leaned in and lowered her voice. "I hope you'll relax and enjoy tonight. I've come to love the formal dining rituals, but when I first arrived, I found myself dreading them. It's not all that difficult. Just don't let anyone or any comments spoil your time. Unfortunately, the dowager thinks of dinner dialogue as some sort of sport. Be on your toes. I have no idea what the discussion will be, but if I know the dowager, you may be uncomfortable. Just let her words slide off your back without injury. That's what I do. And that's what Beranger has done all his life."

"I'll try," Charlotte replied softly when she found her voice. The dowager had been shooting glances their way as soon as Emma had hurried to her side. But so had Mr. Winters. She didn't know how to feel about him. "This whole fairy tale is due to you. I can't believe I'm here."

She glanced at the duke, speaking with Tristen and Mr. Winters. "How is the duke feeling?" she whispered. "He appears completely recovered. Perhaps all your fears were for naught."

Emma smiled. "Let us pray for that."

Pencely stepped into the room. "Dinner is served."

"Thank you, Pencely," Beranger replied, his hand still resting on the fireplace mantel, making Charlotte suspect he wasn't as recovered as the duchess might wish. He gave her a small smile, as if he'd read her thoughts. He made his way to Charlotte and put out his arm. Carmichael had informed her that the duke would escort the most honored female guest, and the duchess would walk in on the arm of the most honored male guest. Behind them Emma slipped her arm through Tristen's, and they went through to the dining room. Mr. Winters followed with Lady Audrey and the dowager duchess, one on each arm.

Charlotte tried to stay her surprise. The table, dressed for seven, was magnificent, with more splendors than she'd seen in all her life. Two candelabra made the silver and crystal glitter like gold. A white linen napkin was tented on each plate, and a beautiful fresco of a multitude of angels in the clouds was painted on the high ceiling. A tapestry of a medieval scene hung on one entire wall. It was the stuff of dreams.

As the duke assisted Charlotte into the chair to his left, she felt a small waver in his stance. She looked up at him and their gazes met. "You're quite fine, Your Grace?" she asked under her breath as the others were occupied being seated.

At the other end of the table, Tristen assisted Emma. She was too far away to hear their words.

"Fine enough to sit through dinner," he whispered back. "Please don't give me away."

After seating the dowager duchess on Emma's right and Lady Audrey on her left, Mr. Winters took the seat next to Charlotte's, across from Tristen and Lady Audrey. Thankful she was between the duke and Mr. Winters, and not one of the women, Charlotte smiled and glanced around.

Once everyone was seated, the night unfolded uneasily. She recognized the two footmen from her time in the kitchen. Allen Copley, who didn't look much older than herself with white-blond hair and a sweet disposition, and Jos Sleshinger, the dark-haired fellow who'd spoken with her on her first day. Jos, being the older of the two, circled the table offering small wedge-shaped slices of a delicious vegetable-and-egg dish, cooked firm. Behind him, Allen ladled on a semiclear sauce that had Charlotte wondering what the ingredients were. After that was consumed and cleared, a tasty consommé was served.

When Beranger picked up his spoon, everyone else followed suit.

After the soup, the servants arrived with platters of cold mackerel and cod and a basket of several types of hard bread. Pencely filled the crystal glasses with white wine. Charlotte felt like she was running a gauntlet with each course that was served. So far, to her limited knowledge, she'd done well and hadn't made any mistakes. Once, when

Mr. Winters had smiled into her eyes, she'd almost tipped the wine goblet she'd been sipping from, but rescued herself at the last moment.

"I'm very heartened to see you're feeling better, Beranger," the dowager said, her expression sincere. "I wanted to stop in but wasn't allowed."

"I second that, Brig," Mr. Winters threw out. "You gave us all a scare. Don't do that again. There's been too much death around here in the last few years. I, for one, was alarmed."

Emma leaned forward as if trying to get closer to her husband at the opposite end of the linen-covered table. "Not anyone more than I, Justin. I've never been more frightened in my life. He's never been sick before. Thank heavens the vertigo passed quickly."

The dowager scoffed softly. With a note of sarcasm, she said, "You hardly know the man, my dear. Three months has yet to pass since you and my stepson even met. I'm sure everything about him is a mystery to you and your American ways."

Shocked that the woman would so openly challenge Emma at her own table, Charlotte reached for her napkin and discreetly patted her lips. She'd been sitting very straight, and not being used to such posture, her back had begun to ache.

Emma blinked several times, the only indication her feelings had been hurt or that she was perturbed. Charlotte would have liked to spring to her defense, but a little voice inside said to leave it be. *Let the things she says roll off your back.*

Emma nodded to Jos, who'd just placed the next course on her plate, and she waited as he moved to the dowager. "Time does not matter where true love is involved," she said.

The dowager's eyes gleamed like the circlet on her head. "Your naïveté is showing, my dear Duchess. The passage of time is *everything*. The Northcott name is listed in the Domesday Book. In fact, our lineage can be traced all the way back to the arrival of King William the Conqueror in 1066."

"That's all very well," Emma responded without missing a beat. "But you're not a true Northcott. I wonder if your maiden name is listed?"

Beranger straightened in his chair, giving Charlotte the impression he was doing all he could to stay upright. He smiled briefly at his wife and then lifted an eyebrow at the dowager. "We have special guests tonight. Let's keep the conversation civil."

The entrée of roasted chicken and an assortment of colorful small potatoes and other vegetables was served. Sitting so close, Mr. Winters had Charlotte on edge. Each time he turned her way, she felt her face heat, and she hoped her cheeks weren't as red as they felt. Much to her dismay, he whispered into her ear three times, once thanking her again for her assistance with the berry stain, then to tell her how much he enjoyed seeing her in Brightshire. And once again, much to her distress, and loudly enough for everyone to hear, to exclaim how gorgeous she looked.

"I hear you have a new lady's maid, Duchess," Mr. Winters commented, turning to Emma. "Is she working out to your satisfaction?"

Doesn't he know the footmen and butler have ears? That's not something to ask except in private; the duchess's answer will absolutely get back to Carmichael. Shame on him.

Emma patted her lips with her napkin. "She's been very kind and efficient so far. But I'm sure you've heard, a cherished letter from my deceased father disappeared today, after she and the dowager duchess visited my rooms." Emma glanced at the dowager and then to Beranger. "I've yet to learn anything more."

"The letter will be found, and the culprit with it," Beranger stated irritably, glancing at his distant cousin. He'd just taken the last bite of his meat and chewed and swallowed. "If I hadn't been reduced to my spinning bed earlier, the chore would already be done."

As calm as could be, the dowager took a sip of her wine and then replied, "Why on earth would anyone leave such an important piece of mail lying about? I think you must have misplaced the thing and don't remember. We never had a problem with pilferage before."

"That's not possible," Emma replied in a cool, unruffled voice. "I've not moved the letter since I arrived. It's been in the same spot the entire time."

Any pleasantness that had been on the duke's face vanished. "This is no small matter and will be treated as such. On a dresser in our private rooms is not 'lying about.' That letter is of great importance to both Emma and myself. Tomorrow, we'll search the castle until it's found."

Jos, now standing against the wall since the next course had been served, glanced at Allen Copley. The younger footman swallowed nervously. The duchess's missing letter had all the servants on shaky ground. Nobody wanted to be suspected.

"In that case," the dowager replied, "we will pray for a speedy resolution. Accusations of any kind put all the servants on edge—and me as well."

Mr. Winters wiped his mouth as the entrée dishes were cleared away and the side dishes were switched in preparation for the roast course. Sorbet was served to cleanse the palate.

"I didn't mean to bring up another contentious subject," he said, turning to Charlotte. "On a nicer note, I was delighted to hear you were to be a dinner guest." He leaned a bit closer, and she felt the distance between them vanish. "The last time we spoke, you were hard at work in your bakeshop."

"Oh," Lady Audrey said. "Pray tell."

Charlotte could feel Tristen's stare on her face from across the table. He'd been dining quietly, hardly saying a word, but she could tell he was taking in every syllable. He didn't like Mr. Winters at all, from the expression on his face.

"Yes, such a delight and shock," the dowager said. "I never dreamed of the day we'd be dining with the servants, but the future has arrived, much to my dismay."

Emma caught her eye. "The duke and I are delighted Mr. Llewellyn and Miss Aldridge could join us tonight. Actually, since my arrival, this is the first time I've felt at home. Ashbury has so much to offer, it's a shame to keep the beauty and splendor all to ourselves."

"Like it's been done for centuries?" Lady Audrey interjected, sounding almost exactly like her mother. "And would have still been had I inherited the title. But I did not, and now we will be the first great home to break with centuries-old social norms. I wonder what that will do to our good name and standing in the community. I, for one, am not optimistic."

The roast course, succulent lamb covered in rosemary, arrived on silver platters, along with roasted courgettes with lemon and tomatoes, butternut squash garnished in butter and onions, and brown-butter radishes. New wineglasses were filled with a light red vintage. The footmen made serving look easy, but Charlotte knew better. The meal was delicious, and she'd be sure to let everyone downstairs know. With Margaret now taking her spot in the bakeshop for a few days, Rose Henderley must have done the side dishes, the sauces, and the rest.

Charlotte saw Emma bristle under her calm and cool exterior. Perhaps the duchess was used to being challenged by the dowager duchess but not by her husband's younger sister. Lady Audrey's comment seemed to have hit a nerve.

"In America, we believe all men are created equal," Emma said, glancing at Charlotte and then Tristen. "Your destiny is up to your diligence and hard work, not who your parents happen to be or from which lineage you have descended. You're welcome here anytime, my new friends. At Ashbury, the times are changing for the better." She took a sip of her wine.

"Well!" the dowager blurted, apparently outraged. She glanced at Beranger. "Do something. Your mail-order bride is out of control! Surely, you don't agree with what she's saying. There is enough of your father in you to make sure Ashbury does not fall to ruin."

Emma broke into laughter, followed by Mr. Winters, and then the rest. All except the dowager. Her ruby-red face looked painful. Charlotte had expected the group to explode into angry voices, not laughter.

How anyone, and especially Emma, could think such a tension-filled event could be enjoyable was amazing. From the moment the group had taken their seats, Charlotte's nerves had been tested. She just hoped she'd get through the evening without some huge social blunder.

She took a small sip from her water glass, not trusting herself to take any more wine. All she wanted was to get through the next few hours without making a fool of herself, especially in front of Tristen and Mr. Winters.

CHAPTER THIRTY-ONE

Y ou're lucky my wife has a sense of humor," the duke said. "Mail-
order brides are frequent in the West. There is no shame in being
one. Emma is not, of course, but perhaps you don't know the difference."

Shocked at the insults, Tristen sliced a portion of his lamb and
shoved it into his mouth. If someone had insulted his wife like that,
there would be a price to pay.

It seemed the Honorable Justin Winters was anything but honorable. He enjoyed stirring the pot and was doing a good job tonight,
one topic after the next. Tristen didn't appreciate how nervous he made
Charlotte each time he singled her out in conversation or whispered
into her ear. He knew what he was doing. His intentions were the
opposite of honorable when it came to her. Tristen just hoped Charlotte
understood the way the upper class worked.

"And if she weren't laughing right now, I'd take offense," the duke
went on. "But what she says is true. We talked extensively on the voyage
here. Not because we knew then that Gavin and the rest had squandered
much of Ashbury's wealth, but because in America we think differently.
Within a few months, hopefully, with some changes that are happening
as we speak, Ashbury may be back on track and self-sustaining. We shall
see." He glanced at Tristen. "There'll be other modifications as well, in

the way things have been managed. Here and with my personal savings abroad. That won't take place overnight, but soon enough."

"I'll be happy to do whatever I can to help," Tristen said, finally feeling comfortable enough with the topic to break his silence. Besides saying yes and thank you, he'd been a spectator so far, but now that the duke seemed to be singling him out, he felt on firmer footing. "Maybe guided hunting parties, perhaps. Your extensive land holdings make that a possibility."

Mr. Winters frowned.

"Changes? What kind of changes?" Lady Audrey asked, picking at the chocolate drizzle over the apricot tart that had been placed before her.

"What you hinted about earlier?" the duchess asked her husband, excitement glowing in her eyes. "Can you share the secret now?"

The duke beamed. "I can. With the help of Lord Harry, I've lent the dukedom cash from my personal savings in America to procure a shipping vessel. Ashbury Castle will export to America and import to England. Many Americans are hot to get some good Hereford bulls to cross with their cattle. And several of our tenants raise sheep. There is no end to what we can export and"—he glanced at Emma—"perhaps we will import beef from the Five Sisters Ranch in Colorado, as well as horses and cattle to breed. And what about sending English fashions to your shop in Eden, dear wife? As well as English items that Americans miss. Tea and other items unique to England that will weather the journey. Steamships have changed the import/export business by making the trip much faster."

"Beranger, what a grand idea! My mind is spinning with possibilities."

"I thought we'd call her the *Emma*, the *Five Sisters*, or perhaps the *American Duchess*," the duke said, a wide grin on his face. "Whatever you want. And then as our fleet grows and dominates sea trade, we'll use all the names you'd like." He looked at his sister. "The *Lady Audrey*? How does that sound?"

The staff looked surprised. Fruit-and-cheese platters were now set on the table, and the wineglasses were being refilled.

A small smile appeared on Lady Audrey's face.

"Please share some of your seafaring stories, Beranger," the duchess said. "I didn't know you loved the sea so much."

"There's too much to tell," Beranger responded. "That topic is better saved for the sitting room, or we'll never get away from this table."

"What about a shipwreck?" Mr. Winters threw out. "Did you ever see one?"

Tristen swallowed a groan at the man's tactlessness.

"No, thank God," Beranger said. "But the *Destiny* came close a few times. Storms can be treacherous. Gale-force winds don't have much meaning until you live through them. The boatswain aboard the *Destiny*, Nelson Wadlly, turned out to be a good friend, watching over me in my youth and making sure others treated me fairly. He had a brother who'd sailed aboard the HMS *Driver*, a wooden paddle sloop of the Royal Navy credited with the first global circumnavigation by a steamship. Unfortunately, she came to a bad end when she wrecked on Mayaguana Island."

"Where's that?" Lady Audrey asked.

"Most easterly island of the Bahamas, in the West Indies. Just saying those names gives me an itch to climb hand over hand to the crow's nest while enjoying the sting of salty air on my face."

He laughed, seeming like he felt much better. Tristen thought perhaps the food had fortified him.

"Was everyone all right?" Emma asked, concern in her voice.

Beranger shrugged. "Like most times, Wadlly didn't have all the information, but the telling made for a good story. Wadlly's brother lived, and that was all that had mattered to him."

"Your desire to become a shipping magnate now makes more sense," Mr. Winters offered. "I may ask to sign on myself." He laughed, his eyes alight.

Good. You need a job, Tristen thought unkindly.

"What grand plans you have, Duke." The dowager smiled coyly at her stepson. "I don't mean to spoil your good news, but I heard something distressing today and wondered if the information had reached your ears as well. I know you've been asking about my dear departed son's death. Well, one of the villagers has come forward to report that Thomas Aldridge"—she leaned forward and looked at Charlotte—"was seen in the woodlands, close to where Gavin was found after he'd perished."

Charlotte's smile froze.

"I hope I didn't distress you with such alarming news. The constable says it was reported that he couldn't have been poaching, because he didn't have a rifle with him."

Blinking, Charlotte wiped her mouth with her napkin.

The dowager went on, "Had you heard that, Miss Aldridge? About your brother? The constable has spoken with him. Has he said where he was on the day my son died?"

"Thomas Aldridge delivers the bread on Tuesdays," Mr. Winters said, as if anyone there didn't already know that. "He's a friendly sort. I'm sure he can't be involved with anything nefarious. Besides, nothing has been proven. The departed duke fell. Questions answered."

The dowager was baiting Charlotte. What would the duke do? And if this were true, why hadn't Charlotte said anything to Tristen?

"No, I haven't heard that," Beranger said. His surprised gaze cut to Charlotte and then to Emma.

"Nor I," Emma added, her brow dipping in concern.

Tristen glanced at Lady Audrey beside him, who had gone as white as a ghost. Did she know something she wasn't saying?

The young woman lifted her gaze from the cheese on her plate, her hand quivering. "N-nor I," she said. "From what I know of Mr. Aldridge, he wouldn't hurt a flea." She looked for a moment at Charlotte and then glared at her mother. "And why bring that up now in front of his sister? The subject could have waited until you were alone with the duke. How mean-spirited."

The dowager's eyes were large. "Not mean at all. And how do you know Mr. Aldridge?"

"He's been coming to Ashbury for years. I hardly go around with my eyes closed."

Charlotte blinked several times and reached for her wineglass.

"Who reported that information?" Emma asked.

"The constable. He was here earlier. He has taken the task upon himself, at the duke's request, to begin investigating anew."

"That's right," Beranger said, finished with the cheese on his plate. "Some of the villagers in Goldenbrook seem to think Gavin's death was intentional. People aren't confident that the truth of the matter has been uncovered. It's best to bring it all up again, let people have their say, and then put the dreadful matter to rest."

Something was wrong, Tristen realized. Charlotte's gaze flicked to her plate as she wrestled with something in her mind. *Had* Thomas been involved with some type of crime? Certainly not murder. Why were Charlotte's eyes filled with fear?

Lady Audrey delicately cleared her throat. "Brightshire has a new duke and duchess, and I think a ball is in order so everyone can come meet them." She glanced around the table.

The dowager's mouth tightened. "A ball?"

"Yes. Since Father's death, we've all gone around with long faces. How does that sound to you, Duke?"

His contemplation turned into a smile. "Emma, what do you think? Would you like that?"

Her gaze traveled between Tristen and Charlotte and then back to her husband. He was touched she'd think of them at a time like this. "Only if everyone can be invited. Gentry and countryfolk alike. And that you keep feeling better . . ."

"My word," the dowager complained. "What will things come to next? I can hardly wait to see."

"Fine, then. Saturday after next?" Beranger said. "Does that give you enough time to plan, Lady Audrey? You and my wife, of course."

Lady Audrey nodded. "It does. But there will be no time to waste."

A ball with gentry and commoners alike? Tristen wondered how that would play out. The expression on the dowager duchess's face had him doubtful.

CHAPTER THIRTY-TWO

"What a night." Emma sat at her dressing table, Carmichael having already left the room. The sheer peachy-pink silk nightgown her sisters had given her for a wedding present clung to her curves, making her feel desirable. Beranger's valet had attended him in the adjoining chamber, and then her husband had joined her as soon as her lady's maid had gone.

Would she and Beranger keep up with the valet and lady's maid forever? She hadn't thought so when they'd married, and then they had arrived at Ashbury. If she and Beranger said they didn't need them, what would these people do for a living? Wouldn't they already have gone off to London in search of a job in a factory or office if they'd wanted a different way of life? She had to keep reminding herself that there were more sides to an issue than just hers.

"I can't abide your stepmother, Beranger. She looks for ways to be inhospitable. Until today, when I learned she'd fired Hyacinth, I've tried to be polite. I've been respectful and bit my tongue every time I wanted to respond. I've ignored her mean comments and turned the other cheek each time she found fault with me or you. That said, I'll not let her degrade our friends just because they've not known the advantages she's had. I won't. And I'm so thankful you didn't as well." She took a deep breath and slowly let it out.

Working a dab of perfumed cream into her neck, Emma searched out Beranger's reflection in her mirror. He'd been very quiet after dinner. Was he angry? Was something wrong? When he didn't respond, she turned on her bench. "Beranger?"

He was sitting very still in a chair by the fireplace, watching the flames.

"Beranger?" she said a little more loudly.

He started, as if just now hearing her. He didn't turn his head. "Yes? And you were saying?"

Realization dawned. The container dropped from her fingertips and clattered to the glass tabletop. She rushed to his side, dropping to her knees. "You're no better, are you? You're dizzy again. Did the vertigo just return, or had it never really gone?"

She watched the rhythmic pulsing along his neck. "Beranger, tell me, please." She scooted around in front of him so he wouldn't have to turn his head. The chalky appearance around his mouth had returned.

She took his arm, and without needing any words between them, he allowed her to lead him to the bed. Once again, she pulled back the counterpane and helped him into the sheets. Less than an hour ago at dinner, when he'd been sharing his plans, he'd been fine. And now . . .

When he lay back, a whoosh of relief passed his lips. "Finally," he said. "This does feel good."

"Why on earth didn't you tell me sooner? And why on earth did you get up in the first place? I want to be able to trust you, my love, but I can't if you don't tell me the truth. How would you feel if the tables were turned?"

He tried to reach up to her face, but the effort must have been too much, because he let his hand fall back to his side. "I wouldn't like it at all," he said. "The vertigo is back with a vengeance. During dinner the wooziness was somewhat better, but not completely gone. I was so

214

hopeful that that was the end of it." His gaze left hers and went up to the high ceiling. "Who would have thought I could fly so fast without leaving my back?" His chuckle held no mirth. "It's alarming."

Frightened, having been thrown back into this nightmare, she paced the room. "I'll cable in the morning for a new doctor. To London, and one highly thought of that doesn't have one foot in the grave, or who knows the Northcotts personally. There is too much prejudice against you still around." She chanced a quick look and found his eyes closed and his breathing steady. If that horrible stepmother were responsible, Emma would have her arrested. She just hoped she could figure it out before something worse happened.

CHAPTER THIRTY-THREE

For Charlotte, staying in the beautiful bedroom on the same floor as the duke and duchess was a fairy tale. Five days came and went in the blink of an eye. Much to everyone's distress, the duke had still not fully recovered. Sometimes he was clearheaded enough to sit up at his desk, eat in the dining room, or even walk around, but often he was reduced to remaining in bed. The periodic vertigo made him cranky, and the longer he had to stay in bed, the more he railed against his weakness. The duchess kept everyone away, still fearful someone was trying to poison him.

But Charlotte knew this visit to the castle would come to an end. The day after their first dinner, Tristen went back to managing the forests and birds. And this morning, Margaret Malone, the kitchen maid, had returned from the bakeshop in tears. She declared she'd work for Ethel Smith no longer. She'd arrived by way of the greengrocer's cart that brought daily foodstuffs from Brightshire. When she got word of Margaret's return, Charlotte had packed her bag, and the duchess had called up the carriage with instructions to take her to the bakeshop door.

Charlotte would be home within minutes.

Since the proclamation at dinner that Thomas was under suspicion for the previous duke's murder, she'd fretted endlessly about her brother. What was happening while she'd been gone? And what was she to do about it? She'd seen Thomas in the forest that day, and clearly someone else had as well. She'd never believe him capable of murdering the duke. And yet she'd also seen Mr. Henderley that day—the day his limping had begun. Didn't that mean anything? The questions twisted her insides into knots. She'd clear her brother's name if she could, yet she didn't want to create trouble for poor Mr. Henderley if he wasn't involved. She was determined to pin Thomas down and finally get to the bottom of things.

With the help of the footman, Charlotte descended the shiny black coach, feeling like she was stepping out of an enchanted life and back into reality. She held a small sprig of fragrant flowers Mr. Winters had gathered from somewhere, probably the castle garden or greenhouse, and tied with a ribbon. He'd also promised to visit her at the bakeshop soon. It had seemed to her that during her stay at Ashbury the handsome man had made every effort to seek her out and speak with her as much as possible. Wherever she went, there he would be. He flirted and touched her hand when no one was looking. And once, he'd suggested she meet him late at night in the garden, alone, so he could show her the stars. He'd looked so earnest and sweet, she'd been tempted for a moment, but Alcott's and Mrs. Darling's warnings brought her to her senses. The moment she'd declined, saying she couldn't possibly, he'd backtracked and made the clandestine meeting sound as if she'd misunderstood. Confused, with no experience with men or older women who'd ever taken the time to educate her in the ways of romance, she didn't know if his overtures were proper or not. At some point, men and women had to get together somehow, didn't they?

And now, she was home. She hadn't disliked her job before, because she'd never known anything different. But now she'd miss the camaraderie of friends at Ashbury, laughing and discussing thoughts and problems. She'd never known a meal could be so much more than just consuming nourishment for her body.

With a heavy heart, she turned and gave the coach and footman one last look, then squared her shoulders and entered the bakeshop. Inside, the air was uncomfortably warm with the scent of sage and onion. The display case wasn't as full as normal. From what Margaret had said, her aunt was none too happy she'd stayed away so long.

Verity squealed when she saw her. "Charlotte, you're back!" She rounded the display case and vaulted into her arms. "Things around here have been topsy-turvy since you left. When Mother wasn't brow-beating and berating poor Margaret, she was grumbling under her breath." She stepped out of Charlotte's arms. "The girl tried her best, but you know how Mother can be." Her smile disappeared. "I liked Margaret. She was nice."

Nice? Margaret? I wish Margaret would forgive me. Perhaps we could be friends too.

"I'm sorry I was gone so long," Charlotte said. She was the cushion, the protection between her younger cousin and Aunt Ethel's sharp tongue. That was no secret. When Charlotte was here, Aunt Ethel left Verity alone. "I should have come home sooner."

Verity shook her head. "I don't begrudge you such a wonderful experience, but my mother does. Please be careful. Even with Margaret's help, she's been on edge the whole time, saying you'll never go back there once you come home." She took another step away and looked Charlotte up and down. "This dress is new. It's beautiful. So finely made. And the fabric is gorgeous." She reached out in wonder and fingered the creamy green cloth. "A gift from the duchess?"

Charlotte nodded.

"Verity! Is that *Charlotte* I hear out there, now that that impostor has run back to the castle with her tail between her legs? If so, send her in."

"Hurry, before she gets angrier."

"Is Thomas home?" Charlotte quickly asked. The dowager's nasty rumor filtered through her mind.

Verity tipped her head in question. "I'm not sure. He hasn't gone fishing this whole time or disappeared at all. I believe he's out in the barn caring for the pigeon."

The irritation she'd felt at the word *fishing* dissolved the moment her cousin mentioned Romeo. "The pigeon? Has Mr. Llewellyn been building the coop?" She'd wondered more than a few times what Tristen was doing since he'd left.

"Yes. Finished two days ago and left the bird. That's another reason Mother has been completely unbearable."

She kissed Verity's forehead. "As soon as I change my dress, I'll be back to help." She glanced around. "Things look a little bare out here."

Verity nodded. "Our routine hasn't been the same without you."

"There you are, Miss High and Mighty," Aunt Ethel said from the tall worktable as Charlotte entered the kitchen. Her hands were deep in a bowl of dough.

Perspiration made Aunt Ethel's face shine, and the lines around her eyes and mouth seemed to have deepened. She did work hard, and that was no lie. Guilt for her time spent at Ashbury pressed around Charlotte's shoulders.

Aunt Ethel's eyes narrowed when she took in Charlotte's new dress.

"Yes, I'm back, Aunt Ethel." She kept her tone cheerful, though her insides felt like a gunnysack filled with snakes. Even with all the problems at the castle, these last few days had been the best in her life. "And I'll get busy as soon as I change into my work dress and apron. I'm sure you're ready for a break." Heading for the stairs, she was about to ascend when Ethel caught her shoulder with a dough-covered hand. Charlotte shrank away, offended her aunt would think so little of her new garment. Surely, she'd noticed.

"No need to change. I need your help *right now*. For the weekend baking. The case is bare out front. How do you expect us to make any profit if we don't have anything to sell?" She stuck an apron in Charlotte's face. "Put this on and get to work."

Hatred glittered in Aunt Ethel's eyes. The attention from the duchess had been too much. Verity's warning rang in Charlotte's head. All these years, knowing she was an outsider, she had strived to be a good niece and a help whenever she could. She worked without complaint, tried to be respectful even under the harshest unfair treatment, and put her work before any personal happiness.

Something dark rose up within. "After I change—"

"I won't tell ya again, girl! Get to work! You've been gallivanting around in rich splendor for the last five days while your family, the one who's put a roof over your head and food in your mouth for years, worked their fingers to the bone with that good-for-nothing replacement the duchess sent. First the pigeon and then you. Who does she think she is, anyway?"

Painfully gripping Charlotte's arm, Aunt Ethel attempted to drag Charlotte to the workstation, but something inside snapped. *I won't be treated with such disrespect any longer. I'm a person, not her beast of burden.* She yanked her arm away, causing Aunt Ethel's eyes to narrow.

"Who does she think she is?" Charlotte repeated. "The Duchess of Brightshire! She's wonderfully kind and noble. The exact opposite of you!"

Her aunt jerked back as if slapped. "Don't you dare use that tone with me, you ungrateful wretch!"

"I will when you treat me like I have no feelings."

Aunt Ethel swung at Charlotte's face with an open palm, intending to strike her, but Charlotte jumped back, almost stumbling over a stool. Thoughts of Verity listening to the confrontation from the front room gave Charlotte more courage than she actually possessed.

"I'll tell you again," she said, panting with horror. "I'll not do a lick of work until I go upstairs and change out of my *new* dress. And that's final!" She straightened her shoulders as she struggled to hold back many years of tears and hurts.

Aunt Ethel's lips trembled with rage. Perhaps she'd pushed the woman too far, but she didn't care. She'd no longer tolerate her aunt's abusive treatment. Later today, after things had calmed down, she'd inform Aunt Ethel she expected a wage from now on, as well as one day off a week. Her thoughts flew to Tristen, of all people, and she imagined walking with him on a warm Sunday afternoon around the forest lake.

Movement at the back door drew both their attention.

Mathilda Tugwer stuck her head inside, her omniscient eyes taking in the scene.

Guiltily, Aunt Ethel reached for a mixing spoon even though she had no batter to mix.

"May I come in for a glass of water?" Mathilda asked, leaning in through the back threshold.

"What's wrong with the well?" her aunt snapped with a curled lip. She and the old midwife had no love lost between them, though Charlotte was never sure what had been the cause. "Did it dry up? Or there's always the bucket at the stream for peasants like you. Go there and leave us alone."

"Uncharitable woman," Mathilda grumbled as she came inside. Her gaze searched the kitchen like a wary animal stepping out into an unprotected glen. "And from such an old friend. I'd expect more from you, Ethel Smith." Nothing seemed to frighten Mathilda—certainly not Aunt Ethel.

Keeping her wits about her so as not to get struck by her angry aunt, Charlotte scooted past, then went to the sink and worked the pump, filling a James Keiller & Sons white ceramic marmalade jar they used for a glass. "Nice and cold," she said, handing it to Mathilda.

"Bless you, my child," she replied and then drank until the jar was empty.

"You've had your drink, old woman, now be on your way," Aunt Ethel spat. "We have work to do and can't begin with you snuffling around and peering into each corner. What are you always looking for, anyway?"

Mathilda only smiled.

Verity appeared in the threshold. "Are you hungry, Miss Tugwer? I have a meat pie that broke apart not three minutes ago when I tried to put it into a bag for Mrs. Jones."

The midwife had stayed long enough to defuse the situation. Had she heard the angry voices from the alley? Mathilda always seemed to appear at the most opportune times. Aunt Ethel was again kneading, the angry lines easing away to a more relaxed expression.

Charlotte was waiting for her aunt to object to Verity's offer. It was their practice to bag broken meat pies and pastries into small paper sacks to sell for a halfpenny. Fragmented items were a good portion of their income. Doing so had been Charlotte's idea—it allowed even the very poor to treat themselves, but didn't wound their pride with handouts.

"That sounds lovely," Mathilda said. "A nice meat pie . . ."

"Costs half a penny, as you good and well know," Aunt Ethel blurted. "We don't work for nothing."

Emboldened by Mathilda's presence, Charlotte said, "I'll pay for the broken meat pie from this week's earnings."

Ethel jerked to a stop. "What earnings? Did you get a job somewhere?"

Mathilda's gaze touched hers.

Verity seemed to be holding her breath.

"Yes, I did. *Here.* I've worked in this bakeshop my entire life without receiving a cent for my efforts. You don't consider me family, so I must be a worker. Either pay me or I'll find employment elsewhere." Charlotte pushed back her jittery nerves, thinking of the duchess and how brave she'd looked as she confronted the dowager. If

Emma Brinkman Northcott could speak up for herself, then so could Charlotte. "I can go back to the castle today if you'd rather."

Even the walls seemed to tremble as everyone waited for the explosion to come.

"We'll discuss this later, Charlotte," Aunt Ethel said, trying to pull her lips into a smile.

Her aunt was at a disadvantage with Mathilda present. And that was exactly why Charlotte had chosen this moment to make her stand. "No. I'd like to get the details settled now, if that's all right. I'm nineteen and need to think about my future. Twelve pounds a year plus room and board sounds fair for what I do."

Aunt Ethel gasped and stopped kneading. "I always knew you were touched in the head. I'll pay eight pounds, but I won't like doing it."

"Eleven and a half pounds," Charlotte countered, knowing without the room and board she'd barely be able to scrape by on such a low wage, but she wanted to make sure her salary would never impact her adoptive family's welfare. That was the most important thing. All the hours she spent baking would more than pay for the small amount she was asking several times over.

Aunt Ethel bit her lip so hard a drop of blood appeared. "God knows, I should'a turned you away when I had the chance," she muttered, picking some dry crust from under her fingernails, "but I didn't want to hurt my sister. She never knew you weren't her real babe, bless her heart. I'll pay ya ten pounds a year, if I must, and not a shilling more."

Aching stabbed Charlotte like a lance. She could have been a member of the family if her aunt had only allowed her to be. And she'd believed she was Ruby's true daughter until she was five years old. The memory of that horrible day was imprinted on her soul.

Rain had begun to fall and the crackling fire was the only sound besides the pitter-patters on the roof. Aunt Ethel had been baking. Charlotte and Amelia sat in chairs by the fire, darning socks, with three-year-old Verity fast asleep by their feet. Thomas, then six, sat on a stool in the corner, being punished for some infraction.

Aunt Ethel reached for the butter container, but after mixing the butter into the batter, she recognized that the contents had been fouled by greasy clumps of lard. Livid, she'd had to throw the entire batch out, after which she'd taken to Charlotte with a switch.

"Can't you do anything right, you stupid little mongrel?" she screeched. "You've cost me a whole day of profit."

At the first surprising sting, Charlotte dropped her mending and darted to the other side of the kitchen, putting the square worktable between them. Shocked and hurt, she didn't understand her aunt's bitter anger. No matter how fast Aunt Ethel moved, Charlotte was faster. Still, the switches she'd received before she'd realized what her aunt was about to do stung like fire. What had her aunt meant, calling her a mongrel?

"I'm sorry," she'd cried. "I'll be more careful, Auntie, I promise."

Since Charlotte was strong for her age, meeting the man who brought milk, lard, and other necessities each morning was her responsibility. She held the cans while he refilled them, scooping gobs of fresh butter, lard, or cheese into their corresponding containers. Distracted by a group of passing children, young Charlotte had mixed the containers up.

The faster Charlotte darted away, the angrier Aunt Ethel became. "I should have put you out on the street when poor Ruby died, you stupid little peasant."

Now awake, Verity began to sob with fright.

"Time you knew the truth!" Aunt Ethel went on in a fit of anger. "You were an orphan! Found by an old crone! My sister's babe died at birth. You needed a mother, and Ruby, who'd just lost her poor husband, needed the daughter she'd lost. Look how I've been repaid by trying to do a good deed."

Charlotte recalled the look on Thomas's face as he stood in stunned silence next to the punishment stool. To this day he'd never said a word about the revelation. And Amelia and Verity were so young, surely they didn't remember.

"You don't even look like the rest of us!"

The memory of that moment could still bring Charlotte to tears, if she let it. It was as if in the recalling of the horrible events that night fourteen years ago, every ounce of love Aunt Ethel had ever held inside had disappeared.

As Charlotte had gotten older, she'd suspected that it was Mathilda Tugwer who'd found her and brought her to Aunt Ethel. Mathilda had as much confirmed it when she described a woman she'd known who resembled Charlotte. But every time Charlotte contemplated asking Mathilda about her, she couldn't bring herself to do it. There was a part of her that feared the disappointment of learning the reason why her real mother had given her up.

"Did ya hear?" Aunt Ethel asked. "I said I'd pay ya! How come you ain't smiling?"

Mercifully jolted back to the present, Charlotte squared her shoulders. "Ten pounds it is, then. And thank you very much. I won't give you reason to regret your generosity."

"I already do."

Aunt Ethel went back to work immediately, ignoring Mathilda and everyone else.

Verity, eyes large, retreated from the doorway back into the front room.

Feeling beaten and bruised, Charlotte pumped herself a jar of cold water and gulped it down, staying the tears that threatened to spill. She hadn't asked to be foisted onto the Smith and Aldridge families. She hadn't gone looking to be a part of the Smith Bakeshop in Brightshire, to cut into their profits. She hadn't caused Ruby Aldridge's baby girl to die. She'd been a baby herself. Who needed care. That was all. But one wouldn't know that by the way her aunt browbeat her at every opportunity.

Mathilda shuffled forward, her all-knowing eyes looking right through Charlotte as she handed back the marmalade jar. "You were saying about the bag of baked goods?"

"Yes, I was, before all this unpleasantness erupted." She thought of the last few days in the castle, the beautiful dress and sumptuous dinners, and her close friendship with the duchess and duke. But most of all, the thought of Tristen, and how he sometimes made her smile when he was really taking her to task, lifted her spirits. But why him? It was Mr. Winters who showed interest and had captured her attention from that very first day. She knew they had no future, but still she liked to dream.

"Verity will help you out front, Mathilda."

And I'll find some paper and start my own tab. What a feeling! She'd have money of her own for the first time in her life. She chanced a glance at her aunt to see how her words were received, but Aunt Ethel's head was down as she kneaded the bread dough, keeping her feelings concealed, as well as any love she might have hidden in her heart.

CHAPTER THIRTY-FOUR

I don't know what you want me to say," Thomas whispered that night in the barn loft. The lamplight made her brother's features waver in the darkness. When Charlotte had gone out to feed the chickens and rabbits and check on Romeo and her pony, Sherry, she'd made eye contact with Thomas, a signal her brother was to follow her out.

One side of his mouth lifted, and he said matter-of-factly but with a bit of humor, "I told you before, I don't know anything about the day the young duke died. I was fishing in the river miles away—and brought home several large perch to prove it. I wish you'd stop badgering me over this. You're beginning to sound like a fishwife."

Charlotte didn't take offense. She knew his tactics. He'd try to put her off, change the subject—but this time she wouldn't be distracted. He couldn't dodge her now that she had him trapped in the loft. She eyed his strong jaw covered in dark stubble. Thick, dark hair hung over his forehead, matted with dried perspiration after his afternoon of chopping wood. He needed a bath. When she went in, she'd warm some water. Since their mother had died when he was small, Thomas was quite competent at taking care of himself. All he'd known was the pathetic substitute for love from Aunt Ethel and the love Charlotte and his cousins showered on him. But, being the only boy, he was the king of the household. And a handsome devil too. Someday he'd steal away a young woman's heart and be off to make his own destiny. He'd told Charlotte many times that he wasn't staying in the bakeshop forever.

"I saw the duke on the knoll with someone who had a coat just like yours," she said. "And then later, when I was leaving the forest, you were skulking away. I can't help you if you don't admit what you were doing."

"You're wrong. You've mixed up your days." Squatting, he put his hand slowly into the pigeon coop, and the frightened bird backed away. Thomas looked up at her, and his eyes darkened.

She returned his scrutiny, unwilling to go inside until one of two things happened. One, he told her the truth, or two, Aunt Ethel came looking. This was the one place they could talk without fear of being overheard.

"I told you somebody has come forward and pointed a finger. If they knew I'd seen you as well, things could be very bad. Tell me everything."

"I don't need any help," he replied. "I don't know who you saw, but it wasn't me. I was fishing that day and—"

She gripped his arm, wanting him to know the seriousness of the situation. This time he could be in real trouble. Something he couldn't talk his way out of. "I've been trying to speak with you about this since I've come home from Ashbury, but you seem to always escape out the door the minute I'm free. We'll have this out now, Thomas. Why were you in the forestlands? You know that's not allowed."

"How many times do I have to tell you? I wasn't anywhere near—" He stood, hunching, unable to straighten his six-two frame because of the low barn roof as he stared at her. "And even if I was, who says they can keep all the wildlife for themselves when they already have so much? Tell me that? I've never heard anything so stupid in my life."

"Thomas, who is they? Why are you so angry?"

"The Duke of Brightshire—and *all* the lords over the lands! They have no right."

"They have every right. The law has been the same for hundreds of years. You can't change that yourself. By entering the land, you're breaking the law."

"You were poaching mushrooms. How many mushrooms does the castle need? Tell me that?"

The open loft door let in a breeze, which cooled her temper.

Thomas stuck his head out and sucked in a large lungful of air. The chasm between the aristocracy and the countryfolk couldn't be crossed—just like Tristen had said. And yet Thomas was suffering. Perhaps he'd just realized all the limits his life in Brightshire held for him.

"I saw you with my own eyes," she said to the back of his neck as he gazed out at the darkened town. "You didn't have your rifle, so I know you weren't hunting. Did you see the duke that day? Was that you and him up on the hill?"

Thomas leaned back inside, angrily seating himself on a wooden box. When had he turned into this full-grown, good-looking young man? His arms were thick with developed muscles, his legs strong.

"You mean, did I kill him? No!"

"What will you say when the constable questions you again? Because he will, you know. It's only a matter of time." Thomas looked so defiant, her heart trembled with fear.

"I don't know."

It was said so softly she hardly heard his response. She'd just begun to believe he was telling the truth—that by some miracle she'd made a mistake. Hadn't seen him at all. But now this.

"Tell me."

"I can't."

"Tell me. You can't keep something so important to yourself."

"I was there, but I won't admit that to anyone else but you. If they ask, I was at the river fishing."

"You have no one to vouch for that. Somehow, they'll trap you and make the circumstances seem like you're lying. You'll hang, Thomas, and there won't be any way for us to stop them. This is serious. I need to make you understand." Did she dare mention seeing Mr. Henderley too? Maybe Thomas was in the woods with the gamekeeper, and they were doing something totally different than speaking with the duke. Why was Thomas being so difficult? Why wouldn't he trust her? She didn't want to drag Mr. Henderley into this if she didn't absolutely have to.

Below, the barn door squeaked open. Charlotte and Thomas froze.

"Charlotte? Thomas?"

Verity.

"Are you up in the loft?"

Verity had a fear of heights and rarely climbed the ladder.

Charlotte came forward and peeked over the edge to see Verity looking very small as she stared up. The argument with Aunt Ethel today had taken its toll on her as well. "Yes, we are. I'm sorry to have been gone for so long. Is everything all right inside?"

"It's almost seven, and Mama is becoming restless. She's mumbling about you neglecting the night baking. I'm frightened. You both best come in so there's not another fight."

"We'll be right there. Go inside and get ready for bed, and we'll follow in one minute so she won't know you came out to warn us." Charlotte smiled, wanting to put Verity at ease. "Everything will be fine. Go on now, and thank you."

Without another word the barn door squeaked again, and silence surrounded them.

Charlotte stared at her brother, whose expression was stony. She'd get no more out of him tonight. And yet he'd just admitted he'd been in the forest.

What would happen to Thomas if the constable could prove it? Rather than settling her fears, as she'd hoped, this conversation had only increased them.

She reached out and squeezed his hand, letting him know that she loved him no matter what. "I'm off," she said. "I'll heat some water for your bath." She started for the ladder. "Don't be long."

CHAPTER THIRTY-FIVE

Oh, man boy, raised in shadows was,
Returns now from across the sea,
Thinks all is good, but does not know,
Recompense is owed to me.

Beranger, your pain I'll see,
And my revenge will be complete . . .

CHAPTER THIRTY-SIX

F inally feeling steady on his feet, Beranger strode down the hall-way in search of his wife. Six days had passed since he'd been forced to his bed, and he didn't want to recall the maddening hours of contemplation he'd endured. He'd felt like a fool waiting for the spinning to stop. As long as he remained perfectly still, it was bearable. But as soon as he moved, even the tiniest bit, his world exploded with vertigo. The experience reminded him of his boy-hood in the woods, gripping the thick rope he and his friends had attached to the large oak. Phoebe had been relentless, winding him up tight until he was far above the ground and then giving him a mighty push. Once released, he'd untwist at great speed. The only difference was then the twirling had been fun. Now the vertigo made him feel fifty years older than his age.

And if that weren't enough, the search for Emma's letter had been fruitless. All it had accomplished was to alert everyone to the crime. All the servants were walking on eggshells, expecting to be accused. Creating such suspicion was unconscionable, but there hadn't been a choice. He'd even called them all together and then searched their rooms. If the missing object had been anything else but Emma's letter, he'd have waited to see if some other way of finding it would turn up. Emma was in utter despair, and he didn't feel much better. But now that he was on his feet, he vowed to get to the bottom of things.

"Your Grace." Pencely met him in the hallway after he'd come down the stairs. "You're up and about."

"I am. And I don't want to talk about when I was not. I'm better. I don't know what was wrong, but now that I've improved, I'd like to forget the whole incident," he said as they continued walking. When they reached the great hall, open to the gallery upstairs, he stopped and looked around. His agitated feelings softened. "It's difficult to believe I'm back at Ashbury. I never intended to be," he said, glancing into the butler's face. "I was content in America. But now that I'm here, I realize I missed Ashbury and Brightshire, even England."

"We're all delighted to have you back. Ashbury lost its heart when you went away."

"I'm sorry to hear that, about losing its heart. A home as grand as this should always feel loved. Thank you for saying that."

"It's true."

He glanced about. "I'm waiting for a cable from Lord Harry, if not for the man himself. I had thought he'd have been back by yesterday. Any news of him?"

Pencely shook his head. "Is there trouble?"

"No. Far from it. You heard when I announced at the dinner that Ashbury Castle will be going into shipping if all goes as I hope. Well, it did. Lord Harry will be bringing the papers for me to sign. The process happened faster than I ever dreamed. A positive cash flow will be something new for this place, at least in a very long time."

"Another reason the staff is thankful you're back. And with a business education from America."

"I was self-taught."

"Understood. But we've all seen the writing on the wall for some time, and especially so when your brother was spending faster than ten dukes before him combined. The staff has been worried about their jobs. Now they'll breathe a little easier. The fortune you made is no secret."

"Good. And a fortune is being made in imports and exports. We may as well get in on the game. If the venture takes off, Emma and I have decided to give our employees a chance to invest in the shipping line, as a way to put their money to work. I don't know many of the staff yet, Pencely. Maybe you can help me out."

Allen Copley, the young, fair-haired footman, came into the room and passed through, giving Beranger and Pencely a respectful nod.

The butler's face clouded. "That's very generous of you, Your Grace. I don't know what—"

"Nothing yet. It's all still speculation. I won't allow anyone to invest until I'm sure it's a sound venture, and that might take a year or two. While we get that venture rolling, I wonder, do some of the staff hanker for a different way of life? Would they prefer to move to London and obtain factory jobs or the like?"

"Hanker?"

"Sorry, my Western influences are showing. Long for, or pine for. Desire to leave Ashbury."

"I see. I couldn't say for sure. Perhaps that's something I can look into for you. I believe most regard working at Ashbury a privilege, Your Grace. As do I."

"Thank you. Please do. There are some changes we can make here to help them, if that's their desire. Hire a tutor so they can further their education on their off hours, or Lord Harry could make inquiries for them with his contacts in London—help them find work. I would never want any of the staff to remain just because they had no other option.

Tell them that. Collect ideas. Both Emma and I are adamant that positive changes will be made here under our tenure."

"Very good. I will do that directly."

He nodded his approval. "Did you happen to see which way my wife went? Now that I've been up and around, even if only in our rooms, she's relaxed her vigil over me. It's been a relief. I'm not one to be pampered and babysat."

"I believe she was on her way to the stable to talk to her horse, at least that was what I overheard her say. I haven't seen her since."

"I'm off, then. Let me know if Lord Harry arrives."

With swift strides, Beranger headed toward the stable wing, telling himself the niggling worry he felt just now was stupid. He nodded at maids as he passed, and as he rounded a corner he realized he was rushing. Emma was fine, all was well. This was their home now. He couldn't be frightened for her every time she was out of his sight. That was foolish. But—something had made him sick. He'd never admitted it to her because, one, he didn't know anything for sure, and two, no reason to alarm her more than she already was. But the feeling was there. Inside. Demanding his attention. And he best not ignore the instinct that had kept him alive this long.

Ahead, Lady Audrey stood at the window, gazing out. In her hand was a piece of paper. When she heard his footsteps, she turned, and it fluttered to the ground. Before she could bend, he swiped the note up for her.

"Here you are," he said as he handed it back. Several words in her distinct writing jumped out. *Can't wait to see you* . . . Did the dowager know she had a secret alliance? Surely she wouldn't be pleased.

"Thank you," his sister murmured, stuffing the note into a book she held, and avoiding his gaze. "You're feeling better, I see."

There was no warmth in her tone. He couldn't figure her out.

"I am."

"Then I won't keep you."

That was plain enough. "Yes, good day," he said and left her by the window and her musings. He took a staircase down to the servants' level, knowing a shortcut. Growing up in the shadows did have some advantages.

He stopped at the laundry room and looked inside, where several laundresses went through mounds of linen each day, sorting, washing, ironing. There, at one of the ironing boards, was a face he recognized, glistening with sweat. *Phoebe.* He hurried in.

"Mrs. Lewis! What a surprise. You never mentioned you worked at Ashbury." A bruise on her face brought him up short. The mark was new since he'd seen her in the livery stable.

She gave a dip of her head and set the hot iron she was using back on the stove. The room was stifling. "Your Grace," she replied, lowering her eyes. "It wasn't something I'd want you to know. With seven children, my wages help to make ends meet. I haven't worked here long."

In the dark livery, he hadn't gotten a good look at her—and perhaps that was the reason she'd stayed in the shadows. And why Leo wouldn't keep their horses. Now he noticed her brittle hair, the mark on her face that could be nothing except a bruise, the fact that she didn't look healthy but had sallow skin. *So Leo hasn't changed a bit.*

A feeling inside pushed at his lungs. Guilt? Responsibility? What? He didn't like to think of her, a girl who'd loved the outdoors, working in this hot room all day long. "Do you like it?" *Stupid question. Who could?* The mark on her face had thrown him off. He hoped it hadn't been made by her husband's hand.

"It's work. And only half time. I'm not complaining."

They were drawing looks from the three other women. "No, I don't think you would." He glanced over his shoulder, angry at himself for feeling uneasy. Perhaps something could be done to this room to improve the working conditions. His stepmother had spent untold amounts of money beautifying upstairs when some of the money should have been spent down here. He'd take the subject up with Emma, and perhaps together they could think of ways to improve conditions.

Phoebe raised her gaze to his, and memories came rushing back. "What brings you down this way, Your Grace? Only servants haunt these halls."

"Well, I used to haunt them all the time, and I know this way to the stables is quicker. I'm looking for my wife and was told she went to see her horse."

"The one she brought from America? That cost a pretty penny."

Her tone was off-putting. He guessed he could understand why. The amount could feed her family for a year. That must not be lost on Phoebe or any of the staff. Yet it saddened him if she thought money was all he cared about now. He and Phoebe had been the best of friends when they were about six or seven, and even pledged their undying love.

He almost said that Emma was an heiress in her own right, to justify the money spent, but stopped himself. He didn't owe this woman, or anyone else, any explanations about anything. Still, he felt as if her poor luck rested on his shoulders. "Yes, she's very fond of Dusty. She didn't want to leave him behind."

Phoebe cut her gaze away to the large vats of hot water and the other three laundresses who had stopped working when he'd entered. He smiled, and they curtsied.

"No. If she had a heart, she'd not leave him behind. That might break his heart—and hers."

"Phoebe—Mrs. Lewis." He tried to smile, but the gesture didn't feel right on his face. "I'd like to help you and your family," he said quietly, surprised at the words as they came out of his mouth.

"My husband wouldn't like that," she said. She slowly raised her arm and with reddened, rough hands, touched the bruised mark on her face. "He has as much pride as the next man, I'm afraid."

Beranger nodded. "I understand. I . . . well, I suppose I'd best be on my way."

As he continued on toward the stables, he thought about what he'd said to Mr. Pencely, about how happy he was to be back at Ashbury. It was true. But it was also true that, for the first time since his return, he felt inexplicably sad.

CHAPTER THIRTY-SEVEN

Emma hurried down the opulent staircase of Ashbury, feeling help-less. Lord Harry was still absent. She'd feel better once he arrived. She met Pencely in the great hall downstairs.

"The mail, Your Grace," he said, holding out a silver tray that contained a letter. *How strangely things are done around here. I'll never get used to being treated like a queen. I don't like it in the least.*

"Thank you." Joy exploded inside when she lifted the envelope. A letter from Katie! Finally, some news from home.

"The duke was here asking for you. I told him I thought you'd gone to the stable. I hope I wasn't wrong. Did you find him?"

Preoccupied with the letter, she shook her head. "No. But I was only there a moment. Then I went upstairs with Carmichael to help her pick what I'll need for the tea when Lord Charles arrives next week." Disappointed, she glanced around. "I guess I just missed him."

With an appreciative nod to Pencely, she headed for the library, where she'd have privacy to open the long-awaited correspondence. Crossing the threshold, she pulled up when she spotted Lady Audrey on the sofa, working on some needlework. A small blaze snapped and crackled invitingly in the fireplace.

Since her and Beranger's arrival, his younger sister was rarely around and had remained aloof. Friend or foe, she couldn't tell. They'd gotten together twice to plan the festivities coming up in a little over a week and had all the invitations addressed and ready to send out. During those times, Lady Audrey had been quick with ideas and talkative, but then she'd lapsed back into detachment. Emma wished for the sort of closeness she shared with her sisters back home.

She seated herself in a chair across from the young woman.

Lady Audrey looked up and acknowledged Emma's presence with a polite yet noncommittal nod.

Lonely for her own sisters, Emma broke her rule of not speaking first to Lady Audrey or the dowager, so she didn't always feel as though she were asking for their approval. "What are you working on, Lady Audrey? The colors are quite pretty."

"Just a sampler piece," Lady Audrey replied, keeping her gaze on her work. Her hands were swift and supple, well practiced at her craft. Emma had never had much patience for stitchery. "What do you have there?" she asked, finally looking up and gesturing to the letter. "Correspondence from Colorado?"

"Yes, from my sister Katie." Just saying that filled Emma with happiness. She longed to rip open the envelope, but also wanted to take advantage of having Lady Audrey all to herself. This was the first private conversation they'd had. Perhaps the dowager's influence had made her elusive. Perhaps she could win Lady Audrey over as a friend and ally. "We never lived apart before I married your brother."

"You must be homesick." Lady Audrey set her needlework in her lap and repositioned herself on the sofa.

She looked so open and inviting at this moment. Yet there was something about her that made Emma suspicious and then ashamed of her distrust.

"I saw my brother today. He looks much better. I've been worried."

The first concern I've seen from her. Perhaps she's thawing.

"Yes. I'm very pleased. I hope we've seen the last of that nasty illness—or whatever was the cause."

Lady Audrey gave a guarded smile and tipped her head. "I've heard my mother refer to you as a mail-order bride. I know that's not the case," she said, hurrying on, "but do you know any mail-order brides? I can't imagine marrying someone I've never met."

Lady Audrey seemed truly interested. She didn't have some sort of secret plan up her sleeve, did she?

"I don't know any personally, but there are many brave and courageous women who have opted to change the life they have, or the life that is expected of them, to strike out on their own. It's true many have never met their betrothed face-to-face but have gotten to know them even better by months of letters. There is much to be said for truthful correspondence."

Lady Audrey's eyes were large. "Oh, I agree."

"But you, I've heard from Lord Harry, have many romantic prospects. Noblemen from around the countryside have been vying for your attention. That must be thrilling."

Beranger's sister glanced at the windows across the room and then back into Emma's eyes. "That is somewhat true," she said slowly. "Some have stopped pursuing me once they learned I would not become duchess after all."

"Then you've been spared, Lady Audrey. You wouldn't want a man after titles anyway! I can tell you, a love match is well worth the wait. Don't rush into anything."

A glimmer came back into Lady Audrey's eyes. "I agree. My mother says I'm still a good match, but I fear the man I'd be interested in would not meet her approval. She'd never agree."

"Time is your friend," Emma said. "Never say never."

A small smile pulled Lady Audrey's lips, and she nodded at the letter in Emma's lap. "Read your letter, because I know you're dying to. I'll just go back to my needlework."

Relieved, Emma opened the thick envelope. A puff of soft violet scent, just like Katie liked to wear, brought a surge of emotion. The sight of her handwriting almost made Emma tear up. Amid all the turbulence here, thinking of home was a pleasure. Would Ashbury ever feel like home?

> My dearest Emma,
>   How strange to think you all the way across the ocean and half a continent . . .

For the next twenty minutes, Emma was transported back to Eden, as Katie regaled her with updates on the ranch, the little shop she'd inherited, the new goings-on in their town. She lavished pages on each of their sisters that made Emma remember the many evenings they'd spent sitting on each other's beds, sharing gossip and encouraging each other's hearts and dreams. Lavinia and her new husband were still acting like they were on their honeymoon—which they were, since they'd married the same day as she and Beranger—though Lavinia had begun work on a new collection of hats; Belle, married the longest of the sisters, teased the newlyweds relentlessly, but she and Blake were making progress on turning a portion of the working ranch into a guest ranch for visitors; Mavis and the sheriff had moved no closer to announcing a formal engagement. Of her own broken heart, Katie said nothing, but in her endless list of questions for Emma about what England was like, and her repeated promises to visit, was a sense that she was moving on, beginning to relish life and her future once more. Emma felt herself laughing and tearing up simultaneously. Oh, this letter had arrived at the perfect time!

It was only as Emma flipped to the final page that her spirits crashed to earth as she was reminded of Beranger's ill health and the letter that had been stolen from her dresser, the last words her father had ever hoped to say to her.

Now, I must know what Father said in your birthday letter. We know you're busy and that's why you haven't written yet, but please have mercy. Write back today, if you haven't already. We all miss you and your smiling face very much.

All my love, Katie

CHAPTER THIRTY-EIGHT

Charlotte stood at the bakeshop window watching the leaves swirl in the street. Her mind was jumbled like the yellow and orange flurry tumbling by. Autumn. Her favorite season. The quietness of the earth was preparing for the onslaught of winter. Shawls and mittens would soon appear on women and children, and the tangy scents of pumpkin and cinnamon would fill every home. With a start, she realized the scent of pumpkin was on the air now.

Thinking about all her beloved things didn't lift her spirits.

Business had been slow all afternoon. Her gritty eyes stung from the lack of sleep. All night long she'd gone over and over the angry words from yesterday's confrontation with her aunt. And what was to become of Thomas? Only one customer had been in since two o'clock, which was unusual for a Friday afternoon. She hoped the sluggish business didn't have something to do with the turbulence that had hung over the bakeshop since yesterday.

Verity was in the kitchen with her mother making pies and other pastries, something they liked to do together at the end of the week. At these times, Charlotte ran the front counter, swept and tided up, and dreamed of a different kind of life, one of love and romance and perhaps a place of her own.

*Am I fooling myself? I had a chance to work at the castle and fool-
ishly let my feelings of indebtedness force me to remain here. Could things
change, or will I end up the spinster niece, always dependent on a woman
who can't stand me?*

Last evening, after she and Thomas had come in from the barn,
she'd found the constable speaking with her aunt after they'd closed for
the night. He'd been the law in town for as long as she could remember, and his wife was a good customer at the bakeshop. Alice, a sturdy
woman whose children were all grown with urchins of their own, came
in once or twice a week seeking something premade for their supper.
Unfortunately, by the looks on their faces, the constable and Aunt Ethel
had not been discussing food. When Thomas appeared, their mouths
snapped closed, and a fear zipped up Charlotte's back. The constable
had quickly pointed out a few scones, settled up, and was gone. Aunt
Ethel hadn't said a word.

Now, amid the blowing leaves, Charlotte could see Phoebe Lewis
headed toward the bakeshop with one of her young'uns and her husband. The child, her youngest, was called Cornie, which was short for
Cornelia. Small for her age, the little thing always seemed to want to
disappear from sight.

The three stopped a few feet away, and Leo and Phoebe began to
argue. Anger simmered in Leo's face. When he raised his arm, Phoebe
quickly stepped back. The little girl was dirty, and her hair looked as if
it hadn't been brushed for days. When Cornie caught Charlotte watching in the window, she ducked behind her mother. Finally, Leo reached
in his pocket and handed something to his wife. Charlotte didn't have
time to move away from the window before Phoebe and her daughter
turned her way.

"Good day, Phoebe, and you too, Cornie," Charlotte said as they
entered. She extended her arm and caressed the girl's cheek before she
was out of reach. "What would you like? Are you in need of something

for supper, or just a sweet to calm a little tummy?" She hurried around the counter.

The child ran to the display case, splaying her hands across the glass.

Phoebe nodded and said in a beaten-down voice, "Just a biscuit for this hungry poppet."

One biscuit with all her children. How awful to be so poor. Charlotte glanced over her shoulder, wondering about Aunt Ethel. Did she dare offer Phoebe anything for free? Charlotte had just bagged an assortment of broken biscuit portions not ten minutes ago.

Leo came close to the window and frowned inside, causing indignation to rise up within Charlotte. Couldn't his wife have five minutes of peace? When his gaze met hers, he turned his back and shoved his hand into his pockets.

"Which one would you like, sweetie?" Charlotte asked calmly. "What looks good on this blustery afternoon?"

The girl shyly pointed to a walnut fig, the largest of the varieties.

"Good choice. Those are my favorite too." Feeling bold, Charlotte handed one over the counter to the child, whose gaze brimmed with expectation. Lifting one brow, Charlotte pressed her finger to her lips at Phoebe. Beyond the window, Leo's back was still visible. Then Charlotte quickly wrapped up one dozen biscuits and the last of the walnut fig, and handed the package over. She'd pay for them out of her own pocket; she had a salary now and could afford this one splurge.

"Put it inside your coat," Charlotte whispered. "So Leo doesn't see." She looked at Cornie. "Our secret. For you and the others."

Charlotte lifted the bag of biscuit pieces. "I also have this sack for a halfpenny, Phoebe. They're broken, but children don't seem to care."

Phoebe nodded. "Thank you, we'll take that as well," she said, placing a few coins on the countertop.

Relieved to see her go before Aunt Ethel came out, Charlotte let out a breath as the doorbells jingled. But that feeling was short-lived.

Holding the door for Phoebe was Constable Kerrigan. He stepped inside.

Charlotte told herself not to panic. He'd watched her and her cousins grow up. He wouldn't want to see trouble come to Thomas. She tried to smile but felt her lips wobble.

"Good afternoon, Constable. How is Mrs. Kerrigan? I usually see her on Friday afternoons. I hope she's not unwell." The man's familiar smile did little to thaw the ice that had formed in Charlotte's veins. Where was Thomas anyway? She hadn't seen him for a few hours.

"As well as can be, Charlotte. That woman will outlive me by fifty years, mark my words." He put his nose in the air and smiled. "You're one lucky girl to spend your days in here. What's baking? Pumpkin scones? Pie? I'd get so fat I'd not be able to fit through the door."

"Pumpkin biscuits." Maybe she was wrong. Perhaps Alice had sent him in to pick up something for supper. He was acting so friendly. He wouldn't do that if he were here to arrest Thomas, would he?

His smile faded. "Your brother around? I need him to come with me to my office and talk over a few things."

Oh, my heavens, this is it. My nightmare has arrived. Once Thomas was down there, they'd lock him up. But not if she gave them some doubt by mentioning that she'd seen Mr. Henderley. Would Tristen think she'd made the accusation up about his uncle just to help Thomas?

"Why do you need him? Has he done something wrong? I couldn't help but notice your long face last night. That wasn't like you at all."

He stepped forward and lowered his voice.

She leaned over the glass display case to catch his words.

"Another man, a villager from north of Brightshire, has come forward to say he saw Thomas skirting the trees the day the duke died. He looked disheveled. Like he was sneaking. As you know, when I questioned Thomas before, it was because the bakeshop ties him to the castle. He'd told me he was fishing, but he doesn't have anyone to say they saw him at the river. I'd like him to clarify a few things for me, that's all."

"But why now? The incident was over nine months ago. Why did the man wait to say anything? That feels suspicious to me."

His eyebrow peaked, and a knowing expression came over his face. "He didn't say anything before because he had a very strong dislike of the previous duke. Called him arrogant. Said if he were murdered, good riddance."

She pulled away. "That's horrible."

"I agree. The law is the law for one and for all. The bloke should have spoken up sooner, before clues that may have been there were lost. Anyway, when he learned the new duke had returned to England to claim the title, he was happy. Then he learned the duke had begun to ask questions about his brother's death, so he felt compelled to come forward, whether his information would help or not. He's telling his tale now out of respect for the man. Back when the new duke was only a boy, and still the illegitimate son with different-colored eyes, he'd done the man a kindness. Dived into a swift river, unmindful of his own safety, to rescue the fella's pup that had fallen from the bank." Constable Kerrigan shrugged. "I have to follow up on all leads, Miss Aldridge. All Thomas has to do is find me someone to verify his claim to his whereabouts that day and he'll be off the hook." He laughed at his own wit. "As it were."

But he won't be able to do that, now will he? He was in the forest that day because I saw him with my own eyes. And then he lied about it to me for months. What on earth has he done?

"I see," she said. An invisible grip on her throat almost kept her from speaking. "Are there any other suspects? Any other suspicious forest crashers that you've heard about, or only Thomas? If he won't help you, are you planning to lock him up?" The man's dark metal handcuffs were hooked on his belt.

"No other suspects, unless someone else comes forward. It's rather difficult to investigate now, so long after the event."

He totally ignored the second part of her question about locking up her brother. Trouble was in the air for Thomas. "I'm sorry, Thomas went out this morning, and I haven't seen him since. I'll tell him you'd like to speak with him and send him to your office when he returns."

Kerrigan dipped his chin and then pointed at a golden-brown chicken pie on the lower shelf. "With that business taken care of, why don't you wrap that up for me. Alice deserves a night off, don't you think?"

"Oh yes, that's very kind of you. Just give me a second and you'll be on your way."

At that moment, Thomas stuck his head through the door from the kitchen looking for Charlotte. "Aunt Ethel wants to know if we're running low on tea cakes? Should she begin a new batch—" He snapped his mouth shut.

Constable Kerrigan gave Charlotte an accusatory look and then waved Thomas out. "Just the fella I'm looking for this Friday afternoon. How are you today, young Aldridge? Can you please walk down to my office with me so I can have a few words with you?"

"I can't today, Constable, I'm busy chopping wood out back. And then I have three chickens and two rabbits to butcher." He screwed up his face. "And pluck too. Can your questions wait until tomorrow?"

"I don't believe they can, son." He unfastened the handcuffs from his belt and held them out. "All depends on you. Now be a good lad, and make my job easy."

CHAPTER THIRTY-NINE

Having missed Emma in the stable, Beranger strode into the library, exasperated by the chase she'd given him. There wasn't much time before tea, and he wanted some alone time with his wife. When he saw Emma seated on the sofa across from Lady Audrey, a sense of relief passed over him.

The letter! The blessed letter safe in her hands. "The letter!" he blurted. "Where did you find it?"

She jumped at his outburst, so intent on her reading.

He hurried to her side.

She looked at him and then the pages she held.

Realization dawned. "It's not the letter from your father?"

She shook her head. "No. From Katie. Arrived today."

He eased down next to her on the sofa and kissed her forehead. "I'm sorry. I've let you down. I told you I'd find your letter, but I've yet to succeed." He was aware of his sister sitting close by, watching, and he remembered the note she'd dropped earlier. He had no idea whether she had a friend nearby or someone whose affections she'd been courting. They'd not had any chance to become truly acquainted, and he regretted that. She was the only living sibling he had. "Lady Audrey," he said, deciding to make the first move. "Are you and Emma getting better acquainted? I'm happy if you are."

"We are. Well, at least we were for a while. The letter she received is long and has captured her attention." A none-too-honest smile appeared. "But I understand completely, and I think she's just finished."

Pencely stepped into the room. "Your Grace, you have two visitors waiting for you in the east drawing room. Should I show them in, or shall you go to them?"

Beranger stood. "Who?"

Pencely's face grew red. "A Mr. Hill and a Mr. Brackston for the duchess."

Emma surged to her feet. "Trevor! KT!"

Before Beranger had comprehended his wife's outburst, she ran out of the room and was gone. He rose quickly, feeling a moment of vertigo, but he pushed through it and strode past a confused-looking Pencely, who had turned and was following Emma as well. He arrived in the drawing room in time to see Emma, and her yards of fabric, vault into the waiting arms of a man wearing cowboy boots and holding a tan Stetson, a cry of joy emanating from her lips.

Trevor Hill and his fellow cowboy, both longtime employees of the Five Sisters Ranch, stood just inside the massive doorway looking rumpled and tired, but as wide-eyed as Beranger would have guessed they'd be as they took in the sights around them for the first time.

"Oh my goodness," Emma gasped, now back on her feet after giving KT an enthusiastic hug as well. "I'm so happy to see you both! Am I dreaming? If yes, please don't wake me up."

Beranger hadn't seen such pure joy on her face since their wedding back in Eden. She fairly shook with excitement, her gaze drinking in each man, then coming to find him. As bad as it sounded, he felt hurt and a little put out.

"Look, Beranger, look who's here. Can you believe it? I'm so happy I could cry. Why didn't someone write and tell me to expect you?" She touched each on the arm and then let her hand fall away. "Thank you. Thank you so much."

Both Trevor and KT wore clean chambray work shirts and new denim trousers that looked like they hadn't seen an hour in the saddle. Their boots, clean and polished, looked strange on the elegant Moroccan rug. The men were like postcard versions of a cowboy, rather than grimy working ranch hands.

Pencely stood silent against the wall, taking in the sight of the Westerners. The footman Sleshinger appeared, his eyes wide. Beranger figured there were enough books about the West to have educated some of the staff, but seeing a real cowboy in the flesh would be a treat to most.

"Your sisters thought we should arrive without notice. That by now you'd be in need of a surprise," Trevor said, his gaze still moving around the room. He gave her an apologetic look. "I couldn't believe when we pulled up outside, Emma, but this is, well, er—I don't know what to say."

Emma laughed, and Beranger recognized the sound as true and pure, causing yet another stone to drop in his belly. She'd been putting on a good show until now, pretending to be happy at Ashbury—but the arrival of her friends caught her out. She'd clearly been miserable with homesickness all along.

The dowager duchess must have heard Emma's screeched greeting, because she appeared from wherever she'd been. Lady Audrey stood at her side.

Emma swept her arm out. "Isn't Ashbury grander than you ever imagined? Did you see the ancient swords hanging on the wall? And the proud suits of armor, England's past come to life? Also the Northcott coat of arms?" She turned to him. "Beranger, come say hello."

He nodded and stepped forward, pleased and surprised to see the men he'd gotten to know during his stay in Eden. He put out his hand first to Trevor.

Trevor enthusiastically shoved his palm into Beranger's, a wide smile on his face. "Good to see you! I had my doubts when crossing that ocean whether we'd actually get here. That water got rough a time or two and, well—"

"We thought we were headed to Davy Jones's locker," KT finished for him. "Tossing our breakfast and supper day and night. Think I lost five pounds. It wasn't a pretty sight, Beranger."

The dowager's sharp intake of breath made everyone turn and stare.

KT put out a hand, embarrassed now that he'd seen the other women. "I apologize for my colorful speech, ma'am and miss. Trevor and me are just mighty happy to be on dry ground. If the good Lord had wanted men to cross the sea, he'd have given 'em gills. Therefore, once I get home to Colorado, I don't believe you'll ever see me again— unless you make the trip to Eden yourself."

Emma, still in a bubble of euphoria, laughed and then hugged the man. "KT, you always make me laugh. I don't believe your colorful words made the dowager gasp, but the way you addressed Beranger. Everyone around here calls him Your Grace, or Duke, even Brightshire or Brig."

She was still laughing and missed the look of confusion, and possible irritation, that passed between the ranch hands. Beranger grew warm under the collar. When he was in Eden, they'd been equals and friends—and now they were supposed to call him Your Grace? He understood their reluctance, but not one other person here would. Not his relatives or the servants. How many boats was he willing to rock? He and Emma were already doing many things differently. Was accepting the title fair if his only intention was to change the way his people had been doing things for centuries? Not at all.

But KT and Trevor weren't his people. Yet as ordinary, untitled men, if they didn't call him Your Grace, they would seem, to the British, uppity and arrogant. For a moment, he desperately wished he didn't have to be a duke. Why couldn't he just be plain, simple Beranger?

Shame for feeling anything but proud of his family's history made him pull back his shoulders. He was the Duke of Brightshire, and he'd better begin to act in a manner befitting the station.

"I'm sorry if you're not used to our titles here," he said sincerely. "But that's the way things are done in England. If you're uncomfortable with Your Grace, just say 'hey you.' I promise to call you both Your Grace when we're back in Eden." He'd meant to interject a little humor, but he was the only one who laughed.

"Whatever you say," Trevor answered, conspicuously leaving off any means of address.

Emma must have felt the tension, because she reached out and took Trevor's arm. Introductions were made while the men, almost speechless, gazed around in wonder. "Now, sit down and I'll ring for something good to hold you over until teatime in two hours. Dinner is served at eight, and I know just how much you both eat. What would you like now—pie, cake, or something more substantial? You can have anything you want, just say." Her smile lit up the room. "I presume you came from Portsmouth?"

KT nodded. "Took a train and then hired a coach. Glad we speak the same language—or Trevor and me would'a been in a world a' hurt, bein' we don't speak any other tongue."

"You hardly speak English," the dowager duchess said from a few feet away.

"What?" KT asked, confused. "That's what I'm—"

"Never mind her," Beranger said, smiling at his stepmother and lifting an eyebrow in warning. Life was too short to always have to be on guard over every word. "Now tell us what has brought you all the way to England? It must be important."

CHAPTER FORTY

E mma feasted her eyes on Trevor and KT as they all settled into
seats. Their kind and unassuming ways were so refreshing compared to the dowager duchess and Lady Audrey. They reminded her of
Charlotte and Tristen, and the staff below. When they'd first arrived,
she'd thought she felt a stiffness from Beranger, but she hoped she'd
been wrong. The castle was large enough for one hundred friends to
visit, let alone two.

Trevor nodded, his boyish face bringing her immense pleasure.
"We've come by request of Blake and your sisters. To see what kind of
livestock you have. Cattle and sheep. See the castle." His face pinked,
and he cut his gaze from Emma to the footman who had arrived with a
tray of pastries, as well as a teapot and cups and saucers. He set it down
in front of Emma, and she began to pour.

"Of course we can show you cattle and sheep, and any other animal
you're interested in," Beranger said from beside her on the sofa. "But in
truth, I don't think that's why you're here."

"Maybe for breeding purposes," Emma interjected, feeling defensive. "A new line to cross." Why did Beranger seem so uncharitable?

Beranger smiled indulgently. "You came to check on Emma, at the
behest of her sisters, and make sure she's happy and well. There can be

no other reason. And I guess I really can't fault you. I would do the same. How long are you planning to stay?"

Emma turned back to her husband. "If Trevor says they came for ranching information, they have. He wouldn't lie." Keenly aware of how much enjoyment the dowager derived from any tension between her and Beranger, she wished her husband would voice his opinions later, after the woman got bored and left.

"Truth is, we *are* interested in your livestock. But Beranger"—Trevor snapped his mouth closed for a moment, his face turning red—"your husband," he went on, addressing Emma tenderly, "is right as rain. We miss you at the ranch and around town. With the fall roundup completed, me and KT had time to travel. In our lives, we've only been as far as Colorado and New Mexico. Time had come for us to see some of the world besides our own mountains and pastures. Hope you don't mind, *Your Grace.*"

Trevor emphasized the title, but not in a nasty way. He just wasn't used to saying it yet. Feeling mulish for snapping at Beranger, Emma reached out and took his large, warm hand and caressed it with her own. He really was wise beyond his years. He looked so handsome, defending his place as her husband and her love, and his ability to keep her safe and happy. She felt loved and appreciated by him, but also by her sisters and friends back home. She was the luckiest woman alive.

When Beranger caught her look, his eyes warmed. "Not at all. The happiness your presence brings my wife delights me. In the future, I should make sure one or another of her friends or sisters are here at all times. She has enough of them to go around. I hope you'll stay as long as you like. Get to know the country. Travel, even. Unless you're needed at the ranch, you're welcome to make Ashbury your new home."

Unable to stifle her reaction, Emma buried her head in his chest, overwhelmed with happiness. She knew her mother-in-law was most likely repulsed at her display of affection, but she didn't care. Some rules were meant to be broken, and this was one of them.

The men ate and drank, seemingly unaffected by the dowager's skeptical inspection, as if they were goldfish in a bowl of water. Lady Audrey had relaxed and taken a chair close to their visitors, answering a question here or there put her way. Perhaps she and Lady Audrey would end up being friends after all. All they'd needed was a little time together—and an icebreaker like the ranch hands. Emma promised herself she'd make a point of seeking her out more often.

"Now, please put us out of our misery, Emma," KT said, brushing scone crumbs from his mouth with his fingertips.

Trevor frowned and pointed to KT's napkin.

No matter what, she'd not ask her friends to address her as Your Grace. Beranger had been born to the title, but she had not. Trevor and KT most likely wouldn't be here that long. She didn't want to cause ill feelings between them. She was still relishing the fact they'd ventured across the wide-open sea for her.

KT smiled his endearing smile, making Lady Audrey blush, then raised an eyebrow at the mess in his lap. "Please excuse my poor manners," he said. "I was born in a barn—*God's truth*. Amongst the calves and chickens, but I'll work on doin' better. Be a gentleman while I'm here. Anyway, everyone in Eden is dying to know what your father wrote to you. Amazing how your sisters' letters sorta reflected how they turned out—in a loose sort of way, how they were born seems to have influenced their growing up. We've been taking bets in the bunkhouse. I say you, being the middle sister and never causing a ruckus, didn't cause your mama any grief at your birth. And that John himself delivered you, not at home but somewhere in a town shop, since you like fashion, or maybe even at a church social."

Now that KT had filled his belly, he was all smiles. Two years younger than Trevor at twenty-seven, he could be a flirt when he wanted but mostly kept to himself, unless he knew you well. A red bandanna tied around his neck enhanced his cowboy flair. His thick black hair, darker than Trevor's walnut-colored locks, had a hat crease on his forehead that ran just above his ears all the way to the back of his head. She wondered what the staff thought of his clothes.

The younger footman, Allen Copley, had joined Sleshinger and Pencely against the wall, to stand at attention and listen. She'd bet some of the other servants might be listening from the other side of the door.

"Trevor thinks, since you were born the end of August, when the weather can run hot, maybe that year there'd been a drought and John and the town were concerned over the river running dry. He'd been out checking with his wife in the wagon and she went into labor and couldn't make it home. Some say a long birth, some say short, some say outside, and some say at home. While others say . . ."

"Heaven's saints alive, KT! Just let her tell us before we all die of old age!" Trevor interrupted, his face a cloud of embarrassment. He was closer to the dowager and could hear all the little distressing sounds the older woman had made, one right after the other, over the indelicate topic.

"I guess you're right. She won't want to know what Tank said."

Trevor sliced his hand along his neck in a cutting motion. "KT!"

"What?" Emma asked, her eyes bright. "What did Tank say?"

KT's face turned red. "You'll have ta ask him yourself if you want to know."

Trevor rolled his eyes.

Emma dreaded this moment. Beranger squeezed her hand, giving her courage. "I don't know what the letter said. It was lost before I had a chance to read the contents." Her eyes stung painfully, and she couldn't meet their gazes. She felt wretched, so irresponsible.

"It was taken from our room," Beranger quickly explained to their blank stares. The news had seemed to render them speechless. "She'd been waiting for a special moment to partake."

Both KT and Trevor sat straight, all the humor and light extinguished from their eyes.

"Gone?" Trevor repeated in disbelief. "Stolen?" With narrowed eyes he glared at the staff against the wall. "John Brinkman was a *good* man, the best. I loved your father like my own," he said to Emma. "This troubles me more than you could know. Have you told your sisters?"

She shook her head, unable to get any words past the emotion clogging her throat. Telling anyone in Eden was the last thing on earth she wanted to do. She couldn't imagine the moment. There had to be a way to find the letter. There was no other option.

Trevor glanced at KT, who returned his stalwart expression. The two seemed to transform right before her eyes from her friendly ranch hands to battle-hardened warriors.

A rueful smile appeared on Trevor's face. "Then I guess we showed up at the right time after all."

CHAPTER FORTY-ONE

Unable to control her fear for her brother, and Aunt Ethel be darned, Charlotte darted through the kitchen and out the back door the moment the constable left with Thomas at his side. She needed some time alone, to think, to plan. Would she be able to find the knoll where the duke had died so she could look for clues, or was that a hopeless possibility?

"What's wrong with you?" Aunt Ethel screeched to her retreating back.

Ignoring the question, Charlotte darted into the barn, frightening the poultry into fits and scattering the bunnies to the back of the hutch. Sherry spun in her stall, sticking her head into the corner. Grasping the ladder, Charlotte ascended into the loft and threw herself onto the hay.

The flutter of wings sounded as the first sob passed her lips. She froze, realizing that Tristen was there, with Romeo on his finger.

Embarrassed, she gulped down a breath to steady her emotions. She didn't dare look up, but she heard movement. Was he coming closer? Why hadn't she guessed he might also be out here today? He came and went without bothering her aunt, spending an hour or two training the pigeon.

"Charlotte, what's wrong? Why are you crying?"

He touched her shoulder, and she heard him sit in the hay beside her. "Has your aunt hurt you in some way?"

Oh, Aunt Ethel would love to catch her like this with Tristen. No matter how innocent a situation, she always liked to think the worst.

Corralling her emotions, she sat up and wiped the tears that had spilled to her cheeks.

His gaze slowly perused her, but in a good way, a caring way, and she knew he was looking to see if she'd been abused. His attention and concern made her feel cherished, not an object of desire. He reached forward and brushed away a tear with his thumb. "Has this something to do with Mr. Winters?"

Mr. Winters? She hadn't even thought of him since she left the castle.

"Tell me. Maybe I can help."

He couldn't help. Nobody could. And when he found out what she intended to do, implicating his beloved uncle, he'd never speak to her again, let alone comfort her in the barn. She shook her head. "I can't."

To her surprise, he moved so close his leg brushed her skirt. The sight caught her attention, and she couldn't look away. Why had her heart and attention been on Mr. Winters? It was as if her eyes had been opened and she saw Tristen now for the first time. He was so kind, so caring with her. He didn't need to flirt, because there was never any doubt that his intentions were honorable.

"Tell me," he said again, his voice strong, determined. "You're not alone in your troubles. I don't like the anguish in your eyes."

Decision warred inside her. Should she tell him? Having someone to confide in would feel so good.

"It's just that Thomas wasn't the only . . ." Shocked she'd almost mentioned his uncle, she snapped her mouth closed and took a breath. "What I really meant is the constable has taken Thomas down to his office for questioning. I fear Kerrigan will pin the duke's death on him. That Thomas will be blamed and then hanged."

"Because of what the dowager said? Just because one person has come forward to say they saw him doesn't make him guilty. Your brother said he was fishing that day. Far from where the event happened. You shouldn't worry so much. He'll answer a few questions, then Kerrigan will have to let him go. I wish the duke would stop his questions. What good are they doing except upsetting people?"

The sound of his voice, and the words said so confidently, lulled away her fear. She raised her lashes to find him watching her intently. His gaze caressed her face. Without saying another word, he lowered his lips to hers.

She shuddered as he slowly laid her back in the hay. Her breathing quickened, and she wondered what on earth she was doing. This felt right and good, not the way her insides had tightened when Mr. Winters had touched her palm. Tristen gathered her closer until she was floating on air.

When he drew away, she slowly opened her eyes.

"I apologize," he said quickly. "I took liberties. I'm not what you need, Charlotte. Far from it. I took advantage of your grief." Tristen stood and brushed off the hay. "I'll go down to the constable's office and see what I can find out about your brother. I'm sure your fears are for naught."

Why had he kissed her? And why was he recanting now? She didn't understand men at all. She glanced away from his penetrating gaze. "You're wrong. They're not for naught," she said softly, wondering how much she should say. She climbed to her feet and brushed the hay from her skirt as well. "I was picking mushrooms that day in the forest. I saw Thomas myself, sneaking through the brush as if he had something to hide. My brother is in more trouble than we know."

CHAPTER FORTY-TWO

"Come on," Tristen said. He reached out a hand for Charlotte to take. "I want to show you something."

"What?" Charlotte said, still reeling from everything—her fears for her brother, *the kiss*. She was afraid Tristen might try to kiss her again. Part of her wanted him to, and yet part of her feared it would only wound him more, knowing she'd kissed him while all the time she'd been contemplating turning his uncle in to the constable.

"Don't be shy," he said, and the warmth in his eyes assuaged her. She let him take her hand, noticing how his work-roughened skin slid against hers. He gently led her over toward Romeo.

"Keep your hand in mine," he said. And lifting her arm so that they were making the same movement in unison, he extended her pointer finger, then made a soft whistling sound.

To Charlotte's astonishment, Romeo hopped from his perch onto their fingers. "Oh!" she exclaimed, conscious of the unfamiliar feeling of the pigeon's talons and Tristen's nearness behind her.

"He has to get used to you," Tristen said softly. "To obey your commands, much the same way I imagine you trained Sherry."

Charlotte nodded.

"Next time, I'll teach you to whistle, but for now, do you want to see how far he's able to fly and still return home?"

Charlotte's heart thrummed with delight. "Do you mean you've trained him so quickly? Should I write out a message for the duchess?"

"Not quite yet," Tristen said. "My uncle told me that it's best to get him used to flying along a particular path first. A little farther each day for him to fly and then return here, so he doesn't lose his way. Eventually, I'll show you how to attach a message to his leg so he gets used to flying with it. Ready for the next step?"

Charlotte nodded.

Tristen slid their arms toward the loft window, gave another whistle, and Romeo flew off in a flutter of wings.

"Now come on!" he said, pulling Charlotte toward the ladder.

They raced down the ladder and out of the barn. High overhead, she could see Romeo veering toward the creek. Laughing, she followed Tristen, ignoring the startled looks of people milling about the town as they ran toward the forest. Keeping Romeo in sight was difficult once they entered the woods. When he finally landed on a branch in an open area by the creek, they stopped as well. Charlotte laughed again and pointed as Romeo watched them from the top of a tree. The bird seemed content to bob on the swaying branch far above the earth. She imagined the air tickling him and what it must feel like to be free for the very first time. The air was cool and crisp, and she filled her own lungs with goodness. Did Tristen feel the same jubilation she was experiencing?

"Here, sit." Tristen motioned to a fallen log. "I'll let him catch his breath as well before I whistle and see if he flies home."

Alarmed, she gaped at him. "Will he do it?"

Tristen lifted a shoulder. "Not sure. But he knows where his coop is, and homing is bred in his blood. We'll know soon enough."

Watching Tristen next to her, Charlotte felt certain this moment would be seared in her mind, heart, and soul. It had been the perfect antidote to her melancholy worries about Thomas.

"Romeo is making great strides," Tristen said. "I'm not as sure about Juliet. She seems to be a bit slower to catch on."

He glanced at Charlotte and winked. His hair brushed his forehead, and she thought she'd never seen such a handsome man.

"Tomorrow I'll take them both out about a mile and see how they do getting back to their coops. If that goes well, I'll switch them before long and try the opposite way. Shall we walk back ourselves?" He stood and pulled her to her feet. "Ready to go?"

She nodded. "Yes, by now Aunt Ethel will be furious that I'm gone."

Tristen whistled, and Romeo took flight. For a moment she held her breath, worried the bird would fly off, but he circled three times above their heads and then headed back toward Brightshire.

They'd started walking back that way themselves when, ten feet ahead at a turn in the narrow path, Mathilda stepped out of the brush, the basket on her back filled with grasses and plants.

"The forest is busy today," Tristen said. "And to think I imagined we were all alone . . ."

"Good day, Mathilda," Charlotte greeted her, happy to see the midwife. She hadn't seen her since the scene in the bakeshop, but the woman had been on her mind. As she'd been thinking more and more about independence from her aunt, she thought that she might finally be ready to learn what Mathilda knew about her mother. Whether her mother was alive, whether she'd loved Charlotte and hated to give her up, or whether she'd been happy to be rid of her. It was a question she wanted answered, but she no longer worried it would define her the way she once might have. Between Tristen and the duchess, she knew who she was, and she knew she had friends who loved her.

"Hello, gamekeeper." The midwife bobbed her head. "Greetings, my little baker." Her eyes twinkled, but there was a very intense look there. "I have something important to share."

Charlotte's first thought was one of dread, the earlier events of the day coming back to her: *Thomas! More people have come forward. Or did Mathilda herself see him that day?*

Mathilda stepped forward and took her hands, something she'd never done before. "Wipe the dread off your face. You have nothing to be frightened of."

The old woman let go of one of her hands and reached deep into her cloak pocket. "I've carried this with me every day for almost twenty years. Today is the day to give it to you. I would've waited for your birthday, like I was told ta do, but after the row Ethel Smith put up the other day, the time has come."

"What is it?" Charlotte asked, unable to stem the quiver in her voice.

"Look and see."

With shaking hands, Charlotte unfolded the time-yellowed paper, the edges worn and tattered. She couldn't imagine what it was.

She glanced to the signature.

With all my love, Florence Witherspoon, your mother.

Charlotte gasped, and her legs buckled.

Tristen jumped forward to catch her and ease her to the ground. "What is it?" he rasped. "Who's it from?"

Mathilda crouched to the ground as well, and Tristen followed.

"My mother," Charlotte squeaked out, and her hands began to shake.

"Before you read, I'll tell you how I came to have it," Mathilda said, wrapping her cloak more closely around her frame.

Charlotte waited with bated breath.

"The evening in late April was mild, and I was out searching for plants, as is my way, preparing to assist the widow Ruby Aldridge of Brightshire who was due to birth soon. I wasn't in these woods, but south of Brightshire a good hour. A snap of twigs made by a human foot caused me to hide. Many don't like me. I have to be careful." She looked straight at Charlotte. "But it weren't no man come to tar and feather me for a birthing gone wrong, but a small slip of a girl with a huge belly and a bright scarlet face. I didn't even have to touch her to know she was burning alive, and not from her labor. She reached out a hand, but before saying a word, she fainted straightaway."

Tristen scooted closer and draped his arm around Charlotte's shoulder, lending her strength.

"I made a bed from sweet grass and flowers. I bathed her face with cool water and wished I had some willow bark, although there weren't time much for a fire. When her pains woke her, I gave her water and had her suck tuber roots for energy. The little food I carried was gone in the blink of an eye, she was that ravenous. Maybe if I hadn't been so far from my home, and I could have dragged her there, I might have saved her." Mathilda glanced at the clouds, shaking her head. "I guess God had other plans. She birthed you with little problem, and when I put you to her breast, she seemed to revive. Rarely did she take her eyes from you or stop fondling your wheat-colored hair. When you finally stopped suckling, she nestled you to her side and asked if I had any paper and a writing tool. Me, I thought, I never had any until that day. Given to me in payment for a tincture. I gladly handed over what she'd requested and watched her write that note. I've never read it, mind you. She made me promise to find you a home if she died. And to give you this note on or around your twentieth birthday, or sooner if you married. I figured now was the right time."

When Mathilda had finished, she nodded, as if agreeing with herself about something as she gazed at Tristen. "Go on and read the letter, girl. Then if you have any questions, I'll do my best to answer."

Filled with a deep hurt but also excited to learn about her mother, Charlotte first studied her mother's beautiful handwriting, blessing her for the valiant effort she'd left behind for her daughter. There were no words to describe the love that had expanded her soul.

CHAPTER FORTY-THREE

Tristen's mind churned. After reading the letter Mathilda had given Charlotte, she'd wanted to speak with the duchess immediately, so they walked on to Ashbury. Tristen had thought he had all the time in the world with Charlotte, that she'd be working in Brightshire and he'd be seeing to the duke's forests, their paths crossing often since the duke and duchess had taken them both under their wings.

That would not be the case now at all.

He studied the elegantly furnished parlor of Ashbury Castle. This was where highborn people lived, not Welshmen who had done a stretch in prison. He didn't belong here—of course he enjoyed sitting on these expensive chairs and admiring the fine artwork on the walls, but he knew his place. Everyone else in the room had a right to be here, including the duke, the duchess, the duchess's friends from America—and Charlotte too.

It was easy to think Mr. Winters would turn on the charm in earnest now that there was nothing standing in his way. Charlotte, Mathilda's letter had revealed, was highborn, just like Winters. Tristen certainly couldn't object to the man making her his wife. He'd give her a fairy-tale life, something akin to one in a storybook.

Feeling cantankerous, Tristen sat back, staring at the flames crackling in the fireplace. The duke and duchess were doing their best to make sense of the new revelations. The two cowboys—the duchess's friends from America, whom they'd just been introduced to—sat silently in opposite chairs, looking totally out of place. And what about Thomas at the constable's? Charlotte seemed certain he wasn't capable of killing someone. And yet, he couldn't help feeling she'd been holding something back. Did she know more about the day of the duke's death than she was saying? What could he do to help?

In astonishment, Beranger gazed back and forth between Charlotte and Emma. "Let me see if I have this straight. Your mother was the daughter of a well-off baronet. When she announced she was about to marry a young naval officer, without much to his name, her parents objected and disowned her. Your father went to sea never knowing you'd been conceived. A few months after, your mother received two letters, one from your father saying that his ship happened upon a shipwreck on the rocks that had an untold amount of gold aboard. In return for giving the treasure to the government, the entire crew earned a considerable prize, and his share of the prize money had made him a rich man. The second letter was an official announcement that proclaimed he had died at sea the day the HMS *Driver* wrecked on Mayaguana Island."

Beranger shook his head. "The same ship we spoke of over dinner. What are the odds of that? So your mother traveled to Kent in search of his family. But your uncle, his brother, had already taken possession of the prize money."

Charlotte nodded, her face and eyes dark with emotion. "Yes, that's what the letter says. Because they'd disinherited her, my mother's parents never knew of my existence. This uncle, this evil brother of my father, let my mother know if she didn't leave and take her unborn child away, neither one would live to see another day. Florence, my mother, was in labor when Mathilda found her wandering the woods.

She was ill and lost in her efforts to find a place to have her child after my father's brother turned her away, intent on keeping the inheritance that was rightly hers. Fearing she would die, she shared everything with Mathilda and wrote this letter." Charlotte held out the correspondence. "She begged Mathilda to find a safe place for me with instructions to tell me everything when either I married, so I would have protection, or when I reached my twentieth birthday. My mother thought I'd be old enough by then to make a sensible decision on what to do with the information. A few days after I was born, Mathilda delivered to Ruby Aldridge an infant girl who died moments after birth. Mathilda helped Ethel Smith bury the babe in a small box in the corner of the church-yard, and they agreed that I should be given to Ruby in her place. Ruby Aldridge never even knew I'd been substituted for the child she gave birth to. And that's where I've been ever since."

Tristen couldn't tear his gaze away.

A light came into Charlotte's eyes. "Mathilda marked my mother's grave and has promised to take me there someday soon."

"Does Ethel Smith know your history?" Beranger asked.

Charlotte shook her head. "No. Mathilda told her she found me abandoned under a log soon after I was born."

Mr. Winters took that moment to appear in the doorway. He was in his riding clothes and looked dashing, even to Tristen. Winters stopped and glanced around at the eclectic group gathered.

"What's this, Brig?" he asked, a broad smile on his face. "Have I missed something important? By the looks on your faces, I believe I have."

"There's been a revelation about our dear Charlotte Aldridge," the duke said. "She's really Miss Charlotte Witherspoon, the daughter of a sea captain who was the recipient of a grand reward. She's also the granddaughter of a respected baronet from Essex, Sir Luther Hastings. Have you heard of him?"

Tristen nearly rolled his eyes at the look of ecstasy that transformed Winters's face. He could practically read the man's thoughts: perhaps there would be some money involved if he chose to make a union with Charlotte. She'd suddenly become a good match for a languishing noble who hung on to the coattails of the Duke of Brightshire. *How fortunate.* The man always seemed impressed with everything having to do with money. Tristen crossed his arms and slumped in his seat.

Winters strode forward as if staking claim to his property. "That name *does* sound familiar. I'm not sure from where, but finding out won't take long. I'll go immediately—"

Charlotte reached out a placating hand. "Please don't, Mr. Winters. Not until I decide when and how I will contact my family. I just can't seem to believe what I've so recently learned."

The way she said the words *my family* so reverently, anyone could tell she was still in shock over the disclosure. Why had Mathilda chosen that moment in the forest to deliver such earth-shattering news? Why with Tristen there? He'd been enjoying the day with Charlotte, replaying the kiss over and over. Moment by moment, he began to feel grumpier. He'd been no good match for Charlotte even before she'd come up in the world. But that didn't stop his heart from wanting her.

Winters looked bemused. "But you must be so thrilled, dear Miss Witherspoon. You've been elevated, I can easily—"

Before Tristen realized what was what, he was on his feet and held Winters's arm in a tight grip.

Winters jerked back, trying to pull his arm free.

"Tristen, stand down!" Beranger ordered.

Tristen released Winters and stepped back, putting a foot between them. "You heard Miss Witherspoon! This is her business—not yours!" He could feel a truculent frown pulling his mouth. Shame for letting his temper take charge grounded him. How far had he been ready to go to protect Charlotte? Hadn't his ten years behind bars taught him anything about the uselessness of violence?

The duchess stood wide-eyed, as did Charlotte. Trevor and KT had jumped to their feet and stood at the ready to do whatever was needed to keep the peace.

Tristen flushed. "She needs time," he said in a more controlled tone. "Don't you, Charlotte?"

"What's gotten into you?" the duke said. "My cousin won't do anything Charlotte does not desire him to. Easy, man."

"I'll not be dictated to by the likes of you, *Llewellyn*." Winters looked to Beranger for validation but only got more censure from his cousin.

"Why don't you just make things easy and agree, Justin. You've put a damper on the good feelings of a moment ago. Give your word. I know how curious you can be at times when you don't have much to keep yourself busy. Go on, cousin. I'd like to hear your intentions myself."

Tristen thought he noticed the duke sway, just the tiniest bit. Was he covering up how he felt?

Winters forcefully straightened his riding coat. "I don't know what's gotten into you all, but yes, I give my word I'll stay clear of Miss Witherspoon's business. Though I only meant to help."

Charlotte spoke up. "Thank you, Mr. Winters. I understood your offer as help." She lifted one eyebrow at Tristen. "Mr. Llewellyn's reaction was uncalled for."

Tristen took himself back to his chair by the fire to lick his wounds in private. Was her head turned that easily? Had the kiss that had meant so much to him meant nothing to her?

It didn't matter. It couldn't matter. Even if she did care for him, he was no good for her. Hadn't he just proven it? He was no good for her when she was a baker's assistant, and he was no good for her now that she had a pedigree. She deserved the new life she'd have, one where she could have all the beautiful blue dresses she wanted, dine on succulent ten-course dinners every night, and never have a care in the world beyond which gown she'd wear for tea. He was happy for her.

His gaze strayed unbidden over to Winters, looking so smug as he chatted quietly with Charlotte and Emma. Yes, the man at her side could give her those things, but would he break her heart as well?

If he did, there was probably not a thing Tristen could do about it anyway.

The footman helped Charlotte from the carriage in front of Smith's Bakeshop, a storm of emotions wreaking havoc with her stomach.

Thomas, please be here.

Whatever happened, she needed to make him and her cousins understand that she would never abandon them. Whether they were blood kin or not, rich or poor, they'd always be her family. Even Aunt Ethel too.

Once Charlotte's feet touched the ground, she turned back to the open door. Emma smiled at her. "Don't be nervous. I won't leave until you come out and let me know everything is all right between you and your aunt. If your mother hadn't wanted you to search out your true family, she'd not have left the letter." She sent a soothing smile. "Once Mrs. Smith has found a suitable replacement, you'll return to Ashbury to stay with me. Don't forget, we have the ball to look forward to in just a week!"

Bolstered by the duchess's words and kind offer, Charlotte went inside, greeting Verity with a hug. "Is Thomas around?" she whispered. She wondered if Verity even knew he'd gone with the constable.

Verity cocked her head and nodded. "Of course. Still out back chopping the wood. Seems rather slow today."

Relief flooded her. So Thomas had gone and returned unnoticed. She hoped he'd put the constable's questions to rest. "Thanks." She squeezed Verity's hand. "Now follow me, I have something to share."

When Charlotte and Verity entered the kitchen, Aunt Ethel set aside the rolling pin. "Where've you been, missy?" she asked sharply, then glanced at the rolled-out dough before her. "This is *your* job. Gallivanting around, I'd guess." She began placing biscuit cutters over the dough.

She'd best just get the news out as fast as she could. If not, she'd lose her courage. "There's something I'd like to speak with you about, Aunt Ethel."

Ethel glanced up. She narrowed her eyes. "Don't tell me you want a raise already, you thankless girl, because if that's the case, I'll have ta send ya packin'. You've only been on the payroll one day!"

Charlotte came a few more steps into the room where she'd spent most her life. The small place felt stifling. "No, I don't want a raise."

"What, then? I can't read your mind."

"I ran into Mathilda in the woods today. She had some interesting things to say." She watched the woman she'd considered her aunt very closely. "She told me who my mother was and where her people are. My name is Charlotte Witherspoon, and I hail from Essex."

Ethel blinked. Certainly, by her reaction, this was news to her. Behind her, Verity gave a small gasp.

"I'm the granddaughter of a baronet named Sir Luther Hastings. My father was a sea captain who died at sea."

Aunt Ethel's face transformed into a mocking grin. "My *lady*," she said sardonically and then curtsied, even while holding a dough-covered star.

"I'm sorry if this is distasteful for you. I've come to let you know I'll be leaving to look for my family, but not until you can find a proper replacement. I had hoped you might be a little happy for me, but I can see that is not the case."

"You always were a big talker. And now I know why. No, you'll not stay here. I've gotten used to your absence. Collect your things and go.

Verity and I will get by. We still have Thomas. We've learned to make do without you."

That hurt. "No. I won't do that. I'm not leaving until you hire someone else."

The butter-and-lard man stuck his head in the back door. "Hello in there," he sang out happily. "Who's bringing me the containers?" He glanced expectantly at Charlotte.

Aunt Ethel smiled while holding her gaze. "If your daughter is still looking for work, Laurence, send her my way."

His smile faded. Over the years he'd seen the way Aunt Ethel had treated Charlotte. "Why?" His imploring gaze reached out to Charlotte, as if he'd been the cause of the trouble between them. He'd always been a nice man, and kind to her. A port in a storm. But paying jobs, in respectable businesses, were difficult to come by for girls and young women. Sandra would do well here, if she could put up with the abuse.

Charlotte nodded to him. "That's right, Mr. Butter," she said, using the name he'd been given by the children. "I'll be leaving soon. If Sandra is interested, she can have my job. I'll be happy to train her."

A smile spread across his face. "You're sure?"

Again, she nodded.

"Then I'll tell her today, Ethel, Charlotte. She'll come by as soon as I finish my rounds."

"It's *Miss* Charlotte now," Ethel said with a sneer and went for the containers. "Oh, and you can tell the duchess I won't be coming to that ball she's throwing. And neither will any of my relations."

Laurence's eyes brightened. "I got an invitation too! We'll be there."

To think she was no longer part of the bakeshop that had been everything to her only a short time ago felt odd. Frightening and yet strangely uplifting.

Turning, she caught sight of Verity's bittersweet smile, but in her eyes was great happiness, and Charlotte supposed it was for her—for her new life, and what was to come.

But what was that, exactly?

For a moment, she felt a pang, wishing she could share her uncertainty with Tristen, hear his advice. And yet she'd been taken aback by how resentful he'd seemed—at her change of fortune? Or simply at Mr. Winters's resumed attentions? The memory of Tristen's kiss in the loft mixed with the feeling of Mr. Winters's touch on her palm, and she didn't know what to think or whom she wanted. How could she, when her entire identity had changed in a day?

The future, although exciting, felt uncharted. Charlotte would simply have to do her best, for that was all she could do.

CHAPTER FORTY-FOUR

H oly smoke, KT, would you stop that hummin'. You're giving me a headache. I can't think straight with you going on and on." Trevor shot his friend a dirty look and continued along the gallery. Emma had housed them in adjoining rooms just down from her and Beranger's suite.

"I can't get used to all this," KT responded. "It's darn hard to imagine being a duke or duchess. I feel like I'm living in the queen's palace, not Beranger and Emma's house." He scratched his hatless head and stopped to gaze over the balustrade to the floor far below.

Trevor, still striding down the hall, looked over his shoulder and backtracked when he noticed his comrade was no longer by his side. Leaning on their forearms, they watched the preparty preparations below.

"Tomorrow's the big celebration and we vowed to ourselves we'd find John's letter before then," KT complained. "It's been a week since our arrival, and we haven't found a clue. Our watching the staff has brought us nada."

"Except gaining a few pounds from hanging around the kitchen."

KT nodded. "I hate to say it, but I'm discouraged."

"I know how you feel," Trevor agreed. "We haven't been looking in the right places. No one would leave that letter in their room for fear of being found out. We gotta use our think boxes. Dig deeper. Emma doesn't say so, but it's weighing heavy on her mind. Her sisters will be plenty upset when they hear."

Two floors down, the footmen hustled this way and that, carrying flower arrangements, extra chairs, and who knew what else. Trevor preferred a spur-of-the-moment shindig with a campfire and a bottle of whiskey, not crystal punch bowls and tables of dainty food that looked too pretty to eat. That kitchen had been running full steam ahead since Wednesday. It was a wonder to see.

"Think boxes, huh?" KT responded as below them Lady Audrey came into view unaware she was being watched from above. Her mother appeared at her side, and they talked for a few minutes and then ambled off. "If you were Lady Audrey, and you pilfered your new sister-in-law's letter, where would you stash it?"

"Pilfered?"

"Yeah, I'm expanding my vocabulary—or at least tryin'."

Trevor chuckled. "First off, Lady Audrey is too pretty to do such a thing. But, for the sake of the argument, let's keep riding down the path you're blazing . . ."

"Fine, so tell me, where's the last place you'd expect for Lady Audrey to hide a letter?"

"I don't know," Trevor said thoughtfully. "In the forest? Or the town? But they're too far away for a quick deposit." He turned and stared at KT. "What're you thinkin'?"

"I've never heard her talk about riding, or liking animals in particular."

KT gave an exaggerated head nod. "Let's go."

Fifteen minutes later, and after several wrong turns, Trevor stood at the stable entrance. Fifty stalls lay before him, twenty-five on each side. "You take the left and I'll take the right."

KT looked dubious. "What'll we say if someone wants to know what we're doing?"

"That we're thinking of building a stable like this when we return to Eden and want to check out the structure." He lifted a shoulder. "I know it's weak, but everyone thinks we're loony anyway. Our looking in every stall will just confirm their suspicions. But be careful. These skittish horses aren't our quiet cow ponies. Don't get kicked in the head."

With a nod, KT opened the first stall door and clucked to move the gelding back. The two men worked quickly and systematically, running their hands along the top boards and checking around the water and feed buckets hung on the wall. They didn't mess with the bedding, because it would have been changed several times since the letter had gone missing.

An hour later, covered in grime and sweat, they stood together at the other end of the corridor, still empty-handed. The stable hands working hadn't said a thing but gave them strange looks whenever they walked by.

"Damnation, Trevor. I thought we were onto something. I don't want to give up, but by now John's letter must be long gone. And that's a pure shame, because Emma'll never get over losing it." KT swiped his shirtsleeve across his sweaty brow.

With their shoulders slouched in defeat, they started back when Trevor pulled up. "What's that sound?"

"Birds?"

They turned together and ascended the short stairwell and came upon the large pigeon cage. Birds fluttered away, and others tipped their heads and peered at the cowboys through beady black eyes.

KT sneezed, grimacing at the cacophony of noise and feathers. "I never did like birds." He turned to leave.

Trevor caught his arm. "Since we're here, let's make a fast search, then we'll get back to the castle."

The row of small, dusty carrying cages on a low shelf looked as if they hadn't been touched in years. Trevor went down the line, lifting each. At the end, he exclaimed, "Looky here. I wonder what these are." He picked up not one letter, but a stack of small envelopes. "It's not the letter from John, but what?" Without worrying about propriety, he slipped a finger under one flap and pulled out the card inside. He read aloud,

The Duke and Duchess of Brightshire

request the honor of your presence at a ball given in celebration of all the inhabitants of the region.

Saturday, the fifteenth of October, at seven o'clock in the evening.

Trevor jerked his gaze to KT. "What's this about?" He turned the envelopes over and thumbed through. "Lord this and Countess that." He quickly went through the fifteen envelopes. "The invitations to the ball."

KT frowned. "Not all of 'em. The stack I saw was much taller than that. But there's no common folk named on any of these envelopes. Seems like they're only the ones to the fine folks around here. All the lords and titled people. Someone didn't want Emma's first event to be a success. Who would do such a thing?"

"The dowager duchess," they said in unison.

Trevor's expression grew hostile. "What can we do? The party's tomorrow. These manors and estates must be scattered all over the place, and we have no idea where they are. Even if we split up, we'd never reach 'em all in time."

"We could if we each took five," KT responded, making a fist.

"Your division is off. There's only two of us, not three. You need to go back to school."

"We'll round up that young man, Llewellyn. He should know where the estates are, and his uncle could help—being he's lived here all his life. Any other house staff might be missed if we involve them. We need to get to Llewellyn fast—and keep Emma in the dark. She'd be crushed if she found this out."

CHAPTER FORTY-FIVE

With maps in hand, Tristen looked uncertainly at the cowboys atop the tall thoroughbreds tacked up with English saddles. Trevor's gray mare wore a Pelham bit with double reins, KT's black gelding a snaffle with a single rein. Dressed in their Western clothes and cowboy hats, they were an odd-looking sight.

The wide-eyed horses pranced nervously beneath their unfamiliar riders. Not wanting to alert the duchess or the duke to the problem at hand, Tristen had agreed that distributing the fifteen undelivered invitations surreptitiously was up to them.

Feeling doubtful, Tristen held the reins of his own horse, which he'd yet to mount. "So you understand where you're going and who you'll deliver the invitations to at each place?"

Trevor and KT both nodded. Their horses, unaccustomed to the long length of their riders' stirrups or the way their weight was distributed in their saddles, pulled at their reins and swished their tails, feeling something wasn't quite right.

"Don't you worry about us," Trevor answered an uncertain smile on his face. "We'll stay aboard, but we can't guarantee the reception we'll get when we arrive. If these people are anything like the dowager duchess, we may get run off their land before we get a chance to open our mouths. And if we are given the chance, will they even listen—and attend? We're not givin' 'em much time."

"That all depends on how persuasive you are, my friends." For the sake of the new duchess, he hoped they were honey tongued and persistent.

KT's gelding half reared and then shook his head when his front feet were back in the gravel. He laid a steadying hand on the horse's crest. "Whoa, now, big fella. I don't like this any more than you do. I'd feel better atop Dusty, even if he is as old as sin. At least then my neck might not get broke." He reached down and felt the saddle. "I feel like I'm sitting on a tortilla."

I hope I don't get these men hurt. They'd opted not to use the familiar quarter horse in case Emma went to the stable and found Dusty gone.

Trevor glared. "You'll do fine, KT, quit your fussin'. Once you get out and warmed up, the two of ya will move like a well-oiled combine."

"Yeah, right. That's right after I land on my head. My gosh, it's a long way down. Good ol' Eden is feeling like a long-lost memory. I hope I make it home alive."

Tristen mounted. "We're wasting time. Your maps?"

Both men held up the hand-drawn maps.

"Good luck, gentlemen. I'll see you back here in a few hours. May our effort meet with success. And please, try to be careful. The duke and the duchess will have my hide if something happens to you."

CHAPTER FORTY-SIX

Emma stood in the center of the ballroom, amazed at all the people who had arrived to welcome Beranger home as the Duke of Brightshire. And to meet the new duchess from America. Most of those present were visiting the castle for the very first time. The entire staff had done a splendid job decorating the large ballroom, and the kitchen help had outdone themselves with tables of food that looked as beautiful as the morsels tasted. The dowager looked as gorgeous as ever, and Lady Audrey was all smiles.

Emma found the fact that Lady Audrey was often spotted swirling very close to the group of common folk from Brightshire quite strange. From the way the dowager had protested a ball that included commoners, Emma would have thought both Lady Audrey and her mother would stay close to the gentry, giving the others the cold shoulder. But that wasn't the case with Lady Audrey. More than three times, Emma had seen her smiling toward a group of Brightshire citizens standing in one corner with their punch glasses in hand. Amazing!

The village residents, including the livery owner, Leo Lewis, and his wife, Phoebe; Phoebe's mother, Mrs. Parker; and Constable Kerrigan and his wife, Alice, looked to be having a lovely time. The gamekeeper, Arson Henderley, sat in a chair waiting for his wife, Rose, and the other kitchen staff to finish up and join them. Charlotte had said Ethel Smith had refused to come or allow her younger daughter, Verity, to attend. That news had made Emma sad, but the woman was Verity's mother, and nothing could be done. And Beranger's uncle Lord Charles had sent his regrets—*again*. He'd canceled the tea with them last Thursday and now this. His continued absence made his feelings about Beranger rightfully inheriting the title quite obvious. More's the pity. Still, Lord Harry assured her his absence was nothing to worry over, that Lord Charles fancied himself an important man, and that when he was good and ready, he'd show up, ready to accept Beranger as his duke.

As her gaze crossed the room, Trevor and KT caught her fancy. Warmth filled Emma's chest—and suspicion too. Something strange was going on with them. The two ranch hands had been all smiles since last night after they had returned from somewhere with Tristen, as windblown as if they'd spent a day gathering cattle in Colorado. Where they'd gone or what they were up to was a mystery, and no one was saying. Whatever it was, they were well pleased with the outcome. And that made Emma deliriously happy as well.

At her side, Beranger spoke with Lord Harry, their low words indistinguishable because of the music. Lord Harry had arrived from Portsmouth several nights before. The two had been locked up in the library every day since, plotting how they would make millions on imports and exports. Emma was learning there was nothing her new husband liked better than a challenge. She smiled, thinking she'd been quite a challenge for him not all that long ago.

My rake! I wouldn't want my life any other way.

Lord Harry smiled and took his leave, leaving Beranger all to her.

The duke turned and lifted her hand to his lips. "I'm sorry to go on so long with Lord Harry over the ship on our grand night. That wasn't fair to you. I hope we didn't bore you to tears."

"I'm never bored when it comes to business, Your Grace, Lord Husband, owner of my heart," she teased. "You should know that by now. I'll have made crates and crates of dresses I've designed especially for my shop and the women of Eden by the time we're ready for the maiden voyage of *our* ship."

"You mean the *American Duchess*," Beranger interrupted.

She laughed, thinking he'd never looked so handsome. "Yes, yes, then, the *American Duchess*. Does she have a crew, or is that something you'll have to remedy? I know how you love to remedy a situation."

Beranger chuckled. "Yes and no. A skeleton crew only. I'll have to hire a captain. But I'm excited about the prospect. Now I'll have an excuse to spend time in the coastal towns by the sea."

She lifted a brow.

"I mean *we'll* have an excuse. I'll not leave you behind again."

Worry chased away the good feelings. She'd begun to suspect in recent days that Beranger was experiencing vertigo again, but he'd kept it hidden from her until last night, when it had sent him swaying to his knees just before bed. He'd been his old self this morning and insisted he felt fine, but until she knew the cause, she was still on edge. She leaned closer. "Beranger, did you see that nasty man from the Gilded Goose in Goldenbrook has arrived? He's been glaring our way ever since he came in. I don't like him."

"Give him a chance, Emma. My brother didn't treat him or his like fairly. He'll change once he learns I'm not Gavin—or my father. Have you seen Rodrick, his father, here too?" He stretched his neck, trying to see over the crowd of guests. The musicians had already begun to play another song, and a group of dancers lined up.

Her smile fell away. "I don't know."

"Is something wrong? Why do you look sad?"

She looked over to the musicians playing a reel. "I can't do those fancy dances where everyone lines up and bows to each other, Beranger. I'm sorry. I hope my inability won't embarrass you. The duke should make the grandest appearance." She glanced around. "Go find someone to dance with. I'd love to watch."

He laughed and then kissed her. "And neither can I. But we have our whole lives to learn. And I don't want to dance with anyone else but you. I know you can waltz, because we did at our wedding. Besides, you look so beautiful just standing here, you outshine all the other women in the room. I'm a very lucky man. Look, here come Trevor and KT."

The two ranch hands were on their way across the room, looking very distinguished in formal Western wear of black trousers, starched white shirts, and black string ties. Their boots were shined to a high sheen, hair combed perfectly, and their lean cheeks looked softer than a baby's bottom. She'd never seen either of them look so handsome. And there wasn't a hat in sight. "Where on earth did they get those fine clothes?" Emma whispered, incredulous. "And especially when they came back so rumpled yesterday. Those two never cease to amaze me. Do you know where they were off to or what they did?"

He shook his head.

Trevor and KT, both wearing large smiles as if they owned the place, stopped to speak with Baroness Eugenia Coldred and elderly Harriet Ninham, the Dowager Countess of Sarre, the two women Emma had entertained at her first formal tea. Harriet, the sweet woman that she was, had a new wig that was covered with an overwhelming amount of black curls and topped with a tiara. Her elegant dress looked beautiful. As little as Emma knew the woman, she'd already grown attached to her.

"What on earth is Trevor saying to the countess?" Emma whispered, amazed. "Have they met the baroness and countess before, Beranger? Do you know? If I don't watch out, they'll know all of Brightshire and Goldenbrook before I do. Those *scamps.*"

The Dowager Countess of Sarre placed a shaky hand on her chest and looked up into Trevor's face, her smile sentimental and sweet. She was obviously enjoying his attention. The baroness reached out and touched KT's arm.

Trevor looked Emma's way and winked.

She laughed. "He's shameless! I'd certainly like to know what they're up to, because you'll never convince me they aren't involved in some kind of shenanigans. Now, please point out some of the others, Beranger, so I'm not caught off guard."

He nodded toward a stooped, gray-haired old man in a black suit and leaned close to her ear. "That's Alfred Batkins, our solicitor in London. With his advanced age, he hasn't been out to Ashbury for many years. We should feel honored he made the trip. Lord Harry thinks highly of the man and said I should as well. We shall see."

"And that gentleman? Speaking with Lord Harry? He doesn't fit the image of a lord, and yet he looks more distinguished than some of the others." She looked up into Beranger's face, marveling at how much she loved him. "Do you know?"

"Well, I'll be. That's Stanton Wellborn the third, the man that was jumped by thugs in London when Lord Harry and I went to speak with Batkins. That seems like so long ago."

"The man whose life you saved."

"I'd hardly say that. Lord Harry must have gotten word to him. I'm glad he did."

"You don't know. He could have easily been killed if you hadn't thrown in to help. I'm so proud of you, *in everything*." She couldn't stop herself from going up on tiptoe and kissing his cheek. "I love you," she whispered. "So very much."

He actually blushed. Some rake! He wasn't at all the flirt she'd taken him for when she first encountered him in Santa Fe.

"Wellborn," Beranger hurried on as if to change her train of thought, "is a scientist at the Royal Observatory in Greenwich. They're working on a standard time for the whole country, as London has had for years. It's quite amazing."

"I don't really understand all that."

"You will. Train schedules, polling places, and the like." He nodded in deep thought. "I believe soon all the world will take this seriously."

"Well, he certainly sounds like an interesting man. I'd like to meet him."

Emma turned toward the dancers to see Justin and Charlotte dancing. Last night, when Charlotte had come to stay, Emma had requested Beranger's valet teach the younger woman the waltz. Now, with Justin leading, she looked as if she were floating on air. Her flushed face was lovely, and she looked gorgeous in another dress of Emma's. So much had happened to the young woman since Emma had arrived. She was glad she'd been here to witness everything and to offer her help.

"Justin has been captivated since meeting Charlotte," Beranger said, watching, "and now there's nothing standing in the way of his marrying her."

Emma cut her eyes up toward his face. "Doesn't Charlotte have a say in the matter?"

He scoffed. "Of course. Why would you ask that?"

"The way you said it. As if just because now that she's a lady, she'd fall into Justin's arms. If he was so attracted, why didn't he do more when she was a baker? I don't like the whole title thing."

"I didn't mean to offend you. Life is just that way. And I saw him giving her plenty of attention when she was still just a baker, even if they didn't see me watching. He's been trying to get her attention for weeks."

"We shall see. I happen to think there are more irons in this particular fire."

Emma looked around for Tristen. At the dinner party, she'd felt the energy crackling between their two friends, and whenever Justin paid Charlotte any attention, Tristen turned his gaze away as if he couldn't tolerate the sight. And when he'd walked her to the castle after the revelations from Mathilda, he'd practically jumped down Justin's throat to protect her. She was sure he had feelings for Charlotte and she for him.

But I haven't seen him all night.

She glanced again at Charlotte and Justin dancing. Emma had to admit she was rooting for Tristen—Charlotte would be cherished all her life by a man like him. Justin was charming, but was he steadfast?

Time, she supposed, would tell. By the way Justin was holding Charlotte, Tristen had better show up soon. A girl could easily lose her head—and her heart—on the dance floor.

CHAPTER FORTY-SEVEN

By the light of a single lantern, Tristen sat on the porch of the gamekeeper's cottage, staring off into the night sky. Bagley lay at his feet, lost to sleep as a light breeze moved the top of the trees. The dog was finally exhausted after a day of running through the forest. Yesterday, he, Trevor, and KT had successfully delivered the stolen invitations. But instead of feeling satisfied, Tristen found himself confused. He'd felt the need to be alone—to walk the forestlands.

In the last week, he'd continued visiting the bakeshop to train Romeo, but Charlotte, who'd been teaching the young woman who would take over her job, had barely spoken to him since his outburst toward Winters.

He was sad to lose a friend, but he was happy for Charlotte, he kept telling himself. She deserved the best. And now she could have everything life had to offer. Her days of working herself to exhaustion were over. If he really tried, he could acknowledge that Winters wasn't all that bad, and might even be a good match for her. Tristen didn't like him, but then he didn't have to. He wasn't marrying the man. Charlotte was the one who needed to love him, and just the thought of her wearing all those lovely gowns, like the duchess, should have made him smile—because he knew how much Charlotte had dreamed of that. But those thoughts didn't make him happy. Anything but. There was no help for it. The events of her life and his were beyond his control.

He reached down and fingered the warm fur behind Bagley's ear.

Without moving his head, the young dog opened his eye, and his tongue lolled out of his mouth.

"So you're just going to let her go?"

Tristen straightened and then stood, shocked someone had been able to sneak up on him without a sound.

Bagley climbed to his feet and yawned. Some watchdog he was turning out to be.

Mathilda Tugwer slowly moved into the circle of light made by his lantern. "What do you mean?" he asked, although he thought he knew.

"Our Miss Charlotte. You'll let her be swept away into a meaningless life with that shallow upstart. I thought more of ya."

"Why do you care?"

"I've watched over her since the moment she came into this world. She's the daughter I never had. I've been observing the two of you together as well."

He guessed that made sense. The woman did have a heart.

Tristen descended the steps and went to her side. "Winters can give her everything I can't. A home fit for a lady, acceptance by all the aristocracy, a future with hope."

"Those are just things. Not worth a halfpenny. He can't or won't give her what means more than those."

She stared a black hole through his forehead.

The soft cry of the lost baby undulated through the trees.

"I have a history. A match between Charlotte and myself wouldn't be good for her."

"Don't we all, my boy, don't we all . . ."

Bagley barked and bounded off the side of the porch into the dark night.

With a shout, Tristen spun and called him back, to no avail. Turning again to Mathilda, all he found was the dark night where she'd been one moment before.

"I'm sorry, Mr. Winters, but I must sit this one out," Charlotte whispered when the music started up directly after the last dance had concluded. "I really must catch my breath."

"Please, Miss Charlotte, why do you insist on calling me Mr. Winters? We sound like acquaintances. After all we've been through, won't you consider calling me Justin? It would please me very much."

What have we been through? I don't know what he means.

He gave her the same smile he'd so graciously bestowed on her whenever they spoke alone. She remembered their first encounter in the scullery and how he'd made her blush. Why didn't his smile move her now the way it had then? Perhaps because he'd totally ignored her request to sit the last few dances out and she now found herself whirling around the dance floor feeling like an impostor. She had to concentrate not to miss a step.

"When will you go to Essex to find your grandparents?" he asked, smiling into her eyes. "Soon, I'd think. They'll be delighted to meet you."

She let the music polish away the rough edges of his question. He was curious, just like everybody else. Her heritage seemed to be on everyone's minds. Well, she amended, everybody's except Tristen, who hadn't asked her one thing about her plans. She'd seen him coming and going at the bakeshop as she'd been training Sandra. As distressing as his lack of interest was, he'd hardly said more than a few words to her since the day at Ashbury when she'd put him in his place. His outburst had frightened her at first, but then she'd seen the look of remorse in his eyes. She had no doubt he was a good man. Each time he came to train Romeo, she found herself in the barn, cleaning the rabbit hutch for the second time that day or fussing with the chickens. Making sure Sherry had enough feed. "Will they be delighted to meet me?" she said now. "I'm not so sure."

She ignored it when Mr. Winters pulled her the tiniest bit closer as they waltzed around the floor. Speaking of Tristen, where was he? Maybe she could find a moment tonight to rectify things between them. She spotted Mr. Henderley, sitting in a chair, but there was no sign of his nephew. Was this her opportunity to get to know him tonight, and perhaps even ask a question or two without seeming suspicious? She scanned the throng of villagers, drinking punch and laughing, Thomas among them. The constable had let Thomas know that he planned to continue seeking other witnesses who could support Thomas's claim that he hadn't been with the duke on the day of his death. But Thomas was to remain close to town. At least he'd been allowed to attend the party, over Aunt Ethel's objections. For that, she was grateful.

"Of course they will. You're beautiful and sweet. The kind of grand-daughter any person would be thrilled to have. I'll escort you myself. But only when you're ready," he hurried on. "Just say the word and I'll drop my responsibilities here and we'll set out—with a chaperone, of course, now that your station has been elevated. We don't want to do anything to tarnish your reputation."

Her head snapped up at that. *You were all too willing to tarnish my reputation before by inviting me out into the moonlight.*

Why did everything he said suddenly grate on her nerves? She'd been anticipating tonight all week, dreaming about dancing in a beautiful gown in Mr. Winters's arms. And yet, if she were honest, all she wanted right now was to be back in the barn loft talking to Tristen, or holding his hand as they ran through the forest in the rain.

"Charlotte?"

Pulled back to the present, she tried to think of what Mr. Winters had just said. Unfortunately, with the music and all that was going on in her head, she had no idea. "Yes?"

"I just asked if you'd had a chance to get to know Lady Audrey any better now that you've moved into Ashbury?"

"I only arrived last night."

As he kept talking, Charlotte glanced away once again. Where was Tristen? *Why* had he stayed away?

CHAPTER FORTY-EIGHT

A pretty bride you bring with you,
What better way to crush your heart?
With emerald eyes and locks of golden hue,
She will regret your days apart.

Beranger, your pain I'll see,
And my revenge will be complete . . .

CHAPTER FORTY-NINE

W hat are your friends up to now?" Beranger asked, still holding Emma in his arms.

She didn't know. As the latest song ended, they'd made their way over to the musicians. People stopped to stare. Trevor clapped his hands together and asked for everyone's attention. She was too far away to overhear what they were saying to the musicians, but by the way the performers calmly moved back and let them take over, she figured this had been planned ahead. Out of nowhere, a Spanish guitar appeared in Trevor's hands.

Emma gasped. "I haven't a clue." She reached for her husband's hand, totally enthralled. "Let's get a little closer."

Trevor winked and smiled when he saw them moving through the crowd. Then the cowboy turned to the guests.

"May we please have your attention!" he called out in his deep voice. "As some of you already know, because your invitations arrived very late, my friend KT here and I promised you something special if you made an effort to attend this first ball of the Duke and Duchess of Brightshire . . ."

"Late arrival of the invitations?" Emma whispered. "What're they talking about?"

"Don't know. But I think we're going to find out."

"You're about to experience a true Western show," Trevor went on. "We hope you enjoy."

With a few strums of the guitar, Trevor started singing in a clear, rich voice. He began with "The Yellow Rose of Texas," accompanied by KT on the harmonica. The crowd was mesmerized, the sound so different from anything they were used to. From there, the two ranch hands segued into "Sweet Betsy from Pike" and "Home on the Range" and ended with "Shenandoah."

As they ducked their heads in a brief bow, the crowd called for more.

KT put up a hand to quiet them.

Trevor began to softly strum.

The long and lyrical verse of cowboy poetry, recited by KT to the strumming background of the guitar, brought gooseflesh to Emma's skin. Visions of the cattle asleep on the open range, guarded and loved by their human companions, skittered across her imagination, making her miss Eden with all her heart. The poem was beautiful, one she'd never heard before, and she wondered if KT was the author.

At the conclusion, the crowd was spellbound. Trevor traded the guitar for a violin from one of the musicians and stuck the instrument under his chin. At a fast clip, he seesawed the strings, trying to keep up with KT, who'd picked up a lariat they'd gotten from somewhere and began building a loop by twirling the rope in front of him. As the loop swooped larger and larger, the crowd backed up, giving them space. Soon the loop was twirled on the floor, and KT jumped in and out with ease. Next, he flipped the spinning loop over his head. It encircled his body like a waterfall, and he jumped out when the rope hit the floor. Poor man was working up a sweat.

"They're a sight!" Emma gasped, clutching Beranger's arm. "Oh my. What a gift!"

Finally, with a flick of his wrist, the loop flew through the air and landed gently around Jos, the tall footman, catching him around the middle. Stopped in his tracks, the tray of crystal glasses he carried never wobbled.

The crowd erupted in cheers and clapping.

Taking the trick in good stride, Jos smiled and untangled himself. He even took a bow.

But not quite finished with the show, Trevor slowed his fiddle playing and soon KT was back by his side, yodeling as if trying to settle a rambunctious herd. That lasted a good four or five minutes, but Emma wished it would go on all night.

With a deep breath and a bow, they accepted a hearty round of applause.

Amazed, Emma waved them over. "What in the world prompted you to do that? It was wonderful—just amazing! But such a surprise. You brought tears to my eyes. Thank you so very much!"

The men looked at each other and then smiled.

Trevor shrugged. "Yesterday, wanting to help, KT and I went in search of your father's letter. We didn't find that, but we did find a stack of fifteen invitations to the ball hidden away in the pigeon barn."

"What?" Beranger barked. "Malicious trickery?"

"That's what we figured," KT said. "What else could it be? We didn't want to tell you and spoil your party, and we didn't want you to notice that no gentry had shown up. The missing invitations were to all the lords and ladies—the baroness and Dowager Countess of Sarre, you know, all them kind of folks. You might have wondered how we became such good friends."

Beranger looked down at Emma and laughed. "Yes, we did. Exactly that."

Emma forced herself to laugh. This time, she had little doubt about who had diverted the invitations. *My sweet, darling stepmother-in-law has struck again. What else is she responsible for? Beranger's attacks of vertigo? I don't put that past her in the least.*

Beranger squeezed her hand as if he knew exactly what she was thinking. "Now is not the time to confront her, Emma. She can see she was thwarted by the arrival of all her friends. She will be dealt with swiftly tonight, I promise. Right now, you'll enjoy your first ball at Ashbury, and my first ball as well. I was never allowed before."

"So," Trevor said, going on with their story, "we rounded up Tristen and told him what we'd found and what we suspected. The three of us rode like the Pony Express to get the word out in time. Some of the people were hesitant, because the ball was the next day, so we promised 'em a special show they would never forget. One they'd not get a chance to see anywhere in England. A real Western shindig."

"Amazing," Emma gushed, throwing her arms around the two. "You saved the day. Thank you!"

"It was Tristen's doing. We wouldn't have known where to go if not for him. He drew maps and helped us get our gear for the show." They looked around. "Where is he? We haven't seen him tonight."

The smile on Emma's face disappeared. "That's a good question. I haven't either. But look for Charlotte. He can usually be found with her."

KT shook his head. "Not so tonight. Winters hasn't released her once. Looks like the writing is on the wall where they're concerned."

"I wouldn't be so quick to judge," Emma responded, the twinkle back in her eye. "Now tell me, how on earth did Tristen get you aboard a tall thoroughbred?"

The night was winding down, and Tristen had yet to show up, making Charlotte almost frantic. She'd been so caught up in the new life that might be ahead of her that she'd forgotten to cherish what was important to her in the life she already had. Wasn't that really what Tristen had been telling her with his warnings about Mr. Winters? That she didn't need the allure of wealth or fancy dresses when someone who loved her for her true self was in front of her the whole time?

"Excuse me, Mr. Winters," she said softly, "but I'm going to catch my breath. I'll speak with you later."

His brows crashed and he loosened his hold while others danced on. "I've worn you out?"

"Yes." *But really, it's not respectable for me to dance every dance with one man. People will wonder. Even I know that without help from Lady Audrey.* She smiled brightly and made her way through the gathering. It was quite strange to see the mix of classes. They weren't yet socializing with each other that much, but they did seem to be having a good time in their own groups. That was something. Small steps in the right direction.

The duke and duchess came into view. When Emma caught her eye, Charlotte smiled and waved. Emma hurried forward, her face glowing with happiness.

"Isn't this wonderful?" she gushed. "I'm having a lovely time, and I hope you are as well. You've been dancing all evening with Justin. Do you have something to tell me?"

On her last sentence, Emma's smile fell away, as if she hoped Charlotte would not have something to share.

"Just that I didn't think one could dance so much in one night." Charlotte laughed. "I need to pat this warmth off my face. Join me?"

"Absolutely. And I want to sit down for a few minutes and rest my feet. We've had scores and scores of people to speak with. Beranger is so diplomatic. I guess his difficult upbringing formed him into the intelligent, tactful man he is. I adore him so."

The two smiled and nodded at the guests they passed on their way to the stairway.

"The pink parlor has been set aside as the ladies' retiring room, but shall we go up to my room?" Emma asked. "No one will look for us there. The solitude is tempting."

Charlotte nodded, but kept her gaze far from Emma's as she searched every corner of the room. "Have you seen Tristen tonight? Did he tell you or the duke that he wasn't coming?"

Emma stopped in the hallway. "I knew it!"

"Knew what?"

"That you're in love with Tristen and not Justin. It's so obvious to me. All the men keep asking about you and Beranger's cousin, and I keep telling them the story isn't over yet."

"You didn't."

Emma's smile was infectious. "I did. I've seen the signs for days. Ones even you've missed." They continued walking. "Open your eyes, Charlotte, before he gets away."

The gallery on the third floor was blessedly quiet. After Charlotte refused to comment, they went along in silence, both lost in their own thoughts. Once they slipped inside Emma's room, Emma went to her dressing table, where she handed Charlotte a clean hanky and took one for herself before she went to the hearth and carefully lowered herself in a chair.

Studying her reflection, Charlotte blotted her forehead and around her cheeks. Besides the one and only kiss, she had no idea how Tristen felt about her. Perhaps he'd kissed her on a whim and she meant no more to him than a bird in the sky. Maybe she'd been reading more into his intentions than she should have.

A soft knock sounded on the door.

Startled, Emma sat straight and looked at her, then slowly rose to her feet. "That's strange. Who could that be?"

Intrigued, Charlotte followed the duchess to the door. After the copious noise downstairs, the quiet up here felt a little eerie. For some strange reason, the crying baby popped into her head, and she became frightened. She hadn't told anyone they were coming up here, and neither had Emma. What did that mean?

As Emma reached out, Charlotte caught her arm. "Wait," she whispered next to her ear. "No one knows we came up. Do you think it's safe?"

The knock came again. More persistent. Louder. "Duchess, are you there? I need to speak with you."

Emma turned to Charlotte, questions and a little fear in her eyes.

CHAPTER FIFTY

B eranger approached the group of shopkeepers who seemed to want to stay in this corner all night. He'd been looking for Emma, since she'd been gone a good twenty minutes and he was becoming concerned. She wasn't with Trevor and KT, who were being regaled by the elderly Dowager Countess of Sarre. She had them laughing and slapping their legs. She wasn't in the kitchen, where he'd thought she'd gone to check on the kitchen staff to make sure they came up for the festivities now that the food had been served.

"Constable Kerrigan." When Beranger approached, the townspeople made room. "Have you seen my wife? Somehow she's slipped away and I can't find her." He looked around the tight-knit group, intending the open-ended question for anyone.

"I'm sorry, Your Grace, I haven't. Not since I last saw her with you," he replied, guzzling down the last of the wine in his glass. "You were speaking with your uncle, I believe."

Some time ago.

"Yes, well, carry on." He strode away feeling unsteady. Not from the vertigo, which had stayed blessedly at bay tonight, but from fear something had happened. But what could happen here? He knew Emma would not want him to cause a scene until he was sure of wrongdoing.

Before him, Tristen, dressed as nicely as Beranger had ever seen him, strode his way.

"Tristen," Beranger said. "We'd given up on you. When did you arrive?"

"Just now." His brows knitted together. "Have you seen Charlotte? I need to talk to her."

It dawned on him that he hadn't seen Charlotte in quite a while either. Beranger grasped his arm and pulled him aside. "No. I haven't," he said, worried. "I'm looking for Emma now. My insides tell me they might be together. Why they'd disappear out of sight is beyond me. They're not in the kitchen. But I've just begun my search."

"What about upstairs? Maybe they went up there."

"That's where I was headed next. Why don't you go find Trevor and—"

"No, I'm coming with you. You may need help."

The trip upstairs to their suite usually took five minutes, but tonight only took two. Beranger pushed through the partially opened door to find their bedroom not in disarray, but not quite right either. Something felt off, and even a bit evil.

"Look at this!" Tristen handed Beranger a sheet of wrinkled paper he'd lifted off the bed. It contained a poem, scrawled so horribly the content was almost unreadable. The last four lines jumped out at Beranger:

> So now good fortune comes to me,
> At long last, victory snatched from defeat,
> Beranger, your pain I'll see,
> And my revenge will be complete . . .

Beranger crumpled the paper in his hand. "What in God's name?"

"Do you know who it's from? Surely you know if you have an enemy here."

"I'd say more than one . . ."

A sound out in the hall made them turn.

The chambermaid who had taken over for Hyacinth stood there, looking dumbfounded and frightened. Her hands were clamped tightly together before her apron.

Beranger leaped toward her. "Have you seen the duchess?"

The maid looked from one to the other.

"Speak, woman! This is important!"

"I did, Your Grace. I saw her and Miss Charlotte climbing the stairs to this floor. Then a few minutes later, I was just about to go down when I heard a scream coming from this gallery and I thought the two had gotten into a fight with each other. I didn't want to intrude. That's all I know."

Tristen rushed forward. "Did you see anything else or any other person up here before or after? Anything. Do you remember anything at all?"

CHAPTER FIFTY-ONE

C harlotte strained against the ties binding her wrists. She was careful to keep her eyes squeezed tightly closed. She'd been hit on the head and must have passed out at some point, because she didn't remember being moved. They weren't in the duchess's bedroom any longer. When the woman on the other side of the bedroom door had mentioned a hurt child, Emma had pulled the door open and been immediately struck on the head. Emma crumpling into Charlotte's arms had left Charlotte vulnerable for the next strike. From there, the events leading to where she was now were blurry.

"Wake up, Your Grace," a sickly-sweet voice sang softly. "I want you to feel the pain and fear I've had to endure for sixteen long years. Open those pretty eyes. I know you're awake. No one will find you down here in the bowels of the earth."

With one cheek resting on the cold stone floor, Charlotte carefully opened one eye. Only their assailant's back was visible to Charlotte. Did she know the woman? Her voice seemed somewhat familiar despite the ringing in her head. If she knew her, perhaps Charlotte would be able to talk some sense into her. Get her to set them free.

Charlotte's head ached horribly. A shooting pain ricocheted through her eyes, and she almost cried out. The smell of singed cotton or some other material caught her attention and brought moisture to her eyes.

Where was the duchess? Was she still alive? The room was dark and shadowy, but Charlotte thought they must still be in the castle, because how could one woman get them both away without being seen? Moist air clung to her skin. Maybe she'd had help. Why had she done these things?

Fear snaked up Charlotte's spine. If she screamed, would anyone hear her with the musicians playing? Would this madwoman want to shut her up for good? She worked her wrists, rubbing them together as much as she could. The tie slackened. She was by the door. Perhaps she'd be able to get her hands free to untie her feet and go get help. The woman put more wood into the belly of an iron stove. *No, I'll not leave Emma here alone. Not with this monster!*

The woman turned her way.

Phoebe Lewis!

Phoebe, from the livery in Brightshire! Whose daughter she'd given the extra biscuits to. What was happening?

Charlotte looked around. Several irons sat on top of the hot stove. They must be in the laundry room. No one would find them here. Charlotte would have to take matters into her own hands. How badly was Emma hurt? She didn't have a moment to waste.

Charlotte tried to move her tongue, but her mouth was dust dry. "Phoebe," she croaked. "Phoebe, please let me go."

Phoebe hurried over. "Charlotte, you awake? Good. Hope I didn't hit ya too hard. I didn't have a choice. This doesn't have anythin' to do with you, mind you. Just stay quiet and you'll be fine."

She must be out of her mind to speak to me in such an easy manner. "Untie me, Phoebe, and let me up. Let the duchess up as well. She's never done anything to hurt you. Why would you do such a thing?"

Carrying on a conversation with someone standing over you when you were on the floor was not an easy feat. She wished she could see into Phoebe's eyes.

"Hush, Charlotte! I won't explain myself to you or no one. I'm done taking orders and keeping quiet. This has been a long time coming. I won't stray from my path now." She started toward the stove. In the darkness Charlotte could see a lump across the room. She thought it was the bound duchess, still unconscious.

Dear Lord, what path? What is she planning to do with Emma?

"Phoebe, *please*, listen to me! My head hurts. I think I'm bleeding. I need help. I've always been kind to you. I'll tell them you're sick, not in your right mind. You're not yourself today." Charlotte tried to raise her head. "They'll understand. Trust me. Please untie my hands."

Charlotte tried to think back through her words for some clue as to why this was happening. What had she said about sixteen years? What did that have to do with anything?

Phoebe whirled around. "Shut up, Charlotte! I don't want to hurt you. But I will if I have to."

Will anybody miss us? Will they even come looking down in the servants' area? Surely not.

Her head ached horribly, more than she could stand, but she had to do something more. Something to save Emma.

"Beranger?" a weak voice called out.

Charlotte heard scuffling sounds, as if Emma were trying to move. "Where am I? Beranger?"

Emma's voice was garbled. She was just coming around.

Phoebe had stopped what she was doing at the stove and now looked in Emma's direction.

Charlotte had to do something before Phoebe had a chance to hurt her, or worse. "Phoebe!" Charlotte called. "I'm going to throw up. Please sit me up so I don't choke. My head is pounding." She wiggled her hands frantically, feeling her restraints give just a wee bit more. She'd have one chance at this, and if she failed, it might mean both their lives.

Phoebe tromped her way. She leaned down and took Charlotte by the shoulders.

That moment, one of Charlotte's hands slipped free. Before she had a chance to be afraid, she wrapped one arm around Phoebe's neck and pulled her down. Charlotte's feet were still restrained, so Phoebe had the advantage.

"Emma! Emma, wake up!" Charlotte shouted. She had a choke hold around Phoebe's throat that wouldn't last long. The woman was strong, and as agile as a snake. If she didn't have help soon, all would be lost. "Help, somebody!" Charlotte screeched at the top of her lungs. "Please help us in the laundry!"

"You viper!" Phoebe snapped, her voice distorted by the pressure on her windpipe. "You're just like them! You've turned against your own people."

"I haven't, Phoebe, I promise you that. Think of your children. If you're hung for killing the duchess, it'll be up to Leo to raise them. Is that what you want?"

They rolled on the floor, both struggling to get the upper hand.

"That pig! He's no better than Beranger, who went off and left me. We were in love, a love that would last a lifetime—I had thought. Beranger and Phoebe, a true love that would last. But he was a liar, just like Leo. I hate him. I hate them both! I'm going to burn her beautiful face and make it ugly like mine. That will hurt Beranger—*my love*—more than killing her!"

The strain was taking its toll. Charlotte wouldn't be able to hold her off much longer. Once she was free, there was no telling what the lunatic would do.

The laundry room door banged open, and Charlotte's heart took flight. Somebody had heard her cries! They would help, come to their rescue. Rolling once again, Charlotte looked up to see Margaret Malone standing there, her eyes as wide as plates.

CHAPTER FIFTY-TWO

Tristen and Beranger made one more sweep of the ballroom and then alerted the staff to begin a thorough search of the castle. Not one corner was to be left unturned, including the stable and out-buildings. The ranch hands had sprung into action, and Justin Winters dogged Tristen's heels, as if he was afraid the gamekeeper would get all the credit if he was the one to find the women and not himself.

Tristen turned suddenly to face him. "We'd cover more ground if you searched on your own. Now go! Leave nothing to chance." It was then he saw fear in Beranger's cousin's eyes. "Do you know something you're not saying? Have you an idea where they are?" It was all Tristen could do not to mop the floor with the whimpering man. He'd transformed at the sound of trouble into a man afraid of his own shadow.

Mr. Winters stood his ground. "No. I'm flummoxed. That note, that poem, it's horrifying. Who would do such a thing?"

"That's what we have to find out. Now, make yourself useful. You have nothing to fear. You're not the duke or his wife. I assure you, you're safe." Tristen strode away, vowing that if he could only find Charlotte before something horrible happened, he'd let her know just how deeply he loved her. Mathilda had been right. Love was more important than things or status. He wouldn't choose to be Justin Winters for all the money in the world.

"Wait!"

Tristen turned back.

"What about searching the secret passageways? Did Brig say any-thing about that?"

"I didn't hear anything. Show me!"

With a screech like a banshee, Margaret Malone flung herself forward and gripped Phoebe's head at the exact moment Charlotte ran out of energy and her arms fell away.

The two rolled to the left, leaving Charlotte free to work feverishly on the tie binding her ankles. Her shaky fingers made gripping the cord difficult. The sound of the screaming women was frightening. Behind them, the glow of the stove top drew her attention, and then her gaze fell to Emma's wide, frightened eyes watching the tussle playing out before her as she lay defenseless, still bound on the floor.

As they struggled, Margaret's head knocked against the stone floor and she went limp. Phoebe sprang to her feet one moment after Charlotte was free.

Charlotte jumped up and crouched forward as she'd seen the village boys do down by the river whenever there was a fight. Her instincts kicked in. The look in Phoebe's eyes sent a streak of terror down Charlotte's spine. Phoebe leaped forward and grasped Charlotte's hair, careening them forward and bumping the hot stove.

With a loud smack, a red-hot iron fell to the floor, landing just inches from Emma's face.

"Get back!" came a shout from the door.

Tristen burst into the room, launched himself forward, and took Phoebe down to the floor.

Her head struck with a crack, and she went limp.

Charlotte rasped for breath, her heart pounding and pain ricocheting through her head. Sweat trickled down her temple, and a lock of hair partially blocked her sight.

One moment later Beranger appeared and ran to Emma's side, scooping her into his arms and striding out of the room.

When Tristen turned to Charlotte, she didn't know what to do. Unspent energy demanded she do something—fling herself, fight for her life and those of her friends as well.

Instead, Tristen made the decision for her by scooping her into his arms and following Beranger out of the sweltering room.

"Wait," Charlotte cried, putting out a hand to Margaret, who was pushing herself shakily to her feet. Thank God she'd appeared at the exact moment they needed her most and was brave enough to jump in to help. Without her, all might have been lost.

Margaret swayed.

"Help her!" Charlotte screeched.

Without missing a beat, the Honorable Justin Winters, who'd been hanging in the shadows, caught Margaret Malone, scullery maid turned kitchen helper, in his arms as she crumpled toward the floor.

CHAPTER FIFTY-THREE

The people had cleared out and gone home. Charlotte, with a towel filled with ice held to her head, sat on the sofa in the library next to the duchess, who had the same treatment on the lump on her head. Constable Kerrigan only a few minutes before had escorted a bound Phoebe out on a stretcher, taking her to the doctor, but only after he and the men had found the passage that had allowed Phoebe to cart the women, one by one, unseen from the third floor to the laundry. The woman was awake but hadn't said a word to anyone. Not her husband nor Beranger when he'd tried to question her.

A basket of green tobacco leaves, as well as gloves, was found hidden in the back of a cupboard in the far reaches of the laundry. The constable's theory was that Phoebe had been trying to poison the duke through his clothing by ironing his garments with the toxic green tobacco leaves inside. That would explain the dizziness and the vertigo.

Trevor and KT sat silently watching. The night that had been so wonderful before now revealed the extent of the danger to Emma in England. Charlotte could see the ranch hands' inner struggle. Would they remain here? Or trust Beranger to keep the beloved daughter of their former boss safe from her husband's enemies? Only time held that answer. Lord Harry sat at their side, his expression also troubled.

"Take another sip of your tea," Tristen said softly to Charlotte. His concerned gaze seemed to caress her face, and he hadn't left her side since carrying her from the laundry. Did this mean that he did feel something for her? She hoped so. The way she'd felt tonight, without him at the ball, only confirmed in her mind what she was beginning to believe. She loved him. She just needed to tell him—and there was one other thing they needed to discuss.

"What will happen to Phoebe?" Emma asked, her gaze skimming over the dowager and Lady Audrey, who'd just entered the room. Their expressions were drawn as they sat, and they both looked like they were in disbelief at the events of the night.

Beranger paced the rug. "I don't know. She'll live, but only because she was unable to complete her intentions." His gaze slid to Emma, who was still as white as a sheet. "I'd predict she'll spend many years in prison. I had no idea she harbored such animosity for me. Or thought I had abandoned her. We were *children*. With children's dreams. I'm as astounded as everyone else. I feel for her family."

Everyone fell silent for a moment. Trevor cleared his throat, glanced at Beranger, and lifted an eyebrow.

"Dowager Duchess," Beranger began, turning toward his step-mother, "your shenanigans with the invitations to tonight's ball are unforgivable. I had hoped, for my wife's sake, you had changed for the better. Sadly, you have not. Your presence here is a stumbling block for Emma. Her happiness is at stake. Since you're unable to let go and allow Emma her rightful place as Duchess of Brightshire, tomorrow morning you are to move out of the manor and into Lily House."

The dowager's face flamed. "So! I'm to be thrown out of my own home when I only tried to help. I should have expected nothing less from you, you cursed man."

The duke straightened his shoulders, and his jaw clenched. "You've done nothing but lie and slander Emma. You fired staff without reason or permission. Now own up to your last heartless deed."

"I don't know what you mean."

"Your intention to spoil Emma's first ball by making sure few lords and ladies would show—an immature action beneath even you."

"What on earth are you rattling on about? Everyone was here. You saw it for yourself."

"Only because the invitations were discovered in time in the pigeon barn, and a valiant effort got them delivered so Emma wouldn't be hurt."

The dowager swallowed and glanced away. Charlotte couldn't believe her eyes when the hateful woman actually teared up.

"I only wanted to save my friends from having to degrade themselves by socializing with commoners. I can't think of anything more distasteful." She glanced at Tristen and then Charlotte and lifted her nose. "And I'd do it again if given the chance."

Beranger snorted. "Of that I have no doubt."

Emma's eyes were huge, confirming Charlotte's thoughts that she hadn't known about Beranger's plan concerning the dowager and Lily House.

Lady Audrey slowly, and a bit unsteadily, rose from her seat. "I have something I'd like to get off my conscience."

"And what is that, sister?" Beranger almost growled.

There were dark circles beneath the duke's eyes.

The cowboys sat in complete silence.

And Mr. Winters kept his gaze far away from Charlotte, much to her relief. She suspected he'd finally seen the obvious. She couldn't blame him, given that she'd been so slow to realize it herself. When she looked Tristen's way, he reached out and took her hand.

"Duchess," Lady Audrey squeaked out. "I'm ashamed of myself, and have been, but didn't know how to put things right. I have the letter from your father. It's unopened. I went up to your rooms looking for Mother, but she and Carmichael had already gone." She bit her bottom lip, her eyes blinking in pain.

"Why?" Beranger demanded. "Why would you do that? She's been nothing but kind to you."

"I don't have a good reason. Just something moved me because I knew it was special to her. As she is to you. Even though you took the title that everyone thought would go to me, I hadn't really minded all that much. But I guess I was—*am*—jealous of how much you love her. Gavin thought me a pest. I had hoped to be special to you, like she is." She glanced at Beranger and then to Emma.

"My letter," Emma gasped and then grimaced, reaching up to touch her forehead. "My letter." That's all she could get out before she started trembling all over.

KT cleared his throat, and Trevor lifted a shoulder in response.

Beranger lowered himself next to Emma and gathered her in his arms. "Thank God," he whispered. "Thank God."

"There's more," Lady Audrey murmured. "I want to start over with a new beginning this night. I don't like the person I've become." She glanced at her mother. "I'll have it all out now and be done with it, no matter what my mother will think or do. Thomas Aldridge is not guilty of anything having to do with Gavin's death. The day my brother died, I was in the forest with Thomas. We were just—"

The dowager gasped. By her expression, she was utterly appalled.

Lady Audrey hurried on. "We were just talking—as we often did." Her face flushed. "We did kiss a time or two, as well. He didn't speak up because he didn't want to compromise my reputation. I used to talk to him when he brought the bread. He used to bring me ribbons, or a poem he'd written, or some sweet that had been baked that morning. Sometimes I'd have the carriage take me into Brightshire to see the shops but really go down to the river and sit with him while he fished."

The dowager turned on her heel and left the room, her chin held high.

My Lord! Thomas had an iron-clad alibi! And from Lady Audrey! Relief flooded Charlotte. She was so happy she wanted to cry. But then her gaze slid over to Tristen. Where did that leave his beloved uncle? Had Arson Henderley killed the duke? Could she keep something like that to herself? And if not, what would her saying so do to the feelings between them?

An hour later, Emma sat in bed, the covers pulled up to her lap, and her father's letter safely back in her hands, where it should have been all along.

"Would you like some privacy?" Beranger asked, standing by the window, nothing but darkness on the other side.

He was dressed only in his pajama trousers, giving her a nice view of his wide, muscled back. When he turned to look at her, the expression on his face tore at her heart. He thought her unhappy here at Ashbury. That she wished to return to America. Nothing could be further from the truth.

She reached out her hand to him. "No, I'd like to share this moment with you, as I look forward to sharing every other experience with you for the rest of my life. Come sit next to me. I can hardly wait to open my letter. Having you near me will make the reading all that much sweeter."

He blinked and then crossed the room in silence, slipping into the bed beside her.

Without further ado, Emma slid her finger under the tab of the envelope and unsealed the flap.

> My dearest daughter Emma,
> Happy birthday, my sweet girl. I pray that this moment in your life, turning twenty-two, finds you the happiest you've ever been.

Emma stopped reading and leaned over and kissed Beranger. "My father knows so much. I *am* the happiest I've ever been—and it's all because of you." She went back to the letter.

I wish that for each and every one of my daughters, and you are no exception.

As you'll learn, your birth was extra special to me because you were the only daughter I delivered with my own hands. After Mavis and Belle were born, I felt as if I was quite experienced with babies, having held, fed, and bathed my girls from time to time. I even changed my fair share of napkins. I figured it wasn't fair that your mother would have to change them all. And so, I believed, nothing much could rattle my soul. How wrong I was.

As your due date slowly approached, your mother and I made ready another small bed that would sit next to ours for the first six months. The days kept passing and soon we figured she must be late, and still no sign of approaching labor. Having expected your birth for the last two weeks, she hadn't been into Eden for a very long time.

"Take me to the café for apple pie," she pleaded more than ten times a day. "Mavis and Belle agree. They'd like some too." Then she rubbed her large belly and said she didn't think you'd ever come out.

What harm could that do, since the midwife we depended on, and who delivered both your older sisters, lived in Eden? We'd actually be closer if her labor were to start. So I agreed, bundled all of us onto the front buckboard seat, and started away, feeling like a king. As you know well now, the ride into town in a wagon takes some time. We hadn't gone more than a quarter mile when my wheel hit a rather large rut and your mother's water broke. She was startled. I calmed her, remembering the last two births and the hours she'd labored to

bear your sisters. We had plenty of time to get to town
and get her settled in the hotel.

A jittery excitement made Emma gaze over at Beranger, who was
listening intently with his head propped on his hand.
He smiled, but his anxious gaze gave him away. "Exciting."
She laughed and smoothed his cheek. "Relax, my love, we know
everything comes out fine, because I'm here now."
"Yes," he breathed out on a long sigh. "Yes, you're right. What was
I thinking . . ."

Even though I had assured your mother we had
plenty of time, I slapped the reins over the horses to
pick up speed. Her pains started immediately, and not
the soft beginning kind. The first contraction made
her cry out, startling us all. Tears sprang to Belle's and
Mavis's eyes, only about one year and two, because
their mama hurt. Your poor mother tried to hold out,
but the knuckle-white grip she had on the side of the
wagon told me I had to pull up. If not, my third child
would be born in a moving wagon. Fortunately, I'd
brought a blanket to wrap the children in on the way
home if they fell asleep. I laid that out in the back of
the wagon and helped Celeste over the seat.

She was scared. And so was I. I'd faced Indians,
pestilence, cougars, and bears, but I didn't want to
deliver my child alone. I looked around at the silent
landscape, and then up into the frightened faces of my
tiny daughters. The fact that women died in childbirth
badgered my heart.

Emma's hands began to quiver.

Well, I didn't have to wait long. With one blanket under your mother and another tented over, blocking your sisters' view as they howled on the front seat, I caught you on your mother's third push, only fifteen minutes after the whole thing began.

With you nestled in my palms, I told Celeste she had something new. So she asked if we had a son, and I said no, we had a beautiful redhead, pretty enough to be a queen. When you were born, your hair was very red and curly and made a fiery halo around your head.

Beranger reached over and fingered a strawberry-blond lock, now straight and sleek. His eyes shimmered with love. "Certainly a queen, or perhaps a duchess?"

Unable to stop herself, Emma launched herself into his arms. After a few kisses, she picked up her letter again.

And so, you now wonder, had your mother and I wished for a son? I can tell you clearly the answer is no. From the first moment you felt the chill of the air right out of the womb, I loved you with all my heart. I wouldn't—we wouldn't—trade our Emma for anything. I could feel you were destined for something great. I hope and pray that your destiny finds you.

"Oh, Beranger," she sobbed. "How I wish I'd met him before he died. I love him as well, with all my heart."

Beranger stroked her hair and murmured softly, until she drew a deep breath and kept going.

My story is not quite over yet. After you were wrapped in my shirt and fed, we remained in the wagon, warming ourselves in the sunshine. Your sisters quieted and fell asleep on the front seat. After about an hour, I prepared to turn back home, tuck your mother into her own bed, and get started on the routine I'd gotten used to with the last two births. But no. She was set on apple pie, and who was I to say no?

Wishing you the most splendid birthday, my dear daughter.

Always remember, I love you with all my heart.

Your Father

CHAPTER FIFTY-FOUR

Tristen waited until the footman took the tea tray with the used cups, plates, and empty pots and left him alone in the library with Charlotte. The time wasn't quite midnight, and he knew it wasn't proper for him to stay so late after everyone else had left or gone to bed. He needed a few private words with Charlotte. But she seemed distracted and worried. Was there something else on her mind?

"Thank you for staying," he said, watching the door close behind the footman. "I'll only keep you a moment. You're exhausted with all you've been through and need your rest."

Her smile wobbled. She looked uncomfortable. Was she worried about her reputation, being alone with him? "Charlotte, I'd like to talk to you about something serious."

"Can it wait until tomorrow, Tristen?"

He was surprised; she'd never put him off before. And after tonight, he was sure she felt the same about him as he did about her. She'd clung to him long and hard when he'd carried her out of the laundry. He'd seen the look in her eyes.

"I *love* you, Charlotte. Ever since our kiss—no, actually before the kiss—you're all that I've been able to think about. The day Bagley spooked your pony and spilled your bread changed my life. I haven't let myself believe it, but Mathilda changed my mind tonight. She gave me the courage to speak with you. Tell you how I feel. I can only pray you feel the same."

Her eyes grew wide, and she put up a hand as if that would make him take back his words. "Stop, please!"

"You don't love me?" *Have I been so wrong?*

She stared at her folded hands.

He sat down and laid one hand over hers. "What is it? You must be relieved about Thomas. And finding out about your parents and grandparents. Is that it? Please don't keep me on the hook. So many things are going through my mind. Do you love Winters and want to marry him?"

She sat back. "No. Never that."

"Then what?" He lifted her hands and kissed her fingertips. He didn't know how he'd go on if she turned him down.

"It's about the day the duke died."

Relief washed over him. As long as she didn't have feelings for somebody else, he felt he stood a good chance of winning her love. There was just some little thing he could help her work through. "Thomas has been cleared, Charlotte. You don't have to worry about him any longer. You're free of it."

She shook her head. "Not really."

"Why?"

"I didn't tell you this, because I didn't want to start something I didn't know the answer to, but the same day I saw Thomas in the forest, I also saw your uncle, and he was limping. He was wearing a long brown coat like the man I'd seen on the hill with the duke. I'll never tell the constable, now that I don't have to because Thomas is cleared, but the secret will always be between us. What if somehow I'm forced to say something? You'd never forgive me."

He sat back. She was right. This wasn't some little thing. He stared at her, thinking.

She turned her face away from his. "See! I can't, I just can't love you knowing there is a secret that will drive us apart."

Snapped out of his thoughts, he squeezed her hands gently. "Uncle Arson wouldn't kill anybody. Even the duke, who he didn't like at all. You saw what you saw, but there has to be another explanation. I wished you'd trusted me and told me sooner." A peace descended over him. There was an answer, and they'd find it. He looked at her pink lips, marveling at their beauty. "This won't drive us apart. If I find out the truth and clear my uncle, will you marry me?"

She blinked several times.

Before she could speak, Tristen raised his hand to stop her. He had a confession of his own to make, and it was now or never. "Before you answer, I have something in my past I've been hiding, for fear of *your* rejection. So you see, we're not all that much different."

She gave him a watery smile. "There's nothing that would keep me from saying yes, except for what I just told you."

He was feeling better all the time.

"Over ten years ago, I was in a fight. No—I want you to understand completely—I started a fight. My punch knocked the other man down, and he hit his head. The man, the son of a politician, died, and I spent ten years in prison for manslaughter. My uncle and aunt know, and Pencely does too. Perhaps the duke now too, I don't know."

"Over ten years ago! You were little more than a boy."

"I was fifteen and should have known better."

She pulled away from him. "Did you try to kill him—was that your intent?"

He shook his head. "No, but that's what happened. I paid my debt, as much as it could be paid, and then Uncle Arson invited me here so I could start my life over with a clean slate. I hadn't intended on falling in love." He gazed deep into her eyes. "My uncle, and Pencely, gave me a chance to do better and be a better person. That's all I've tried to do, and I'm going to spend the rest of my life making sure they don't regret trusting me. I'm asking you for your trust too. I want to build a new life here in Brightshire. Will you share that life with me?"

Her gaze was serious. "Marrying you and building a life together would be a dream come true. I love you, Tristen, but I can't say yes until this other business is settled."

"Then first thing in the morning, we'll go into Brightshire and search out Thomas. See what he has to say since we know about him and Lady Audrey. From there we'll talk to my uncle. I want to hear his side of the story."

CHAPTER FIFTY-FIVE

The next day, in the confines of the barn loft, Charlotte and Tristen listened to Thomas, unbelieving. "Say that again, brother. Why on earth didn't you tell me this before? I've been sick with worry about you and also about Tristen's uncle. The man already has enough problems with his health. He shouldn't have to be a suspect in a murder."

"No one would have believed me unless I revealed I'd been meeting with Lady Audrey—and she confirmed the fact. That would bring all kinds of trouble onto her head, which I wasn't willing to do. Her mother is always threatening to send her away for various reasons. Besides, I never had any love for the duke. He did nothing but belittle me every time our paths crossed. His death truly was an accident, even if he did have a confrontation with someone."

Charlotte swallowed down her surprise. She'd imagined he had a sweetheart, but not that she was Lady Audrey. The silence in the barn was almost deafening. "Are the two of you in love?"

Thomas sighed and shook his head. "We thought we were once, but with this whole trouble, we realize we're mostly friends—very good friends. I've never done anything that would hurt her, or compromise her future. The fact I had nothing to offer was only too clear."

Charlotte reached out, thinking of what that admission must have cost him to say. "So Gavin came upon Leo Lewis poaching."

Thomas nodded. "I'd just left Lady Audrey in the forest behind the castle and had gone deeper into the woods. We had talked about our future, and I needed time to think; I was hurting. When I heard voices, I hid. The duke and Leo were arguing. The duke was furious to discover him with an armful of game. Intended to have him arrested and put into prison as an example for others. Leo was hot, but he held his tongue and tried to talk his way out of it, placate the duke by telling him about all the children he had to feed. When Gavin began to laugh, Leo threatened to kill him then and there. The duke drew his knife and lunged at Leo, sticking his thigh. Leo bellowed in pain and knocked the knife out of the duke's grasp. They wrestled. Gavin fell sideways on the uneven footing and landed on his own knife, which had wedged in the rocks. I wanted no part of that, so I took off. I'm sure Leo must have a recent scar on his thigh, to support my story."

Charlotte reached out and took his hand, her heart filled with compassion.

"I'm glad the truth is out," Thomas said on a deep breath. "It's a weight off my shoulders."

Charlotte nodded. "The truth will always come out, Thomas. That's why the truth is always a good place to start." She couldn't stop her smile. By her side, Tristen's presence had her senses humming. This meant she could accept his offer of marriage—which they'd put off until having this conversation. She couldn't feel more blessed or happier. He'd be at her side when she went in search of her past.

Romeo fluttered in the loft door and landed on his cage.

Charlotte laughed. "Look! There's a message on his leg. Who could have done that?"

"It's a mystery," Tristen said, shrugging. "Why don't you read it?"

She glanced at Thomas, and he shrugged as well. Very gently, she lifted the bird, being careful not to frighten him. Romeo cocked his little head from one side to the other and cooed as she withdrew the tiny piece of paper and set him next to her on the hay. With shaking hands she opened the note.

"'Heart of my heart,'" she read aloud as heat rushed to her face. "'I love you. Marry me and make me the happiest man in the world. Please don't keep me waiting, my love, because this ache in my soul is very painful. Say yes and put me out of this torture.'"

"Oh, Tristen. Yes! My answer is yes, now and always. I love you with all my heart." She flung herself into his arms, and Romeo, frightened at the burst of excitement, flew back out the window, having completed his job.

CHAPTER FIFTY-SIX

Two weeks later

Feeling pretty in one of the several new dresses the duchess had had her dressmakers construct for her, Charlotte stood next to Tristen in Ashbury's drawing room, a jumble of butterflies playing tag in her tummy. The duke and duchess had so lovingly allowed her to remain in their house since she'd moved from the bakeshop. So much had happened in the last six weeks. Her heart and mind were full of wonder and excitement. Her life was an open book, and all that needed to be done was for her and Tristen to write their story.

Beranger and Emma entered, all smiles. Behind came the ranch hands, minus Mr. Winters. After the ball, he'd had a telegram from home, or so he said, and was needed there. He promised to return as soon as his responsibilities, which he never spelled out, were taken care of, but he didn't know when that might be. He'd never given more of an explanation than that, although he didn't really have to. He'd steered clear of Charlotte, and that had made her sad. She didn't want him to feel embarrassed, although that was what she expected.

After Lady Audrey's revelation about Thomas Aldridge, the dowager duchess had apparently decided that moving into Lily House wasn't far enough away. Instead, she announced that she and Lady Audrey were taking an extended, and long overdue, holiday to London, followed by a visit to Beranger's uncle Charles, and possibly other relatives as well. Lord Harry had gone with them to London but was scheduled to return within a week. On the day of their departure, Thomas had appeared and, standing tall in defiance of the dowager, had bid Lady Audrey goodbye like a proper gentleman. Charlotte had never been so proud of anything in her life.

Emma hurried over and took Charlotte's hands. "Hyacinth has seen that your things, and hers, are well packed and nothing is left to chance—per Carmichael. She's ready anytime you two are."

"It's so kind of you to send her with us, Your Grace," Charlotte said, thinking of the pretty blond sixteen-year-old. She was young, but since Emma's efforts to find and persuade her to return had been fruitful, Carmichael had taken the girl under her experienced wing and was training her to be a lady's maid as well. The girl couldn't have been happier. "Are you sure you can do without her? And does she really want to go?"

Emma laughed, adding a sparkle to her eyes that hadn't been there when the dowager was always peering over her shoulder. "*Want* to go? She's so excited she nearly swooned when I mentioned Essex. I was happy to see her enthusiasm. And as for us doing without her, it's only for a couple of months, until you return for your wedding." She gave a satisfied sigh and glanced up at Beranger, who was standing patiently by her side, his expression indulgent, as if all women ever talked about were weddings, lady's maids, and swooning. "I can't think of a more beautiful time to be married than Christmas. It'll be lovely."

Charlotte blushed and glanced at Tristen. "It seems so far away. Everything is changing so fast. I can barely take it in."

Emma added, "And Margaret Malone will be taking over Hyacinth's work, even though we do have a new girl, so there's another person who is tickled about the new developments. She's moved up to chambermaid."

At the breakfast sideboard, Trevor and KT helped themselves to a cup of tea, poured for them by Jos Sleshinger, the footman. Unlike most guests to Ashbury, the two cowboys drew him into spirited conversation. On his off time, they'd been teaching him to twirl a rope, and Charlotte wondered how he was progressing. The tall footman was all smiles.

Beranger fixed her with a serious stare. "And what if you find the same resistance your mother did to the man she married, Miss Charlotte? Sir Luther Hastings may very well still be alive and have the same prejudices about the man you picked that he had with his own daughter." He glanced at Tristen. "Are you ready for that?"

"Beranger!" Emma's smile fell away. "How can you ask such a question? Of course he'll be thrilled. They all will."

"Because Tristen and Charlotte need to be prepared. No knight rides into battle without some sort of plan—several, in fact. Well, a foolish one might, but that's not what I know of Llewellyn."

"Hastings's opinions don't matter to us," Tristen answered. "And we're only going to meet them, not live there, or ask for anything. Who knows, perhaps they've softened."

Charlotte nodded. "That's correct. We don't need their blessings to be happy. If they want to give them, they will be well received and cherished—and if not, we'll shake the dust from our feet and never look back. Who's to say my grandmother didn't feel differently than her husband and, too frightened of the man who held power over her, went along with him and has been grieving since the day she lost her daughter? I'll never know the truth unless I go. I'm prepared to hear either story. I'd love to know more about my mother—and my father."

"And if they have mischief in their hearts, we will know it," Tristen added stoically. "Nothing will tear us apart."

For the time that Tristen would be away, Thomas would watch and walk the woods. Things were changing. To help the villagers, the duke and duchess had opened Ashbury's forests two days a week, allowing hunting of the seasonal animals.

But the talk about mischief brought a troubling thought to Charlotte's mind. "Please look after Verity for me. She didn't say so, but when I told her I was leaving, she became very quiet. I worry about her. I know Amelia is fine here with you."

Beranger's brow lifted. "Not to worry at all. Those two"—he nodded toward Trevor and KT—"have developed a sweet tooth for your aunt's baked goods, and until they decide it's time to go home, they will no doubt be visiting the bakeshop daily."

"And don't forget about Romeo and Juliet, Charlotte," Tristen added. "Verity has a simple way to speak with the duchess and Amelia. And Thomas is there. There's no need to worry."

Pencely stepped into the room. "Your coach is ready anytime you are," he said with a respectful dip of his head.

"Thank you, Pencely," Beranger responded.

The butler cleared his throat.

Everyone looked his way.

"There is a person waiting to say goodbye. Outside."

Emma started. "Please, invite them in."

"She won't come, Your Grace. It's Mathilda Tugwer, the midwife."

A warm feeling radiated through Charlotte. "I must go to her," she said, almost bolting from the group. "She has loved me from afar my whole life. My destiny has arrived, and it's because of her."

She turned at the doorway to find Tristen at her side, more love in his eyes than she ever thought possible. "I love you so much, I think I'll shatter into a million pieces," she whispered for him alone. "Let us express our gratitude to Mathilda together and never forget the love and happiness we feel right now."

ACKNOWLEDGMENTS

As always, my first thank-you goes to my publisher and all the wonderful people at Montlake. They've been so supportive of me and my ideas, I could never properly express my gratitude if I tried for a thousand years. I appreciate all the ways they make my writing life better. It's difficult to believe *An American Duchess* is our ninth novel together. How time flies.

Thank you to Alison Dasho, my Montlake editor. Her dedication and professionalism are such a blessing, as well as her cheerfulness. I've adored every moment working with her.

Thank you to my developmental editor, Caitlin Alexander, who has kept all my Montlake novels on track—from the folks in Logan Meadows in my Prairie Hearts novels, to the Brinkman sisters in my Colorado Hearts novels, and now off to England with my new Brightshire novels. Each and every book has been a joy!

A huge thank-you to Saralee Etter for her knowledge and help with all things Victorian England. I couldn't have written this book without her!

My heartfelt love to my family: my husband, Michael, and our sons, Matthew and Adam. My daughter-in-law, Misti, and my soon-to-be-daughter-in-law, Rachel. My darlings, Evelyn and Hudson.

Gratitude to all my sisters, my sister-in-law, and mother-in-law—all here on earth—and my parents, father-in-law, and sister in heaven. You all are my world. Thank you for your love and support.

Never to forget my readers! You're the best. Thank you. I treasure your comments and love.

And most, thank you to our awesome God, who continues to bless my life, my family, and the work of my hands.

ABOUT THE AUTHOR

Caroline Fyffe was born in Waco, Texas, the first of many towns she would call home during her father's career with the US Air Force. A horse aficionado from an early age, she earned a bachelor of arts in communications from California State University, Chico, before launching what would become a twenty-year career as an equine photographer. She began writing fiction to pass the time during long days in the show arena, channeling her love of horses and the Old West into a series of Western historicals. Her debut novel, *Where the Wind Blows*, won the Romance Writers of America's prestigious Golden Heart Award as well as the Wisconsin RWA's Write Touch Readers' Award. The author of the Prairie Hearts series, the McCutcheon Family novels, and *Heart of Mine* and the Colorado Hearts series, Caroline lives with her husband in the Pacific Northwest and has two grown sons, two daughters-in-law, and two darling grandchildren. For more information, visit the author at www.CarolineFyffe.com.